Opalescence

The Middle Miocene Play of Color

By Ron Rayborne

Edited by Lynn Steiner

Illustrations by Rod Rayborne
and
Marianne Collins

For Ruddy

While the author has endeavored to be thorough
and accurate regarding life and conditions during
the Miocene, this work is one interpretation. Thus,
it is possible that errors have crept in. Additionally,
due to scanty data, and in an effort to recreate that
long bygone world, certain scenarios are envisaged.
These imaginings and errors are solely those
of the author. The use of material from others
does not imply endorsement of the ideas herein.

~~~

Back cover: Ron and Ruddy, circa 1995

"For obvious reasons none of the Miocene ecosystems examined in this study has been directly observed by ecologists, nor will they ever be barring the unlikely invention of a time machine." ~ *Functional Convergence of Ecosystems: Evidence from Body Mass Distributions of North American Late Miocene Mammal Faunas.* W. David Lambert

"Lasting for millions of years, the mid-Miocene must have seemed a kind of endless summer." ~ *Neptune's Ark: From Ichthyosaurs to Orcas.* David Rains Wallace

"I am Miochin, the Summer Spirit, and in my home corn grows and flowers bloom all year long." ~ A Story of the Laguna & Acoma People of New Mexico's Pueblos

"If the outer world is diminished in its grandeur, then the emotional, imaginative, intellectual, and spiritual life of the human is diminished or extinguished. Without the soaring birds, the great forests, the sounds and coloration of the insects, the free-flowing streams, the flowering fields, the sight of clouds by day and the stars at night, we become impoverished in all that makes us human." ~ *The Great Work: Our Way into the Future. 2000.* Thomas Berry

"There is pleasure in the pathless woods, there is rapture in the lonely shore, there is society where none intrudes, by the deep sea, and music in its roar; I love not Man the less, but Nature more." ~ *Lord Byron*

"May your trails be crooked, winding, lonesome, dangerous, leading to the most amazing view. May your mountains rise into and above the clouds." ~ Edward Abbey in *Desert Solitaire*

Prologue

"Everything is hard-edged and gray. There is no light. No color. It clangs painfully, and drones dully. The heartbeat of the world is slowing. Slowing. What do you do when there's nothing left? What do you do when every resource on earth has been exhausted? When water, air, and food must evermore be recycled to use? What do you do when earthly beauty has become a distant memory, relegated to myth? When official liars deny that it ever even existed? When it becomes a crime to measure one world against the other, the other being our 'wonderful' modern era? When all that remains, after eons of evolution, of the bold struggle to adapt and survive is ... people? What do you do when there is nothing left? Nothing but anger and sadness. The heartbeat of the world is slowing, slowing. Soon, it will stop."

Tom Pine read the words of his wife. He'd found them when he decided one day to look through her things. Her "effects." It had been almost four weeks since she'd left. Left on the highly classified mission, which had been put upon her by nameless, featureless Blacksuits.

The Blacksuits were the only visible representation of the government most people ever saw. When you did see them, you looked the other way. Never look a Blacksuit in the eye. Some people wondered if they were even human; they seemed almost to glide over the ground. Clones they were, of course, human, but humans which had been engineered for their intelligence, their loyalty, their discretion, and their cold-blooded ruthlessness. When summoned by a Blacksuit, one did not argue, one did not question. One obeyed. There were stories about the few who did and did not. Unpleasant stories. The stuff *bad* dreams are made of.

They simply showed up one night, wordlessly showing Tom a photograph of his wife, Julie. When she noticed, Julie came to the door, lightly touching Tom's arm.

"What..." he asked, not completing the sentence, apprehension rising in his throat.

"I have to talk with these gentlemen a moment, honey," she replied, looking earnestly in his eyes. Tom tried to decipher the look. Was she asking for his help? Should he leap into action and aid her getaway? Instead he stood there, rigid, tight, muscles ready, yet waiting uncertainly for something more definitive.

"It's okay, honey," Julie said, "I'll just be a moment."

"Fine," said Tom, but he remained where he was. Then one of the Blacksuits who had been looking at Julie slowly turned his head toward Tom. That turning, mouth set in a hard line, dark glasses reflecting light in his eyes, seemed gauged to inspire fear, like an ominous creature that has suddenly noticed its prey. It didn't work. Tom, though apprehensive, did not look away.

"Please, Tom!" Julie blurted, voice now quavering. She never called him by this, his first name, unless she was serious. She wanted him elsewhere. Hesitating, weighing possible options, Tom decided to step back. "Thank you," Julie mouthed.

She turned around to look at the Suits. While one of them spoke to her in a voice too low for him to make out, lips barely moving, the other continued to look at Tom. They spoke for only a minute or two. Toward the end, he too looked in Tom's direction and said something further. Julie spoke reassuringly to them and smiled. Then they were gone. She closed the door, and for a moment they stood in silence, saying nothing.

"Why didn't you tell me before?" he'd demanded after Julie said that the Suits had met her at the Los Angeles County Natural History Museum where she served as Under-Curator. She worked below Richard Burns, doing the major work of assignation, writing papers, caring for the exhibits, meeting with people. The work that Burns despised. Lately, though, there was something else, Tom noticed. She had become simultaneously more somber, and more ... excited. Something was amiss.

Tom knew Julie better, he felt, than she knew herself. Her moments of joy when they were together. The moments of despondency when she became depressed over the state of the world. Yet, sometimes she looked at him wordlessly, her eyes very far away, and he had no clue what she was thinking. Once, drunk, she spoke words of heresy, and he quickly intercepted, clamping a hand over her mouth and clearing his throat. She laughed. It was well known that not just in public places, not just along the streets and squares, but even private homes were bugged. Harmful thoughts had to be pulled out by the root before they could take hold, even in the mind of the doubter. Otherwise, like a contagion, they could infect and spread, endangering the entire system. One minded one's thoughts. Even Julie's hard earned status as Under-Curator wouldn't save her if word got out that she was having misgivings.

No, for this was the Glorious Age of Man. A *new* era. When we'd finally achieved separation from "dirty nature", had finally conquered it. The old book spoke of having "in subjection the fish of the sea, the flying creatures of the air, and every living thing that moved upon the earth." In the Twenty-

First century, that happy time became a happy reality with the extermination of the last "wild beast."

It began in earnest with a new policy of "land cleansing." The time had finally come, we'd decided, to evict the "squatters", non-human species who, by their very existence, had been wantonly wasting human resources for so long. Thus, great hunting parties were launched the world over and every wild beast found, slaughtered.

It had taken millennia, even longer. Our slow, inexorable, relentless thrust into all of nature's secret places, every hidden corner of the planet, humanizing it, making it *safe* for us. And when at last it was over, that day was one of gleeful celebration across the world and even declared a global holiday: the "Great Awakening." True, some used to believe that such a goal, the elimination of wilderness and its wild inhabitants, would be a mistake, a travesty in fact, that it would mark the beginning of the end, but their minority of voices were drowned out by the corporatists. Tom remembered Derek Black's famous line, *"Now we are free, free to be what we are, free to be Man!"*, followed by thunderous applause, a tremendous uproar of cheering which could be replayed at any time with the push of a button.

One

Deep underground, the Institute de Physica in southern California, an ultra secret government facility, was alive with activity. Very few were aware of its existence, even in official administration circles.

After the LHC, or Large Hadron Collider, made its astonishing finding some decades back, thousands of acres of National Forest land were purchased. Then began the arduous task of tunnel digging, fifty miles long. To minimize space, it was carved in the shape of a giant spiral. The new collider cost a staggering amount of money, the diversion of revenues for such a large non-GDP item even leading to a mini recession. When it was completed, it was given the name *Temporal Transporter* (TT).

Then came a long dry spell. What worked well on paper and seemingly in small experiments failed to work when the TT was finished. Anger and disappointment at the scandal was high among the élite, and the project was all but mothballed, only a skeleton crew of physicists and technicians remaining.

Suddenly, it happened. It all began with a routine run. Having loaded their atomic bullet, a three-man tech crew aimed and fired. They realized that something was awry when only a nanosecond later the two-inch thick titanium walls surrounding the target room buckled like a plastic bottle with the air sucked out. Then, just as suddenly, with a loud outward rush of air which threw the team to the ground, the target chamber was inexplicably filled with the impossible: the snapped off stump of a conifer, shrubbery, grass, rocks and dirt. That chunk of expensive equipment which had been there just before was gone, simply gone. Alarms rang out and lights flashed. The overhead sprinklers came on.

Scrambling to his feet, one of the three white smocked workers, Longerman, ran to a panel and slammed on a toggle. *"Alert. Alert. Code Red in the Target Room. Repeat, Code Red in the Target Room!"*

"Cut that siren!" Rondle, another of the workers, yelled, "and that damn water, there's no fire in here!" Seconds later, all was calm again, and a strange quiet fell while the crew gathered themselves, brushing lapels, straightening glasses and picking up clipboards. A dusty sort of haze floated in the air, obscuring their view. The mood had changed in Observation, from one of slightly bored surveillance just moments before, to stunned silence.

Finally, Jeff Flanitz, crew lead, asked in a voice so small only he heard it, "What just happened?" There was no reply.

As Longerman squinted, trying to penetrate the dust, something small and fast suddenly collided with his legs, then ran between them. He jumped, half landing on a toppled chair and, ungracefully, fell again.

The room that had been 12' X 12' now more closely resembled some old, disheveled diorama. On top of that, a rank odor filled their nostrils.

Three months later, a secret meeting was called for those scientists who had been part of the experiment, along with others from around the world who it was deemed would have a special interest in it. Scattered throughout the crowd, though, were many unknown faces. But if a look of deep concern alone was enough for a pass into this learned assembly, then they certainly fit in.

It was "Old Man" Joseph Edwards, assistant director of the complex, who briefed the gathering. He spent the first ten minutes summarizing the experiment that day, a basic proce-dure with which he was sure most everyone was acquainted, but he trudged on for the record. Some were fidgeting. *Well, if the strangers can't understand the technical jargon, or the math involved,* he thought, *that's their problem.*

"Getting that out of the way," continued Edwards, "let me cut to the chase. Certain, er, rumors, have been floating around regarding the events of 12, September. Sensational stories of bizarre effects, et cetera, et cetera." He paused, looking around the hall. With this statement, a look of relief was beginning to soften the tension on the faces of some in the room. Other expressions, however, tightened. The scientists. They would be disappointed to learn that it was all merely hearsay. The former group he put down as government men, those sent to find out if the discovery might somehow pose a threat to the stability of the regime. None of those invited knew for sure what was up, just that it was some significant breakthrough.

"Rumors, gentlemen," Edwards said, "sometimes turn out to be correct." There was a reversal of expressions, he noted with an inward laugh. "My friends, what I am about to tell you must remain, for the time being at least, *strictly* confidential." He knew that such an admonition would mean nothing to the G-men. "It is vital that you exercise extreme discretion from this point on." Another pause, then, "There has *indeed* been a very strange effect. A, uh, *corollary,* or *side effect,* if you will, to the test that we ran in September."

Among those in attendance was Julie Pine of the LA Natural History Museum. She, too, was interested in learning what this was all about, but did not know why she'd been invited. Every now and then she noticed Edwards gaze at her, holding her return gaze, and it made her uncomfortable.

"To make a long story short, while testing a hypothesis of Gerald Gray from MIT," Edwards gestured toward a young man with thick spectacles and a shock of equally thick hair in the front row, then broke off. "As some of you know, Gerald has been working on a contribution to the Grand Unified Theory, and making fine progress, I might add."

Julie looked toward the scientist he referred to; he sat impassive, as if it were someone else Edwards was talking about. "Anyway, this happened. Dan..." he said, nodding at Longerman, who stood near a large video screen mounted on the wall behind him. Longerman reached over and touched an LCD switch, causing the screen to lighten, and the recording from the wall-mounted camera in Observation to play. Only a few moments were necessary to show that an anomalous event had in truth occurred. When the unusual contents of the test room became obvious after the filters kicked in and cleared the air, gasps of excitement arose, Julie Pine's perhaps being the more notable.

"The *HELL?!*" she exclaimed, standing up suddenly. Edwards looked at her.

"Yes, Dr. Pine, did you have something to say?"

"Well, *that can't be!*" she answered, waving a hand at the screen, "It's ... impossible!"

"Would you care to elaborate, Doctor?"

Julie flushed, suddenly aware of herself. "I'm sorry. It's just, well ... excuse me," she said, as she made her way around the knees of those seated near her. Walking to the screen, she asked, "Could you wind that back up a bit?"

"Certainly." Edwards gestured to Longerman who, using a remote, backed the video up about a minute, then replayed it.

Julie waited, then said, "STOP." Longerman did. There, amid the rubble, scampering atop a rock, was a smallish, spotted, weasely looking animal with a fluffy, striped tail.

"*Sthenictis!*" Julie said definitively.

"Erm," Longerman intoned, clearing his throat and looking displeased. "A stinking skunk," someone chuckled.

Julie looked at him wonderingly. "Well, yes and no.

Sthenictis were actually members of the weasel family, which included skunks. But the first real skunks that we know of didn't arrive until around nine to nine and a half million years ago with *Martinogale faulli,* before..." she trailed off, "uh, but how..." It still had not settled on her what must have taken place here. She was still waiting for the logical explanation.

"Dr. Pine, perhaps you'd be more interested in the actual specimen?" Edwards asked innocently.

Julie frowned. "Um..." she answered awkwardly. "Yes?" *What is going on?* she wondered, brows furrowed, a feeling of confusion coming over her.

"Allow me." Edwards walked over, and, holding her right arm, led her to a darkened window. Handing her a small remote, he said, "Would you care to do the honors?" She stared at him now, apprehension rising, and feeling her legs beginning to wobble a bit. Slowly she nodded her head. "Steady," Edwards cautioned. Julie looked down at the small control, then tentatively took it and looked back at Edwards. There were two buttons on it, "Trans" and "Op." Transparent and Opaque, she guessed. Placing her thumb on the Trans button, she looked at the window and pushed. Instantly the view cleared. Julie hit the floor.

When she came to twenty minutes later, her head was throbbing. She reached up and felt a sizable lump on the brow over her right eye. "Ow!" she yelled. Immediately someone appeared at her side wearing a white smock, hair tied back in a rather severe bun. A small tag said her name was "Peloste."

"Well, hello there, Professor!" Peloste said with a smile. "You gave us a bit of a scare there."

"Uh, what happened?" Julie asked.

"You don't remember?" Peloste queried, concerned.

Julie thought. "I was talking to Dr. Edwards ... and ... then, I was about to, I saw something..." she trailed off.

"Right. Then you fainted and knocked yourself out. Apparently the shock - " Julie lifted a finger silencing the nurse, thinking, then remembering. She let out her breath.

"Oh. Oh yeah ... oh ... SHIT!" She began to rise.

"Hold on there, Doctor," Peloste said, putting a hand on Julie's shoulder and gently pushing her back down. "We need to take a film of your head." Julie lay back down, but her mind raced.

Peloste walked to a small panel on the wall. "Dr. Karstens said to notify him the moment you come to."

"Karstens?" Julie asked.

"He's the Director of the Institute." She clicked a button and punched some numbers, paused, then spoke in a voice too low for Julie to hear. When she was done, she turned again to Julie. Chuckling a little, she said, "Edwards felt so bad. Said you slipped right out of his grasp."

She adjusted the magnifier attached to her glasses and looked closely at the bump, then touched it lightly, causing Julie to yelp.

"Sorry, Doctor. It looks like just a surface injury, but after Karstens sees you we'll take a closer look."

"Mmm, okay," Julie mumbled, again touching the lump. It was tender and felt like a small knot. Trying not to think about what she thought she saw in that room, she looked about the one she was in. The walls were painted a cool blue; strangely reassuring. On the wall directly in front of her hung a large videograph, a scene from nature, snippet of a view, a minute in length. It was of trees and grass waving in the breeze, making a gentle rustling sound. Occasionally, she also heard birdsong. It was a lowland. In the background was a mountain of medium height, round on the backside, flat on the front. Its face had clearly been shorn off due to some past geological episode. Down below, wound a small river. The scene looped almost imperceptibly every sixty seconds, which became noticeable when the same pattern of sounds occurred over and again.

"Half Dome," Julie said. Well, Half Dome as it appeared some fifty years earlier. Yosemite Valley had since been sold to a private developer for several billion dollars. He'd promptly cut down and sold off most of the trees, then built a large town and amusement park geared toward the very rich. It was now called Arnoldland, as the buyer's name was Ross Arnold. He carved a large, golden "A" on the flat face of Half Dome.

Within a year, most all of the larger wildlife had been shot and mounted on walls or erected free-standing. Bears, mountain lions and elk, caught off guard nibbling or grazing peacefully, now stood immobile, collecting dust, cast in their perennial roles as vicious and terrifying beasts, ready to rip out a man's throat at a moment's notice. With each elimination, the people sighed to think that there was one less horror in the world.

"Very good," came a voice behind her. Julie looked around to see a mid-sized, suited man walking toward her, distinguished looking with glasses, beard and gray hair at the temples. With him was Edwards. "You recognize it. It's changed a bit since, hasn't it?"

"My father took me once when I was a girl," Julie responded. She didn't offer more. "Not your typical hospital room," she noted.

"Mm, no," the man replied, a look of distaste darkening his features. He extended his hand and said, "Bob Karstens. Glad to meet you."

Edwards, who had been behind the director, took her hands after and cupped them in his. "Dr. Pine," he began, "how are you feeling?"

"Well, except for a headache and sore neck, I feel fine."

"Yes, Dr. Peloste will be looking at that. However, her initial diagnosis is encouraging. I am *so sorry,* Doctor. You fell so suddenly, and my vintage reflexes aren't what they used to be."

"Please, call me Julie. Formalities have never meant much to me. And I'm sorry about fainting like that, but..."

"Of course, perfectly understandable. And you can call me Joe. A regrettable situation, your fainting and my dropping you." Edwards shook his head in self-reproach.

"Um," Julie started, "about that room, what I saw, or, *thought* I saw..."

"Julie, my dear," Karstens answered, "let's talk about that later. First thing we need to do is make sure you are okay." He touched her shoulder, then, with Edwards, began to walk off.

"*But*," Julie called.

As he was about to round the corner, Karstens turned back, and with a gleam in his eye said, "Yes, it was real." And then he was gone.

Two

True, for a time we tolerated them in our graciousness, those unthinking, unfeeling beasts of the earth. All the crawling, squirming, slavering creatures that we shared this small planet with. Nature, red in tooth and claw. Monsters, really. For millions of years they had inhabited our nightmares, and generations of children shook in the dark for fear.

But we grew up, broke the chains that bound us, and now were free. Free of the guilt we'd felt at their slow, systematic extinction. For now we knew that their existence had been mere *chance;* they were never actually *meant to be here permanently*, not the way *we* were. Their continued survival had been *incidental* to ours. They'd been, in actuality, *parasites* that had taken, yet given back nothing in return for their miserable lives.

Still, there were voices "crying out in the wilderness," which tried to raise the alarm. But not for long. It was apparent that an unstoppable force, in inexorable time had come to the human sphere, the Anthropocene, and it was no use trying to fight it. It was like expecting a speeding train to stop for one man on the tracks. It simply wasn't safe to be at odds with destiny. Posters randomly appeared at the time with a wise old Japanese saying, "The nail that stands up gets hammered down." People weren't sure who put them up, the government, or the opposition.

It became a crime then, an unforgivable sin, to speak of protecting the environment, and of what once was. For those with such delusions had a sickness, a disease, and most of the time it was incurable. Even so, some tried to rehabilitate them, and in a few notable cases were able to help these people to see the wrong in their thinking, the harm such fantasies could cause the Great Vision. It was a war of ideas, of values, but the outcome was never in doubt, for the government, in essence, an amalgamation of corporations - really a cabal of the very rich - had already made its decision.

As might be expected, there arose a Resistance, which, at last, giving up on verbal protests, opted for monkey wrenching and vandalism. Hackers attacked government surveillance systems, offices of The Enlightened, and just about anybody else they perceived as part of the "suicidal order." At the same time, construction equipment was torched, engines wrecked, headquarters burned down. It was a last desperate act, the final, inevitable card to be played before the end, and was, of course, anticipated by the government. In fact, elements therein, with official approval, even took surreptitious part. It all made for horrendous public relations for the troublemakers, terrorists and traitors, serving to verify and harden popular opinion against them.

Thus, when every avenue had been tried, and still people insisted on looking back to a past that was dead and gone, all that remained was to excise the cancer of earth worship. That's when the purges began. It was a sad, but necessary evil, and when it was over, fully ten percent of humanity had disappeared. No one knew what happened to them, although everyone did. Dumped at sea, it was rumored. They had gone the way of prehistory, as everything pre-Awakening was dubbed, just another stepping stone, another footnote in the Grand Story of Life.

With the guilt-makers gone, suddenly it was as if the whole world opened up for us. Those mental shackles broken, we'd been set free, and it was *liberating*. Land previously wasted by being set aside for "wildlife" was rightly reclaimed for human use. *Finally.* And with it, a new era of wealth and consumerism took off. We had not realized *how much* had been withheld from us. But now, all had a surfeit, and it became a time of luxury and laughter. New transit soon crisscrossed through previous forestland, while their trees were felled and harvested for more housing on the very same land. Vast new acreages were opened up for farming crops to feed our rapidly increasing population. Free of the curse of environmentalism, nothing was held back, nothing untried. People were happy, and everything was "clear." A new era began, the "New Man" (NM) era. Everything "prehistoric", pre-Awakening, was OM, or Old Man. All calendars were changed accordingly.

And indeed, our numbers exploded; it became a virtue to have many children. At the same time, genetic advances translated into longer life spans for all. Where once "overpopulation" would have been a concern, now no one worried. "The World Is Our Oyster" was a catchphrase seen everywhere. When children asked their mothers what an oyster was, mom would shrug, pat the child's head and answer, "Some fish thing that lived in the ocean." It made the children shudder.

And like the dumping of toxins on land, synonymous with the time of the Great Awakening, the world began to openly dump all manner of waste into the seas. Effort was no longer spent on attempts to keep them clean. It was reasoned that these waters were so immense, so dynamic, that they could absorb *anything* we discarded.

The new agricultural lands, rich in nutrients, easily fed the masses, food from them aggressively grown and harvested, forced from the ground with poisons. On them we grew genetically engineered Pomatos (a potato/tomato combination), Whorn (a wheat/corn combo), and even Peef (beef and potatoes) along with various fusions of all of them together.

Then *every* combination was tried, *every* possibility tested, and entirely new foods invented from molecular scratch in laboratories. It seemed that every day an all new kind of fare was making news, and the people, unwitting subjects in the mass experimentation, clapped their hands in delight.

It was a golden age. And it lasted about 40 years. Then certain things began to go awry. Actually, they had already been doing that for a while, it was just that, in their revelry, no one really noticed.

Songbirds were one of the first to go during the Golden Age. Somewhere in that initial decade, the last lonely melody was heard. A warbler it was, calling futilely for another, until, finally giving up, it fell to the ground, dead, and was crushed underfoot. Nobody really missed them, but for a year or two one could buy a sound recording, made decades earlier, on the black market. It was highly frowned on.

It was more of a worry when major insect pollinators stopped coming around to visit the flowers and make our food grow. Scientists weren't sure why, but some secretly believed that bees had no taste for Peef, or any of our other laboratory concoctions.

This potential calamity, however, turned out to be a boon for the government when it quickly unveiled a new technological breakthrough in crop pollination. *Synth-o-Life* pollen, each type tailor-made for the particular plant that it was to be sprayed upon, produced bumper harvests. It was another milestone in the new system, and it was exclaimed upon by enthusiastic school teachers and corporate spinmeisters alike as evidence of man's natural superiority over nature.

And when we thought about it, it suddenly seemed absurd that we had so long depended upon the unpredictable vagaries of such a fickle and primitive mistress as *nature*. How could we? It was utterly preposterous! Of course we had to wrest our fate from the hands of "mother nature" and claim it for ourselves. Hadn't we, in fact, been doing *just that* all these years, anyway? Housing, water supply, energy, agriculture, etc., all were evidence of our unwillingness to be tossed about like reeds in the wind, or like flotsam thrown upon the rocky shores of fate.

From this triumph, we turned our attention much more to controlling the climate and attempting to defuse earth's chaotic weather bombs. That, though, turned out to be a much harder proposition. It seemed that every piece of modification here was accompanied by a random act of violence there. When the poles and Greenland were finally ice-free, the thermohaline current, which had previously circulated the ocean's waters north and south, began to slow and the waters to stagnate. On land, drought was spreading, ravaging cropland.

Then, throwing all previous caution to the wind, we tried everything to mitigate the heat and rising tides; well, everything short of actually cutting our emissions of greenhouse gases: every geoengineering trick without regard to possible negative side effects. Iron was dumped wholesale into the seas with the expectation that the growing masses of algae would absorb the increasing CO_2. That appeared to work for a short while, until it was noticed that enormous algae blooms were robbing the oceans of oxygen and contributing to their demise. We dropped millions of tons of nano-sized aluminum from the skies, many a flight cutting grid-like paths back and forth. The hope was that the particulates would reflect sunlight back into space. Then people began to complain of serious lung issues.

For a long time, scant attention had been paid, except by a nervous few, to the implications of receding forests and expanding deserts. In the oceans, plankton and coral reefs, victims of global warming and pollution, began to die out wholesale. Fish too, ruthlessly depleted, were now to be found only in pockets, surrounded by extensive, dark "dead zones."

In time, the very air one breathed, no matter where he or she was in the world, carried a foul, oily, chemical stench about it, which never seemed to go away. Grass that had been growing in the few spaces where concrete and asphalt met began to brown, even without treatment. Rain, which used to fall freely on agricultural fields, now increasingly had to be coerced from the sky. When that failed, reclaimed and desalinated water was quietly substituted.

With the lax regulatory atmosphere came increasing environmental disasters, including massive leaks from many of the thousands of offshore oil rigs. The infamous 2010 Deep Water Horizon disaster was repeated again and again. Similarly, one by one, nuclear power plants also failed and melted down when people tired of the vigilance required to prevent accidents; of fighting an industry behemoth intent on deregulation. Or when loss of power for any reason, from solar flares to warfare, for more than a few hours, meant loss of reactor cooling. Vast no-man's-lands, contaminated with radiation, were nonetheless inhabited by those with nowhere else to go.

And thus, silently, one by one, links in the chain, strands in the great web of life, were snapping. Nature was, at last, buckling beneath the strain, had hit its final tipping point - the point of no return. And, like the earth itself, it seemed the whole of man was ailing, sick with respiratory disease and cancer.

When it became obvious that things weren't going well for us here on our home planet, it was announced that the time had come to set our sights on bigger and better horizons: the colonization of space and the terraforming of other planets, no matter the cost. On moving out among the stars and populating their worlds with more of us.

For it had been decided that man was, indeed, the highest form of life by far to have ever existed, the very *pinnacle* of galactic evolution. Must have been, else we would have heard from others by now. But no, the radar dishes still rang silent, even after all these years. Flatline. It could only mean that no one else was out there. Perhaps there were places with lowly forms of biology as had once existed here, but when found, they too would be transformed, made to our likeness, their vermin exterminated as well. If we so chose, we might bring some promising specimens along via genetic modification. They could turn out to be useful.

That was the vision, our *new* mission. *That's why we are here*, we realized, *to fan out into the galaxy, and from there to the larger universe*. It is a holy crusade, and one we've held, unconsciously, within our breasts for lo these many, many years. It's why we have always cleared the way before us, purging our path with fire, cleansing the earth, this noble which gave us life and nurtured our youth. Surely, if she could, she would understand, understand that we had finally come of age and had outgrown her; that the time had come for us to leave home. And, like young men and women who have their whole lives ahead of them, that's exactly what we would do. The time had come to put childish sentimentality aside and move forward; time to be free of the prison of this planet. A glorious future awaited.

Once the earth was written off, huge resources and brain-power were put to work. A new era of spaceflight ensued, and rumor had it that great Dyson Spheres were being constructed that would be capable of taking people away from their ruined world and onto a happy journey to the stars. There were videos! People were told there would be sacrifices and everyone was expected to contribute. Unknown to all but a relative few, however, was the fact that, even though the mission had consumed much of the available resources left, there was not *nearly* enough to complete it. At least not for everyone, nor even a *tiny fraction* thereof, since most of the raw materials were already gone, expended during the heady building boom.

And while we did make it to Mars, the job of terraforming it in a way that would make it amenable to our existence proved to be impossible. Maybe in a couple hundred years. Problem was, it became painfully clear to intelligent people, that we didn't have a couple hundred, nor even an appreciable fragment of that time left.

When the reality of our dire situation was undeniable, a great disillusionment began to settle on us. That's when we began to hear fewer and fewer patriotic speeches. That's when the Blacksuits began to be seen more frequently. There were still some who shilled the inevitable "breakthrough" that would finally take us off "this old barge", as one called it, but blind trust in official reassurances was evaporating. Signs of this disaffection began discreetly: officially approved posters quietly removed in the dead of night; flags that people had worn on their lapels or put in their windows, disappearing.

A general feeling of gloom, even dread, seemed to descend upon the world like a shroud. Most hoped that this was just a temporary state and that any day now would come the good news that the ships were finally ready to carry everyone off to the heavens to continue life in the great spheres which *surely* must be there. No doubt the reason essentials were running out here below was because these great spheres were being decked out in magnificence. Indeed, lay artist's depictions of the high-tech vessels were popular for a time. In any case, people knew that *something* was imminent, they just weren't sure *what*. But deep beneath it all, it was hard to shake the unease.

Around that time, forty years after the inauguration of the Great Awakening, a chilling stage in our fall commenced. It began when one man, a famous journalist, wrote an essay claiming that, while it was true that the great spheres existed, *there was simply not enough room for all the billions of humanity to come aboard.* More likely, their number would be in the *thousands.* Thus, it had been decided that only *the most faithful* would be allowed passage. The rest would be left to their own devices on a rapidly declining planet. Evolution was like that, he stated cynically at the end; only the best survive. That was his last article.

It was a stunning betrayal, but few dared reveal their bitterness. Those who snapped and did, did so but once.

And that's when the "Worth" campaign began. With thirteen billion people all vying for the same limited resources, it was inevitable. At first, it was just a handy measure of a person's value to the community of man, a value determined by a formula based on right-wing ideas of patriotism and servitude. Was a person an actively contributing member of society, or *just a leech* that only took while giving nothing back? "Worth" caught on quickly, and soon a "Worth Index" was developed and aggressively propagated. People were interviewed and assigned their personal worth, or usefulness, ratings. These were numbers on a scale of one to one hundred and fractions thereof. Those with higher ratings often attached a small pin to their shirts, under their flags, proudly stating that number. All, however, were required to keep their numbers somewhere on their persons to be presented upon demand. A person with a low Worth rating was advised to get his or her numbers up.

The Worth campaign naturally made many suspicious of its ultimate intent. Eventually, it set off a cascade of spying and counter spying, charges and counter charges, finger-pointing and kangaroo courts. Sentences were delivered and executed, and people fell over themselves to prove that they and their family were more worthy than their neighbors.

The next phase was the surreptitious physical installment of "trackers" within the human body. This was done by way of mandatory injections, purportedly to prevent devastating epidemics. RFID devices, small enough to go through hypodermic needles, were inserted and their numbers logged. Most now had a permanent personal ID and could be followed and watched anywhere they might be in the world. That information was added to an individual's computer profile, indelible records of data continually collected in myriad ways and stored, documenting every aspect of his or her life, birth to death. Privacy, once a natural birthright, was a privilege reserved for the select few.

Around the edges, ferocious battles for resources were spreading, the barbarians ever at the door, while on the sidelines, dedicated scofflaws, anarchists and apocalyptos bided their time, always ready to bring it home. Though the government tried hard to suppress unfavorable disclosures, a new paranoia descended, one unequaled in history. From this resulted the Second Great Purge (and some noted the serendipity that, in a world devoid of other animal species, a world with so much shortage and privation, there rarely seemed to be any lack of protein).

Those that remained after the second purge lived day-to-day with their flags firmly fixed. None of them, however, were the naïve, undoubting believers they'd been previously. They were simply too afraid to air those doubts.

Thus, pale and gaunt, dark rings under its eyes, humanity stumbled its way to its appointment with fate, as, piece-by-piece, the world careened towards chaos and collapse.

Three

Though Julie protested that she was fine, Peloste insisted on the head scan. Legalities, she murmured. When it was done, the images showed no damage beyond a bruise to the skull. After an additional hour lying in bed and drinking fluids, she was released. It was a long hour.

A de Physica orderly was waiting just outside the door in a small electric cart.

"How are you, Professor?" he asked politely, extending a hand toward her. "I'm Don Mack. I work in tours and was asked by Dr. Karstens to show you around." Julie took his hand, warmed by his boyish smile. Smiles were rare currency these days; one accepted them gratefully.

"Thank you, Don," Julie replied. "But what I'd *really* like to see are your recent, uh, *zoological* additions, if you know what I mean." Julie was quite eager to examine the floral and faunal specimens she'd observed earlier, though hopefully this time sans the fainting spell.

"Of course, Professor. I understand."

"*Julie* is fine," she said.

"Of course, Julie." Mack continued. "Thing is," and here he lowered his voice and shielded his next words so that only Julie could hear, though she suspected that Mack was being playfully dramatic, "I was instructed not to speak about that matter with you. You are to be given a 'walk-through' of our facilities here, first."

"And I appreciate that, Don, but what I'd really like to do is get back in that room and inspect ..."

"Understood," Mack cut in. "And you will. I believe that Dr. Karstens will be attending to that personally. Please climb aboard, this train's about to leave." After seating herself and buckling in, Mack activated the vehicle, which hummed quietly and started slowly down the hall.

The walls were the usual antiseptic white, lit overhead by embedded fluorescents. Other than that, they were bare. People walking by, singly or in groups of two or three, clipboards in hand or arms loaded with books and papers, would step out of their way to let them pass. Occasionally, one would lift a head to acknowledge them. Strangely, several seemed to know who she was. A couple of times a passerby nodded, saying, "Don", "Professor." She wondered about that last. *Did they mean Don?* She turned her head slightly to look closer. He wasn't wearing the standard white, she noticed. His was a casual, yet, neat and not unbusinesslike combination: Tan Rakii slacks and tweed sweater. *That must be it,* she thought, *why he gets to wear what he wants.* Mack noticed her watching him out of the corner of her eye and smiled. Julie quickly looked away and flushed.

"Uh," she stumbled.

"Yes?" Mack asked helpfully. Just then another business suit walked by. "Afternoon Don, Dr. Pine," he said in passing.

Julie turned around to look at the man. He too was looking back and waved, unsmiling, then continued quickly on. Julie thought, "How did he..." she broke off, wondering.

"Excuse me?" inquired Mack.

"That man, he knew my name." Then pausing, she said, "Ah, silly me. That must be it. I was wondering how that man knew me. He must have been in the Observation Room when I, um, when I was there."

"Tom Gordon? Oh no, Tom's in administration. He never involves himself in the details. *Great guy, though.*"

"Okay, then how..." Julie began.

"Coming up on the right is the door to the firing room. This is where we send our protons on their way," Don said, apparently intent on ignoring her question. He stepped out of the cart, and walked to an innocuous-looking door marked "Section One" above and opened it. Julie climbed out, looked peculiarly at him, then walked past and into another, narrower, hallway. It was short and led to yet another door. Humming could be heard through it, machine-like. It increased in volume as she entered and was suddenly in a very large room, more the size of an airplane hangar. All manner of piping was here, and in all sizes, floor to ceiling. At regular junctures in both directions, metal staircases wound up to other levels, and on each were more smocks, some white, some blue.

"These pipes carry mostly electric cables, but some, like that one," Mack said, raising his voice above the drone and pointing to a cluster that surrounded a larger pipe, "carry refrigerant. That's so we make sure the 'A' tube, that's the acceleration tube you see there in the middle, doesn't get too hot." Indeed, Julie could see frost on the outside of the cooling pipes. A sort of foggy mist hung in the air immediately around them. She noticed an aluminum pan underneath that ran the length of the pipes. In it was flowing maybe an inch of water. She looked both ways. The piping setup stretched off into the distance, finally occluded by other apparatus.

"Where does the water go?" she asked.

"Oh, we use it. It's clean. We could probably drink it if we wanted to. On top of this, we have dehumidifiers set up all along the path to remove the rest of the excess."

"Hmm," Julie nodded.

"Now this is the important one, Julie," Mack said, pointing at the larger tube in the middle.

"The 'A' tube," Julie repeated.

"Right," Mack said. "That one is a perfect vacuum. Just *making* it cost quite a little bundle. I can't tell you how much exactly, because officially I don't know myself, but it and these other tubes are fifty miles long. There could not be one internal flaw in it, not one thing that might cause the slightest deceleration or throw something else off. That could happen if, say, even a millimeter height weld were to incur even the slightest friction. To reduce that possibility further, the inside of A tube is also lined with mirrored Teflon.

"We are trying to recreate the conditions leading to the Big Bang, what some refer to as the Genesis Event, as closely as possible, without actually *doing* it - another Genesis Event - that wouldn't be good." Mack paused here as a technician strode up, looking at Julie. Short crew cut, he had a certain military aspect about him. He and Mack walked off a ways and spoke briefly. A few minutes later they shook hands, then the technician approached, and smiling, said, "Hi, Professor. It's a pleasure to meet you."

Julie shook his hand, "Thank you, er..." she looked at his name tag, "Dave."

"I understand that you have an interest in our little project?"

"Aspects of it, most definitely. That is, if I can ever get past the preliminaries. No offense, Don," she said. Dave smiled.

"You're in good hands, Professor," he said, smiling at Mack. "Hopefully we will be seeing you again."

"Yes, thanks," Julie replied uncertainly. Dave walked back to his station where two other men stood, looking at readouts.

"Dave supervises this part of our complex. Good man," Don stated. He broke off a moment, then pointed to a large, round shaped object, almost like a doughnut, encircling the tubing about a hundred feet away. "That little gem, or rather, a whole bunch of them, are *key* to our work here. Can you guess its function, Julie?"

She looked at it. Thirty meters past it was another doughnut.

"Well, I suppose it has something to do with the A tube, since it's surrounding it."

"Go on," Mack encouraged.

"All right. Well, the idea behind particle accelerators is to fling an element, often a proton, at another element, often an anti-proton, so as to cause them to smash into each other, thus giving off huge amounts of energy."

"Right."

"So once you launch 'the package'," she continued, "you'd like to try to get it to, or as close to, light speed as possible, right? So that you can get the biggest bang for your buck. A good way of doing that, then, would be the use of powerful magnets, or electromagnets."

Mack was smiling.

"So my guess is that these doughnut shaped things are your version of gas pedals," Julie concluded. Don laughed.

"Seems you know more about our operations than I was led to believe, Professor!" He exclaimed.

"No, not really," Julie answered. She reached into a breast pocket and pulled out a glossy brochure, neatly folded, and handed it to Mack. He took it, immediately recognizing a flyer that he himself had written, complete with helpful diagrams of the accelerator. It was meant for the few official visitors that occasionally came by to see where all the money was going. Of course she'd gotten it at the meeting earlier, a little stack of them on the table next to the refreshments. He laughed out loud.

Mack drove Julie around the rest of the complex, showing her the various departments and important sections, but the longer the tour drew out, the edgier she was becoming. All she really wanted to see was the miofauna, an animal that she knew had been extinct for millions of years. And Mack hadn't answered her more detailed questions having to do with the experiment itself, things not covered in the presentation earlier.

She wanted to know, for instance, about reproducibility. Could they do it again, and what were the larger implications of the incident? She knew that once a discovery had been made, science could not leave it alone. Rather, it grabbed hold of the tree of knowledge and shook hard until every last morsel of information and material benefit fell like fruit from its branches. What were their plans now? Were they going to try again? And what about the specimens, where would they be kept, and would she be allowed to have unfettered access to them?

Julie thought about the other notables in her field. There was her mentor, Jim Hodges, Curator at AMNH in New York. He knew his stuff, certainly. Maybe they'd send the animals there. And Fukushita at São Paulo University. He, too, was quite published, specializing in Neogene felines. Jere Roddick, Paleobotanist in Amsterdam, had made more contributions to our understanding of Tertiary plant life than anyone since the great Daniel Axelrod. As for geology, Abdul Ammad, the diminutive professor at the University of Morocco, was unsurpassed. There was also a host of excellent, if perhaps less qualified, names: Hansen, Fredericks, Johannsen and others.

Still, with the exception of Hodges, none of them truly had the kind of broad expertise, or, she believed, level of interest in Miocene fauna that she had. On the other hand, though well published and well regarded, she was still only an "Under-Curator." Robert Burns' hold on the office of Curator was white-knuckle, even though he was well past the normal age of retirement. She could probably add his name to her list of experts, but didn't want to. His interest seemed to be mainly in preserving his lucrative position. He'd never had any real love of the subject, she suspected. So she bided her time knowing that one day the stubborn cuss would have to step down, if he didn't pass away first, and then maybe she could change things.

Burns had been an all too willing accomplice of the technocrats when they'd suggested their ridiculous revisions to the "Past Ages" dioramas. What they wanted was the removal of background scenes depicting a different world, one that was wild and free, only allowing to remain the bones themselves and their physical descriptions. Julie hated petty micromanagement which had political censorship as its aim.

Unlike Burns, she'd loved these dioramas, and should, seeing she, with the help of museum staff, both designed and built them years earlier. She spent many an afternoon having her lunch, not in the cafeteria, but in these rooms. When the government people finally came by one day "requesting" their complete removal and replacement with various "halls of the future," she nearly lost it. Bit by bit, piece by piece, it seemed the magnificent story of earth was being changed. New Man revisionism. Everywhere it was becoming the story of our inevitable conquest. But where was our modern Galileo to stand up and declare that we were not the center of the universe? Then she remembered that in the end, under threat, Galileo, too, recanted.

Still, Julie knew that there were other quietly disgruntled witnesses to this raping of science and culture, people just as angry, but alas, like her, resigned to a mute grumbling. Her feelings, though, festered and burned. It was like a dark chasm in her soul. She knew that the earth had survived many a natural disaster over billions of years, but this one, the cancer of man, was an assault on so many fronts that she was often sick with dread.

Mostly, though, Julie kept these feelings to herself and wrote them in journals, which she locked away. Certainly Tom knew of her sentiments, but not their depths. No one knew or could know, even accidentally. It might be the end of her. Of them. She and Tom. Strange world where the truth was now impounded in the repository of a few minds. And increasingly, even that wasn't a safe place. The rest of humanity, fraught with other concerns, were content to exist in the bliss of total ignorance.

"You must be hungry." Julie startled a bit, turning to look at Mack. He was slowing the cart some as they came to another large room where people were coming and going. He parked behind a row of other such vehicles and looked at her while she gazed around the corner. From where she sat, she could see that this must be the complex cafeteria. Yes, she *was* hungry.

"I don't think you've heard much of what I've been saying for the past ten minutes or so. I understand; I tend to drone on."

"Sorry, just thinking," Julie responded. "Actually, I'm famished." As if to underline her statement, Julie's stomach suddenly let out an audible growl. She covered her arms over her waist and half smiled, embarrassed.

"Well then, this place has the best burger in town. I recommend it," Mack quipped.

"Ah, Mack! Right on time." It was Karstens, walking out of the dining area. "Let's have lunch!" He clasped Mack and Julie on the back.

"I'd love to, Bob, but if it's okay with you, can I take a raincheck on that? Some people coming by from Beijing and I'll need to meet them." He opened a small hatch on the back of the cart, pulling out a plastic bag, which Julie guessed contained his lunch. "Potential sponsors. They're looking to make an investment."

"Oh yes, the Wang group," Karstens remembered. "Yes, by all means continue. Every little helps. I'm going to hold you to that lunch, though."

"Looking forward to it, Bob." Mack looked at his watch. "Gotta run, guys." He shook Julie's hand, then, looking at Karstens, gave him the thumbs up. "I think she'll do nicely."

With that, he winked at Julie, smiled, then boarded the cart and left down the hall, turning right at the corner, and was gone.

"'I think she'll do nicely?'" Julie repeated aloud.

Karstens took hold of Julie's elbow, "Chow time!"

Four

Amid greetings, smiles, and nods, Karstens led Julie to a corner booth. Those on either side of it were unoccupied. He glanced around while gesturing for her to sit, himself taking the side facing the wall.

The place was moderately engaged, with more arriving. Groups of people were in quiet discussion. A few of them, Julie noted, occasionally glanced their way. Then Karstens took a small device from his pocket and set it upon the table. He touched it lightly on the side and paused. Slowly, Julie noticed, the volume of background noise was increasing. More conversation, mixed with kitchen sounds of dishes and silverware. She looked around, but the decibel level seemed somewhat out of proportion to the number of people in the room and was apparently coming through the ceiling speakers. She looked back at Karstens, who was looking down, innocently adjusting his napkin. She looked again at the little box sitting on the table, then reached for it. Quickly Karstens shielded it with his own hand and Julie withdrew.

"White Noise Amplifier," Karstens said, "aka WNA. Makes it harder for others to hear a private conversation."

"Oh," Julie answered, lifting an eyebrow and looking at Karstens peculiarly. The place was filling up. She looked again at the booth closest to them, still empty. Then she noticed a small triangular sign on its table, near the edge. "Reserved," it said in red letters. Karstens was now fidgeting with the condiments. Scratching her right temple and clearing her throat, Julie turned in her seat to glance at the booth behind her. "Reserved."

"Okay," Julie said. "Are we expecting company?"

"No," Karstens answered.

The waitress arrived. "Hi, Bob. Having lunch a bit late to-day, aren't we?" She looked at Julie and smiled. Julie returned the smile.

Karstens waved her query away. "I had something earlier." He grinned.

The woman, Sonya, frowned disapprovingly. "I hope you're not still sneaking that toasted - "

Karstens coughed loudly, cutting off her statement. "Oh, heck no. Matter of fact I had that lovely piece of carrot cake you sent up yesterday," he asserted, "and *was it good!*"

"Umm," Sonya murmured. Since his divorce, Sonya had made herself Karstens' de facto dietician, and while normally she would have continued this light banter, she sensed some-how that now was not the time. Her eyes dropped to the little black box on the table. She nodded to herself, then reaching into an apron pocket, took out an e-pad. "What can I getcha?" she asked him again. She knew that the man liked to eat.

"I'm thinking a fat faux egg sandwich with fries would do nicely," Karstens answered. "And a glass of red wine, please, maybe that number you've been telling me about." Sonya raised an eyebrow.

"Got it," she answered. A very rare wine. *This was her, then?* "But for the record, I don't have faux anything," she corrected. Then turning to Julie, "And for you, Dr. Pine?"

Julie gaped, "How do you know who I am?" she questioned. "How does *everyone* know who I am?"

"You look like a garden burger kind of girl to me," Sonya deflected. "We make a killer GB with a lovely salad on the side. How's that sound?"

"Uh, fine," Julie answered, starting to feel annoyance at the skullduggery.

"Great," said Sonya. Then, sticking the stylus over one ear, she turned on her heels and walked to the order counter.

"Dr. Karstens," Julie began, "I mean, Bob, if you don't mind my asking, what the hey is going on? Why do I get the idea that everyone here is in on something?" Just then her stomach growled again. "Sorry." Grabbing a glass of water, she drank half.

Karstens' beeper went off. "Excuse me a moment," he said. He flipped open his cell and began an unenlightening conversation. While Julie could hear a tinny voice coming from it, she couldn't quite make out what was being said. Small chitchat about percentages and the like. She looked at her watch. It'd been almost two hours since she left the clinic. She should be leaving soon. The transit home would take a while, and she needed to make a stop at the museum. Yet, she *had* to see the specimens.

Karstens noticed her. "Right. Yes. Okay. Uh huh. Go ahead with that. Let's talk about that other thing later, Howard, I'm in the middle of an important meeting... It's fine. Right. Right. Okay, talk to you later." Karstens flipped closed the cover to his cell.

As if on cue, Sonya showed up with their plates.

"Thanks, dear," Karstens said.

"Thank you," Julie said. She saw, now, the small round pin on Sonya's shirt. It read:

Party like there's no tomorrow

"My pleasure," said Sonya. Then she gave Julie a somber look and half-smile, squeezing her hand.

Too hungry to parse it, Julie immediately grabbed her sandwich and took a large bite. It was delicious. She took another.

"*Mmm*, this is good. Where do you...?"

"We grow it ourselves, underground, hydroponically, with water from the accelerator," Sonya informed. Then with a little bow, she headed to another table. Ah yes, the recycled water. *Important meeting*, Karstens had said. Hmm.

"Sonya's a promising grad student. Gifted, even. She waits on the side. Doesn't have to, she likes to. Gets to meet people." Karstens offered. Then he set to his sandwich.

A grad student. Julie almost asked what the point was, but she knew the answer already. In times of crisis, we maintain our traditions to maintain a sense of normalcy. The alternative, admitting futility, was madness.

Karstens seemed to be in thought and Julie didn't want to interrupt him. Still, she felt that she'd waited long enough. Finally, she said, "Bob, I need to leave soon. When can I see the specimen?"

Karstens hesitated, looking at his plate, then, at last, up at her. He'd apparently come to some decision. When he did, the look on his face shook her. Gone was the easy disposition of just moments before. Now he looked dead serious. She stopped chewing.

"Absolutely, Doctor," he said. "First though, I have to get something out of the way .... Julie, I, uh," pausing again, "I know about you."

She gulped hard, almost choking. *What? What's this?*

"Know about me?" she asked. It wasn't that she had anything to hide, really, but the way he said it, it sounded bad.

Karstens faltered, smiled, then said, "I'm sorry. That didn't come out right at all." He took a quick sip of his drink. Julie had stopped eating and was now staring blankly at him. Karstens sighed and muttered an expletive. "What I'm trying to say is, well," he shook his head, "um, well, a complaint was made, and well..."

"A complaint? About me? I don't understand," she said, feeling a tightening in her throat. *Is that what this is all about,* she wondered, *preamble to a lynching?*

"Okay," Karstens said, putting his hands edge down on the

table, like knives on a cutting board, "here's the long and short of it. Your supervisor at the museum - Burns, I think it is? - anyway, he made a complaint about you to *his* boss. Seems he found one of your notebooks and thought it - subversive. So he wrote you up." Julie started to stand.

"Sit down, Julie!" Karstens ordered. He looked around the room, but no one appeared to be listening. "Please, hear me out." Julie stared at him, reseating herself, while her heart picked up its pace.

"What does this have to do with you, sir?" she asked.

"Julie, do you know who Burns answers to?" he asked.

"To be honest, I didn't know he answered to anyone," she replied.

"Well, he does. Though he doesn't want anyone knowing that. Julie, Burns is an ass, everyone in your field knows it. You know it, perhaps better than anyone."

"I still don't get..."

"Burns reports to Jim Hodges."

"Okay..."

"Jim, as you know, and with all due respect, is the greatest, all around paleontologist we have today."

"Yes," Julie acknowledged, though she felt somewhat stung in the admission. "Of course he's the best. I agree. I know my place." Karstens looked at her.

"No, Julie, that's not what I'm saying. Like I said, Hodges is the best *all around* paleontologist we have today. But he's not the best there is for *our* purposes. And I'll get to that." He lifted his glass and drank more, eyeing Julie over the rim.

"First off, you don't have to worry about that report from Burns. Hodges filed it appropriately, I believe it was in his fireplace, and he instructed Burns not to say another word about it. To gain his cooperation, he left him with the impression that you would be investigated," he said. "Seems you and Hodges know each other," Karstens continued.

"We do, somewhat." Julie acknowledged. "We met at a conference a few years ago. He had a grandfatherly way about him."

"Yes, well, he certainly thinks a lot of you. Notes all your papers. He's a friend." Julie felt herself beginning to relax. "And so am I." Karstens reached over and extended his hand as if in symbolic greeting for the first time. As if to say, "Let's start over." She understood and took his hand.

"Thank you. But I still don't follow..."

"Julie, Hodges *led* us to you. He said no one else would be right for this job." Julie sat, impassive, listening.

"So I'm going to cut to the chase. Finally," Karstens grinned. "Julie, m'lady, remember this day, this is the day that will change your life forever, and I mean that in a good way. This is the day that you have dreamed of for so long. Are you ready for that?" He thought that it was a good thing that she was already sitting down.

"Julie, the freak experiment that you saw earlier is not a one-off. It's reproducible, and everything you saw in that room, *everything*, is *Miocene*. Julie, *we have found a way to travel back in time*. And those specimens we've got, they're just the *tip* of the iceberg, if you will," he said.

"No. That's impossible." Julie replied. "Impossible. There's some other explanation."

"Believe me, I *know* it's a lot to absorb. But I'm not deluded and I'm not lying. And it's now history. Though I don't think you'll see it in any history books for a while."

"Not to be disrespectful, Dr. Karstens, but *why should I believe you?* This whole thing, it's incredible! And all the cloak and dagger. It's like something from a science fiction movie. How can I believe any of this?"

Karstens decided to put it on the line. In spite of the white noise amplifier, he held his voice low, glancing covertly around. "My lady, here's the long and short of it. We both know, you and I, that people have screwed the earth and ourselves. Unfortunately, it's irreparable." Julie gaped. It was treason. He continued, "This idiot system, the morons running the show, sold the farm. Our planet is doomed, there's no saving it."

The pulse was pounding in her temples. She felt light-headed.

"Oh sure, something will survive, cockroaches, bacteria. With enough time, other species will evolve. Who knows?" Julie had gone white. He could be executed for this! She would be an accomplice. She looked furtively for cameras.

"Don't worry m'lady. No cameras, no microphones," Karstens reassured. *So you say*, she thought. *Was this a setup, designed to get her to confess?*

Karstens suddenly felt a wave of pity for her, and for what the world had become. She was, in that moment, not an eminent scientist, but just a young woman, a girl even, like his own daughter. A girl who had had to live in fear for too long. Silently, he cursed the state that could do this. Reaching across, he placed his hand over hers, placed it as a caring father would. She looked hard at him. *No, he isn't lying.*

"My lady, we've found a way to travel back in time, and," here Karstens paused, then, "and we want you to go." Julie leaned back against the seat and rested her head against the corner. Karstens said no more then, and just watched her.

Julie closed her eyes, head bent over, just breathing, waiting for the light-headedness to fade. When she opened them again a few moments later, she gazed around the room. Nothing had changed. The world had not stopped. In fact, no one was paying them any attention at all. Wait, there was one. Guy in a dark suit. Dark blue tie. Soon as Julie looked his way, though, he averted his eyes. She watched him, and a few seconds later, he looked back. The stranger held her gaze for another moment, then away again, nodding to the conversation of the woman whose back was turned toward her. He looked down then, writing something in a small notebook in front of him.

Julie looked at a woman working behind the counter. Young, cute, dressed in circa 1950s drive thru. She hadn't noticed before. All the wait people were wearing the costume. Hmm. This waitress was also writing something down. An order, probably burger and fries. No wait, throw in a milkshake. But she was writing on an electronic pad. The stranger was using a paper notebook. People didn't generally use those unless they feared their electronic messages might be intercepted.

Too much mystery. She let it go.

"Is this retro week?" she asked. Karstens looked around.

"Heh. Looks like." The girls were attractive, short skirts, low bustlines. They brought in the customers. The restaurant was a concessionaire, but most of the employees were students with degrees.

"Oughta be a law," he said facilely. They said nothing else for a while, each simply eating his and her lunch. *Let her digest it all,* he thought. Perhaps ten minutes went by that way. Each relaxing or trying to relax. Then Julie spoke up.

"So how does this work, Bob - you've invented time travel and - I'm to be your guinea pig?" she asked. She had to ask.

"Something like that." Karstens replied. "No, not really. Well ... maybe. Well.... Julie, I'm not telling you anything you don't already know. We're in trouble. Real trouble. We're going down." Now that she steeled herself for this conversation, Julie was ready, both feet firmly planted. She was ready.

"My lady, I am you. Male version, but ... I know how you feel, I know what you think - about people, about the government, about the whole of human enterprise, because I feel *ex-*

actly the same way. Furthermore, I believe that most thinking, caring souls among our race feel the same. We all know it.

"We screwed up this world, probably the only livable planet we could have found in lifetimes of spaceflight. Our earth, our precious, lovely, fragile planet. She was a paradise, clinging tenaciously, proudly, to life in a vast sea of lifelessness. Struggling mightily to overcome the many assaults she has endured through the billions of years. Struggling to make life as comfortable as possible for her many children. How happy we should have been.

"Gaia Theory, yes," Karstens said when he noticed Julie's expression. "I am a proponent. Secretly, of course."

"As am I," she replied subversively.

"We had everything, Julie, everything we needed right here. But it wasn't enough. We also had an insatiable drive, an unquenchable hunger to *be God*, and it's killed us. What have we done? What have we done?" He trailed off here.

"But," Julie objected, "what about the spheres?" Karstens seemed not to hear. He was in another place.

Then he said, "Yeah. The grass is always greener somewhere else. Even when it's in *the frozen vacuum of space.*"

A strange sort of delirium seemed take hold of her, almost a drunkenness. But an unpleasant one. He was right; she knew it, had known it for a long time. But it was painful to finally admit it to herself. We'd killed the planet.

"Sometimes at night," Julie began, releasing years of pain, "I cry. I cry when I think of the way we've treated this wonderful world. Damn it! We had it on a silver platter. All we had to do was take care of her. People just don't know. They have no idea what we've lost. How close we are to the end."

"Yeah," agreed Karstens harshly. He looked around. "People have grown up thinking the world of man is all there is, all there's *ever* been. All that *counts*. They've been deliberately lied to by shrewd people cleverer than us. Oily corporate politicians and their think-tank liars for hire. Sociopathic freaks of evolution whose only concern was enriching themselves. Ayn Randians of the worst kind. Hard, mean, evil. Brilliant Neanderthals who found the pen mightier than the sword, but had no problem endorsing the sword when the pen wasn't enough. They were like thieves that break into a house in the night, who, seeing it on fire, whisper to the tenants to go back to sleep 'cause they figure there's still time to plunder the place.

"And we let it happen, Julie. We let them bring it all down based on an elaborate, transparent pile of lies. That the earth was indestructible. That it's resources would last forever. We didn't stop them. Oh, some of us tried, just not hard enough, I guess. Mostly, those of us who understood what was happening, well, we were above that kind of fight. We refused to lower ourselves to their level. Big mistake, 'cause these people don't stop until they win, and they've won. And now ... now." Karstens' voice broke, a tremolo barely heard. "You know, as children we were closer to nature, most of us anyway. We knew that special joy, it filled our hearts and we couldn't help but laugh. Then we grew up and learned that having such feelings was wrong and marked one as weak. A few of us never forgot, though."

A tear formed at the corner of Julie's eye. This was a man who loved the planet. And yes, she'd felt the same, exactly the same way. For a long time. It was a heavy load to bear. Insanity, perceiving the truth, knowing the truth, but unable to speak it. Unable to do a thing about it. To make people understand. To care.

Silence.

"So here's the deal," Karstens said, gathering himself, "we've done more testing - other testing. Like I said, this was not a one-off." He paused to let that sink in. Julie's expression was unchanged. She had stopped seeing and was now only hearing.

"Go on," she said.

"We now know that time travel is a fact. I'd even say it's easy, now that we know how. The problem is, it takes an enormous amount of energy, and, well, each time the energy needed grows almost exponentially. We don't know why."

"The blackouts," she said inquiringly. "The LA Blackouts."

"Quite, my lady. That was us," Karstens acknowledged, looking embarrassed. The Los Angeles Blackouts had caused a stir because of the fact that there was no known reason for them. No weather, solar, geological or other conditions at the time that could have precipitated them. The first had knocked out the city for a day. The next for more than a week. Rioting and looting ensued. The latest would have lasted quite a bit longer had not the government been ready with supplemental power supplied by the huge McCready nuke plant in the Mojave. People got suspicious and were looking for answers. In the month following, though, other issues of import had consumed public attention and the blackouts were forgotten.

"The first time displacement incident was accidental. The second time, after much debate, we'd almost decided to send someone back, but finally opted to house a video camera in a "Strong Box". The third time was the retrieval of that box - though it turned out not to be so strong. The box was smashed," Karstens chuckled. "That caused a lot of angst and 'I told you sos'. *However*," and here he grinned and stuck his index finger in the air, "the camera was not. Julie ... *we have video!*" At this point he reached into an inner pocket and gingerly withdrew a sleek, flat, black square, laying it on the table. It clicked upon it like a tap shoe. "We discovered, my lady, that not only can we send something there, *we can bring it back!* That opens up *a lot* of possibility.

"Now it's true," he continued, "that what we have here is

fixed upon a single location, which just means that we couldn't get a 360 degree view. That was a condition of the Strong Box, so it doesn't show everything. But what it *does* show is *extraordinary!*" He unfolded the plastiscreen and faced it toward her, then smiled. "Are you ready?" Julie watched as Karstens' fingers lightly touched the top left of the square, her heart racing.

"No fainting now." Instantly, the screen lit. There was a moment of static, then, suddenly, there it was in glorious color. Though the bottom third of the screen was blocked by green, most of the rest was bright blue sky and low mountains. The camera was positioned beneath a tree, which was fortunate, for it cut down on solar glare. The landscape here was moderately high, a mountaintop, yet locally level, rising somewhat in the distance. Off to the right, however, it dropped gently into a pleasant valley, and in that valley she could see small lakes. Farther still, was a long blue line, which she knew was the sea. All through, the ground-cover was dotted with color, wildflowers upon which some of the animals grazed. Lupines and Shooting Stars swayed in the breeze. Trees were also in bloom with beautiful pink flowers in varying hues here and there. Soon those flowers would become fruit as delicious as the flowers were fragrant. But it was what was moving among this lovely scene that quickened her pulse.

Indeed, Julie felt her breathing speed up, a typical sign that she was feeling overwhelmed, though she'd resolved to control it. For it was true. Quite obviously it was true. There was no mistaking. The *Zygolophodon*, a genus of Miocene mastodon, was grazing in the mid-distance, while around it, a variety of period horses, camelids, and other long extinct fauna, made that clear.

She stared it the scene, then began to recite the names of those she recognized. *"Archaeohippus! Desmathippus! Parahippus! Hypohippus!"* she exclaimed. "And there's *Meg-*

ahippus! Yes! And *Aepycamelus! Miolabis! Oxydactylus!* And who's that?" she laughed and clapped her hands together, *"Tomarctus opatus!"* Unbeknownst to Julie, tears were flowing down her face. There was a catch in her voice, excited as she was by a scene long gone. Suddenly, there stepped into view a very strange animal with a bizarre crown of horns: those on the left were much larger than those on the right. *"Ramoceros!"* she nearly shouted, "They're all here!" She was beaming now, and despite the WNA, people were looking in their direction.

"And what's that?" she continued, "What's that they're eating?" She'd suddenly noticed the long, green, tufted groundcover. It was backlit by a warm afternoon sun and seemed almost to be glowing. "GRASS!" Julie yelled. "THAT'S GRASS! I KNEW IT!" It went quiet in the diner, but she didn't care. She was oblivious, lost in the moment.

Karstens looked puzzled. "Go on," he prodded.

"You know, *grass!"*

"Yes, so..."

"This era!" she continued excitedly, "It was a huge debate. Though grass phytoliths were found as far back as the Mesozoic, because of a lack of *direct* fossil evidence, some maintained that it didn't evolve until much later. But that may have been due to a low silica content. On the other hand, however, grazers were present at this time with hypsodont teeth, indicating abrasion and wearing. So the question was, what came first, the grass or hypsodonty?"

"'*At this time?'*" Karstens said, repeating her words. "Are you saying, Dr. Pine, that you know what time period this is?"

"Well, yes, of course!" she answered triumphantly. "This is the middle Miocene. Specifically, the *Barstovian.* The Barstovian Land Mammal Age, and by the look of it, I'd put the date at around fourteen or fifteen million years ago. And what a time it was!"

"How are you placing it?" Karstens asked wonderingly.

"That's easy. You see that elephant-like proboscidean there? That's *Zygolophodon proavus*. Though Zygolophodon existed throughout the Miocene, *proavus* lived mainly during a two to three million year stretch within the Barstovian. On top of that, I'm seeing species that became extinct with others that were just evolving then. It's unmistakable."

Karstens laughed and nodded. "You're very good. We estimated the actual time at 14.5 and 14.8 million years ago."

Julie looked at him thoughtfully, yet he offered no more, but only looked at her, waiting. Then it dawned on her. "The stars. You can tell from their positions," she said.

Karstens smiled and nodded. "Relative to today's, yes."

"You have night video." All at once the enormity of it struck her and she blurted, "Oh my God! Oh my God!" and found herself barely able to hold back the tears that flowed, for with all of her learning, and even in her dreams, she'd never conceived anything so beautiful.

"Well then, my lady, I have to ask you," Karstens began, "are you interested? You'd only have thirty days."

"Am I interested? In going to the Miocene? YES! YES, OF COURSE I'M INTERESTED!" Julie answered emphatically through her tears.

Karstens noticed others watching and handed Julie a tissue. Diners turned away nervously at his glance, eyes sent back to their own business. One, though, held his gaze a moment, then nodded slowly, a gesture which Karstens returned. Then the man and his companion stood and left. Karstens looked back at Julie. "My lady, we have an appointment."

Back in Karstens' office, five other people waited. They

had apparently been in conversation when Karstens and Julie walked in. They all stood, except one, and shaking Julie's hand, introduced themselves.

"Have a seat, Julie," Karstens said, waving her to an empty chair. The others sat also. Two were from the government. They didn't give their names. One was a normal Blacksuit, while the other was evidently his superior. Both had a dark, no-nonsense aura about them, of atrocities committed and secrets kept. Though indoors, the Suits wore dark glasses.

Another, smiling, introduced himself as "Halverson, Roger Halverson in personnel." Julie looked at him; he seemed familiar, then she placed him. The man in the diner who had been watching her, who, upon discovery, had looked away. *Personnel, my eye,* she thought. She stole a glance at his clipboard and noticed a logo in the center of the gold envelope, on top. A snake climbing a pole, the internationally recognized symbol of the medical industry. She looked back at him.

"Psychologist, I'd say," she offered. Halverson raised an eyebrow. "Very good, Professor. Actually, that is one of my fields. I do other things as well."

Julie looked at the man sitting behind Halverson, recognizing him too. She'd only met him once, at a "party" a few years previous. A bunch of life scientists, science librarians, and a few others, held a get-together. The real purpose of the meeting was agreeing where to house their most valuable artifacts; some sort of lockdown until the crazies were gone. For all they knew, that could be a long while. The location chosen turned out to be a vault deep underground: a large, old, forgotten bomb shelter. Truck loads of specimens were sent for weeks disguised as radioactive waste with official logos on the manifests. No officer was willing to check the contents of the trailers once they saw the paperwork. Since most museums had already been closed for sometime, no one outside of this circle knew what happened to the precious items. Museum workers were told that the relics were being sent to a safe place, but not *where* to. Still, it was assumed that the government knew. The government *always* knew. It would be virtually impossible to keep an operation of this size completely secret. That fact made the participants more than a little edgy.

Some advised against putting everything in one location. Finally, however, they took a vote, one last vestige of democracy in a world gone mad.

Julie remembered the leader of the subversives, Hodges, as a warm, intelligent man, an air of confident defiance about him. A man who inspired trust. He stood six foot five, which seemed to help. For some reason, people look to tall men as leaders. Something primitive about it. In Hodges' case, though, it was deserved. He was old and gently spoken, always waiting for others to speak before he did. He'd weigh and consider the words of friend and foe alike before coming to a conclusion. He wore his grandfatherly glasses on the bridge of his nose like a trademark. Most everyone else who needed glasses, and could afford it, had had corrective surgery to repair less than perfect vision. But those were the old timers. For many years now, no one had been born with eye defects. Genetic modification pre-utero had, like so many other ancient health issues, simply erased them.

Julie stood again and so did Hodges. Suddenly, seeing him, she felt relieved. *If Jim is involved in this, it's okay.* Hodges walked over. She looked up at him as to a father, and he smiled down at her, extending his hand. She didn't know why she did it, but she ignored his hand and instead embraced him. Here was a man she'd admired for so long. As much as she knew about her field, she knew that Jim knew so much more. A feeling of excited anticipation flowed through her now.

"Thank you," she whispered. Hodges smiled solemnly and nodded. They sat again.

"Julie, this is Dietrich Jaqzen," Karstens said, gesturing to the last man, the one who hadn't stood. She looked at him. Jaqzen gazed back, unsmiling.

"Glad to meet you," Julie said.

"Um, thanks," Jaqzen said in reply, his husky voice booming in the small room, then he added "You, too." He put out a hand and Julie took it. Almost immediately, she wanted to withdraw it. Huge, strong and vice-like, his hand engulfed her own. It wasn't that which made it objectionable though. It was the cold clamminess. She shook and let go. Jaqzen held on for a fraction of a second longer, then also let go. Almost imperceptibly, his eyes dropped and took her in, head to toe. Then he smiled, "Call me Deet." A tiny shudder went through Julie, which she shook off. She also surreptitiously wiped her hand on her skirt, while smiling in return. Frowning inwardly, she wondered who he was and what his role was in all of this.

Jaqzen, pronounced "Jackson," was tall and tanned. Muscles bulged under his shirt. His hair was cut in a tight crew, shaved at the temples. From the left ran a long angry scar. Above his right ear, she noticed a tattoo, but couldn't make it out. He wore khaki pants with several pockets on each leg. The two on his calves contained undetermined items of some weight. From the lower one though, through just a bit of opening, reflecting an overhead light, was a glint of steel.

"Deet is a specialist, Julie. He knows how to, um, survive in rough situations. That is a skill that will come in handy on this mission," said Karstens, breaking the uncomfortable silence.

"Tell me about this mission, Bob," she asked.

Karstens looked to Hodges. "Doctor?" he intoned.

Hodges rose once again. He looked around the room.

54

"As most of you know," he began, voice deep and sonorous, "almost all of earth's native biota, plants and animals which existed here from time immemorial and up to the last century, are either now gone or pending extinction. All that is left, really, are the smallest creatures. Rodents and insects, things like that. There are, of course, a variety of reasons for this, all having to do with us." Brushing aside the nervous coughs, he spoke now for the benefit of the others in the room, as Julie had no need for a refresher on mass extinction. "Skyrocketing population growth. Relentless habitat destruction and over-development. Deforestation. Mountaintop mining and removal. The cutting off of migration routes. Extreme hunting pressure. Climate change. Ocean depletion, acidification and incursion. Vast areas of land, sea and air, now polluted beyond remediation with radiation, PCBs, oil and other toxins. A variety of ozone destroying chemicals, et cetera, et cetera.

"Soon, we will be moving out to the stars. Humanity's destination is there. A glorious future awaits us." Julie was startled by these last comments. The last she knew, Hodges believed that all of this futurism talk was nothing more than a load of public relations BS. He continued, "If we can send a mission back, collect as much of the flora as we can, it would add immeasurably to our ability to survive."

"But," Julie spoke up, "we already have the seed bank at Svalbard. Tons and tons of seed pre-collapse set aside for just such an occasion."

"Very true, Professor. We do have a lot of stuff stored at Svalbard and alternate locations, seeds, and later, the DNA of every species we could get it from before they went under. It's all been carefully preserved for decades, frozen in underground vaults. Saved, as it were, for a rainy day. There's a problem, though. While we do have seeds, we aren't sure of their integrity. It's been many years and likely a lot of them are no longer viable. Further, a large proportion of them are contaminated with biotech traits. Unfortunately, we are no longer sure which ones they are. If you'll recall, a political decision was reached some time back to stop segregating those seeds. Thus, seeds were mixed together based solely on variety and without regard for the GMO factor. When the Transgene Crisis began and famine first swept through the world, some of us wanted to rid them all from our agricultural lands and start over. Couldn't, by then all of our crops were contaminated due to cross-pollination. Turns out that was the corporate goal all along. So the only uncontaminated seed left is at Svalbard, though we'd have to literally examine them all one by one to be able to tell what from what. That's a lost cause."

"But I thought - " Julie began.

"That we'd destroyed them all? No. That's what was told the media. It made people feel better. It was decided that GM contaminated seed was better than no seed at all, and so those seeds were left where they were.

"Fortune," he continued, "has smiled upon us, though, and given us a chance to find clean, healthy seed. Virgin germ. All unmodified. It's a spectacular opportunity which we cannot pass up."

"Okay, say I go back to collect plants; what if it's the wrong time of year and they aren't seeding? Then what, wait around for who knows how long until they do? I thought I only had a month," Julie badgered.

"Good question. While we prefer seeds, we don't need them. All you need to do is to collect plant tissue samples and bring them back. We will then clone those, and from that first generation, we'll get our seeds. This is vital in our plan to terraform the new planets we will encounter. It is a huge under-taking, a heroic undertaking." Hodges' eyes stole quickly in the direction of the two government men, then back to Julie.

Ah, of course, he knew he was talking smack. She, too, flashed a glance in the direction of the Blacksuits. They sat stone still, their faces masks of impassive non-expression behind their shades.

Likely, they knew Hodges true feelings, could read it in the slightly exaggerated edge to his words. They were able, it was rumored, even to read a person's thoughts from a variety of clues, the inflection in a voice, the tilt of a head or eyebrow, the movement of the hands, the way that one stood. *You're not fooling anyone, Jim*, she thought.

Karstens rose and walked to his desk. Opening a bottom drawer, he produced a box. He set it on the desk, placed his thumb on it and said, "Open." It did. *The man likes his gadgets,* Julie thought. "A remarkable invention, this," he said. "We call it 'the Case.' I think you will find it quite useful. This container will automatically record the genetic phylogeny of any bit of flora placed inside it. We estimate its accuracy at virtually one hundred percent. No homework involved."

Julie looked at it. Oblong, sleek and red. It looked about four inches long by two wide and half an inch deep. She frowned.

"Unbelievable? All you have to do is snip off a bit of any plant and lay it on the platform inside. I suggest leaves." He turned it so that Julie could see the inside. There was a smooth, opaque white, raised area. On one side were various keys for the addition of notes. On the other was the display.

"Wait," Karstens said, "I'll show you." Underneath the lid, he removed a small item and held it in his open palm. It looked like a slim pair of tweezers with a very small cup at the end. This he took, and, leaning over his desk toward a potted plant, squeezed the handles, taking a tiny bite out of one leaf. He then brought the tool to the opaque platform and squeezed again. Out fell a round bit of leaf. Next, he touched a small button inside the container. Immediately the bit of green disappeared, absorbed seemingly through the platform. Red, green, and yellow lights suddenly came on, flashing rapidly. The display also lit up and a long string of data instantly began to flow down it. It was apparently analyzing the plant's DNA, comparing it to that of every other plant in its database, which was encyclopedic. What started out as many connections began to narrow from kingdom, to phylum, to class, to order, to family, to genus, and finally to species and variety. Then suddenly it stopped and the words "*Epipremnum aureum.* Golden Pothos" and "Cataloged" appeared at the bottom. The lights, too, went off. Meanwhile, a blue LED with the word "Data" lit.

"You push this button if you want to view the information again, but slower." He handed Julie the box. She took it and looked it over. "Essentially, it's a tree, and every new piece of data, like another leaf. Each has its place on the tree. Yet, not only does it record the phylogeny of individual species, it also stores the actual genetic sample for later use. All you need is a small amount from each plant. We figure you can get several thousand samples in here. And it's refrigerated. The tiny portions are frozen inside, preserving the samples indefinitely. With this device, we can build a new world. Needless to say, we hope you don't lose it."

Julie was in awe. Carefully, she closed the box and handed it back to Karstens. He took it.

"It's constructed solidly. No need to be overly worried about it getting a little banged up. Though, of course, you are expected to use all caution." At this point, he again reached behind his desk and produced something else. A backpack, *A nice one,* Julie thought, *full of pockets.* He unzipped one and easily slipped the oblong box inside, then re-zipped. The other pockets had items in them, as well.

"Dr. Karstens," Julie said, following his nomenclature, "I

can try to locate the edible plants, but, to be perfectly honest, I might not be able to identify them correctly." Julie then laid out a list of reasonable objections. "No doubt I'll recognize some of them, but keep in mind that many of the plants I'll be sampling became extinct five to ten million years ago, during the long Clarendonian / Hemphillian extinction event. True, some survived to modern times, but most we only know about from fossils - which don't tend to reveal a lot. Also, it's likely that many of the biota from that era never fossilized because the conditions weren't right. Fossils generally need to be deposited in wet conditions. That potentially leaves out a lot of life. Furthermore, it's also likely that some of these plants will look different than they do today, being earlier in their evolutionary journey. And lastly, some of these plants may have been poisonous in their younger years. There are just a lot of variables," Julie said.

"All taken into account, my dear," Karstens said. "You are not solely looking for the relatives of those few plants that humanity grew up on. No, you will be sampling *everything*. This handy device," and here Karstens patted the pocket of the backpack, "will tell you instantly which flora are poisonous and which are suitable for our needs. In this way it will also be a good means for you to know which plants you can eat while there. We would be happy to find the ancestors of those foods that we have evolved with, but truth told, if it's comparable, it's edible, no matter the species. Just think, we could be adding a whole library of nutritious and delicious foods to our diet!"

Julie pondered that, then said, "If it can do all of that, then why, um," her voice now dropped a decibel, "why do you need me? I mean, why not just send Tarzan here?"

"We need an expert, Julie, and you know *that particular time* better than anyone else, present company not excluded." It was an obvious reference to Hodges. Jim nodded in agreement.

His feelings were not bruised; he was the one who, in fact, had urged the committee to pick Julie. In a situation like this, it was best to dispense with the usual courtesies.

Suddenly Jaqzen spoke up, "'Tarzan, here' is going to be watching your back. Make sure you aren't cave bear food. So I'd be a little less flip if I were you." *Hmm, I see,* Julie thought, *but will you be watching my back, or my backside?* Instead, she said, "It was a crude comment. I apologize. I'm glad you're coming along. Anyway, there shouldn't be any cave bears in the Barstovian to worry about." At that, Jaqzen's countenance seemed to drop, but ever so slightly. It was barely noticeable. *Now why would that disappoint you?* Julie wondered.

"While you are there, you are also going to be recording." From another pocket, Karstens withdrew a broad-brimmed hat. He pointed to a spot in the center front. "You will be wearing this hat at all times. Here is the camera, it's full color and high-definition. It will remain on the entire time. Thus, upon your return, we will be able to see what you saw and you will be able to review the entire trip at your leisure for your own studies."

"If I could," Jim Hodges said, "what an adventure, Julie! People talk about 'once in a lifetime'. This is far, *far* more than that. If I were younger, I'd have loved to go, and I know you're eager, too. That particular period. Wow! So much going on, what luck!"

"Yes," Julie agreed. "It *is* amazing. I mean, *what are the chances?*"

"Would you mind clarifying?" Karstens asked.

"Sorry. Yes. Well, your 'time machine' could have gone anytime, but it chose the middle Miocene, a geologic period that runs concurrent here in the West with the Barstovian NALMA, or North American Land Mammal Age. And since this is California, we call it the *Luisian,* after foraminiferan fossils found in San Luis Obispo County."

"Yes, so?"

"Bob, if we're right about the time your machine chose, and I think we are, this period represents the convergence of a lot of exciting changes on earth. For one thing, it was the beginning of what S. David Webb dubbed the 'Clarendonian Chronofauna.'" She thought for a moment. "When mammal diversity, their 'species richness', reached a peak as never before, or after, and all living in a lush, almost tropical paradise he called the 'Middle Miocene Savanna Optimum'. In the oceans and skies, too, diversity also peaked. People have tried to figure out this sudden burst of evolution, and the closest we've come to an explanation is that it was due to a big increase in 'primary productivity.' You see, it was also a time of volcanic upheaval, coupled with a worldwide increase in rainfall. So you had huge episodes of volcanism throwing monster clouds of ash - and carbon - into the lower atmosphere and rain bringing it back to the surface. Besides heating the earth while it was in the sky, all that carbon became fertilizer for plant life, both terrestrial and oceanic, so animals had a lot more to eat. As a bonus, this intensified vegetal growth maximized and enriched the oxygen available to them."

She paused, then continued. "'Populations increase as a function of food availability.' Hopfenberg and Pimentel showed that around the turn of the century. Its what's unfortunately led to our own overpopulation, despite some researcher's insistence that numbers would level off or even drop on their own mid-century. So, because of this increased food supply, these animals bred and evolved like crazy.

"It was a warm, green world," she maintained, "averaging 18.4 degrees Celsius, with sea levels seventy-five to a hundred and twenty feet higher than modern times, and that's because there was so little ice locked up at the poles and in glaciers."

"Volcanism," Halverson interrupted. "So is this going to

be a big hazard?"

"When you look at things over a much longer timeframe, events can look as though they occurred very close together, when, in fact, on a human timescale, they are actually far apart." Here, Julie knew that she was stretching the truth, for though her words, themselves, were obviously correct, she also knew that the Miocene was rife with activity and that the chances for significant tectonism while she was there were high. She added more accurately, "The thing about this volcanism is that it wasn't really the violent kind, big explosions and all. These were instead mostly fluid flows, called 'flood basalts'. Lava oozing over valleys for long distances. There was a lot of it. Fortunately for life, though, they weren't as big as some of the older flows, like those that formed the Siberian Traps.

"As I indicated, the same carbon that encouraged so much plant growth also increased temperatures quite a bit, spurring what came to be known as the 'Middle Miocene Climate Optimum'. It is going to be hot. Yet, paradoxically, not as hot as we've managed to make *our* world from the burning of fossil fuels." The government official shifted uncomfortably in his seat, as though feeling some of that heat himself.

Julie continued, "Not long after this era, again, geologically speaking, there was an enormous asteroid strike at Nordlinger-Ries in Germany. That rock was almost a mile wide, which left a crater fifteen miles across. It had the power of nearly two million Hiroshima bombs, and may have had something to do with this whole thing. At least, they are somewhat causally linked in time."

"I do remember something about all this," Karstens said, hand stroking his thick beard. He thought, then said, "I believe that there was also a smaller strike at Steinheim, Germany, as well. And if I have my time right, you can correct me on this doctor, if I have my time right, coincidental to everything else, or maybe not so coincidental, the earth's magnetic field reversed in record, or near record, time."

Julie clapped her hands together. "That's right. In just one to four years! North became South and visa versa. I'll have to look at that when I look at my compass."

"That must have been one hell of an asteroid hit," Karstens injected. "I know it's remote, but what if it happens while you are there? My God!"

"No, I'm pretty sure the strikes were after what I saw on your video. I'd guess by about two hundred thousand years, or more. Those animals, they are one of the last links in a wondrous chain of events that some think began to end at Nordlinger-Ries," Julie answered somewhat confidently. "The Clarendonian Chronofauna, that diversity event lasted roughly ten million years, from fifteen to five million years ago, with fifteen being the peak. Well, fifteen to twelve. Then, at about 14.5 Ma, the accumulation of volcanic aerosols, sulfur dioxide in the atmosphere, combined with the drawdown of carbon dioxide by the same abundant plant growth it spurred, and in concert with certain geographical phenomenon in the southern hemisphere, began to reverse the temperature direction and the world began its long cooling and drying slide. Coincidentally, that's also when the asteroids struck. Slowly after that, species and genera began to drop away, one by one, like leaves from an autumn tree. By six million years ago, or so, over five dozen genera had become extinct and the earth was hobbled by a huge drought. It's called the Messinian Salinity Crisis, when the Mediterranean Sea dried up. That drought - and the Miocene epoch - ended when the ocean finally crashed through the straits of Gibraltar at around 5.3 Ma, creating a monumental waterfall, the Zanclean flood, that refilled the dry Mediterranean seabed. A fitting finale and transition to the Pliocene.

"But the earth continued to get colder until the Pleistocene, when almost half of the northern hemisphere was covered in ice." Julie looked over at Jim Hodges. He was smiling in an almost fatherly way. Karstens looked over at him too, and nodded as if to say, *Yes, she was the right choice.* Julie wasn't finished, though.

"What *I'd* like to know is, why did the incident here at the Institute choose *that* temporal point to land in?" All eyes were on her, waiting for an answer. "Might it be that a temporal loci was created around that time, perhaps by the asteroid strikes? Something that drew you almost like, like," and here she looked around, then walked over to a small table which had a cloth covering the top. On that was a bowl with various items, geologic souvenirs that Karstens had collected over the years, rocks of interesting shapes and colors. "May I?" she inquired.

"Oh, by all means, uh..." Karstens sputtered. Julie picked up the bowl with her left hand while removing the cloth with her right. She then set the bowl back down. Then she walked over and handed Karstens, Hodges and the two government agents each a corner of it.

"Now pull it taut, but not too taut," she said. They obliged. Julie then picked out a beautiful, red, round rock from the bowl, came back, and then, with her hand hovering half a meter above the cloth, said, "Nordlinger-Ries," and released the rock. It fell, bounced a bit, then rolled to the center. The weight of it caused a depression in the cloth with every part inclined toward it.

"Marvelous!" exclaimed Karstens "the cloth represents space and time."

"Exactly," Julie agreed. "Space, *and time.* You could use other analogies as well, sand in an hourglass or water running down a drain. The asteroid dented space/time."

"But you said that the period we encountered was a couple

of hundred thousand years before that," Karstens said. He thought a moment. "Perhaps it's a function of the mass of the asteroid. If it had been bigger, or if it were made of very dense material, it would have made more of an indentation, and we might have landed at the very moment of impact."

"Hmm," Hodges said. "I wonder. If that had happened, might that, that 'Temporal Drain,' might it have affected our own space/time?" There was silence now, as those who cared to, pondered that.

"Well, then, let's be glad that it wasn't bigger," Karstens replied.

"But maybe the asteroid isn't the full, or only possible, explanation," Julie cut in. "Maybe the very confluence of life itself at this particular time, this apex of biology, created its own temporal loci. And maybe this is a case of life attracting life, almost hyperstatically."

"Well, we've certainly got a lot to chew on," Karstens said, and with that, he stood and walked around his desk, then sat on a corner of it facing Julie.

"My dear," he said, abandoning any pretense of personal non-involvement, "intellectually, you are prepared for this adventure. More than prepared. But I suspect that it will be physically arduous. It's going to be dangerous, even with Dietrich looking after you. It is paramount that you return safe and sound. One month, that's 30 days, or 720 hours from the time of your launching, and that's what we are calling it, a 'launching', 30 days from your launching we will be bringing you back. You'll know you're getting close because there will be a periodic beeping from your chronometer. Beginning two weeks before your return, it will increase in rate until that hour.

"Why two weeks? This is to give you adequate time to return to the locus, the Strong Box. Two weeks out, two weeks back. Naturally, it would be unwise to cut it so closely since things can happen that could trip up the schedule, so don't tempt fate. Personally, I recommend that you remain in the vicinity of whatever camp you make. A few miles in any direction should be all that's required. Plenty of time to get back, even if injured. The same spot, of course, that you viewed in the video, so mark its location in mind and note it upon arrival. You will reenter the box, bolt the door, turn on the environmental equipment, be seated and fasten yourselves no later than one hour before launch time, then simply wait.

"I guarantee you that we will not forget, so don't you either, or you will be stuck back there permanently. Mark my words." With that, Karstens turned to Dietrich, who sat at Julie's left. "Dietrich ... Deet. We chose you because of your singular ability to survive in difficult situations. You came highly recommended." He stole a glance at the two government men, then back to Dietrich. "Your job is to do everything in your power - up to and including risking your life - to keep Julie safe. She will be your superior. You will follow her orders to the letter, no questions asked." Jaqzen shifted in his seat. "In return, you will receive the compensation we previously agreed upon. If you incur an injury of such severity that you cannot return, but Julie does, our agreement about distributing the compensation as you requested will be honored. Understood?"

"Yes, Sir!" Jaqzen answered, saluting.

"Uh, right," Karstens replied and returned the salute. Continuing, he said, "This trip, I don't think I need to mention, will assure both of you *a lot* of personal benefit. Needless to say, neither you, nor your families," looking at Julie now, "will ever have to work again. Julie, you will have all the time you want to research and publish. It really doesn't get much better than that. Your place in history will be alongside the other great explorers and discoverers that have contributed so much to our cause: Galileo, Magellan, Gagarin,

Armstrong. I wish it were me that was going. But, alas." He threw up his hands, then smiled.

"Don't let me down, kids. It's only thirty days. Think of it as a vacation." Karstens reached into his shirt pocket. "In the meantime, Julie, you will be training with Deet." He slapped two sets of keys down on the desk. "We have a fitness room here at the Institute. You will have complete access to it, 24/7 if you need.

"I'm not going to lie to you, Deet's going to push you, and push you hard. It won't be easy. You're in good physical shape now, but I want you in the best shape of your life, and then some. The training will last three weeks, with a week off at the end to rest and prepare for launching." Julie, who had been a bit lost in her own thoughts, looked up at him, over to Jaqzen, then back to Karstens.

"I understand, I'll do my best," she answered.

"Wonderful!" Karstens said, clapping Julie and Dietrich on the shoulders, "Then we're all set."

Doubt, however, gnawed at the pit of his stomach. It was a hard, almost painful fear he could not show. A fear not just for Julie's life, but for the future of all humanity.

Five

For the next three weeks, Julie trained, Jaqzen putting her through every conceivable exercise. Over that time, she began to feel her muscles harden, like her resolve. Though inwardly she was uncomfortable with the man, a discomfort she could not define, she pushed these doubts back down, below the surface of her consciousness. So excited was she at the impending journey that she simply would not allow room for anything else.

Jaqzen, sensing her resolve, took advantage of it. And, thus, day blending into day, the pair became almost inseparable. Julie found that, in fact, he began to grow on her. There was relief in this, as it cut the prior tension and gave Julie hope that they could pull this thing off. In between sessions, they often ate lunch together or just sat and talked. The administration encouraged this closeness, hoping that a bond would make the team stronger.

There was a confidence in Deet that Julie admired, a strength that made *her* more confident. After a while, she no longer worried about him, coming to believe that her original impressions had been mistaken. Well, mostly. Every now and then, she would catch his glance in a mirror, or the reflection of a window, surveying her toning body from behind, a glint of something - different - about his gaze, and it worried her. But she kept it to herself.

The sessions lasted six hours, five days a week, for seventeen days, and she'd go home exhausted. Tom, who had been apprised of the secret mission and knew of his wife's physical travails, always had a delicious meal and warm bath ready for her.

Tom had been shocked, quite understandably, when he'd learned of this operation. She told him that night, after the

Blacksuits left. Had been given permission to. It was felt that keeping such a secret from her husband would not only be impossible (how to explain a month-long absence), but would be too much of a distraction for her. She had assured them that he was discreet, that he was loyal. They'd also quietly run a profile on him and found it acceptable, so he was subsequently pulled aside and officially informed. In these highly uncertain times, the mission would give Julie and him a much better future (for what it was worth) than that which most people dreaded. And all it would cost was a few weeks' training and a thirty-day trip. Simple. At least that's how it was presented. The actual time travel part of it was not clearly explained to him, and truth told, in all the good news, he managed to gloss over that bit of detail. Time travel was an esoteric idea to Tom, an abstraction he'd never given any thought to. For all he knew, the ability to move in time was something not inherently impossible; something which perhaps science had possessed all along.

Julie Welsh was 22 and Thomas Pine 25 when they met. She, a slim, five and a half-foot, 110 pound beauty, was also a grad student in paleontology at UCLA, with intern work at the museum, while he studied music theory. A year into their relationship, she moved in with him and he dropped out to provide for them. Not able to find anything else, he settled for a job as a "stamper" at a local dirtbag factory while practicing music after work. Her profession was satisfying and relatively high paying, while his job was dull in the extreme. It involved standing most of the day in one spot, punching the company logo, name and address onto small pieces of metal, which were then affixed to the company product, Crystil Flush Toilets. The pay was low, benefits nonexistent, the environment smelly, noisy, dirty and dark, and his boss a psycho jerk. But it was work. For two hours in the late afternoon, he also worked a second job as a musician at a local club. He did it because he felt he had to - first, for the money, and second, to restore self-esteem he lost on the factory job. Her worth index was 35.7 while his was a 16. It seemed an obvious mismatch at first, but any doubts her friends had soon evaporated when it became clear that they were in love and that Tom was a good man. Good for her. True, he made less money than she, but what he brought home was more than many whole family's combined income.

The fact was that the majority were barely making it these days. The population / available work ratio was way out of balance. If a home had a single provider, actual take-home pay notwithstanding, that was a successful home. Most families were on government welfare to survive. The GAP, or "Government Assistance Program", was initially designed to fill in the gaps between paychecks. It later devolved into the principal means of support for most. Since so many were on it, the stigma historically associated with welfare programs faded. The larger part of these people were not hireable anyway, even if jobs *were* available. Dejected, despondent and angry, they stumbled their way through life. Often sick or drugged out, GAP and shelter were all they had.

There was, however, a darker side to GAP: as a condition of qualification, one was required first to sign an Allegiance To The State Agreement. Ergo, anyone at anytime deemed a "threat" to the order could simply be denied it. This Damocles Sword served effectively to keep potential troublemakers quiet. An initial cutoff for a relatively minor infraction, such as tri-fling criticism of the regime uttered in public, was "actionable" by a *minimum* two month revocation of the transgressors card. Further, anyone found guilty also had their worth numbers reduced, sometimes to zero. Like the Worth system, subversive comments were subject to a rating scheme based upon both the quality and quantity of the words spoken. Usually the unfortunate soul, thinking that his whispered comments went undetected, would find a summons in his mailbox to which he was obliged to respond. Once at the hearing, he sat dumbfounded while his inflammatory mutterings were played back to him. People eventually learned how sensitive the microphones were.

A large proportion of these criminals, suddenly finding their GAP assistance gone, would move in with other family or friends. This, of course, created a tremendous strain on that family, which, often down to one meal a day anyway, could kick them out at any time. That knowledge served as additional deterrence to other potential transgressors, for many, having no family that was willing or able to take them in, ended up on the streets, homeless and scrounging for scraps, until finally starvation, sickness, homicide, suicide, or the elements took them. Or they joined a gang.

Indeed, the world had become a perilous place for those without somewhere to go, and even for those casually caught on the street. Crazed gangs roamed the night, always on the lookout for prey, desperadoes joined by their shared deprivations. Many suspected that an unofficial truce existed between these wild mobs and the government. After the sun fell, they could take whomever they wanted, *if found outside*, and do whatever they wanted to him or her, while Big Brother looked the other way. But only at night. If caught during the day, they were executed.

It was also rumored that the night gangs were cannibalistic. As a consequence, when the screams came, no one ventured out to see. This de-facto martial law helped clean up the street and struck paralyzing fear into the hearts of the populace. Every homeless person wandering the highways stood as silent warning to any would-be agitators. Their government, rather than rounding them up and sending them to camps, simply left them to their fate. There were very few repeat offenders. The ban on seditious speech was, of course, not limited to the lower classes, though they were the easier to deal with. Still, The State had ways of dealing with *anyone* who persisted in subversion.

Neither Tom nor Julie was on the GAP program. Though for a while times were tough, they struggled to remain free, feeling a natural aversion to handouts from The State, especially with such atrocious strings attached. That shared hardship, rather than causing divisive stress, as it did so many other unions, bonded them in a mutual determination and an uncommon love, each for the other. After a time, Julie gained more status, and thus, money. Meanwhile, Tom developed a bad cough, and over Julie's objections, often went to work ailing. She doted on him with soups and medication, begging him to quit the factory, but he knew that if he did, his chances of finding other work would be nil. For one thing, he was convinced his boss would give any potential employer who called a bad reference. So he toiled, lost weight, and his complexion paled.

Then one day, at the urging of his club's proprietor, he quit Crystil and began to play for him five hours a day. With that, his pay actually increased, though only slightly. Thus, together, struggling, he and Julie were doing okay. If there was a surplus, they gave money and food to the beggars in the streets. Tom's cough, however, remained, waxing and waning, but becoming a permanent feature.

Now, seven years since first meeting, they were more in love than ever. Each seemed to compliment the other perfectly. If one partner lagged some days, the other picked up the slack without a word of complaint. Neither took undue advantage, for they knew that, in a world falling apart, they really only had each other. They were an island of stability in a sea of upheaval.

When they could, they took day trips, visiting those few remaining patches of wilderness left which were owned by well off friends or others interested in Julie's work. These latter, agreeing to put them up for the night, indulged her strolls arm-in-arm with her husband through their acres of wilting forest. Then they would disappear for hours, and sit in silent repose listening to the breeze in the pine boughs or making love on a dry grass strewn hillock. In a different time their lives would have been complete. Now, though, there was always an undertone of sadness in the air, especially for Julie. Tom knew that when she sat next to him on the grass, head turned away from him, that she was crying, silently. Softly he'd whisper, "It's not so bad is it? We have good jobs, food on the table, a place to live..." But she'd not answer. Then he would sit and encircle her in his arms, she laying her head on his shoulder. The wetness of her tears stung him deeply.

Tom, while enjoying these times with her, did not share his wife's abiding love for nature. Why should he? Most of what he saw was brown, dying, and stunk, and had for most of his life. This was reality. What was past was past. Julie, though, informed by her memories as a child and her knowledge of the natural world, by what she knew *should* have been, saw tall trees adorned with green leaves dancing in the breeze. She felt soft green grass under her bare feet. A Capri blue sky filled with birds and puffy white clouds slowly drifting by. In the distance, she saw the stately magnificence of a proud elk, heard its faint, shrill call to its harem. *Come, I am here. The day is wonderful. Let us graze together.* She'd see a fox bounding through grass higher than he. A meadowlark, frog or cricket thrumming its little song for all to hear. The delicious scent of spring flowers floating on warm currents.

The way life was *meant* to be, the *real* world. Not this artificial, synthetic, plasticized, ruined husk of a planet, barely clinging to existence, destroyed by greed, hubris, and spite. By a species that never learned how to be satisfied, to be grateful for what it had all along, but refused to see, that always wanted more, more. A species that rarely seemed to fit in and was always at war, if not with itself, than with the rest of nature. And so it bulldozed and razed, hunted and parceled up, poisoned and polluted its way to its paradise of oblivion. Already, it was rumored, much the world had fallen to anarchy as the collapse spread.

Julie remembered an obscure study that had emerged some years back, only to be quickly put down. It found that, for some reason as yet unknown, the human race had, deeply embedded within its genetic makeup, a desire to self-destruct. But not only to self-destruct, but to also bring everything else down with it. It was part and parcel of the more positive qualities it possessed: the arts, innovation, and charity. A yin to its yang. A bizarre finding.

And whilst not fully appreciating it, somewhere in the depths of his soul, perhaps only where it touched lightly with hers, Tom understood. Perhaps he'd unconsciously hardened his heart to the kind of pain Julie felt, cancelled it out because it was too much to bear. Yet, somewhere, somehow, he knew that something good was leaving us, and it was a sad goodbye.

For all their love, Julie couldn't chance asking Tom's permission to go. If she honestly revealed the hazards involved, he most certainly would have said no. As it was, he was uncomfortable with the whole idea, but he'd assented, imagining the enterprise to be but a short, relatively risk-free excursion in the name of science. When he saw how badly she wanted to do it, he couldn't say no. So he asked if he could come along too. She said she'd ask. When he got a chance to meet Karstens shortly thereafter, he requested that they send him in place of Jaqzen. Who could be more dedicated to protecting Julie than her husband? A man who loved her like the sun loves the moon?

Karstens smiled at that, then, placing a hand on Tom's shoulder, gently let him down. He told him what Julie hadn't, though not quite everything. He told him that the Miocene was a time of beasts and geologic phenomena, conditions for which Tom simply was not equipped. That to send her back with anyone other than a professional would be to risk tragedy. He then assured him that every measure would be taken to ensure Julie's safety, that Jaqzen was a top-notch game-hunter and survivalist. He was also a highly decorated military man. If anyone could take care of Julie, it was Jaqzen. He added that, though he would have liked to send Tom in addition to Julie and Jaqzen, the energy budget, not to mention the authorities, simply would not allow it. In sum, to attempt to send Tom back would be to jeopardize the entire mission. It was impossible. But not to worry, thirty days from the day of launching, they would be reunited and could then enjoy a worry-free life.

Tom looked hard at Karstens, trying to decide if he was being told the truth or a load of crap. Finally, assuming that the government would not go to all of this trouble only to have the mission fail, he softened his expression and relaxed his stance. He cast his eyes to the ground, then back to Karstens. "You take care of Julie or you'll be dealing with me," he said. Karstens' smiled. "Of course," he replied. And in that moment he knew what love was, understood the bond between them, Julie and Tom. *I promise you, my friend, I will do my best,* he thought.

For the three weeks' training before launch, Tom drove and dropped Julie off at the Institute, and picked her up afterwards. He rearranged his hours, his supervisor at work readily agreeing. Tom had never met, nor even laid eyes on Jaqzen.

Then one afternoon, as he waited in the parking lot, they came out together, Julie and he. Standing outside, they chatted for a while, and Tom got his first view. Jaqzen was a big, forbidding man, towering over Julie like a boulder, a human boulder. He had a short, tight crew cut and hard, angular edges to his face. There was something on it, on the left cheek, but he couldn't tell what it was. Jaqzen's movements were those a beast restrained, but able to pounce at a moment's notice. He held a black jacket slung over one shoulder and wore a black T-shirt. Under that, it was obvious, was solid muscle. And he was an alert man, simultaneously paying close attention to every word Julie spoke, while glancing, from time to time, at the goings on around him. For a moment, Tom's fears about Julie's safety abated.

As he sat there watching the two, Tom realized that he hadn't really given Jaqzen much thought. For one thing, Julie rarely mentioned him. But now seeing him, his imposing size, the easy way he conversed, Tom suddenly felt out of place, even intimidated. He wondered then, though not for the first time, at his luck in meeting and marrying Julie. Not only was she a true beauty, lithe of figure and form, sweet and unselfish, she was also intelligent, professional, and fit in easily with any in the upper classes. He knew that she could have had anyone she wanted. *Anyone.* And yet, she chose *him.*

He remembered how once she told him something like that when he'd brought it up. Just a casual remark on his part, quickly spoken, half-consciously, betraying perhaps a bit of inadequacy. They'd been strolling, her arm in his, looking in shop windows when he said it. There was silence, then suddenly she pulled him back and held on, looking hurt, and said, "I married you because you were the only man for me. The only man I could *ever* marry. Don't ever forget that!" And in that moment she looked so young and fragile that he wanted to hold her and protect her from the world. And that was their relationship. When the spark in other relationships around them fizzled, theirs was everyday renewed.

Tom opened the door to a rush of muggy heat and got out. He wanted to meet the man he was entrusting his wife to. His life to. Julie turned, sensing his approach and waved to him. The giddy wave of a girl half her age to her boyfriend. He smiled and returned the wave. Then Jaqzen saw him and Tom noticed the scar, a long one running from his temple to his chin. Unsmilingly, Jaqzen sized up him in an instant, then looked back at Julie. A small affront, but it felt dismissive. When he had closed within ten feet, Julie met him, and grabbing his arm, said, "Deet, I'd like you to meet my wonderful husband." Tom smiled, stuck out his hand and said, "Hello, friend. Glad to meet you." Dietrich looked down at him. At six foot seven, he was truly a giant of a man. He returned the smile, but it looked forced, plastic. "Hi," he said in simple reply. He noticed Tom's outstretched hand and grabbed it in his huge paw. It entirely covered the smaller, weaker hand, and gripped. "So you're Julie's husband, huh?" he said.

Tom's smile dropped a bit at the pressure on his hand. "That's me. Uh..." he pulled away. Dietrich smiled again, it seemed with humor. "Well, you bagged yourself *quite* the little lady here," he said. A loud, resonant voice.

"Yes, I, I guess I did, uh, Dietrich is it?"

"That's right, Son," he answered, "Dietrich to you. Or, Mr. Jaqzen. Or, Sir." There was an awkward pause. Then Dietrich laughed and elbowed Tom, almost knocking him over. "Hey, lighten up. Seriously, this will be a great adventure for Jewels. She's going to have the time of her life. I *guarantee it*."

"All right, sure." Tom looked over at Julie, who had a surprised look on her face. "So you'll be watching over my Julie," he said, as if to correct the too familiar "Jewels". "Do you anticipate any problems?"

"Problems? *Heh.* Not a one. This thing's going to go over easy as pie and she'll be back home safe and sound. *Okie dokie?"*

"Okay. That sounds wonderful. Thank you," Tom said, coughing.

"Oh no, thank *you!"* Jaqzen replied, amused. Then he turned to Julie, and touching her shoulder, said, "I'll see you tomorrow, Jewels, got to go. Nice to meet you, Tommy," he chuckled, then waved, walking off toward his vehicle.

"'Jewels?'" Tom repeated.

"That's what they call me around here," Julie replied, unconvincingly.

"Hmm. And does *he* have a pet name as well? Maybe something like 'Goliath' or 'Godzilla'?"

Julie laughed. "Don't be jealous, Sweetie. That's just him. He's actually a really nice guy."

"The guy's a tank. Do they really think you'll need that much protection?"

"Honey," Julie said, putting her arms around him, "I really don't think it's going to be that hazardous. But, just in case, Deet will be there watching my back." *Right,* Tom thought, but said nothing.

"Just think of him as our life insurance policy. Another one that will probably never be used, but there just in case."

"Baby, I could take care of you. Give me a gun and I'm as strong as that guy. I doubt he's going to be relying on his brains to fight off the beasts."

"I know you could, Sweetie," Julie agreed. "And believe me, I've asked. Problem is they won't stand for it. I don't know why." Tom was unconsoled. "Don't *worry*, Honey. Everything's going to be fine. I promise." She kissed him lightly on the lips. Then they walked toward the car. Neither of them noticed the man who had been watching them all from behind darkened windows.

Six

Tom was playing the piano when Paul Kiley, the affable Irishman who owned the club, suddenly set a glass down in front of him, startling him. He looked up at his boss, then down and continued playing.

"Looked like you could use a drink," Paul said, a note of concern on his face. Tom said nothing, then, "Thanks." He took a slug, then went back to playing.

"Something wrong?" Paul asked. Again Tom was silent, only his fingers moving over the keys. It was a beautiful tune, yet strangely like a dirge.

"Cause you look like your mother just died or something."

Tom shook his head. "What could be wrong?" He asked disingenuously. He waved expansively at the barred window near where he sat. Paul looked out. People shuffling past in the stifling heat, dejected, aimless, dirty and disheveled. And, with mandatory food rationing based on a person's worth rating, in addition to normal rationing, always hungry. Many looked sickly. Most had given up hope. Had given up the fight. What was the point? Living on GAP and old movies, people no longer tried to keep up appearances. The brushed hair, trim clothes, and phony smiles, affectations people had always associated with "success", weren't fooling anyone anymore. Trash blew in the streets. Old cars parked in public places left to rust. Traffic laws rarely enforced. Broken windows in businesses patched up with tape and boards. The sidewalk tree that Tom remembered green and alive. Its long struggle to hang on to life. Branch by branch it succumbed. Now it was dead and bowed, like an old woman. And over everything, a stinking, yellow-brown pall. *Everything yellow-brown.* The color of smog, of dying skies.

Still, buried deep in the human psyche, on the edge of extinguishing, a tiny spark flickered, sputtered, refusing to be snuffed. Hope. Hope, when there was no reason to hope. Hope, when all of naked reality bore cold witness against it. Hope, that tiny, internal flame that had kept humankind marching all through the long ages. Never quite giving up. That deep, instinctual conviction that if one can just hold on a little farther, can swallow the pain a little longer, then, maybe then, finally then, peace would come. Peace, and maybe even happiness. But it had proven to be a slippery, elusive dream, like a mirage which he'd walked toward, reached out for so many times, only to find it evaporating in his grasp.

Had it all been a delusion, a phantom? A lie based on nothing more than wishful thinking, this hope for a better world, passed on from mother to daughter and father to son for hundreds of thousands of generations? A hope finally encapsulated in religion, in myths of heaven when people despaired of ever finding Eden on earth?

Eden. Julie had spoken of it. A place where man, woman, and nature all lived in harmony. The quaint stories of primitive peoples. It was never mentioned anymore, perhaps too hard to imagine. Or perhaps its loss too painful to remember. Paradise lost.

"Tom!" Paul snapped. He jumped. "Man, where were you?" Tom looked down at the keys. Then up again. The club was quiet, as all eyes were upon him. Then, smiling crookedly, he set to playing once more.

"Sorry, bro," he said lowly, coughing. "It's just, well, something's happening right now." He shot Paul a glance.

"What is it, man? Can I help?" Paul asked kindly. He was like that, which was why Tom worked for him rather than his strictly business competitors. They'd tried on more than one occasion to lure Tom away with offers of more money. This place, ironically called the *Oasis*, wasn't fancy; in fact, it was barely above being just another dive, but it was clean, it had atmosphere, and it had quality people. Employees chosen over the years for their character as human beings, in addition to their work abilities. Paul paid everyone every dollar that he could, while he himself lived almost a pauper's life. He knew the score, knew that this old world did not have much longer to go. His values were his people. And he loved his business, lived in a couple of rooms just above the place. Had been its sole proprietor for twenty-three years. Tom thought of Paul as a brother. He'd never dream of playing anywhere else.

And now he wanted to talk to him, confide in him, tell him what was going on. Almost did, then he noticed a man watching him from one of the booths. Intently, it seemed. He held the man's gaze for a moment, the other never blinking or looking away. Finally, Tom did.

"Thanks, bro, but I don't really want to talk about it." He picked up the drink and downed more.

"Suit yourself, but you know my door's always open. If there's trouble or anything, I know some people."

Tom knew that what Paul meant was that among his customers were government types who kept running tabs at the Oasis. Tabs only occasionally squared with Paul. But they paid in other ways, smoothing the regulatory hassles he sometimes encountered, such as when they shockingly acquiesced when he requested, half jokingly, to start an alcohol delivery service. In the past, that kind of commerce was strictly prohibited, and had he been caught doing it would have resulted in the likely closure of the Oasis and jail time for Paul.

Now, though, they merely inquired about the greater societal benefit. A surprised Paul explained that people needed something to soften the hard edges in their lives. He felt that home delivery would keep people at home rather than wandering the streets in a state of drunkenness. He further cited the value in petrol saved. One vehicle delivering liquor on a route calculated for maximum economy would save a lot of fuel over the long run. A final benefit then, Paul said, was the creation of a new job: deliveryman. Still, many drinkers simply walked to the club and home again with their crutches in bags under their arms, or sagged in doorways and drank themselves to sleep. Only the rich could afford to drive anymore, and they tended to, even if it was only across the road. They tipped, however, occasionally.

The truth of the matter, though, was that, except for acts of subversion, few in regulatory positions much cared anymore, while the government at large looked the other way at the relaxing of certain rules. It was an extension of the general Libertine policies, or at least the *perception* of such, that the Feds had tried to foster. Would an Orwellian government be so generous?

But Paul's contacts tended to be lower level civil servants, and Tom knew, that were there a problem his boss needed help with, they would be of little use to him.

"I know, man," he replied to Paul's offer. "I wouldn't say it's really a problem. Just some extra goings on with Julie and me lately."

"Oh, well, yeah. Can't do much about that. Sorry. Sure hope it works out, though. Julie's a great gal, a great catch," Paul said, suddenly embarrassed for having butted into a family matter.

"No, it's nothing like that." Tom stole a glance at the man sitting in the shadows. Then something caught his eye. A glint of reflection. Something on the music stand in front of him. It was at the bottom, tiny. Had it not been for a single shaft of light from the passing sun falling at just the right angle on the stand, he might not have noticed. He reached for it, and it came off easily in his hand. Small, circular, flat. Like a battery with perforations on one side. He turned it over in his hand, puzzled.

"What's that?" Paul asked, reaching for it.

"Don't know."

Paul took it and paused, inspecting it. "What the..." He took out his reading glasses to get a closer look. "Huh?" He thought for a moment. "If I didn't know better, I'd say this is a bug. And actually, I don't know better."

"A mic?" Tom took it back again. "Yeah, you're right. But why..." He suddenly looked up, toward the man in the dark suit. He was gone. "Uh, Okay..." he said.

Paul followed Tom's eyes, then back, then down at the bug, and back again at his friend. He paused, then dropped the bug into Tom's glass. It sank quickly to the bottom with a *"tink."*

"Don't drink that," he advised.

"Yeah, thanks," Tom replied.

Paul regarded the empty booth. "There was a Suit sitting there a little while ago."

"Yep."

"You, um ... in some kind of trouble?"

"No, but I can't really talk about it."

"Hmm. Something's going down. *Blast*, does it have to do with the Oasis, 'cause I got nothing to hide," Paul said, though he wondered nervously if his good luck with the authorities had run out.

"No, like I say, it's something to do with Julie and I. Nothing bad ... I don't think. Can't talk though. Maybe later. After."

"All right, all right. You can't tell your best bud, I understand," Paul said. Tom smirked.

"So you'll inform me *'after.'* After what?" Paul pressed. Tom just looked at him.

"Yeah, all right. Just watch your back, man. I'm serious. Do not mess with these people. They're trouble, and I might not be able to help."

"Yeah," Tom answered him.

"Yeah. OK," Paul said, staring at his friend a moment longer, then heading toward the bar. He went back to serving customers, periodically glancing in his pianist's direction. Tom, for his part, went back to playing his slow, melancholy tune. His mind, though, was racing. Why had they bugged him? Did they think that he was going to blab everywhere? And if he had, what would they have done? Why was this assignment so secretive? The incident shook him. He vowed to be more careful.

The next week was a flurry of activity. Julie and Tom had been moved to a small cottage on Institute grounds. There was instruction for Julie and Deet in various new instrumentation, in first-aid and in certain new medications, should they prove necessary. One concern was the possible disease issue due to insect bites, particularly from mosquitos and ticks. It was surmised, based on research, that the climate in the Miocene was both hotter and wetter, more tropical, and that these two pests would be prevalent. Though Julie was a specialist on the time, she wasn't on the entomology. Others were consulted for that.

Some believed that exposing the team to pathogens the human race had not co-evolved with, and thus developed an adaptation to, could be especially dangerous. Others felt that, given the long history of primate evolution, it was likely that some sort of adaptation was already incorporated in our DNA. There, they suspected, it lay dormant, waiting re-exposure to reactivate them. A long wait, indeed. Still others felt that there would be no threat from that quarter, as humans had never been exposed to those pathogens. They simply would not "fit" with our physiology and would be no more dangerous than exposure to diseases from other species of animal normally would have been. These latter were in the minority, however.

In any case, it was deemed prudent by everyone that every precaution be taken. Thus, standard repellents and nets would be deployed. Further discussed was an experimental toxicant, a pesticide, to be administered intravenously, which, though said to be harmless to people, would repel or kill biters before they had a chance to transmit disease. Julie decided against it for herself, while Deet accepted. Leeches, chiggers and sundry other tropical parasites were also on topic.

The time came for Julie to train Jaqzen in what to expect as far as the larger predatory and other animals, so a few hours were set aside for a short introduction. The projector room was used and depictions of the various beasts the two might encounter were displayed. Barstovian mammals, she explained, were big and burly. Covertly, Julie watched Deet's reactions to the images. Huge animals that could maim or kill with even an accidental impact. Deet observed the screen intently, his attention complete. If he felt fear, it was not apparent. Instead, he seemed to be sizing each animal up as a professional fighter would a prospective opponent, Julie thought, taking notes even when she was not speaking, his eyes narrowed and mouth set.

Julie hesitated, troubled, suddenly worrying that, for Deet, this mission was not just about protecting her. He was a hunter. A game hunter primed for the kill. A frustrated Nimrod in a world that had little wildlife left to finish off. *Ah*, she thought, *is this is to be your secret, privileged safari? Are you planning to use at least some of the month we will be there waylaying the local fauna for sport?* That, Julie would not have. This was not to be another exercise in man's inhumanity to nature; our malignancy exported to a world still innocent of our atrocities. The same arrogant speciesism that had succeeded in driving the race and the earth itself to the dire state it found itself in.

She had to know. Julie paused with Jaqzen awaiting the next slide, then decided on firmness.

"There will, of course, be no hunting," she stated matter-of-factly, and waited for Deet's reaction. He'd evidently not been expecting that, for he continued staring at the screen. Then he blinked and slowly turned around, looking at her without saying anything. Julie shifted some notes in front her as if there were no question about it.

"Come again," Jaqzen inquired calmly, as if perhaps he'd not heard right. Julie glanced up, her hand on the clicker, ready for the next slide.

"Excuse me?" she looked at Jaqzen innocently.

"You just said something about hunting ..." He pressed.

"Hunting?" Julie recalled. "Oh yes. There will be no hunting on this trip. It's strictly scientific."

Jaqzen looked down, then smiled. "All right then, how do you expect us to eat? Or are we going to bring along a month's supply of canned food and carry it wherever we go?" Then, having felt that he'd easily disposed of Julie's inane notion, he turned back around in his seat, ready for the next image. In front of him, unknown to Julie, Jaqzen had been writing the particulars of each beast with a small check mark next to the names of those he planned to target. Big, beefy animals, any one of which could provide enough meat to see the two of them through the mission.

Julie felt her temper rising. *I have to choose my words carefully,* she thought. *A bit of compromise.*

"Of course. You're right," she began.

"Damn straight!" Jaqzen spit out. *That wasn't so hard,* he thought.

"The taking of small game," she continued, choosing that word, "game," deliberately, a word Jaqzen understood, "will, of course, be permitted, just enough to see us through." She didn't mention that she was a vegetarian, and she needn't;

Jaqzen had noticed in their lunches that she never ordered anything containing meat. "But I expect that we will find plenty of non-animal nutrition available, especially since, in the more tropical world of the Miocene, it should be present for most of the year. We will find fruit aplenty, I would think."

Jaqzen grunted, "Fine. You eat your fruits and veggies, and I'll eat what I want." Then a little less audibly he repeated Julie's 'permission' with derision.

"Mr. Jaqzen," Julie said, more forcefully now, "I said that small game is fine, enough for our needs. But this is *not* a trophy-hunting safari and you will not be killing for sport. The purpose of this mission is clear - it is scientific. We are going there *only* to collect data while leaving as little impact as possible on the surrounding environment. Is that understood?"

"Ms. Pine. I am a hunter. That is what I do, and do well. I was asked to join this mission because I have skills unmatched by anyone else. I'm good with guns. I enjoy *using* them. I *will* be using them to keep your pretty little ass safe. I will *also* be using them to provide us with food. And if I decide to use them for sport I most *certainly* will be doing so, and no one," he said, now pointing at Julie, "*no one*, will tell me otherwise. Is *that* perfectly clear?" Then he added, "NEXT!"

"Mr. Jaqzen. I don't think you understand. While we are there, there is a possibility that our presence alone may be enough to disrupt history. We don't know all the perturbations that led up to us, the human species. If somehow we do something that changes something else which in some way influenced our evolution, that could radically alter our future. Therefore, we must endeavor to minimize at all costs our impact on that prehistoric world. *Now* do you understand?"

"That's *bullcrap*," Jaqzen shot back. "Do you think I'm *stupid?* There is no way that *anything* we do to them will do *anything* to us. There will be so many animals, the chance of our taking out the exact one that led to us is pretty much impossible. Period."

Julie felt herself trembling, her face flush with anger. "I'm not arguing this with you any longer," she said, eyes shining. Suddenly, all of the joy of the past month was gone, in its place was dread. The dread of a promised mutiny before the mission had even begun. She realized now that, in her excitement about the trip, she'd pushed down her nagging doubts about the man. "I could have you thrown off this mission, Mr. Jaqzen!" she raged.

At that, Jaqzen stood. Then he laughed. It was the laugh of someone absolutely certain of *his* mission. "Yes, you go ahead and do that, *Bitch*," he said. Then, waving a hand with his middle finger extended, he walked out.

"He was completely out of line!" Julie insisted. Karstens listened and nodded. "He basically told me that he is going to do whatever he wants, regardless of what I say."

Karstens thought for a moment. Inhaled and exhaled. He, too, had had serious misgivings about the matchup from the beginning. About the government's choice of bodyguard. When the Suits first introduced him, he took an immediate dislike to the man. *Surely*, he thought, *they could find someone with a little more science background and a better understanding of protocol.* There was no doubt that Jaqzen was qualified for the task for which he had been chosen. He'd been the chief bodyguard for a noted head of state and in that capacity had kept the man alive through seven assassination attempts. It didn't matter that the man was political pond scum, a dictator who ruled his district with an iron fist. The governor was eventually forced out, and Jaqzen went on to other things. It wasn't disclosed exactly what those other things were, though Karstens heard in passing that it may have had something to do with quelling political disquiet. He'd wondered what that entailed.

Besides his official work, Jaqzen was an expert martial artist, having won several Ultimate Man Championships (UMC). Through all of this, he was also a dedicated "big game hunter" who spent much of his private time dispatching more than his share of the world's remaining wildlife with satisfaction. Had Julie known that Dietrich was a member of SCI, a group long known to target endangered species, she would have been horrified and would never have agreed to team with him.

On the other hand, Jaqzen was also known for his loyalty once hired. Though his loyalty in this case was apparently to the government, not to Julie per se. Still, Karstens knew that the regime wanted this mission to succeed. Surely they would not have picked someone who was a threat.

As it was, Karstens kept most of this to himself. His duty was to make certain that this job went off without major incident. Higher authorities were involved, and they could have easily found someone else to commandeer things. The best way to ensure that the best decisions, as he saw them, were made, were if *he* made them, and right now he had to reassure Julie.

"I understand. You're right about the insubordination, if that's what it was. I will talk to him," he said. Julie waited. She'd hoped for more. "I want you to know, confidentially," and here he lowered his voice, "that I was not happy with the decision of Jaqzen's inclusion. I felt that we could have done better. I was overridden. And to be honest, that means that I don't have a lot of room for action." Then raising his voice, he continued, "Having said that, Julie, there are other things that you need to consider. The first is that, as you know, Jaqzen is his own man. He's headstrong and muscle-bound. He's someone who's used to giving orders, not taking them.

He has a lot of experience in his field, and, frankly, I believe we need his services."

"But his actions could change history," Julie protested.

"Julie, I am a physicist; I deal in matters of time and probability. Let me give you my opinion on that. Were we sending the two of you back into recorded history, then yes, there is a fair chance that, were he to bash about, he could indeed change things. Or even if you were to go back into prehistory a ways, to the time of the Cro-Magnon, let's say. That too, while the risk would be lower, would still be unacceptable in terms of a chance to mess things up. But you will be going back *fifteen million years*, to a time when our most important primate ancestors weren't even in existence, nor were they in North America! The odds of our changing the course of our history, it seems to me, are vanishingly small. Think of it like throwing a rock into a pond. There are ripples, and they do stretch out for a time, but then they are gone, healed over by the Gaian need for equilibrium. He may be a Neanderthal, but in this case, I think Jaqzen is right. I don't think, short of a mass reshaping, something simply not possible by one man alone, not to mention in the time frame of one month, that there is any threat to the human species from this mission.

"Second. Again, it's only a thirty-day expedition. It will soon be over and you will be back and never have to lay eyes on him again if you don't want to. Third, I'm going to point out the obvious, and that's that there are two days left before your departure. Even if the authorities wanted to find someone else, there is simply *not enough time*."

"I know, I know," Julie acknowledged. "I'm sorry. I should have been more attentive. But jeez, Bob, why do we have to bring the worst of our qualities back to a pristine world?"

"My lady, don't make too much of this. While you know I

share your convictions regarding our attitudes toward other species, I think that we can rest assured that, even if Dietrich spent the entire month that you'll be gone blowing away native fauna, he wouldn't and couldn't make a dent in the total numbers. You know that better than anyone." Julie's eyes flashed at the thought, but she said nothing.

"I know that this union won't be easy, but I need you, no, the *world* needs you, to temporarily rise above your convictions and make it work. There will undoubtedly be areas of disagreement, but I'm afraid you're going to have to bend a bit," then lower, "and I strongly advise you to do so. Trying to make a large change now could jeopardize the mission. I'm afraid there's no other way." Julie's mouth was set, but inwardly she acknowledged the truth of his words. She nodded agreement.

"You're right, of course. I'll do my best."

"My dear, you've known Deet for a month now, and in that month have there been other issues?" Karstens asked.

"No," she acknowledged.

"Then don't make more of this than it is. I'd wager that this whole thing goes off without a hitch and you'll have a wonderful adventure and a wonderful future of study upon your return. You are in quite an envious position, scientifically speaking, you know. Very few people ever get everything they want, and many, nothing. I say, go talk to Jaqzen, then put this behind you and move forward. I'll speak to him as well, and remind him of our expectations. You will be in charge, just do it wisely."

"Yes, okay. Thank you, Bob," Julie replied, suddenly embarrassed for even bringing it up. "I apologize for the distraction."

"No apologies required," Karstens said.

"Bob, there's something I've not said before, but should have. I can't tell you how grateful I am for this opportunity. This trip is a dream come true for me." Then, forgetting her reservations, she suddenly broke into a broad smile. "Truth be told, I'm absolutely giddy at the prospect." Karstens returned her smile and took Julie's hand in his. He felt a real affection toward her.

"I know, child," he answered. Julie blinked back a tear.

"I do wish Tom could come," she said.

"I know you do. I tried. It's just not happening. I am sorry." And Julie's heart sank a little, for even though she knew his answer, she'd still held out a thread of hope.

What she didn't know was that Karstens' heart also sank, and that was because he'd lied to her. He knew that indeed Tom could have gone as well, at least as far as the technical feasibility was concerned. There *was* enough energy for him: extra power that, while unnecessary for this trip, would, in fact, be wasted and unrecoverable if not used.

What shamed Karstens was his belief that, were they to allow both Julie and Tom to travel backwards in time, back to a world beautiful and unspoiled, a world of wonder and diversion, a world devoid of the many sickening reminders of the shambles we later made of it, very likely they would not return. Even now, there was a possibility that Julie wouldn't. Tom, thus, was to be "held" as unsuspecting insurance against that possibility.

Karstens knew that, much as Julie loved the prehistoric world, that long bygone age she'd made the study of her life's mission, she loved Tom even more.

Seven

The launching party was an extravagant affair and not really to Julie's or Tom's liking. Tom was amazed at the crowd. The place was virtually bustling. He had thought that this was to be a secret mission. Apparently, those with a "need to know" were more than a few. Besides relevant scientists, those from the original crowd that day at the lab when they all learned about the astounding events which led to this day, the gathering also included various worldly VIPs. Probably a hundred and fifty people in all, and everyone dressed in their finest attire. Laughing, joking and even the occasional song broke out among them. Perhaps, Julie mused, the reason for the lightness of the mood was the belief among those less skeptical than she that this endeavor would somehow contribute to the success of the greater glorious mission, humanity's destination among the stars.

But she doubted it. The majority of this group were simply too intellectually solid to fall for that tripe. So she decided that the cheeriness must simply be due to the occasion, another techno-milestone achieved after a long dry spell. But not just any old milestone. Time travel by a human being was extraordinary, the impossible finally attainable. Certainly a time to celebrate. Then, of course, there was simply the need to find a reason for optimism. Even in the face of depressing bleakness, people found reason for hope.

Julie noticed Dietrich, surrounded by a cache of admiring females, was waving his arms around, recounting and regaling his personal audience with past tales of daring-do. Though most of these women were married, he had plans to bed at least one of them tonight, the finer points of civilized society notwithstanding. But that was none of her business and she turned away. She, herself, had had her own small entourage until she dismissed herself to find Tom hovering near the refreshment table. She lightly took hold of his elbow.

"Your man Karstens seems to have missed the boat to Happy Island," Tom said, nodding in the direction of the administrator. Julie turned to look. Indeed, Karstens was standing alone, back near a wall, drink in hand and looking pensive. He held a sheaf of papers, and though to a casual observer he appeared to be reading them, Julie saw that his eyes weren't moving. The papers, then, were apparently meant to keep others at bay. She also noticed that he was repeatedly clenching and unclenching his jaw. A small sign. *Something wrong,* she thought.

Someone approached. "Mrs. Pine, I wonder if you wouldn't mind saying a few words?" he asked politely. Julie nodded. She'd anticipated it and had a short speech prepared. "In, say, five, ten minutes?" he asked.

"Certainly. Thank you," she answered.

"Knock 'em dead, sweetheart," Tom said. She gave him the lopsided smile that he knew meant that there were any number of other things she'd rather do. Julie had her abilities; public speaking wasn't one of them. She felt a few flutters coming on. *Calm,* she thought.

Julie walked to her bag to fish out the notes. Suddenly she was aware of a presence behind her. She turned. Blacksuit. He held out his hand.

"Yes?" Julie asked.

"Speech," was the reply.

"Excuse me?" she asked again.

"Speech," The man repeated and reached for her notes, grabbing them by a corner.

"I beg your pardon!" Julie answered, pulling away. By the side of the first man, another then appeared, not a Blacksuit, but obviously an accomplice.

"Ah, Ms. Pine, my apologies," said the man in a thin, nasal voice. "I hope you understand. We'll have to go over your notes, to, ah, clear them for public consumption." He took hold of the papers and pulled slightly, removing them from Julie's hands.

"To ... *what?*" she exclaimed. Heads turned toward them. Karstens, too, looked up. Tom was already moving her way. She looked for a name tag on the man, but there was nothing. "Mr...?"

"I'm sorry, but as you know, all public dissertations must be approved ahead of time. It's quite routine."

"The hell it is!" Tom said, snatching them out of the man's grasp. The Blacksuit next to him made a quick move, but the anonymous man shot out a hand and stopped him with, what seemed to Tom, unnatural speed.

Karstens showed up. "What's going on?" he inquired, looking at the anonymous man.

"Nothing at all. A minor misunderstanding. It is protocol for all speeches to be cleared first. I believe that Ms. Pine was unaware of that," the man said.

"*Mrs!*" Julie corrected.

Karstens looked at the notes, then back at the man and the Blacksuit next to him. His face flushed, but he gave none of that away in his voice. Instead he said, "I see. Yes, that does seem reasonable, don't you think so, Julie?" She gazed at him, considered his set, unsmiling features and realized his point. A small injustice. Civil society crushed under a mountain of small injustices. But don't make too much of it. It's not worth it.

"Yes. Yes, of course," she agreed, breathing out. She reached over and took them from Tom, the two of them briefly connecting, and handed them to the man. "Forgive me. I forgot," she said apologetically. *But it's not like I would be saying anything this crowd doesn't already know*, she thought.

95

"Certainly," the man replied, smiling. It was a skinny pseudo smile, though, the kind one might see on a mannequin.

"Um hmm, um hmm," the nameless man repeated as he scanned the notes. Reaching the end, he said, "Excuse me a moment." He walked to a table, his back toward them. Leaning over it, his movements were vigorous. A minute later, he returned and handed Julie back her speech. She looked down at them. Whole lines were crossed out, while in other areas, words and sentences were added.

Clenching her teeth, she glanced again at Karstens. "An improvement," he said. "Thank you."

"Yes, thank you so much," Julie said, barely keeping the mockery out of her voice.

"Most welcome. Delighted to be of help," the man replied. "I certainly hope that you have a successful journey and hurry back to give us the good news," he said.

She frowned at that. *What did he mean, "news"?* She replied only, "Yes. The good news."

"Mrs. Pine? You're on," said the man who had asked her to speak. Not enough time to read the changes, Julie walked toward the podium. She shook hands with the host, then turned toward her audience.

"Greetings, fellow citizens," she began. "My name is Julie Pine. I am Under-Curator for Antiquities at the Los Angeles County Museum of Natural History. I have been asked, and have accepted, an assignment from our great and enlightened Pangaean government. The nature of this assignment, at present, is officially classified; however, suffice to say that humanity stands to benefit in no small way from our efforts. Isaac Newton once stated, 'If I can see far, it is by standing on the shoulders of giants'. Today I wish to acknowledge some of those giants.

"First and foremost, the Institute de Physica, and its great family of theoretical physicists, without whom my mission would never have occurred. Guys, I am proud to have been selected and only hope that I will prove worthy of your trust in me." There was applause.

"Then there are my own stomping grounds at the Museum of Natural History where I have served for almost ten years. And of course I want to thank AAAS, the American Association for the Advancement of Science, the National Academies and the National Science Foundation, whose tireless work to close the knowledge gap between us and the cosmos has led to so much of the progress I will be depending upon. NASA and the National Geographic Society, which have contributed so much to our understanding of the world over the years. Amonston," she stopped suddenly and read to herself with horror the words which had been inserted, "um, Amonston Biotech. Uh, Wod and Duntop Chemical." She swallowed. "Oxxen-Milob oil. Yessam Coal. Monarch Nuclear. Ubiquity Nanotech. JR Dorylens. Lipphi Rimsor. New World Chamber of Commerce. GlobeTech Surveillance Systems. Er, these, um, luminaries of industry have also given us all so much and," her face reddened, "uh, indeed I, uh, I," swallowing, "I am so ... appreciative of their labors, and their leadership in making our world and the world to come a ... a ... better place." She looked at the crowd. Stony faced, they knew it was crap. They also realized that these wouldn't be her words. On the other hand, these industries had made notable scientific and monetary contributions to science over the years, so in a way they could be construed as having been a part of it all. *In a pig's eye,* Julie knew. More likely, it was their perennial "donations" to certain governmental officials which merited their mention. It was an outrage, of course, but there was nothing to be done about it. She pressed ahead.

At first, Tom was as angry as his wife, then he saw the irony in it. Here was Julie, the last person in the world who would be singing Amonston, et al's, praise, doing just that. Then the humor of it occurred to him and he laughed. A short, sudden burst and Julie looked up. Other heads turned in his direction. Tom gave a sheepish shrug and smiled. Julie gave him a look that said, 'just you wait.'

He turned back to the refreshments, poured himself another drink and downed it. He poured another. As he brought the glass to his lips, suddenly there was a sharp jab in his back. A momentary loss of balance caused the liquid to splash out - and onto his shirt.

"What the hell?" he said, turning. It was Jaqzen. He was standing between Tom and the crowd, casting a shadow like a small mountain. Tom looked up at him.

"Why did you do that?" Tom asked, flummoxed.

"What kind of man laughs at his wife?" the big man said with derision. He shook his head as if at a sad example of a human being.

"What? I wasn't laughing at her," Tom shot back. "Why did you knock me in the back?"

"You know, people like *you*," and here he looked Tom up and down, grimacing, "somehow you manage to snag the babes, don'tcha? Never been able to figure out why they go for you, though. *Losers.* Must be sympathy. You're like half a man. Nothing at all." Tom balled his fists. Jaqzen looked down at them. "Ha! Go ahead, give me your best shot, Mouse," he said, standing and waiting. Tom did nothing. "That's what I thought," he said.

Tom looked around. No one had noticed. He doubted he was even visible behind the big man.

"Gonna call for help, Mouse? Won't change a thing. If I were you I'd just *shut up*. After all, I'm the guy who's gonna be taking care of your wife. *Yeah!"* he said, suddenly smiling.

Tom swung and Jaqzen caught it. Caught his blow as if it were of no consequence, a mere trifling, then slowly twisted Tom's arm, as if it were a child's. He chuckled. "Who's laughing now, Mouse?" Out of the corner of his eye, he saw Karstens approaching. He let go of Tom's arm, then said, "Sorry about your drink." Turning outward he said as he walked away, "Wish us luck!"

Karstens arrived in time to get a sense of what had occurred. Tom was red in the face, holding his arm. Karstens said, "Come with me." They walked out into the hallway.

"You're not sending my wife with that, that *shit!*" Tom said in a fit of coughing.

"I don't like him either. It's Julie's call. If you want to talk to her, and she changes her mind about going, I will completely understand," he said to Tom's surprise. "We can probably find someone else. Would really throw a wrench into the works at this late date, and whoever they are, they won't have Julie's expertise, but I'll do my best if you two decide that's what you want," Karstens said, an ancient look on his face, one worn by too many years of disappointment and resentment. *Probably be the end of my career*, he thought

That hit Tom. Call it all off. Julie would be crushed. "Can't you just find someone else to replace this creep? I mean, who's more important to the mission, Julie or *him?* Damn it, I told you, I can do it. Give me the biggest gun you have and I swear we'll be back in a month with everything you want."

"You're absolutely right. Julie is by far the more important to this mission. Unfortunately, while I ... I *think* I can replace her, I can't change him. Can't really tell you why, except to say that, for some reason, the powers that be want him in it. Of the two, Julie is actually the more expendable." Then seeing the incredulity on Tom's face, he added, "I know, I know, makes no sense. I'm still trying to figure it out. Best I can guess, he's got some kind of governmental ties."

A couple of people were coming down the hall.

"I'll talk to her," Tom said, coughing again.

"Launch is day after tomorrow. That gives you tonight. Whatever your decision, there will be no questions asked."

"Okay," Tom said, a note of relief at the flexibility.

"I will tell you, though, that I'll be mighty disappointed if you do call it off. Jaqzen's a royal ass, but I don't think he'd harm Julie."

"That's reassuring," Tom said lowly as the two strode up.

Tom didn't broach the subject with Julie right away. Instead, they walked to their bungalow on the complex grounds in silence. Julie, of course, knew something was bothering him. She'd not seen the incident, distracted as she was by other things, namely the Blacksuit's changes to her speech.

When she asked him what was wrong, he told her what had happened. Her anger flared. Then she said exasperatedly, "Why are they so insistent on *him*?" and echoing Karstens said, "I don't get it!"

"Probably someone owes him a favor," Tom said. "A month-long hunting safari in exchange for who-knows-what. Something we don't want to know, I'm sure." He then said tentatively, "Honey, I don't want you to go." Julie looked at him sharply.

"What? ME? What are you talking about, I'm going!" It was just what he was afraid of; she wanted to go that badly. He then told her about Karstens' offer to withdraw. That only made her angrier.

"What are you doing?" she said hotly. "Why are you trying to torpedo my dream? You *know* I have to do this."

"I know baby, believe me, *I know*." A sadness came over him. More than anything he wanted her to go, to live her dream. But not with *him*. Not with that Neanderthal. Fact was, he was worried about entrusting her to the guy for a solid month. No one in the world to hear her scream should he decide to go cave man on her. "I'm just really worried."

"You're always worried!" she shot back. "I swear that you treat me like a kid! I'm not a kid. I can take care of myself, thank you very much!"

"Then why do you need him?"

"It's not my choice!" she retorted accurately, tears now streaming down her face. Tom reached an arm over to comfort her, but she threw it off, then stormed away. *Funny how much like a child she looks right now,* he thought.

"Honey, wait," he called out after her. But she ignored him.

The next day was no different. Time had not brought her to her senses. Seeing Karstens walking alone on an Institute path, Tom informed him of Julie's decision.

"I'm sorry," Karstens replied. "Well, not sorry for Julie, but for the two of you. I'm sorry to have caused this fight." Then, walking to a rail and leaning against it, he said, "As I said, I don't think that Jaqzen intends to harm her. He's got too much at stake. I'm not supposed to mention this, but there will be a large settlement with him upon the successful completion of the mission, which means Julie's safe return. He's going to be rich, and I've got to tell you, the man's greedy. He won't do anything to jeopardize that."

"So you hope," Tom said.

"So I think," Karstens replied. "Incidentally, and you probably already know this, but I should also tell you that, no matter the outcome, you needn't worry about money."

"I'm *not* worried about money ... I'm worried about *my wife!*" Tom said, a catch in his voice.

Karstens regarded him with sad eyes. "I know, friend," he said. Then, "I'm doing the best I can. I'm going to give Julie a couple of weapons. This is something that no one else can know about. The first is EMP based. All she needs do is hold it, press a button on top, and anything within ten feet of her will be knocked to the ground and likely out. Don't know if it'll work on larger animals, but it would on any man, even a giant like Jaqzen. The second is a gun. All she has to do in the event of a separation from Jaqzen is be at the designated spot in thirty days. She knows that. Then we'll get her." Tom nodded.

"Tomorrow's launch day," he reminded. "We will be going over the basics with the two of them later today for a couple of hours. I'll not mention the incident yesterday. Let Jaqzen think no one else saw it. And I will, once again, prompt him of what he has riding on this. After that, Julie is yours, so I'd make the most of your time together," he advised.

"Yes," Tom said. Karstens put an arm on his shoulder. "Try to relax. One month and it's over and this will all be history."

"All right. I'll try," Tom said weakly.

"Good," Karstens said more positively. "Now, how about we get something to eat?"

After the final preparations, Julie came home to the cottage. Tom was in the small kitchen and had conjured up something delicious. Alcohol, however, on the night before launch, was strictly forbidden. He wished that he could tell his friends at the club of the momentous day. Their company at launch time would be reassuring.

Julie's mood had softened, and she was sad to have fought with Tom. Of course his worries were justified. She was worried too, and not just for herself. She'd made Tom promise to take his medicine and eat right. Still, her apprehensions were mixed with a sense of her duty, the job she had to perform. Over all that, though, was an overwhelming excitement, an excitement like she'd never known.

That night, she and Tom made love as if it were their last.

Eight

In the course of their research, the men at the Institute had decided early on that the size of the capsule that was to be their "Strong Box" could, theoretically, be enlarged without negative effect. That meant that the team could bring along a host of items in addition to the load of scientific equipment that was going.

There were video and audio recorders that were to be set up in safe locations to record Miocene daily life. These would be later studied by a team of paleontologists headed by Julie. There were a variety of food stuffs available, packaged items "just in case." Neither team member thought they would be needed, and neither wanted them in any case, but they were mandated as a last resort. One item that Julie did expect to need in the area of nourishment was a supply of salts and electro-lytes, as they might not find available salt just lying around. Jaqzen wasn't worried about it, though; he knew that he could get enough from the blood and flesh of game he shot.

Other items included:

Tent/Hammocks (aka T/H) (2)
Handsaws (2)
50' & 100' length of rope (2 each)
Compasses (2)
Fire Lighters (several of different kinds)
Well stocked medical kits (2)
Binoculars (with night vision) (2)
Hand shovels (2)
In-ear sound amplifiers (2)
High intensity flashlights (2)

Insect repellent (1)
Walking sticks (2)
Thermal blankets (4)
Pedometers (2) (as an aid in back tracking)
Sleeping bags (2)
Backpacks (2)
Needles and thread (2 packs)
Rolls of duct tape (2) (Jaqzen's preferred moleskin)
Weapons / Ammunition (guns, knives, pepper spray)
Toiletries (a variety)
Towels (4)
Writing journals (2)
Magnifying glass (1)
Sunglasses (2)
Broad-brimmed hats (2)
Extra clothing
Gloves (4 pair)
Vitamins (2 bottles)
Eating utensils (various)
Sonic repellent (2) (to hopefully deter beasts)
Extra shoes (3 pair each)
Cooking implements (various)
Lanterns (2)
Portable motion sensors (4)
Candy (various)
Rappelling equipment
Walkie Talkies (2 pair)
Signal lights (various, in case of separation at night)
Inflatable pillows (2)
Water filters (4)
Camputer (1)

All of these items were stored in crates in a hold in the

Strong Box. The box itself was padded and strengthened. A new device was to be employed that, it was believed, would prevent implosion by countering forces that pulled inwards with an equal outward force. The box also had automatically inflating parachutes and balloons on the outside, similar to those used when landing craft on Mars in years past, should they appear in the sky. After noting, however, that the previous launching and landing with a camera was uneventful, accident wise, it was concluded that the chances of that happening were so remote that some strange law must be in place which ensured that nothing would materialize in midair or underground, some sort of attraction of mass to mass. More of a worry was that the Box might appear at the exact time and location as previous launches. *That* would be an issue. It caused a bit of mind-bending debate before it was ruled out. If it could happen, it would already have.

After breakfast, Tom and Julie walked hand-in-hand to the complex where the target room was located. Tom tried not to let on the depth of his worries. He smiled and fronted a cheerful demeanor. He doubted that Julie was buying it. What he didn't know, though, was that she was as anxious as him.

Karstens was waiting. Seeing them, he smiled, waved, and headed over to meet them, putting an arm around both.

"This is a big day, guys. Really, really big." The three stopped and stood in silence for a moment, each almost overcome by the import of this day to their lives and to the future of humanity.

"Are you ready, Julie?" Karstens asked.

Julie took a deep breath and let it out. "No," she shook her head. Tom looked over at her. She continued, "I'll never be ready to leave those I love. And yet ... and yet, I've been ready for this journey my whole life." She choked up, and half smiled.

Someone called out. The three turned. It was Mack. He was standing at the door to the complex. "One hour!" he said, tapping his wrist watch. Karstens waved a thank you.

"Okay, let's collect ourselves, shall we?" he suggested.

The three headed for the large glass double doors that stood open, waiting. *Waiting like a trap ready to catch some unsuspecting prey,* Tom thought. Julie could feel her heart pounding. Several people came out and stood by. "Fifty-five minutes, Mrs. Pine," said one. "Time to suit up." Inside the Strong Box, she and Jaqzen were to wear a protective outfit similar to astronauts. This was until the Miocene outside environment could be assessed. As a last resort, should the situation be deemed too dangerous, they could hole up in the box for the entire thirty days until they were brought back home. While it wouldn't be comfortable, there was space to move around and adequate supplies, including a portable toilet. Taking such an option, however, would doom the mission and, Julie thought, she and Tom's hopes for a better life. Thus, as far as she was concerned, it wasn't an option.

"Where's Dietrich?" Julie asked.

"Just inside, waiting for you, Doctor," said another. Walking into the building, they were met by Jaqzen.

"Hello there," he said, extending a hand. "Welcome to your future." He then offered his hand to Tom, smiled and nodded. Tom looked the big man in the eye without shaking his hand. "Hello," he answered curtly.

"Hi, Deet," answered Julie. She regarded his hand, then thought that perhaps he was apologizing. Let bygones be bygones. She took it and smiled half heartedly.

In the time since she first met with Karstens that day in the Institute cafeteria and agreed to this mission, a team of engineers had constructed a control room from which they would launch Julie and Jaqzen fifteen million years into the past.

107

Once gone, "the Js", as these engineers dubbed them, would be on their own. Before that happened, though, every technical detail possible that could contribute to success was hashed out and loaded. When she walked into the room, everyone suddenly stood, let out a loud cheer, and clapped. Karstens beamed.

The mood lifted, and Julie waved to the group. Someone walked by, a woman with a head mic on, and, grabbing Julie's hand, said in passing, "What an adventure. Wish it was me." Then the rest also approached. Suddenly, she was surrounded by warmth and good wishes. Tom, too, was hugged and reassured. "It'll be fine." "Don't worry." "You're a good man," and such.

Someone touched Julie's arm and said, "It's time. Let's get you to decontamination." Julie nodded. First, though, she was allowed one last moment with Tom. Turning to him, they embraced, holding tightly on to one another, "I thought I was doing this for me," she whispered, "but I'm not. I'm doing this for *us*." Tears flowed down her face. Tears at the thought of being separated by so great a distance. One not measured geographically, but temporally. Though she and Tom would be standing in the same location, they would be as far apart as if removed almost by the span of the universe itself. Tom tried to prevent them, but his own tears formed, and, running down his face, mixed with Julie's. She held him tighter. "I love you," she said softly. "So much." "I love you, too, baby," he breathed. "Hurry home." "I will." They kissed then and held on until someone said, "Time, Julie." Slowly, she let go and looked at him a moment longer. This would be her last view of him. Though he would be able to watch most of the launching on the viewer, she would not see him. Not again until she returned. Reaching the open door, she turned one last time, blew a kiss - and was gone.

There were two chambers for decontamination, one for Julie

and the other for Jaqzen. In these rooms, illuminated only by ultraviolet light, they were to strip off their clothing, then shower in a flow of warm water and disinfectant. A glove with bristles was provided with which every inch of skin was to be firmly scrubbed, their hair washed, teeth brushed, finger and toenails clipped to the skin. Lastly, Julie and Jaqzen were to swallow a large green pill that would kill off their gastrointestinal flora. This last was not pleasant, inducing a feeling of queasy nausea, but necessary. Every reasonable consideration was made to ensure that as few bacteria as possible from the modern world would be carried back, to avoid risk to the indigenous animal life.

Karstens put an arm around Tom and said, "We've got some time. There's nothing more for us to do right now. What do you say we take a walk?"

"Sure," Tom replied. He tried to collect himself. They walked out of the control room and out the building.

"What a whirlwind this has all been," Karstens offered amiably.

"Yeah. Pretty wild," Tom replied lowly.

They walked on a ways longer, neither speaking. Then Tom said, "So what happens now?"

"Well, now from decontamination they'll go into the sterile target room where the Strong Box is located by way of two internal doors. Once inside the capsule, they will close and seal the door behind them. Then they buckle in. There will be a series of functions to perform. The capsule is also sterile, so internal pressure will be increased to prevent potential leakage from the outside environment. Then we begin cycling up the accelerator. Actually, it's already warmed up. Then we drop the nuclear package into the accelerator tube. Pretty much immediately after that, the proton collision will occur in a small chamber just above and attached to the Strong Box. At that very moment, a tiny E.H., or "event horizon", will form. It is an instantaneous occurrence which initiates launch. One minute they are here; the next they are on their way, or already there, fifteen million years ago."

"You don't sound sure." Tom looked at Karstens.

"Well, we did have a recorder on our last trial box and thus were able to observe the time of actual retrieval and compare that to our time, but we are not sure of its accuracy. The time elapsed showed four minutes, thirty-two seconds. That's way, *way* faster than would be possible if Einsteinian physics applied. As an example, the speed of light, which is considered the universal speed limit, is more than 186,000 miles per second. Light travels close to six trillion miles per earth year. As you can see, if we were to travel at that speed and distance for fifteen million years, we would be traveling an ungodly distance, approximately 88 quintillion miles. Imagine traveling that distance in mere minutes! We're talking one and three quarter *trillion* times the speed of light!

"Another example, Messier 83," he continued, "known as the Southern Pinwheel Galaxy, is fifteen mega, that's fifteen million, light years away. That's how many years it takes light leaving that galaxy to reach us. That's *the same temporal distance* as from our current time to the Barstovian age. Imagine traveling to Messier 83 in such a short period of time!"

"Boggles the mind," Tom said.

"Mine, too, and I study this stuff! But what's *interesting* is that if we look at M83 today, we are seeing it the way it looked fifteen million years ago, during Julie's Barstovian. *There's* a bit of time travel for you! Of course, we're *not* talking physical distance here with our mission, but temporal. Thus, in this case, it means they'll be moving at roughly 50,000 years a second!" Karstens didn't mention that they still didn't understand the actual processes involved in their discovery of time travel, or that its finding was pure chance.

"And once gone, there's no way of contacting them?" Tom asked.

"No, unfortunately. Not until our retrieval in thirty days' time. It's not like we can pick up a cell phone and call, though I wish we could." Out of the corner of his eye, Karstens noticed Tom's dejected look. "Thirty days time, my friend, and it's over."

"A lot can happen in thirty days," Tom said.

"Yes, it can. And we've done all that we can possibly do to make this go smoothly. I only ask for your patience. Really, this is not all that different from many, many voyages in the historical past by other great adventurers, men like Magellan, which led to the formation of the United States."

"Yes, and look at us now," Tom added cynically.

There was a pause.

"Yeah," Karstens conceded faintly.

"I gotta ask you, do you really believe all that stuff you said, you know, in that speech back at the send-off?" Tom asked, somewhat nervously.

"You mean about 'our glorious future', that kind of thing?"

"Yeah."

"Sure," Karstens said.

Tom didn't buy it. "Hmm," he replied.

Karstens glanced around, then back to Tom. "Between me and you?" Tom looked over, then nodded.

"Pile of crap."

"Then what's this all about?"

Karstens looked suddenly uneasy. He cleared his throat. "In a way, it does have to do with our future, the future of the race. That part is accurate. Further than that, however, I can't - talk about. It's classified."

Tom stopped and turned to face Karstens, who also stopped. "I knew it. Something's not right here, is it? So what *aren't* you telling me?" he asked, "I want to know what's really going on, and *now*," he grabbed Karstens by the front of his shirt, "or so help me ... I swear I'll raise a ruckus like you've never seen."

Karstens, not anticipating this, looked around apprehensively, afraid that someone might notice and call security. No one had. "Please. Everything I've told you and Julie about the mission is true. Nothing has changed. It's just that... I think there might be more to its, um, long-term, uh, aim, then I've been told." The answer wasn't satisfying Tom. Karstens exhaled, "Look, I am sworn to keep quiet and could lose my job if others find out, and I don't know everything, but in thirty days time when Julie comes back, I will gladly inform you both of what I do know." Tom looked hard at him, then let go.

"Why is it always like that? You government people hiding stuff, thinking you know better than everyone else. You can't just level with people," Tom bristled.

It's because people don't want to know the truth, Karstens thought. Instead he said, "I'm not the government. I'm just as much a pawn of them as are you, perhaps more so."

"What's your Worth number?" Tom asked accusingly.

Karstens exhaled again, "I'm a sixty-nine," he admitted, seemingly ashamed about it.

"Yeah. Government man," Tom said. Karstens said nothing to that. Then he noticed someone approaching them. It was the Blacksuit he'd seen at the launching party, the one who had altered Julie's speech.

"Suit," Karstens warned, quietly flicking his eyes in the man's direction. Tom turned to look. The man had a grim look on his face.

"Wonderful!" Tom said, rolling his eyes. "I suppose he heard everything."

"Maybe," Karstens replied. But as he advanced, the Suit's hard look changed to a smile and a wave. "Maybe not."

"Gentlemen! Fine day for a launching, is it not?" The Blacksuit declared.

"Absolutely!" Karstens agreed, "Couldn't be better."

The man's eyes shot back and forth from Karstens to Tom. Small, beady eyes that reminded Tom of a spider's. "So I trust all's well then, Dr. Karstens?" he inquired.

"Of course. We're all set for launch in, let's see," Karstens looked at his watch, "about twenty-five minutes."

"Good. Good," The nameless Suit said. Then his former dour appearance returned, and he gave Karstens a hard look. "Because it certainly would not do to have a loose indiscretion throw a wrench into the works at this late date, would it?"

Karstens gazed at the man, paused, then parroted his tone, "No, it certainly wouldn't," he smiled.

"Yes," the man continued. "We all need to be mindful our actions, and their consequences. Keep our eyes on the prize, so to speak." He looked at Tom.

"Um hmm. Yep, that's certainly true," agreed Tom.

"Delightful!" exclaimed the Suit. "Well, now that we are all on the same page, perhaps we should repair to the viewing room?"

"A good idea," agreed Karstens. "Julie should be ready. You'll be able to watch her on the viewer." He looked over at Tom.

"Let's go," said Tom. He immediately set his step in the direction of the room, and off the three went, Karstens and Tom in the lead, with the Suit behind.

Arriving at the room, he found that it was packed with, he guessed, at least a hundred crammed into the small chamber. Two seats had been reserved for Karstens and he at the front. The Blacksuit went to stand in the back. Strangely, no one showed up to see Jaqzen off. This worried Karstens. A wireless mic was given to Tom, and he put it on. Julie, wearing a green jumpsuit, was seated at her place within the Strong Box, Dietrich, in red, was opposite her. Both wore mics as well.

"Can she hear me?" Tom asked.

In answer, the speakers sounded overhead, "Honey, is that you?" It was Julie's voice.

Tom perked up, "Yes, it's me!" He looked at her image. The name *Pine* was attached above her left breast. Vari-colored lights were blinking around her. There were also tubes attached to their arms. Slowly, sedatives and anti-nausea agents were being administered.

"I'm so excited. I sure wish you were here," Julie said, her exhilaration apparent.

"Me too, sweetheart," Tom answered.

Another voice came through. It was a technician from the control room. "Julie, this is Howard. How's the weather in there?"

Julie looked at the instruments that she and Dietrich had trained on. "Oxygen, twenty-one percent. Nitrogen, seventy-eight percent. CO_2, normal. Pressure, fourteen point seven pounds. Temperature, twenty-one degrees Celsius."

"Affirmative, Julie. That's what we're reading here," the tech said. There was some background commentary, then he said, "Julie you're showing elevated adrenaline levels and your heart rate's up. Everything OK?"

"Affirmative, Control. I'm just amped."

"Understood," Control acknowledged. "In a minute, you'll be feeling the effects of the sedative."

"Affirmative, Control," she said.

More commentary, then, "Deet, you're level across all boards," meaning that nothing was out of the ordinary. "How are you feeling?"

"Excellent, Control. I'm ready to go!" Jaqzen replied.

"Affirmative. Launch time in fifteen minutes."

A muffled, but nevertheless, loud noise overhead, like a large thrumming gong, blared, followed by the sound of a relay and servo starting. "Winding up," said the voice at Control. That meant that that the accelerator was turned on and was warming. A powerful hum filled the room. Tom could feel the vibration in his teeth. This kept up for about five minutes, then suddenly lowered to a dim background purr, like an engine smoothly idling.

"Julie, this is Bob," Karstens said.

"Hi, Bob!" Julie answered.

"I can't wait to see your video."

Julie laughed. "I'll do my best, sir," she replied.

"I know you will. You just have fun, okay? And take care of yourself."

"I will, thank you," Julie said.

"You too, Deet. I'm looking forward to your report!"

"Yessir," Deet replied. "Already working on it," he added, smiling.

Then someone spoke something in Tom's ear. He nodded, stood, and followed the man to a very small room. It had only one chair and a view screen. Julie wanted to say something privately to him. Since she and Jaqzen were wearing headgear, the control room techs were able to mute the comments so that only her husband could hear. The main view screen also switched off. The tech voice screen in the control room showed only the bouncing lines of a dialog graph.

After a few moments, a voice sounded. "Five minutes, Julie," it said. Tearfully, she and Tom said their goodbyes. The main viewing room screen remained off as the impact doors shut. From this point on, until Julie and Deet returned in thirty days, they'd be incommunicado. The sedatives finally kicking in, they sank back into their chairs, which had gone into a reclining state. Soon, they were out, each tightly buckled. If he had wanted to say anything else to her, she would not have heard, Tom thought. But he said it anyway.

"Be safe, my love."

"T-minus one minute and counting," the voice said. Another loud noise of relays opening sounded. Tom jumped slightly and gulped. He crossed his fingers. Someone behind him put a hand on his shoulder. It was Karstens. He'd let himself into the small room and now stood behind him. He handed Tom some hearing protectors, his own already on. Karstens looked at his watch and compared it to the time on the wall chronometer. The decibel levels rose as a whirring servo opened and continued to rise.

"T-minus twenty-seconds and counting," said the voice. No one else said anything. Unbeknownst to Tom, Karstens was holding white knuckled onto the back of his seat. He was also saying something over and over again in a voice too low for anyone else to hear. A prayer, perhaps.

"T-minus ten-seconds and counting. Nine. Eight. Seven. Six. Five. Four. Three. Two. One. *Launching!*"

A loud BOOM, like a clap of thunder.

And then the room where Julie and Dietrich were just a moment before was void.

Nine

The month was a long one for Tom. Every day that went by seemed like an eternity, and the nights were longer. When the loneliness seemed overwhelming, the worry and fear, he'd scold himself for his weakness and lack of trust. Karstens was a good man, someone who made you feel that he had thought of everything. Every angle. Every possibility. And indeed, that was the case, so why was he so anxious? Karstens encouraged Tom to think of the fact that every day gone was one day less to wait. To busy himself and take his mind off this interval.

Karstens turned out, in fact, to be a true friend. If he didn't call every day just to chat, he'd come by the Oasis and have a few drinks. Rather than annoyance at Tom's disquiet, he understood.

Once, Paul came over and sat with his new patron at the table. He could tell from his observations that the two had become confidants, compadres of a sort, and he wanted to meet him. If Tom liked him, he was okay. Paul also thought that Karstens looked somehow familiar, but he couldn't place him. He suspected, though, that the man had something to do with Tom's troubles. Something to do with Julie, but how, he couldn't quite get. A lawyer, maybe? No. Perhaps he was family. There was something about him that seemed to Paul rather more refined, more, *intelligent*, than his typical customer. The way he spoke. The way he seemed to be a man in charge, yet not overtly so. It was rare to have someone who exuded such *professionalism* and *integrity* in his lowly establishment.

When the overhead television began showing a program about space aliens and "Grays", Paul decided to test him.

"If you asked me, it's all a crock," he said, waving at the monitor.

"Oh? How so?" Karstens asked, intrigued.

Paul thought about it, then said, "The ships. You know? They are supposed to one day take us all away to our 'heavenly future', so to speak."

"Yes?" Karstens furtively took a small box out of his pocket and stuck it upside down underneath the table. The white noise amplifier.

"Uh," Tom said, suddenly uneasy. He could see his boss had been drinking.

"No, no. Hear me out, hear me out," Paul said confidentially. "It's true that there are ships. But guess what? You ready for this? They've already left! They've *already left!*" Karstens and Tom looked at each other now.

"We all know that there is *no way* they could build enough ships to take billions of people off this planet. No way. Okay? So they built a few. I have it on authority, I can't tell you who, either, so don't ask, but I have it on authority that they left some time ago, and with them they took the élite. You know, the rich, the powerful, scientists, engineers and others that are useful. They're already gone. They couldn't even go down with the ship! And the gang that's running things now? They're the *rejects*."

Karstens' calm smile dropped. He said nothing.

"Oh come on, Paul," Tom whispered, "you don't believe that!"

"Believe it? I *know* it," Paul said, "And you know something else, I have a theory about them." He turned to look again at the screen, at a picture of the thin lipped, large-eyed, large brained grays. "Those things up there, you see 'em? They're not aliens from another world. Those are *us, people*, but from the future! They are the descendants of those traitors that left us all to rot! But they've come back now, back in time, after spending who knows how long out there evolving, or maybe I

118

should say, *de*volving into *them*." He jabbed a finger over his shoulder at the TV, his expression a look of disgust. "They've come back in failure, finally learning that people can't live in space. Look at how wasted their muscles are, how sickly they look: gray, the color of death. They also discovered that the closest candidate planet for colonization in our galaxy was either uninhabitable or too far away."

"*Paul!*" Tom urged. He coughed now, trying to prevent a bout of it.

The bar man lowered his voice. "And those medical experiments we hear about? They're *real*. Their scientists are stealing *our genes* to try to fix what *they've wrecked!* But it won't work. Those cretins were *too stupid* to realize that this planet is all we have. No, they were more interested in ter-raforming some cold, dead rock than protecting a living planet. What's that old saying? Good planets are hard to come by. And now it's *shot*, thanks to creatures like them. We'll be lucky to retreat under domes or underground."

There was a long break now as Paul stopped to let it all sink in. Tom, stunned, stole clandestine glances around them to see if anyone else was paying attention. If there were, it wasn't obvious.

"That's extraordinary!" Karstens said lowly, looking at Kiley with solemn admiration. "How did you...?"

"Like I said, I got it on good authority."

Karstens nodded. Tom worried. And Paul satisfied. Evidently he'd wanted to get that off his chest for some time.

"My friend," Karstens said, "you're a very bright man, and what you say may well be true, but from this point on you must, *must* keep this to yourself." There was grave earnestness in his voice. Paul nodded, suddenly embarrassed. In a rush of enthusiasm, he'd foolishly let his guard down.

"Sorry," he said.

"Don't be," Karstens whispered. He extended a hand across the table and shook the bar man's. "A pleasure meeting you."

At home, Tom occupied himself with housework, things that lagged since Julie's departure or things that he'd put off for months, even years. He finally repaired that broken step to the upper floor that she'd nagged him about for so long. He also spent an afternoon trying, without luck, to fix the freezer. Ultimately, he gave up, put it back together, and found a repairman. The bored fellow had it going in five minutes.

Tom also passed time perusing the books of Julie's favorite author, Loren Eiseley. She'd suggested he read them when they were dating, but he just couldn't drum up the enthusiasm to digest melancholy nonfiction. The writings of a man in love with time itself. Now, though, he found the old books strangely compelling.

Then, hesitantly, he opened her drawer in their shared dresser, the one she kept her own writings in. Not her official work-related papers, those were kept elsewhere, but her personal ones. He felt guilty for doing so. Likely, if she were here, she'd fuss about it. She could be like that with him: didn't want him to see her depression about the state of the world she so loved. But he wanted to hear her voice and began to read anyway. Took a gloomy Saturday and sat on the floor, absorbed.

As he looked through them, he came across one piece with "Julie Welsh, 12" scrawled in the corner. It was a poem.

The Field

Sit I upon this hillside fair

toward the close of day
and gaze in peace the land below
so green and still
but for the breeze

Far away a bird flock pauses
this moment in time given to them
pauses to eat some unseen food
unseen to me that is
almost to sleep am I ...

The birds are gone when I lift my eyes

I see a form, dark and so small
moving thoughtfully
among the grasses of an endless field

I hear no sound from her, the cat
she hears no sound from me
her world is what she sees
in that moment ——

Lies she down for a rest
then continues her journey
till I see her no more

Farewell my friend, farewell

Sorting through, he found another. In the corner was scrawled "Harrison Welsh, 7 - 22." A poem by her father. Reading it, he was reminded of the dog she'd told him of, a cherished childhood pet, the mere mention of which could bring her to tears.

Ruddy My Heart

Years ago it was
when first I saw you
there at the pound
and yet it seems like only yesterday,
only yesterday

One of nine you were
a pup the size of a cat,
and now look at you, how you've grown
my boy, my beloved companion, my right arm

Almost did I choose a sibling
but what a mistake
that would have been

Then I saw you and
O how sad you looked
deliberately separated from frantic mother
alone, like myself

You did not look at me
did not jump or beg
but stayed behind, for you knew
that I would choose another

-and so I chose you-

I remember that first night
how you cried for mother
cried in the dark
and I brought you up onto the bed

and there you found comfort and warmth
your cries became whimpers

<><><><>

Like leaves blowing along
on a gusty day, we've drifted
down some trail here or there
and time has stretched out
for us, fine as a gossamer thread
silken, glistening, in the early morning light...

How many miles - who can tell?
and spring becomes autumn
and autumn spring once more
as one by one the years
drop away
like ripe plums from the tree

How gentle and fine
are lands that remain
wild and free,
still untouched
by the improving hand of man
May it ever be so

<><><><>

How do I write of this
the death of my heart
for you were
Ruddy My Heart.

Opalescence

For fifteen years we were
inseparable, you and I.
Will anyone ever be able
to understand our bond?

So pure of heart, unselfish and true
you never asked for more
than my love in return

(and how you delighted
when two we howled together!)
No shred of the evil was in you
that exists in the heart of man

———

I asked you remain
before ever I met her
and you did because you knew that alone,
alone...

thank you

———

How will the world cope
with your loss
a loss so profound because you were
the embodiment of goodness & happiness

A week before
you took a fall
and suffered a twisted stomach

unknown to me
until that night
when I took you out
for your last walk
and though you were in pain
still (slowly) you followed
- as always
but this time,
this time ...

I could not help

and into my eyes you looked
there at the clinic
deeply, one last time
trusting, never wavering,
and I stammered
"Okay"

and wept.

~ I am so sorry ~

I buried you there
at our favorite place to hike,
and that night
under the crescent moon
I howled for you

And now Tom wept as well. Julie had adored her father, an avid hiker. Reading this, he understood how she had become *who* she was. He wept for the goodness that was his wife. A ruby in a world of rubble.

Then, digging through, he found another. This one, much darker. In the corner it said, "Julie Pine, 25." Four years ago.

Extinction

Time t'was to go
and though we perceived't
we refused to accept
or admit us defeat

Oh! our history's been grand
none to compare
from earth we took sand
and built without care

All the wars that we fought
and ships that we made
and lovers we've held
on bright sunny days

All the days that we cried
the days that we laughed
was it all just for naught
has the die just been cast?

We still have our plans
So much for to do
now our time is at hand
and our end is now due

The stars to explore
other lands to bring low
as we conquered our own

Ron Rayborne

oh so long ago

We shall silence those say
our time is but up
that our day is now done
and of death shall we sup

We will not lie down gently
will fight to the end
for we are not ready
and we will not bend

For we still do not know

~ the meaning of life ~

But now at the end
now we do see
t'was not all the hurried
crazed activity

T'was not all the things
we might accumulate
nor even the faithless
we did habilitate

But alas do we learn it
too late, oh too late

T'is days warm and bright
that we shall never see
loud, crashing waves
the life in a tree

a mouse as it chews
a tiny grass seed
a bird as it sings
the song of the freed

Sunrises, sunsets
the thunder and rain
for us are no more
we cannot remain
Time t'is to go
we shall not refrain,
and after us will come
the hard cleansing rains

Ending, he felt stunned. He'd no idea that Julie had been so troubled. It broke his heart that he hadn't been enough to ease her despondency. Looking at the paper, he saw the stains, marks of her tears as she wrote. Leaving her writings scattered around on the floor where he'd been sitting, he lay down to sleep.

When he awoke, he looked at the clock. Time for work. But he couldn't. Not today. So he called in. Paul understood and told him to take some time off. The Oasis would still be there when he returned.

Tom ate and washed up, leaving the papers on the floor. Then he called a friend who, detecting a note of sadness in Tom's voice, suggested he come by to visit. It was a long way, northwest Nevada, the place that he and Julie had last walked. He'd leave his motorcycle at the station and take a train. They still ran. He'd have a couple hours at his friend's, then, back again, he'd cycle the nine miles home, through the crowds trying to beat sundown. There was time.

The scenery was bleak, and Tom resisted the urge to stare out the window. He knew what he'd see. Garbage, old, over-turned cars and smashed appliances piled up along the tracks. Winos in fights and addicts with their heads in their hands. Racial epithets spray painted on the sides of buildings. The crass, flashing, phallic-shaped neon of the Hard-Up Hotel. And farther down the road, a dilapidated Baptist billboard that shouted: *YOU'RE GOING TO HELL!!!* The words surrounded by faces in flames. Across it were the scrawled curses of those angered by the ghastly message. In another sector, armed troops wearing gas masks raced through the streets. The ugliness of man at the end of his rope. It was all very depressing.

When he arrived, he sat and talked to the couple and felt better to know that there were still good people around. Then he left them to wander their land. To see if he could glimpse what it was that Julie perceived in nature. And in the quiet, it began to come to him.

Though what should be green was brown, a hue which matched the pigment of the sky, still, even now, there were patches of "natural" left. Here and there, like the stubborn hope that exists in the hearts of the good, he would find a leaf or two, green and beautiful. Though they were affixed to plants once con-sidered "weeds," now they were a welcome sight. Tom sat and saw something moving in the soil, ants wandering restlessly, as if preparing for a long winter. *You don't know how long*, he thought. And then, lighting on a dead twig not three feet away, a dragonfly suddenly appeared. Its tiny head looked right and left. It flicked its wings. Turned around. Then around again, now seeming to look straight at Tom. It lifted effortlessly, then came near Tom's face as if to study him. Soundless. A tiny beat of glassy wings catching stray sunlight, splitting it into color. It hovered there a moment longer, then, suddenly as it had appeared, it was off. Gone on some unknown mission.

"Farewell my friend. Farewell," Tom said.

He lay down there, as Julie had often done, folded his arms behind his head and closed his eyes, imagining the world as it once was. The world that Julie saw. Green earth and blue sky. Strong, proud oceans, teeming with life. Birds flying overhead and deer grazing sweetly a wild grassland. *Yes, it is beautiful. As are you, my love.*

Come home to me.

He closed his eyes.

Something.

Tom jumped and turned around. There, like an apparition, looking down at him, stood a man, if that it was. Ancient, red skin, wrinkles upon wrinkles. Hair, long and gray. Strangely attired, tanned habiliments, like, canvas perhaps, hung on his shoulders and around his waist. Even upon his feet. There were beads around his neck. A look vaguely familiar, perhaps something he'd once seen in a book. The old man looked down at Tom, saying nothing. Tom scooted back on the ground.

"Can I help you?" Tom asked.

The old man looked around as if seeing the entirety of the earth.

"You have forgotten. But the last shall be first," he replied with a voice deep and halting.

Tom stood and stepped back. "Who - who are you? What do you want?"

"I am Grandfather. I am Algonquin and Cree, Hopi and Lakhota. I am Mohawk and Navaho, Nez-Perce and Onondaga. I am Chumash and Pueblo, Shoshone and Sioux, I am Ojibwa and Miwok, Wichita and Zuñi. I am a thousand tribes that walked this land. I am the hopes, the fears, the loves, the joys, the despair and the sadness of The People. I am the brave who holds his lover tightly under the boughs of ancient oaks. I am the maid who suckles her child in a field of flowers. I am the water as it runs over the stones. I am the cry of the hawk that says all is well. I am a thousand thousand dreams, and one."

Tom gaped, but not understanding said nothing in reply. Yet, he sensed that the old man was more than that, and that this visit had some significance - to him.

"You have forgotten", the old man said again.

"Forgotten? Forgotten what?" Tom asked.

"But the last shall be first."

He'd not noticed before that a strange sort of fog had gradually appeared. It drifted between the two, then dissipated. With it went the old man. Tom blinked.

As he thought about this, he suddenly heard the sound of dry foliage crunching underfoot. Footsteps. Tom turned. Another man, this one younger, and more - real - was approaching. He, too, was dark with long hair. But his clothes were obviously more modern. Then he spoke.

"The Great Chief, Luther Standing Bear, once said, 'Miles were to us as they were to the bird. The land was ours to roam in as the sky was for them to fly in. We did not think of the great open plains, the beautiful rolling hills, and winding streams with tangled growth, as "wild." Only to the white man was nature a "wilderness" and only to him was the land "infested" with "wild" animals and "savage people." To us it was tame. Earth was bountiful, and we were surrounded with the blessings of the Great Mystery.'"

Tom shook his head. "What the devil is going on?" he demanded.

"Be calm, my brother. I am Kidütökadö, Numa chief of the Northern Paiute tribe. I understand that you do not. You stand upon sacred ground."

Tom looked around at the browning foliage. Kidütökadö laughed.

"Even when a man has crushed the flower underfoot, he cannot erase its memory from time. Cannot remove its place in earth history.

"This valley," he continued, "you once called Virgin Valley, it is my home."

"I'm sorry," Tom stammered, coughed. "Did I wander too far?" He glanced around, but no fence was apparent and he'd not crossed any.

Kidütökadö laughed again. "No, brother. Long before your friends settled here, The People were present."

"Who was that old man?" Tom asked.

"He has told you and I cannot say more. With time it will be clear." Then Kidütökadö said, "Sit, and I will tell you a story."

Tom sat. Then the red man sat as well. He gathered together dry foliage around him into a little mound in front of them. Then he put his hands over it and began to sing. It was a soft, lilting song, and the man sang it in a low, melodic voice, rocking slightly. Tom looked at him, then something glinted and he looked down to see a small fire forming. It was warm, soothing.

"Long, long ago, longer than before even the dawn of The People, this land was sacred. Sacred above all others. At that time, there were many wild beasts, kin that we would never know. They lived here in great numbers," he said, gesturing with his hands. "Where we now sit upon dry ground, a vast lake was. In beauty, brother deer and horse wandered the green hills that encircled it. And trees, spruce, hemlock, birch, chestnut, even sequoia, sang, sang with the songs of many birds. It was a paradise." He paused, looking at Tom, who looked peculiarly back at him. "But it was also a time of great danger. Mother earth spoke violently and poured forth her blood. Over and over it flowed, mightily, and when finally she calmed, from her blood came life.

"The land itself was beautiful beyond compare. Like a young maiden bedecked in jewels, she was adorned in flowers all year, and the land was many colored. Eventually, Mother rested from creating, and for a long time, all was so. A golden season that was never before or after. But in secrecy she hid her blossoming, hid it in time, shy as a girl."

Tom was captivated and continued to sit, listening.

"By and by, she matured and outgrew this phase, as all must do. With time, things changed and she aged. Still, she held onto her youthful beauty. A blue-green jewel in the infinite deadness of space."

"What happened?" Tom asked, seeming to understand the special wisdom of this man.

"Were it not for one of her creations, a people she formed in her haste and giddiness, she would still be magnificent and long would live in stately splendor. That child which she held to her breast, though, was greedy and turned against her. He grew to hate his mother. With knives he cut her hair and carried it off to sell. But like a mother that cannot be angry at her child, she did not rebuke him. And so he grew and became bold and continued to take and take. And now, like one mad, he holds the knife finally to her throat, the throat of his mother. The one that birthed and cared for him for so long, and slowly he draws it. Yet, still she loves, and will die for it."

The red man paused, then, quietly, he began again to sing. Another language. Tom did not understand. As the man sang, he picked up dirt and debris from the ground and commenced to pour it over his head, then to weep. Tom, alarmed, got ready to rise. Yet, instead, he continued to watch. Then the red man reached into the fire with his hands. Flames licked around them, but seemed not to cause him pain. He continued his song. Tom made as if to pull the man's hands out, but stopped. After a moment, the red man withdrew them, closed. His hands, though dirty, did not appear burned. Once again he sang, though this time Tom understood. He strained to hear.

"When the sky has turned dark, and your eye has grown dim, then, Mother, then will you rise again. In loveliness you will go, and I am struck. I am struck. Then will you rise again, and the circle will be complete."

The red man spoke. "So lovely was Mother that her beauty fell from the sky like raindrops that reflected the world around them, each a memory of that distant time, a world of many colors."

With that, smoke from the small fire in front of him arose. It burned Tom's eyes and obscured his vision. Suddenly, he felt very tired and lay down on the spot, falling asleep quickly.

Ten

When Tom awoke, it was raining lightly. Acids in it burned his skin. He sat up and looked around, donning his jacket and hat for protection. Nothing out of the normal. He stretched, embarrassed at himself for having fallen asleep on the ground, then brushed his jacket and pants. How to explain his appearance to his friends? Then he thought about what had happened, or what *seemed* to have happened. A dream. *Ah, a dream.* But he couldn't remember.

The rain stopped, and sun broke through in the West. Then, gradually fading in, colors in the East. Brilliant. A rainbow. He gaped and marveled. Colors, yes, colors. Wonderful that even at this late date, the earth could manage a rainbow. Such a pity.

Placing his hands on the ground, he prepared to rise. Then he felt something - something hard and smooth. He pulled his hand away and looked. An outline of something roundish. Dusty-white, with a glint of green. Intrigued, Tom again reached down and attempted to remove it, but it held fast. He brushed the dirt away from the top, then began to dig the sediment around it. A stone. But more than just a stone. It was evidently some sort of quartz-like rock. Finally freeing it, he lifted it to have a closer look. It had a nice heft, balance. But it was what was under the dusty-white surface that interested him. A smattering of color. Tom stood and wiped it on his shirt. Doing so, his eyes grew wide. Muted greens, reds, blues and yellows emerged. Excited, he took some water from a small canteen he'd carried with him, poured a bit on the rock and wiped. Now color shone forth as if lighted from within. Brilliant hues within a translucent, almost watery matrix, went in every direction. Tom drew in his breath.

A jewel of some sort. It must have weighed several ounces. That suggested value. He turned it over in his hands. Flawless. Though it had been in the ground for who knew how long, it had not a scratch on it. Tom felt his jaw drop. It was most beautiful thing he'd ever seen. With the sun shining through it, his hand flared its own rainbow of colors.

Tom was nothing if not honest, and immediately decided that he had to get this to his friends who had so graciously allowed him to visit their land. Straightening his attire, he set back down the path. Yet, even as he did, he knew that it was his. It was, in fact, *meant* for him and that he would never be without it. He seemed to feel a sort of melding with the stone, as if he'd always had it. Then a thought, unbidden, impressed itself upon him like a waking dream.

"The color stone Mother has given to you,
for you are to go to her."
Go? What do you mean, go? Tom thought.
"The greedy child has stole into her secret place.
He cannot, for he would violate and destroy.
But the last shall be first."

It was past midday. Tom looked at his watch and was horrified to find that he had missed the train. He'd have to take the next. Troubled, he decided not to call in at the house, not wanting the inconvenience of an interrogation, no matter how friendly. Instead, he cut across the landscape, climbing the fence, then ran to the station and bought a ticket. Finally, it came. By the time he made it back to his motorcycle, the sky had dimmed.

In a few days, Julie would be returning, then all would be well. The thought made him happy. She would have stories to tell, and he to listen. Then they would love. Safe in each other's arms, the world could go to hell.

And it was.

The streets were deserted. He looked at his watch ... 6:14 PM. Uh oh, the curfew! The sky above was darkening. *Crap! What should I do, try to make it home, or find a place on the side of the road to wait out the night?* The risks were twofold: If he wasn't taken by the police, he might be by the roving gangs which plagued the night, only dispersing, like cockroaches, when the police came through on "Cleanup" in the morning. But both could be brutal. Having the police show up, though, was actually preferable to being caught by one of these gangs or some roving scofflaw. They were merciless if you didn't have something to give.

Tom decided to try to make it home. He put his hand to the gas on his motorcycle and it sped down the road. Loudly. He'd gone halfway by the time the day was done and everything black. Rounding a corner, he didn't realize what had happened until he was in the street, it transpired that fast. A guy wire placed across it, one side to the other, by someone who heard him coming, caught him at his chest and hauled him off. A little higher, and it would have been his head. He tumbled while the motorcycle continued on without him, until it, too, crashed to the ground. There was a sound like distant shouting.

There Tom lay, not quite comprehending what had happened. Looking around at the darkness, he sat up. *A crash,* he thought. He'd hit the ground, hard, yet curiously, nothing felt broken. Surely his arms and legs should be twisted at impossible angles. Shock. No. Then, *fear.* Flashlights, moving toward him from several directions. Running.

Oh no.

Tom climbed to his feet. They'd not gotten to him yet, were searching with their lights. *Thank God for a moonless night,* he thought as he darted in the one direction that the flashlights weren't. Reaching the corner, he turned around to see spots of light converging on the area he had just been. More shouting. Curses. He coughed, coughed again, and someone shone a light in his direction, yelled something, and the other lights were suddenly pointing at him. He turned and ran.

All was dark and no house welcomed him, no stranger standing in a doorway to say, *"Over here."* Panic rose in his throat. He knew this street, Division. He crossed Central. A bad area. Four miles to go. He'd never make it.

Suddenly, a bullet rang out and hit the wall of a building close to where he raced. Tom jumped and dove into a doorway, wheezing. They closed in. *No.* He bolted from the trap and ran at full speed. Yet, even now he could feel a burning in his side, a pain that told him he would not be able to continue much longer without a rest. His breathing came in rasps, hard and ragged. The air was bad, and hot. Still, he cursed himself for his lousy shape. More shots. They hit the sidewalk around him, chipping bits of concrete that stung his face. He didn't dare look back; didn't want to lose any momentum. Though his lungs ached, he wouldn't allow himself to turn around and see how close this gang was. He came to a corner and saw at the end another group running toward him. They'd somehow communicated his location and were converging. Veering off, Tom sprinted across the highway toward the shopping district, now closed and barred. He noticed that the moon was beginning to peek out in the East. A half-moon. He felt his pulse beat in his temples, but would not give up because he knew that he'd be a dead man should they catch him. That he had so far eluded them had enraged the mob, and now it was a fox hunt. To them.

On he ran. Finally, around a corner, he was forced to stop. Breathing hard, then coughing, he turned. Though he could see them coming at him, he couldn't go on. If he had a minute maybe. He looked around. Shadows. The moon had risen, quickly it seemed. Back again, long shadows closed in. Now maybe fifty yards away. They'd be able to see him, too. He turned. Nowhere to go. Then he noticed that the bars on one small window near him were loose. Not bolted down properly. A sign that they had been loosened at some point and not discovered by the owner. A robber's window. He grabbed at them, and to his amazement, they simply came off as one in his hand. He threw it inside and it landed noisily, then he clambered up and went through the window after it. Running footsteps. *Coming.* They'd notice. He dived at the bars and snatched them up, then, deliberating, decided to try to hold them onto the window from the inside. Risky. Should they shine a light toward the window, likely they'd see his hands stupidly holding the bars. He thought about dropping them and continuing, but it was too late. They were at the corner. It sounded like a lot.

Tom's breathing was rapid, and his heart pounded in his ears. He was certain that they would be able to hear him and tried to keep quiet.

"Where is he?" Someone demanded, puffing. They, too, were breathing hard, and Tom hoped that their own breathing would disguise his. A light shone around outside, making a faint glow inside.

Please, Tom thought, *don't point it this way.* His fingers holding the grating must be so obvious, yet still they did not notice. He felt another cough rising, irresistibly, and fought to suppress it. More cursing. Then someone yelled out a loud, foul, imprecation. Deep, probably a big man.

"You let him get away!" he yelled, rasping. His voice sounding just on the other side of the wall. Tom was standing against a shelf of some kind, and suddenly he brushed against something that had been balancing precariously on the edge. It clanged to the floor.

"Shhhh!" another said, *"Did'ja hear that?"* Then all was quiet as the group tried to judge where it was coming from. Tom gulped and felt light-headed. *Don't pass out now,* he thought. He realized that it was because he'd been holding his breath, an impossible feat seeing as his heart was still thumping. He tried to breathe gently. Abruptly, the light flashed directly at the window. A pause, then an exclamation. *"THERE HE IS!"* and a loud crash as a steel rod banged down on the bars near his fingers. Tom let go the grating and it fell heavy on the foot of the big man, who howled in pain.

It wasn't much, but the pause had allowed Tom to gather some energy, and he set off toward a door which he could barely see in the faint light that shone in from outside. The light brightened when several beams were aimed at it. He slammed the door and was now in total darkness. He assessed wildly. *Do I try to hide in here somewhere or do I keep on going?* He opted against the first choice when he remembered that, with their torches, they'd likely find him in no time, so he ran with his left arm stretched out, touching the wall. Several times he knocked something to the ground, and once ran full into another item, possibly a table. If they were inside, they'd know which way he went. But he continued to run, as fear rose up in him. He didn't run into anything else, and that was lucky, because they were in the room.

Tom judged that it was a department store. The lights danced around the room as the gang searched for him. He found a door and tried it. Locked. Running on, he found another. Locked again. When a light came near him, he ducked and it passed over. Yelling. The light had revealed an open door, and Tom crept toward it, then slipped in, quietly closing the door behind him. Metal. He felt for the lock. A button. *Click.* Too loud. More shouts.

In the pale moonlight, he saw a window, made his way

over to it, and looked out. Nobody around. Did they all come in? Then he noticed that beyond was some sort of private courtyard, probably a lunch area for the employees. As such, there were no bars. He looked for a way to open it. Steps closing in. Only seconds. He was about to settle for simply throwing a chair at it, when he spotted a small latch. He turned it and it slid. The window opened easily and out he climbed, then glanced around for an outlet. One door. His heart sank when he found it was locked.

On the door were words painted in blue. Some employee graffiti that no one had removed. He had no time to read, yet felt strangely compelled to do so anyway.

It didn't used to be this way. There was a time when people were truly and actually free, wandering over the countryside wherever they happened to go, living without fear. Fear of losing their jobs, losing their home, making a boss mad, getting sued, not being able to pay their rent, not being able to feed their families. No screaming commercials, no waiting in lines, no political divisions, no governmental busybodies trying to get something on them, no worry about D-day. Just living. Yeah, they had their difficulties, but at least they were free.

Someone banged on the inside door, the one he'd locked. Tom looked up. Over his door was wall. But a height of about ten feet, it was open to the outside. Unhelpfully, though, on the brow of the wall, sat a length of razor wire. Pulling a table over to the side, he scrambled up, discovering that he could just reach the top, but no further. Frantically, he jumped off to the sound of someone throwing his weight against the inside door. Grabbing a chair, he put it on top of the table and clambered up. The wire tore at his sleeves. It threatened to hold him fast if he became entangled. He seized the section that connected it to the wall and pulled, painfully. A rusted bolt broke loose and the wire fell away. Now he could reach over and haul himself up. It was a bit of a drop, but drop he did just as the door crashed open. Down to the pavement he went, without looking to see if anyone was around. The landing stung his feet and scraped his bloody hands, but he paid no mind. In an instant, he was off again.

Fortunately for Tom, all the commotion had attracted the attention of most of the mob members in the area, and, as they were presently inside the department store, none were around outside to give chase. In this way, he sprinted into the night, darting in and out of the shadows, which lengthened toward dawn, until, finally, he was home.

The last few days before Julie's return went quickly. On the last, Karstens called at Tom's door at the complex, and together they walked slowly toward the target room. There was no rush on Karstens' part, as the scheduled time for activation was still some hours away. Tom, on the other hand, was excited and edgy. He did his best not to show it.

There was a small diner a stone's throw of the T-room, and there they sat, eating lunch. Karstens was relaying the wonderful things they'd learned from the accelerator, those things both confirming and throwing doubt on Einstein's theories. Sitting there, surrounded by the largeness of the Institute complex, Tom felt reassured. It was true what Karstens said. Just think of how much science had led to this day. You could go all the way back to the ancient Greeks, and likely they themselves built upon thought too old to record. It was funny how every time historians thought that they had found the ultimate origin of something anthropological, something else even older would be discovered which would force them to turn their scientific clocks back yet again.

It was a litany of names that Karstens recited and Tom heard only vaguely. Names like Crookes, Thomson, Röngten, Rutherford, Cockroft-Walton, Van de Graaff and Lawrence. Instead of listening, Tom surreptitiously consulted the large clock on the wall behind Karstens. He'd dressed in the very outfit he had worn on the occasion of his and Julie's first date. Everything was ready for her homecoming.

At last this silly trip was over and his worrying would be at an end. Karstens was going on about the potential for broader use of time travel in the future once the energy kink was worked out. Tom nodded politely, sometimes appending an "um hum" or two. Truth was, he couldn't relax, not until Julie was safely back in his arms.

Finally, Karstens was called away, and Tom walked outside. Though most of the world's flora was declining rapidly, in pockets where people could afford to and took the care, the landscape looked almost as beautiful as it did before the decline. These patches, however, were tiny in comparison to the whole, and a lot of people wondered what was holding the facade up.

There was another small table outdoors, and Tom decided to sit there in the warm, brown sun. A waiter came and offered him a glass of wine, which he accepted gratefully. Closing his eyes, the sun and the drink relaxed him and he began to feel better, even drowsy. Lifting himself, he walked to a small, grassy mound under the flickering shade of a birch tree and lay down. Placing his hands behind his neck, he paid no attention to the sidelong glances of the passersby. In a moment, he was asleep.

Julie! She was running, jumping. Fleeing. Long hair trailing behind her in slow motion. Something - or someone - was chasing her. Tom's heartbeat quickened. He tried to catch up, but couldn't. She was just out of his reach. He called out, but no sound came from his mouth. Then she turned, and he saw the look of fear on her face. Terror. She called out to him, but he could not hear her. On the edge of a cliff, she extended her arms toward him before falling. "NO!" he yelled out.

Tom woke with a start. People were still walking by, paying him no mind, or at least, pretending not to. Embarrassed, he sat up, then stood. Then he remembered the dream. It shook him. Brushing his clothes, he walked back to the diner to check the clock, as he'd forgotten his watch. Ten minutes! He hurried out of the diner and across the complex quad in the direction of the T-room. When he was almost there, Karstens walked out with an anxious look on his face.

"Where have you been, we're about ready to initiate!" Karstens said.

"Sorry!" Tom offered. "I, uh ..."

"Never mind. Follow me!" Karstens ordered. They wound their way through the maze of now familiar halls until they got to T. Tom was expecting another big crowd, but when Karstens opened the door, there was no one in the room. He locked the door behind them. Tom looked at him questioningly.

"Where is everyone?" he asked.

"Besides those in Control, everyone else will be watching via closed-circuit camera. After decontamination, you get first dibs," Karstens smiled at him. Though they were physically alone, the air was alive with control room chatter. That, and the heavy drone of the accelerator. Karstens sat next to his friend. He prayed that all had gone satisfactorily, and though he exuded confidence, he knew only too well how powerless they would be if it hadn't. This episode had been about as draining on him as it was on Tom.

"Five minutes!" came a voice over the speaker.

"Do you want something to drink?" Karstens asked him, pointing at a table in the corner. "Water, soda, beer, whisky?"

"No, nothing, thanks," Tom said, coughing.

"I think I'll have one," Karstens replied, tensely. He walked over, and, picking up a flask, poured himself a rather tall scotch. Tom smiled.

"Not professional, but it takes the edge off. You don't mind, do you?"

"Not at all. Go ahead," Tom answered, slightly worried at Karstens' sudden display of nerves.

He reseated himself, and they fell silent, listening to the various discussions.

"One minute and counting!" The suddenness of the notice made him jump. *One minute.* Karstens nudged him and they put on their hearing protectors. Tom's leg was shaking. *Longest minute ever,* he thought.

"T-minus ten-seconds and counting!"

"Nine."

"Eight."

"Seven."

"Six."

"Five."

"Four."

"Three."

"Two."

"One. *Initiating!*" A low, deep groan. The lights dimmed, then came a clap of thunder. Moments later, the impact doors opened. And ... there it sat. Intact. The Strong Box, with a bit of Miocene debris upon it. Inside would be Julie and Deet. It was over. *Thank God it was over.* It worked! Tom Jumped up.

A loud hurrah sounded from the control room. The sound of cheering. Tom almost fell, so relieved was he at the success of the mission. He felt suddenly ashamed that he'd ever doubted Karstens. Karstens stood and extended a hand toward him. Tom grabbed it and shook hard.

"Thanks, bro," he said.

The cheering began to subside. There was a pause. Then some crisscross discussion.

Something.

Something wrong.

Karstens called out a query, but it wasn't immediately answered.

"Control," Karstens said. More discussion.

"Control," he said again.

"Bob, this is Edward in Control. Code yellow. Repeat. Code yellow." Tom watched as the color literally drained from Karstens face.

"'Code yellow'. What does that mean?" Tom asked.

Karstens was silent; a vein pulsed on his neck.

"What does it mean?"

Karstens eyes were closed, his breathing measured.

"What does it mean?" Tom shouted, now coughing violently.

Karstens was staring straight ahead, his mouth closed, set in a grim line. Then he said, "It means... It means..." He turned toward Tom and swallowed. "It means the box is empty."

"WHAT?" Tom roared. *"What do you mean 'the box is empty'?"*

"Julie and Jaqzen, they're not there," Karstens answered.

"Try again!"

"We can't. There's not enough energy," Karstens said.

"What the hell are you talking about, 'there's not enough energy'?" Tom demanded.

"Each time we've launched, it takes longer and more energy to regenerate the power necessary. Fact is, I don't know if we'll be able to do it again. Least not for a while."

"YOU MEAN ...YOU MEAN JULIE'S LOST?"

"I am so sorry. So truly, truly sorry my friend."

146

Eleven

Tom had gone back to the suite, locked the doors, and drank himself into a stupor. His eyes were red and face wet with tears. Karstens came by, but Tom didn't answer. Tomorrow, he would go back home, alone. Alone forever. Julie was gone. Dead for fifteen million years. What a fantasy to think that such an arrogant idea would be without consequence. So like us. Then he remembered the dream he'd had just before the final initiation. Julie calling out to him for help. Falling. Falling. And now he was falling.

Tomorrow he would go home and Karstens would call to tell him that he could still count on the money. Would never have to work again. Sure, it would be hard for a while, but others had been through the pain of tragedy and survived. It was an everpresent, though unpleasant, side-effect of science and discovery. There was always the chance of misfortune.

But Tom knew there was no living without Julie. Not in this world. His death would be the poetic finale on the long, sorry existence of man. A fitting epitaph.

Shortly, drunkenness overtook him, and he fell asleep on the floor.

———

Not long after the failure of the mission was communicated to his governmental superiors, Karstens received a call. It was brief. He was out. The operation would be pursued under a new leader. He had three days to gather his belongings and vacate. Further, his pension would be reviewed. He was ordered to record a public apology of no more than one minute's length, accepting all blame. Karstens didn't care. A man of uncommon conscience, he had been devastated by the mission failure, by the pain he had caused to innocent others. He wondered what had gone wrong.

His suspicions were confirmed when his crew brought him the note from the Strong Box, from Jaqzen. A roughly scrawled, hand written sentence on a crumbled piece of paper. It read simply:

So long, suckers! Enjoy your miserable existence and I'll enjoy mine!

Below the fold it read:

P.S. Come after us, and you're dead.

It never occurred to Karstens to point out to the government that it was *their* man who compromised the mission. *Their* choice. He'd never trusted Dietrich. Tried to warn them, yet had been rebuffed. And now Karstens felt shame, a profound shame and an incredible rage. He was responsible. Should have trusted his instincts. He might have found a way if he'd just pressed harder.

Then a thought crossed his mind, *I can't let these creatures do it again. To populate the past with their ilk.* He now knew beyond doubt that that was their real plan. Had, in fact, found out by way of an official memo he'd been furtively passed months before, but had discounted. Too incredible. He'd blinded himself. The real modus operandi, send the filthy rich, corporate, military and governmental scum back in time. The ones who hadn't absconded in the spheres. Let them escape their fate while the present earth dies in a hell of their making. And then they would live their foul lives in a glut of hedonistic pleasure. Pleasure in the raping and plundering of that ancient, virginal world. Eventually transforming it into another hell.

He had three days. Karstens wondered how much destruction he could cause in three days. Make it so that they could never use the accelerator again. Least, not for *this* purpose. Destroy machinery and records. Then, finally, himself. Otherwise, they'd get the information out of him. He grit his teeth.

Karstens was heartened when he was visited later by a trio of Institute management: Edwards, Pilagro and Olsen. They'd heard what was planned for him and were aghast at the cold callousness of it. When Karstens produced the memo he'd been handed, they were shocked. Each digested its implications in his own way, then spoke quietly among themselves. Moments later, they came into the kitchen, where Karstens sat at a table.

"Bob," Edwards began in hushed tones, glancing around for the inevitable microphones, "you should know that we are all behind you." Karstens looked at his associate and smiled.

"Yeah, well, I don't think you'd much care for what I'd like to do," he replied probingly, not looking Edwards in the eye.

"What if there was another way?" Edwards asked. Karstens looked at him. They were already on to him. Some little clue he'd spilled just before, perhaps. He'd underestimated his friends. When he'd hired them years before, Karstens was always careful to select those, everything else being equal, who he felt had more than just the intellectual qualifications necessary to do the job. He'd also looked for soul, a rarer combination. And now it was paying off.

"Another way?" he inquired.

Edwards cleared his throat. "We believe that we can find the Q required for another launching," he informed. Karstens eyes widened.

They stared at each other without saying anything, waiting for Karstens to comprehend. He looked down at the table while his mind raced. Where could they get the energy to launch again, especially so soon afterwards? It would take ten times the energy of the last launching. He frowned. Then it began to dawn on him. He drew in his breath. Of course! They *could* do it if they tapped into the main governmental power grid, the nuclear capacity designed for the ships. Terawatts of energy stored at a site in New Mexico. It would be a simple matter. Use a back door to tie into the grid, an instantaneous and monumental rush of power across the states, the drawdown of which would put the grid out for who knew how long. Along the way, relays would trip, transformers burn out and the grid melt. It might take years to rebuild. But *why*? Why another launching?

"So the plan is to save ourselves?" Karstens asked, disappointed.

"No," Edwards answered. "To save one man. One good man before we all die." To do one good thing. It was kind of poetic. Let the concluding act in the long, tragic human drama be a compassionate one. To sacrifice the ultimate in human achievement all to save one, well, two worthy people. Adam and Eve. To prove to the universe that we are not all bad.

A shadow came over Karstens heart. It was treason, and they all knew it. Certain death would follow. He nodded in agreement.

"Yes," he said.

There wasn't much time. Karstens came around to Tom's cottage at six in the morning. There was no answer. Alarm shot through him. Frantically, he used his master-key and looked around. Tom had cleared out early. Everything of his was gone. Karstens thought. *Where would Tom go? Home?* That would make sense. He had to catch him and set to go out, locking the door behind him. Somehow, he wanted to hold onto the memory of them there. Turning, his heart sank as he saw the nameless Suit approaching, a hard, stern look on his face.

"Going somewhere?" Nameless asked thinly.

"I just wanted to say goodbye to Tom. Seems to be gone, though. You wouldn't happen to know where to, would you?"

Karstens asked, not really expecting any help from this man.

"And if I knew, why would I tell you, a traitor to the cause?" Nameless asked.

"Dietrich was not my choice," Karstens said

"So what were you and your friends talking about last night, hmmm?"

Karstens stared at him, suddenly angry. "What? Were you *spying*? Are my friends not allowed to console me, their leader for the last twenty years or so, for the unjust theft of my work?"

"There is nothing that we do not know, nowhere that one can hide and not be seen and heard. *Despite your little box!*" Karstens' pulse quickened. He gulped.

"Planning a little something are you? And what might that something be? Something a little ... *subversive,* perchance?" That was it. The game was up. "And you do understand the consequences of your mutinous scheme, don't you." It was a statement, not a question. "To think that you planned to hijack the accelerator. Did you really think that you could get away with it? Tsk, tsk. So clumsy."

Karstens looked for the police, that, even now, would be descending on their location. It would be a quick trial, and then he would meet the fate of those judged high traitors. He and the others, his friends.

"Please don't harm them. I'm the guilty one," he pleaded. Still no police. Perhaps waiting for a confession. "It was my fault, my plan. They didn't want any part of it." Of course, Nameless would know that was a lie. Nameless shook his head. Then he reached out his hand. In it was a device of some kind, which he pointed at Karstens. *Ah, so we're going to dispense with the trial altogether and just go straight to the punishment. So be it, then.* Karstens waited for it. Nameless laughed.

Tom, arriving home, morosely carried his and Julie's belongings upstairs to the landing of their skyrise. He loaded it onto the elevator and then ascended to their 36th story apartment. His eyes were swollen with tears from which others looked away. Lugging them down the narrow hallway to his door, he opened it and brought them inside, turned and locked the door, then went to his room where he kept the gun. It was illegal, of course, but these days it was getting easier to find things like guns. If the money was right, you could get it from a stranger, who got it from a stranger, who got it from a stranger. He'd kept it for protection, his and Julie's, in a dangerous world. Now it would be used to destroy him, the reverse of its original intention. He picked up the pistol and walked with it to a large window that overlooked the city. It was evening now, the evening of the world. Odd how beautiful it still was, looking at the lights below.

"Goodbye, my love," Tom said. He put his finger on the trigger and the gun to his head, then closed his eyes. He would fall through the window and plummet down, downward to the earth.

Rushing feet. Coming closer. Tom did not hear. His finger tightened on the trigger. Then, pounding on the door. He jumped. The gun dropped and went off, shooting a hole in glass. Thousands of pieces falling, cold air rushing in, lashing at his clothes, his hair. So close, he was dizzy. The color rock glowed. The sound of someone hurling at the door. Yelling. His name. Pound, pound, pound. He lost balance, surrendering to the outside ... fell.

And was caught. Someone holding him by the arm as he spun, then, yanking, yanking him back. Back to this life, this horrible life. *No. No. Let me go. Let me die.*

And he was on the floor, the wind still rushing in.

A face above, embracing him, holding him. He looked. Karstens.

"No, my friend. You'll not die tonight. You have some-where to go. Someone who is waiting for you."

It was a jolt, this news from Karstens. Did he want to travel back in time, fifteen million years to find Julie? The question stunned him. Then, suddenly everything was different. There was hope.

There would be dangers, Karstens explained, not the least of which was Dietrich, an experienced hunter who vowed to kill anyone who dared try to find them. Further, they were going to tap into power that in one moment would be the single largest surge the world of man had ever known. On top of everything else was the fact that Tom was completely unprepared for life in the Miocene. He might not even make it a foot outside the Strong Box. There were many unknowns and no guarantees. But if he gave the word, the team at the Institute would follow. It was not a question for Tom. His answer was immediate.

"One more thing. You'll be traveling alone," Karstens informed him. Knowing the trouble Karstens would face, Tom had assumed that he would be coming, too.

"What? No! Come with me! You're a good man. Too good for this world," Tom protested, a mixture of fear and excite-ment washing through him.

"I can't. I have to stay here. It was part of the agreement."

"What agreement?"

"I can't elaborate."

"Are you going to be all right?" Tom asked, putting a hand on Karstens' shoulder?

"Of course," Karstens lied. What Nameless had pointed at him was a GPS device that let Karstens track Tom's car, not a weapon. He was going to help Karstens send Tom to the Mio-cene. In exchange, he wanted Karstens to join a growing group of powerful dissidents plotting a coup of the government. An unexpected, large-scale blackout would serve their interests as it would catch the authorities off guard. The putsch leaders believed that the biosphere could still be saved, but that it would take severely draconian measures to do so. Their concern, however, was not salvaging the earth for its own sake, but the prolongation of the human, and thereby their own, enterprise.

To Karstens, it smacked of more cloak and dagger. The kind of stupid political shenanigans the world of man had endured so many times before. Et tu, Brute? One group craving power over another. It rarely had anything to do with a desire to set things right. And he'd go along with it. But not for long. Then he'd die. An odd miscalculation on their part.

A potential glitch came the next morning when Tom was leaving to say goodbye to his old friend and employer, Paul. He was stopped by a Blacksuit who put a hand on his chest, not allowing him to get into his car. The Suit looked at him, stony, unblinking. Tom looked at the hand, then back at the Suit.

"You'd better get that hand off me," he warned. The Suit's eyes flashed, ready to put Tom down. Just then, a car drove up. He looked over - it was Karstens.

"Get in," he instructed. Tom looked at him, then back at the Suit, then turned and walked to Karstens car, opened the door and got in.

"Let's try not to screw things up at the last moment," Karstens said.

"Just going to say goodbye to Paul," Tom replied. Karstens thought about that a moment.

"I'll take you," he murmured. He waved at the Suit, which still stood looking at them. It didn't wave back.

"By God, this is a risk," he said, shaking his head. "You cannot, I repeat, *cannot* give *anything* away. Understand?"

"Yes."

"And you're going to have to make it quick. If they catch us, there might be trouble. Sorry, everything's super secret right now. Very dangerous."

When Tom walked into the Oasis, Paul put down the glass he'd been drying, threw the towel over his shoulder, and strode over to him. He looked in Tom's eyes, trying to gauge his condition.

"About time. I was starting to worry. Everything okay, bro?" Paul asked.

"Yeah," Tom said.

"You look like hell, you know, but it's good to have you back. Why don't you set up and I'll bring you a drink." Paul turned to head back to the bar. Tom put a hand on his shoulder stopping him. Paul turned.

"I've got to go, bro," Tom said sadly.

"Huh? You just got here!" Paul protested.

"I mean, I'm leaving, quitting."

Paul's mouth dropped. "What? *Why*? Is everything okay?"

"Yeah. It's just time. I can't explain. Just wanted to say goodbye." Paul looked like a man stricken.

"I don't ... I don't understand. You're *quitting*?"

"Bro..." Tom paused. Paul had truly been the brother he'd never had. He choked up. "Don't worry about a thing. I'm going to be fine. It's just time for me to move on." He waved at his instruments. "You can keep all that." Paul looked at him, shocked. He'd known that something was amiss for a while, had half-expected this. He nodded.

"I'm going to miss ya, bro," he told Tom.

"And I, you." They shook hands, then hugged. Brothers.

"You take care of yourself," Paul told him.

"You, too." Tom turned to walk out.

"You ever need anything, you know where I am," Paul

called out after him.

"Yeah," Tom said. *I'll know where you'll be, an eternity away.* He was leaving Paul to this life of pain, and it made him sad. At the door, he paused, noxious fumes from some undetermined location assaulting his nose. No one noticed anymore. He turned, waved, then walked out onto the busy street toward Karstens' waiting car.

At the Institute, Tom was loaded with equipment and given an hour's instruction on how to use them, then another hour on what to expect and how to survive. No one actually believed that he would succeed, but if determination alone was a survival quality, then he might. *Maybe.*

The following day, the Institute was to be commandeered by the new man. A government physicist whose strong suit had been nuclear weapons. He would be arriving at precisely 3:00 PM, at which time Karstens would make his speech, then step down as head of the Institute. Of course, there were other plans, and plans within plans. A very tangled web. Seven o' clock in the morning, then, was set for launching, *Nineteen hours from now,* Karstens thought as he looked at his watch. *It was fantastic how many people were in on the subterfuge. What were the chances that all of them could keep such a secret quiet for nineteen hours?* Karstens took half a handful of antacids. *We'll see.*

The plan was to all but trip the access to Q power until the last minute. A single keystroke would send terawatts of energy streaming their way at lightning speed. A moment later, a government specialist would notice the drain, but by then it would be too late. In the meantime, Nameless would keep the Blacksuits at bay. There was no telling how many of them were in on his conspiracy. Cameras were loaded with concocted video. Audio recorders with fabricated sound. It would serve as cover, at least until someone discovered that it was a loop.

After everything went dark, Karstens would be rushed to a secret bunker, and there kept safe until the shooting stopped. Just a matter of days, Nameless suggested. The plan seemed hasty, rushed, but it was all he had. It would have to do.

That evening, nine hours before launch, Tom and Karstens had time for a last meal together. They ate it in a small, private restaurant a little ways from the Institute grounds. The place was meant for entertaining important people. As such, it was more luxurious. *It seems to be rote with Karstens, this discussing of business over food,* Tom thought. Tonight, though, didn't feel like business. It felt like a send-off. Tom's last meal in human society. It frightened him. No more civilization. It would be Karstens' last such meal, too, though he said nothing of it. They ate in silence for a while, big, heaping meals. Tom wondered where it was all coming from. And wine, though not too much for Tom. The attendants seemed subdued. Were they in on it too? Tom worried that someone would spill the beans, imagined at the last moment a horde of police running in and arresting everyone. He couldn't wait to get it over with. His leg shook with nervousness.

"Easy, my friend. Don't worry," Karstens said.

"Where have I heard *that* before?" Tom countered. Karstens looked at him, then down again without replying.

"I'm sorry, Bob," Tom said, feeling guilty. "You've been a good ally through all this. Heaven knows, without you, I'd have no chance of finding her."

"Without me, you'd still have her," Karstens corrected. Silence. Then, "Again, I am so sorry this all turned out as it has. I wish I could do more."

"You did all you could. That's all anyone can ask," Tom replied. "And you saved my life."

Have I? Karstens thought.

"There is a chance that, at some point, we can bring you

back, you and Julie. I just don't know when. It's all very mercurial right now. If you can stay alive and in the vicinity of the Strong Box, and if we can launch again, we'll look for you." Tom thought about that. It added a new component. *Come back. Come back to ... what?* Then he thought, *Yes, we'll have to, this is our world, Julie's and mine, not some tangled, prehistoric jungle.* Civilization. Hostile it might be, but it was all he knew. Besides, then they'd be set. No more worries. It gave him hope.

"Thank you," Tom said.

"This is going to be the last time I see you. So I want to wish you luck."

"What? Why?" Tom asked. "You're not going to be at the launching?"

"I'm being sequestered tonight. Got to go with a new group for a while. Least until things settle down. So you'll be on your own, so to speak."

"I can handle it," Tom said.

"Yes, I know you can," Karstens paused, took another gulp of his drink, whiskey. "Tom, I'll tell you what I told Julie, though she already knew it. This is not going to be easy. You're going to have a whole world to yourself. Well, you, Julie, and Dietrich. To a lot of people, that'd be a dream come true." Tom knew that he meant himself. "I want to show you something." Karstens took a small viewer from his vest pocket and opened it, showing Tom the same video he'd shown Julie.

"My God! *Is that it?*" Tom asked incredulously.

"That's it. That's where you're going," Karstens answered wistfully. "Doesn't look too bad, does it? If you can survive, not just Dietrich, but everything else, you might like it. But it's going to take a revolution in the way you think. Nothing is going to be recognizable to our world. Nothing normal. Nothing you're used to. It looks exquisite, but don't be fooled, you're going to have to get tough *real fast*. There are no rehearsals. My advice: treasure it, go with it, love it - but *never* lose respect for it. *Ever*. Be careful and don't take any unnecessary risks. Can you do that?"

"I have no choice. I'll do my best," Tom replied, shaken by the images on the screen. Karstens nodded.

"I can't believe we messed that up," Tom said.

"Well, in all fairness, this was before our time. The world *Homo sapiens* inherited was cold and icy. Maybe that's why we developed such an adversarial relationship. *After that, though, after the thaw*, it wasn't much different."

He closed the little viewer. Turned it around in his hand. Sleek, glossy, compact. Able to do all kinds of wonderful things. "Do you mind a little philosophy, Tom?"

"Go right ahead," Tom replied, unsure what to expect.

"Some people believe in the story of the Garden of Eden. That Adam sinned and was kicked out because of that. But that's wrong. We were never *forced* from the garden. No, we left *voluntarily*. You see, somewhere in our remote past, we made a choice, an exchange. That world of uncertainties, primitive fears - and unimaginable beauty, we traded for lives of security and comfort. That tree of lore. And here's the apple," he said holding the little device out for Tom to see. "Convenience. Security. Predictability. But with the gain in knowledge, we sacrificed something deep in our souls, a vital part of ourselves. It's something we've tried, futilely, ever since to regain. I'd trade it all back in a heartbeat."

Karstens continued, "Instead of respecting the earth, instead of cherishing it, we treated it like a big supermarket from which we could just rip whatever we needed, whenever we needed it, without regard for the consequences to other species, our future, or the biosphere as a whole. All the world's resources on a one-way trip to the dump. Meanwhile, we longed for an imaginary paradise, an invisible pie-in-the-sky. How ungrateful.

"In our arrogance, we overestimated the resiliency of the earth and underestimated our ability to impact it. When you look at the biosphere from space, the actual *size* of it, you can see that it's *really quite thin,* comparable in thickness to the skin on an apple! Yet, within that razor-thin space, we've heaped indignity upon indignity, using our ingenuity to destroy. Everyone vying to see who can be the biggest, most insensitive asshole."

Karstens paused here, took a drink, then said, "I should qualify that. While there's plenty of blame to go around, it's not the average Joe and Jane who are the culprits, in my estimation. They didn't ask for this. Most were just trying to survive and feed their families. No, it's those in power, corporate and political, who conspired to deceive, to maintain the status quo, just so they could keep their gravy trains running as long as possible, who I hold responsible." Another sip. "In any case, here we are.

"There's a wise old Italian saying," Karstens added, "'Feather by feather, the goose is plucked.'"

A shaft of light, red in hue, flared out, reflecting a small overhead lamp. Then a brilliant blue, followed by green, then yellow, orange and violet. Tom looked down to his right. It was coming from his open jacket pocket. Karstens looked at him oddly. Tom reached in and withdrew the color rock. He set it on the table between them. It flashed in a moving rhythm of color that danced around the room. Karstens eyes went wide.

"Any idea what that is?" Tom asked, picking it up and handing it to him.

"An opal, but unlike any opal I've ever seen!" Karstens looked at it closely. It seemed to be dimensionless, to take one into itself. Drawing the soul. Benevolent. "The play of color is *magnificent!* Where did you get it?"

"I found it. In Nevada," Tom answered, himself in awe

over the light show the opal was delivering.

"Nevada. Nevada." Karstens thought. Then he stuck a finger in the air, "Ah, was that in the Virgin Valley?"

"Yes, how did you know?" Tom asked.

"Well, apart from my day job, I'm a bit of a rock collector." He turned the stone over and over in his hand. "Wow." Pausing, he added, "Are you aware that the opals from the Virgin Valley began their formation in the middle Miocene? As I remember, at the time it was a large hill-locked lake. When surrounding trees died, many accumulated within. Then volcanic ash covered them. Hot water seeped through the ash layers to the trees, slowly replacing the wood with biogenic silica. The result was opals."

"I didn't know that," Tom replied.

"The middle Miocene. Kind of a coincidence don't you think? I don't really believe in coincidences, though."

"So what are you saying?"

"Not sure, except that, maybe you were meant to have this." He handed the opal back to Tom.

"Why?" Tom asked.

"A charm, perhaps."

"What, like one of those old rabbit's feet?"

"I know; it's nonsense. Still, there's something about this one that seems, well, different." They both stared at the precious stone a while longer. Finally, Karstens pulled his eyes away and looked at his watch.

"Look at the time; it's eleven! Man, I've kept you too long. You're going to need sleep. You've got a journey ahead of you."

Tom re-pocketed the gemstone. Fear crept back into his veins. "Can I ask you a last favor?"

"Anything."

Tom pulled a small folded sheet of paper from a shirt

pocket and slid it to Karstens. "This is a list of the people who have been there for us over the years. Our friends. Good people. If we don't come back, could you please give our earnings and possessions to them? It's the least we can do."

"You got it," Karstens agreed. He took the small square, stood, and reached out his hand. Tom took it.

"Good luck to you, my friend. Give my regards to Julie." He forced a smile.

Tom, his voice trembling, said, "I will."

With that, Karstens turned and walked out of the side door, Tom out the front. Both to an uncertain fate.

Strapped tightly in the Strong Box, Tom felt wide awake. He'd been offered the same relaxant given Julie and Dietrich, but declined, wanting to be at his peak should the Neanderthal be waiting for him. Though he was assured that the box could only be opened from the inside, he wasn't taking any chances. Next to him, under a tie-down, was a gun. If Dietrich planned to kill him, it wouldn't be without a fight.

Holding the opal in his hand, he said a sad goodbye to the world of man, the only world he'd ever known, and to the brave men and women at the Institute, all risking their lives just to help right one wrong. A last, symbolic act.

Voices calmly spoke commands. Gave stats.

Tom's heart raced. He tried to compose himself. Just then, Karstens' voice came over the speaker.

"How's it going, my friend?" he asked. Tom jumped.

"Bob? I though you were..."

"I'm not at the Institute. I'm speaking to you from a remote location. But they allowed me this moment." A sudden deep rumbling as the accelerator was switched on. A vibration. It unnerved him. He swallowed.

"How long did you say this will take?" Tom asked.

"No knowing, though we think it shouldn't be long, something like four to five minutes. Transport in time at the speed of light. There's a lot of people who wish they were in your shoes right now. Science and all. You know, discovery."

Then the countdown. The box began to shake. Decibels rising. Suddenly, there was a different sound. Shouting. Someone screaming orders.

"STOP!" A sound of crashing and fighting. "STOP HIM!" Then a loud staccato report, like gunfire.

"Thomas Pine, we salute you!" Karstens yelled out.

"Three. Two. One."

"GOOD LU..." His voice disappeared.

A sudden jolting, violent explosion, then a feeling of accelerating, of rushing. Tom slammed his eyes shut. *Fast! Incredibly fast! Horribly fast! Faster than anyone had ever gone before!* Time, he knew at once, has two states: "solid" and "liquid." Like energy. He had stepped off the solid, stable like the earth, and into the liquid, ever in motion, like the sea. The opal began to glow, sending out rays of color. A pressure, crushing pressure on every cell of his being. He felt himself screaming. Odd, that sound, as if coming from outside himself, as though from someone else. Pulling, pulling, stretching him, like taffy, into infinity. Surely he would be torn apart. But somehow the opal was protecting him, his undrugged mind. He didn't know how, he just knew. Still, even with that, the box around him seemed to be shaking to pieces. How could it withstand this terrible shuddering? Horrified, he kept his eyes squeezed tightly closed against his imminent destruction. Julie and Dietrich must be dead. No one could survive this. Yet, still he accelerated, and his thoughts became elastic, whisper thin. Gossamer. The dull thundering of the launching rose to a shrill pinpoint of sound, then disappeared, as did Tom.

Twelve

Stillness. Quiet. Nothing moved. Tom, eyes closed, head lolled to one side, was motionless. The opal, still in his hand, had returned to its normal gleam. But his hand relaxed and the gemstone threatened to fall. To the edge of his fingers it rolled.

And he awoke. Caught it. Picked up his arm. So weak. Looked at the stone vacantly. Beautiful. He loved it. He stayed there, just staring at it. Babe in a new world. The stone seemingly looking back at him. Finally, he put it in his pocket. He looked around without comprehension. Except for a small white light over his head, everything was dark. Made darker by the light. Shadows. Then, barely cutting through the darkness, he noticed some other lights, small, flickering. Greens, reds and yellows. What were they? What did it mean?

His head slumped back in the rest and he drowsed, slept. Then, slowly, a thought began to impress itself upon his unconscious mind. Like a mosquito it was, tiny, but persistent. *Wake up. Get out.* He swatted at it. Shooed it away, but it only grew stronger. Eventually, he opened his eyes again. Harder to breathe. The light above his head seemed dimmer. Except for one tiny, pulsing red light, the others had all gone out. It was dark. The air thick with his breathing. Oxygen diluted with carbon dioxide. He needed to do something. But what?

An image began to form in his mind. Someone, calling him. Calling his name. He looked at her.

Julie. He awoke, his lethargy fading. Julie. A pause, then Tom sat bolt up. JULIE! Now he remembered. It all came back. He had time traveled! *"Holy ..."* He'd made it! He was here! He looked around, but all was blackness. The air was thick. A feeling of claustrophobia came over him. He was in the Strong Box. Had to get out. But how, where was the door?

The control lights were faint now. Panic overtook him. He strained to see, trying to remember. Feeling for the release, he unstrapped himself and jumped up. *Crap*, he couldn't remember where the door was or how to open it! Groping his way, he stepped to the wall and fumbled about, barely able to see. Switches. Lights that had died. He walked completely around the inside of the box, but nothing felt like a door. Fear grabbed at his chest. To come all this way only to die because he can't find the exit. He ran around the inside, pounding, clawing like a caged animal. *NO!*

Then, gasping, he remembered something his father once told him when he was a boy. *Don't stop thinking. When people are afraid, they stop thinking.* Willing himself to calm down, he looked up at the last tiny light, reached for it. It was movable. He pointed it at a wall of the box. Nothing but wall. At another. Instrumentation. At the third. An outline of something in the wall. A prominence. The door! He ran for it and felt for the button in the middle of that prominence, pushed it. Nothing. No power. As if the ages had drained it away. *Oh, God.*

Wait! He remembered that he'd been shown a manual release, *just in case.* It was to the left of the door. A big lever. Grabbing for it, he held it and began to pull up. Stuck, it wouldn't budge. Had it been damaged in the transport and now hopelessly jammed? Bending low and placing both hands and a shoulder under it, he heaved upward, straining, growling, then, slowly, began to rise. There came a sound of metal groaning and Tom feared that the handle would snap. Still, up he went, holding his breath, then bellowing, while gradually straightening himself. Hope shot through him as the lever rose. Then, suddenly it was up and the door creaked open, but just a bit. Light shone in, a long shaft that fell on him, as did a warm breath of air.

Relief flooded through him as he looked out the narrow opening. His heart beating and breath coming hard, he placed a hand on the door and prepared to open it, moving it just a bit to assure himself that that he *could*, but no more. Dietrich, alerted to his arrival by the noise of it, the unavoidable explosive sound of air being displaced, could be standing out there right now, ready to end his life, fulfilling his vow to kill anyone who attempted to find him. The thought of Julie being held by the maniac filled Tom with rage. He turned around to find the gun that had been placed under a net next to him. It was even darker in the cabin now that his eyes had adjusted to the light from the outside. He imagined Dietrich now heading toward him, not waiting for him to leave. *He had to find that gun!*

Taking a risk, Tom pushed open the door a little more, and the expanded shaft fell on the weapon. Rushing over, he pushed the release on the netting and grabbed the gun, swiveling back to meet Dietrich. But he wasn't there. Likely, casually sitting just outside. Tom crept to the door and peered out. What he saw shocked him. A mass of greenery with blue sky in the background. A waft of warm air lightly blew in. There were sounds, as well. Unfamiliar sounds. Sounds he'd not heard in a long, long while. Bird song. A variety of bird song. Sweet bird song. But he didn't have time for this!

Slowly, he pushed the door open, looking around for the big man, until, finally, it was thrown wide.

No one. No one and nothing except the big, wide world, his arrival apparently undetected. *Good!*

He seemed to be in a small clearing in the middle of a forest. Light streaming in from above made the leaves on the trees shimmer green and gold. They flickered in the breeze, occasionally letting in spotty sunlight that danced warmly on Tom's face. On the ground were a variety of flowers. Blues, reds, yellows, whites. Then he noticed something else, the air, the very air around him was filled with a lovely fragrance, a whisper of perfume. It was so delicious to breathe, just to *breathe* it.

It was a shock. He knew he'd never in his life breathed air so fresh. It literally seemed to be filling his being. Invigorating him. *This is what air was meant to be*, he realized. Not the polluted brown stuff he was used to sucking down. Involuntarily, he smiled.

There was a sound of water. Flowing water from nearby. He looked in the direction it was coming from, a ravine shadowed by numerous trees. Tom walked over to it, enjoying the satisfying crunch of leaves underfoot. A pleasurable feel. *Crunch, crunch,* a snap of some small twig, to the edge of the coulee. Below, perhaps a foot or two, was a small stream. Water rolled along, bumping over rocks and boulders melodiously, carrying stray leaves. Where the sun touched the waters, they looked like liquid glass, flowing in smooth arcs, confidently. Water, the blood of the earth, reaching everywhere, giving life, just as it had from time immemorial.

A big leaf floated slowly by, raft-like, and upon its surface, a beetle walked. Tom crouched to look at it. When the beetle got to an edge, it seemed to be testing the margin to see if it was safe to disembark, then, finding water, would walk along further as if it might find land there. Tom stood and followed for perhaps twenty feet. Finally, the leaf caught on the rim of the bank and there rocked in the current, threatening to dislodge again and continue the voyage downstream. The little beetle found the spot where the leaf was touching and, tentatively, put one foot down on the other side, then hurried over and was gone under a thick mat of forest detritus. One life, one little life in a world of so many. In the great stretch of time, this little beetle was insignificant as could be. But to Tom, it had great value.

Farewell my friend, farewell.

Tom looked up into the canopy. Through it. Morning. The morning of the world. He felt drunk with it all. Then he remembered Julie. *Snap out of it.*

He looked around again. Any sign of them. But there was nothing. Nothing that would betray their path. Where could they be? A thought hit him. Turning around, he wondered if something was wrong. He turned around and around. Something *was* wrong. This was not the place he'd seen in Karstens' video.

Oh no.

He'd been sent to the wrong time. On an earth four and a half billion years old, the time machine had accidentally gone to another era. Another time. Gone were the open, grassy hills he'd seen. That pastoral parkland dotted with peaceful grazers. That sweet vista of harmony rimmed by the sea. This could be *millions* of years before, or after. After continents had drifted, mountains fallen, and forests grew. It could be *anytime*.

Tom shot a look around and spotted a hillock, maybe 600 feet high. Immediately, he headed for it, so as to look out over the landscape, praying that he was wrong. In short order, he found himself winded and had to stop to take a break. He realized that he was in terrible physical shape. Exercise was not something he'd ever taken much interest in before. Now he'd pay for it. It took Tom the better part of an hour to climb that 600 hundred feet, coughing and hacking as he went. His lungs ached.

When finally he made it and looked out, he was stunned. Not a hill at all, he was near the top of a fairly high wooded mountain of maybe two thousand feet, the Strong Box having landed in a flattish area on its northern face. The altitude had been hidden from him by close-set trees and shrubbery. Now he saw below - a vast sweep of greens, yellows, blues and pinks unlike anything he'd ever seen. His heart sank like a rock in a pond. This was not the place he'd seen in the video. *Not at all.* Instead of open grassy hills was forest, and in the distance, a low plain, narrow and long, bordered by woodland. Far away to the right, he could see blue, which must be the ocean, but it was farther away than that which Karstens had shown him.

At that moment he sank to his knees and began to cry.

Tom was part way into a good sob when he suddenly remembered the locator that Karstens had given him. He hastened down the side, almost falling over his feet on the way. Evidently, he startled something large, for it bounded off into the brush, escaping his view. That unnerved him, and he continued the rest of the way down a bit more carefully, eyes wide with apprehension. At the bottom, he discovered that he'd lost the Strong Box. It was nowhere to be seen. In his rush, Tom had gone down willy-nilly and now could not remember the way he'd come. Never had panic so intimately known a man, for not only was the locator in the Strong Box, but so was everything else he was going to need to survive here. *In this God forsaken jungle,* he thought. Tom cast about desperately, but all was seemingly a tangled mass. Nothing looking familiar. Even the stream he'd seen earlier was gone. Too late, he remembered the advice of his instructor at the Institute: *Always watch where you're going. Always find landmarks. Always know the way back.*

Tom cursed himself. They'd gone to a great deal of trouble, even risking their lives to get him here, to give him a chance of finding Julie. He'd be damned if he was going to give up so easily, like a spoiled child. Then, again, his father's advice: when people are afraid, they stop thinking. But what to do? He'd have to retrace his steps back up the mountain. He looked up; *Yes, maybe from up there I'll remember the way.* And so, up again he went. This time it took longer.

Reaching the top, Tom bent over for a rest, then looked around, but could not recognize the way he'd originally come. Then he looked out at the scene he'd spied before. He remembered that when he'd come up the first time the view was directly in front of him. He stood as he'd stood then, looking out. Then he turned around and looked back the opposite way. A ray of hope shot through him. He recognized the oddly shaped branch on a tree he'd walked out from under before. He walked to it and looked down. The way was choked with vegetation, yet he thought he could see some impression in it from his passing. Turning around again, he looked toward the far off view, to see if the angle was right. Yes, it did look familiar.

This time, Tom set off thoughtfully, attentively. Instead of a haphazard, headlong rush, he poked, scanned, and crept along painstakingly. After a few minutes, he let out a loud yelp of glee when the unnatural angles of the Strong Box came into view, dark amid the green of the forest. Now he picked up his pace.

The heavy door was still open, but, for safety's sake, he decided to prop it with a stick, just to make sure it didn't close again with him in it. In a compartment on the floor was a container, and within it, a plethora of items Karstens and others had thought he might need. In another was food, but this was only a temporary stash. He would have to learn how to find his own food, he thought with a shudder.

Tom opened the first container and hauled everything outside where he could see it. A backpack, sleeping bag, clothes, medical equipment and assorted electronic gadgets. He tossed things around, trying to find the locator. Finally did. *PinPointer,* it said. Before Julie and Dietrich left, they had been fitted with bracelets that emitted a strong signal, in case one of them became lost. Each of them had a PinPointer that he/she could use, which would show the other's position on a small screen and estimate the distance between them. All one had to do was to keep the point of light which represented the other person at the bottom center of the screen to know that they were headed in the right direction. When they finally closed in, the point of light would slowly move toward the center, until, standing next to each other, it would be directly in the middle. It was deemed failsafe - provided one did not remove, lose, or break either the bracelet or the PinPointer.

Hastily, Tom turned it on. Nothing. *No.* He stood and held his arm out, moving around in a circle. Still nothing. Then he thought about the summit again. Grabbing a pair of binoculars and making a careful look as he went, he slowly headed toward the top of it for the third time. When, at last, breathing hard and an awful ache in his side, he came over the rise, he turned around to make sure he would know the way back. Then he continued on.

Beep.

He caught his breath. There was a rocky outcrop in front of him. To its left was the panoramic view he'd stood over before. He walked that way.

Beep. Beep. Beep.

Tom let out a jubilant cry. *Julie was alive and he'd made it!* He looked at his screen. There, just as was supposed to be, were two dots, a red and a green. Each pulsing rhythmically like the beating of two hearts. His relief was palpable and his knees shaky. He sat quickly before he fell. He'd made it! Karstens had not let him down, God bless him! Now all that remained was to find them, and with the PinPointer, that should be easy enough. He'd steal Julie away before the Neanderthal discovered her missing. Then he'd think of what to do next.

Tom's smile was so large it was painful. The PinPointer continued to beep. Tom looked at it. Then he noticed that the dots were not together. There was some distance between them. How much, he couldn't tell. In the way he was shown, Tom pulled out the estimator and laid it over the screen, then moved the compass, placing one end of the estimator on each point.

Must be some mistake. Forty-four miles. *Forty-four miles between them? Why would that be? Unless...*

He remembered what he'd been told; Dietrich was red, Julie green. And there were forty-four miles between them. Then he wondered, if there are forty-four miles between them, how many were there between him and Julie? He pushed a small button on the side of the PinPointer. He, too, had a locator bracelet. Instantly, the red and green lights shrank to minuscule dots at the very bottom, while another light, a blue, popped on at the top of the screen.

Oh no.

His heart sped up. Pulling the estimator back out, he took the measurement, blinked, took it again. *It can't be.* He pushed the little button on the PinPointer's side that said, "Map." Around the colored lights, an outline, black on white, of the state of California now appeared, a depiction of its shape as it was during the Luisian, with the names of future cities and distinctive features noted for reference. And there it was; there was no doubt about it. He was six hundred and fifty-three miles away. Six hundred and fifty-three miles! As the crow flies. In this world, it might as well be ten thousand. Tom let out a roar.

The silence that followed was startling. It seemed all the earth grew quiet as if to give this strange new biped his due. He had something to say, and the world waited for him to say it.

The quiet unnerved him. Finally, though, tentatively, a *chirp* here, a *peep* there, and before long, all was as it was before.

Tom sat down there on the summit and looked out. Looked in the direction the PinPointer said his wife was. Six hundred and fifty-three miles away. All he could see was country. Of course. What else would there be? He began to think of his situation, of the *enormity* of it, of what he had to do. The more he thought about it, the more frightened he became. It was impossible. *He simply could not do it. He'd never make it.* And there was something else. Something very odd. According to the PinPointer compass, Julie and Jaqzen were *north* of him, for there was the needle pointing at the big "N." Yet, he was sure he'd been looking *south* - after all, there was the ocean on his right. If he were looking north, it would be on his left. Additionally, the map showed Julie in southern California, while he was in northern. It made no sense. On the other hand, he worried, maybe the device had broken during the transference.

Slinging the lanyard around his neck, he lifted the binoculars, and, scanning below, Tom surveyed the open spaces. Between him and them was unbroken forest. It looked like it went on for miles, after which was the start of long, flat, grassy areas, fringed by still more forest. That stretched on as far as he could see, and appeared to be dotted with innumerable bodies of water of various sizes. Far to the left and running south was higher land, not mountains per se, but a gradually rising flatland with low hills and valleys. Flowing between them and running down into the lowlands were rivers that ended in lakes or continued on south for a long, long way. From here, those highland hills looked like roundish mounds and everything covered in green: grass or other soft ground-cover. Much further south, the shallow hills became true mountains that continued into obscurity. On the right was more forest, with areas of relief here and there.

Distantly to the west, past the woodlands, was the long, thin, blue stretch he'd seen before. The prehistoric Pacific, he decided. A little further out in that sea, he could just make out prominences; islands, he assumed, running north to south.

Adjusting the focus, Tom again looked to the view ahead of him. While other, lower mountain chains were visible, especially near the far southern coast, on the whole the impression was of quasi-flat, eroding land, sprinkled with gentle hills here and there. Of dense forests with long ribbons of grassland, opening sometimes onto wider parkland, and other times, a semi-arid landscape, running through them. Farther still, beyond the plains, he could barely make out a fine, bright, turquoise line. It looked like water, too.

Above it all was an expanse of azure sky and huge, puffy, white clouds. And there, flying high above the pristine valley, were birds, large, light-colored ones, and smaller, copper-brown versions, silently drifting in wide, lazy circles.

To a man used to gray and brown, it was shocking, all this green and blue, all this *life*. Overwhelming, even.

Tom tried to make sense of it. Was this, indeed, California? If so, where? Those low hills, what were they? And that line of turquoise blue ahead stumped him. But it must be, for the PinPointer map confirmed it. He turned to look behind him. Dark, unbroken forest to the horizon. He was glad he wasn't going that way.

Then he thought about that. *Going*. He'd have to leave. He'd not planned to be away from the Strong Box, had intended to use it as his base. But now? He'd have to. There was no other choice. North or South, he'd follow those lights. The thought chilled him. Tom knew next to nothing - okay, nothing at all - about outdoor survival. He was in sorry shape, weak and full of self-doubt. What's more, he knew there was no way he'd be able to pack enough food to last him the time it would likely take him to go six hundred and fifty-three miles. *Six hundred and fifty-three miles!* He couldn't stop thinking about it. God, that was a long way! How did he end up so far off?

Then he remembered a sound of shooting just before everything went dark. Something must have been changed. He imagined a body falling over a dial, possibly turning it. *Probably.* He remembered Karstens and hoped he had not been caught in the crossfire.

What Tom didn't know was that, besides being dislocated in space, he'd also been displaced in time; luckily, though, it wasn't by much. A further turn of the dial and he could easily have ended up in an ice age. As it was, he was four months past the time he was due to land.

He remembered something else then. Reaching into his pocket, he felt a now familiar smooth shape; pulled out the opal. Just as beautiful as ever. It felt warm in his hand. Warm as the day. It gleamed and glistened. He put it back in his pocket. Somehow, it comforted him, this memento from his time. What was it that Karstens had said? It began its formation in the middle Miocene. That's *now*. So it had come full circle. Back home.

Fearful as he was, Tom felt a drive to be underway. *Just follow the blips,* he thought. He looked again at the way ahead, down, down the mountainside and through that congested forest, tight with tall trees. Tried to see a way through it, finally spying a thinnish, lighter area, illuminated from above. An open path, cut off from sight here and there by the canopy. He followed it with his eyes, *yes, a path,* possibly a wildlife route.

Finally, it came out onto the grassy plain, and there, at its mouth, was a collection of black dots.

He hadn't noticed them before, but now as he looked out, he saw them, like scattered specks, some singly, but most in groups. He raised the binoculars again. They were herds, large and small. Farther out onto the plain were more of them, thinly dispersed, as if they didn't feel safe being too far out on the exposed savanna. A few groups, though, other kinds of animals, increased in numbers. There were more pockets of forest near bodies of water, and around them, more of the small black flecks he knew must be wildlife.

Wildlife, he thought. *How strange that word. Animals roaming free, free to go wherever they choose. No cages, no walls, no roads, no fences. It boggles the mind. And I'll have to go* through *them!* The thought sent a shiver up his spine. Still, the view ahead of him was lovely, no, more than that, it was *stunning, majestic, alluring.* It called to something deep inside him, something long buried by civilization, paved over with cement and asphalt. Touched a heart hardened against it.

Something moved briskly in the grass nearby. He looked. Spider! A big one! Tom jumped up and back, but it paid him no mind, continuing on in its hurried fashion away from him until it was lost in the undergrowth. He looked around himself for more; shuddered at how close it had been. One didn't see spiders much in his time, casualties of man's ceaseless war on pests. One did, though, have to deal with flies and roaches.

Again, the magnitude of his situation hit Tom and terrified him. This world, this raw, untamed wilderness, teeming with life, all manner of life, was alien, as alien as if it were another world. Karstens was right, it would take a revolution in his thinking to get used to it. Where before, his basic necessities had always been met by long established means and mediums of convenience, now he was entirely on his own. He would have to find his own food when his rations ran out. Make his own clothing. Defend himself. No one would come to his aid if he called. There was no one to complain to for injustices. No doctor to attend to his injuries. If that spider was poisonous and had bitten him, he could very well now be lying on his death-bed, so to speak, and no one would ever know - or care.

Then, suddenly, unbeckoned from within him, from that dark core of fear and loathing he'd acquired in the warped, twisted world of the future, arose another feeling. He *missed* his world, his own time. A world that, for all of its sickness, all of its miserable gloom, still was the world that *he understood*. A world that he could at least navigate in somewhat. The world where his friends and everything he ever knew were. He want-ed to go back.

Almost as quickly as he'd thought it, though, Tom shiv-ered, his revulsion immediate. *No!* The perverse feelings of regret were short-lived, melting away in the light of sanity, blowing away on the wind. He shook them from him. Yes, he did miss his friends. Yes, the prospect of being alone in this world *was petrifying.* Yes, for a while he would miss the secu-rity of utter predictability. But there was *nothing else for him there*, nothing else to yearn for in that dark and dreary place.

He looked again at the PinPointer. There were the two dots, still separated by a puzzling distance. He wondered if they could see him, as well. Then Dietrich would know that someone else had made it back and would be on the lookout. Tom wondered if he should turn off the device so as not to announce his presence. He thought about it: *Might be a good idea, better not to let the big man know until the last.* On the other hand, if Julie noticed the other dot, it would give her hope. Of course, there was the possibility that, as soon as he had switched on his locator, both Dietrich and Julie were aware of it the same way he was of them. He was undecided, but finally chose to leave it off, for the time being anyway. He took another look at his intended path, then turned around and headed back down the mountain, this time with a bit more assurance.

At the landing site, Tom noticed that the lighting had changed subtly. He looked up. The day had advanced some, but he couldn't tell by how much. Wondering what time it was, Tom looked for his watch, then remembered that he'd been told to remove it before launching. He dug around among the assorted paraphernalia in the container and found it. Not working. He tapped it, shook it, but to no avail. *Damn!* He'd *need* that watch, *always* wore one. How would he know the time without it? Then he thought about it: *What do I need it for? It's not like I'm on a schedule now. There are no more clocks to punch, no more deadlines to meet. No more curfew. Still.* Tom looked up through the canopy, tried to judge the time by the position of the sun. It was high overhead. Probably near noon.

He wondered what time of year it was. In the summer, the days were long, but in the winter, they were short. How to know? Looking around, he again noticed the flowers he'd seen earlier. *Flowers used to come out in spring,* he thought. *Spring, then.* The days would be of medium length, with sunset perhaps seven or eight hours from now. Should he leave right away? Tom pulled the other bunker out, the one with the food. Put everything on the ground. Spread it out. He grabbed the backpack, opened it, then tried to decide what to bring. He wouldn't be able to take everything, so he had to choose wisely.

The pack was a nice one. Top of the line, as would be everything else. He looked inside. Roomy, yet not nearly enough space. Should he fill it with food or equipment? If food, it would take him farther, but he knew it would run out well before he was even a fraction of the way there. If equipment, he would have to find food on the way, and Tom was decidedly wary of his ability to do so. What if the plants were poisonous? He had a firearm; he could hunt. But he was leery of that, too. For one thing, he had no idea how to go about it. What if he only wounded the animal? He'd heard as a child that a wounded animal was a dangerous animal. For another, was the fact that he had ethical objections to killing other beings. In his time, wildlife were all but nonexistent. It would be sacrilege to those with caring hearts, like crushing a rare flower. Besides, both he and Julie were vegetarians, having made that decision years ago when they began to distrust the meat the government supplied. A combination, then.

From the gear in front of him, Tom chose:

Sleeping bag
Tent/Hammock
Inflatable pillow
Lightweight thermal blanket
Broad-brimmed hat
Sunglasses
An extra set of clothing
Needles and thread
Handsaw
Two small hand towels
Two bars of soap
Medical kit
Insect repellent
Water filter
Collapsible water bottle
Small, foldable pan and spoon
Flashlight / lantern / signal light
Fire-lighters
Magnifying glass
Pedometer
50' length of rope
Hand shovel
Compass

PinPointer
Photo Identifier
Knife
Gun and ammunition
Writing journal
Binoculars (still slung around his neck)

Lastly, he found the board piano, or "Kalimba", he'd brought. The little wooden, oval and steel-tined instrument from Africa his father had given him as a child that played such simple, yet sweet tunes. His first musical instrument. He couldn't leave it.

Then he loaded the foodstuffs. A meatless, jerky-type concoction. Freeze-dried packages of various meals. Packets of candy. Powdered sugar drinks. He hefted the pack and groaned. Too heavy. *Way too heavy.* But when he tried to think of something to leave out, he couldn't. He was already leaving too much stuff behind.

Something moved in the brush behind him, something heavy.

Tom vaulted for the door of the Strong Box, tripped, painfully banging a shin, then, rising in a hurry, fell inside, grabbed the door and made to close it, stopping himself just before it shut. *Yeow!* he grimaced. That really hurt! And he didn't want to be stuck here in the dark again, that was for sure. Heart racing and leg throbbing, Tom listened for it now - at first, nothing more, then, finally, a slow, methodical advance through the brush. Gradually, he pushed the door open a little to get a look. Peered around the side. What he saw made his heart leap. A great, russet-colored beast, with wide antlers upon its head, stared attentively in his direction, ears pricked forward. It looked ready to bolt. Evidently, Tom's ungraceful exit alerted it. With great caution, it stepped, one foot in front of the other, occasionally stopping to look around. Extremely watchful, its muscles rippled under thick skin. In a short while, it was standing over the supplies Tom had carelessly left on the ground. A huge beast. Magnificent.

After taking another look around, it lowered its head to sniff the gear. *Great!* Tom thought, *It's going to eat it, and then I'll have nothing. What to do?* Seeing that the enormous animal looked like it might flee, Tom decided to try to scare it away. Holding the door, he pushed it open some more, ready to close it again if need be. Instantly, the beast raised its head and looked at him. He gulped, continuing to open the door until he was fully in view of the animal. It took a step back. Then another. Tom just stood. Finally, the animal turned, and with high springy steps, pranced away, back into the shadows.

Tom's chest heaved. He'd never seen anything like it! Well, maybe in pictures from a time before he was born, or in Julie's dioramas. There was no comparison.

If Tom was apprehensive about the journey before, he was positively terrified now. Quickly, he began to gather the supplies into the bunkers and drag them back inside the Strong Box. He put the lantern on the small, raised counter next to the seat, which provided some light. Back outside, he looked up again, trying to gauge the time. The sun was now further west. He decided that the day was too far advanced and thus now was not a good time to leave. It was a stall. But leave he would, first thing in the morning. That meant a night in the Strong Box.

Suddenly hungry, Tom rummaged in the food locker and found some bread and jerky. He ate it hastily, then opened a pack of the powdered drink mix. He'd need some water. To be sure, there was some in one of the "cabinets" below, but for some reason, Tom didn't want that water. He thought of the stream outside - clean, lovely. Taking the collapsible bottle, he dumped in a portion of the powder, then tentatively made his way back outdoors, carefully scrutinizing the area before proceeding. It was probably fifty feet to the stream. He judged that it was safe. Limping, Tom kept an eye out for any more uninvited visitors. None showed. Crouching down now, he dunked the bottle into the stream and it began to fill, turning a bright red from the drink. Likely an artificial dye. When it was filled, he turned back to the Strong Box.

Leaning back in the seat he'd arrived in, he made to chug his drink, when he suddenly realized that he'd not filtered the water. He looked at it. It *looked* clean, but he'd been instructed not to drink unfiltered water, could catch a disease or something. *Damn.* He really wanted that red stuff! Sighing, he got the water filter and unscrewed the lid, pouring the drink in. Then he drank it. None of the coloring or sugar made it through, but the water by itself was refreshingly cool. Tom drank half the jug, wiping his mouth with the back of his hand. Then he ate some more. He'd decided that, if he was going to be leaving most of the food behind, he'd better eat as much as possible before he left. He gorged himself.

Tom withdrew the journal from the backpack and wrote:

Julie, I'm here. I'm coming. Hold on, my love.

Reflexively, he dated it the date it had been when he'd left: February 21. Then he thought again about that: *What is the date?* It seemed improbable that he'd landed on the very same day of the year he left on. He furrowed his brow. *Actually, it does seems to be spring outside,* he thought; *Okay, let's make it April 22nd. Earth Day.*

April 22, Year 1.

The night was a long one for Tom. His leg ached, his fall had inflicted a nasty bruise, and he shivered, not due to cold, for, if anything, it was warm. But from nerves. All the night sounds of the forest. The various calls, both deeply guttural and high. Roaring, bellowing, yipping and mewling. The sound of crashing through brush. He dared not look out. It hit him now how foreign this world was. Yes, it was the same earth, but *so very different*. All the normal sounds he knew, had grown up with - cold, hard, mechanical noises, of grinding engines and sharp, abrupt staccatos - were gone. Gone forever. In its place were *these* sounds, the sounds of nature. Of unpredictability and chance.

And there was apprehension. Tomorrow he would be leaving. Leaving the Strong Box, the last bit of security the future world provided. He knew that, once away, he'd never find it again.

After a while, a light rain began to fall. A gentle shower. The sounds of the forest died down, then another sound began from farther away. Rhythmic, melodious. Tom tried to identify it. Something from his past. His mother taking him somewhere. A lake, at night. Her walk down a dirt path nearby it, holding his hand. And ... *frogs*. Yes, that was it! She wanted him to experience them before they were gone.

This was frog song. A million of them now, it seemed, lulling him to sleep.

Thirteen

Tom awoke the next morning, stiff and achy from his night on the floor. It was hard and unyielding, even in the sleeping bag. Besides that, he'd stretched muscles he didn't even know he *had* climbing that hill yesterday. Sitting, he raised his arms and twisted his torso right and left in an effort to loosen them, groaning as he did.

Light streamed in from the narrow opening of the door. He'd been tempted several times during the night to shut it completely against the eerie sounds of the outside, but stopped himself each time. Scooting out from the bag, he looked at his leg. The bruise had spread a little, widened, but now it didn't feel as sensitive. He hoped it was a good sign.

Rising, he walked to the door and looked out through the narrow gap. A cool, fresh breeze brushed his face. The sound of the stream met his ears. Pushing the door open, he looked out. A lovely morning. A symphony of birdsong. Scent of cedar in the air. The sun above the eastern horizon told him that he'd overslept. He stretched once more and thought about the difficult road ahead. Likely, that was the last safe night of sleep he'd ever have again. *Well, no sense dallying.*

Tom stepped outside, naked, to relieve himself. Felt the cool, moist grass beneath his feet, between his toes, the coolness of the air upon his skin. It felt wonderful. He listened, half expecting the usual sounds of the city. The ever-present drone and scream of automobiles and airplanes, the honking of horns, of someone hurling a curse at someone else, the alarm of gunshot and the cries that followed, the jarring notes of siren and jackhammer, the painful shriek of metal on metal, the many clangs and bangs. But there was none of that. It was unsettling; told him just how alone he really was. He walked to the stream, and, forgetting his filter, bent down and drank. The water was cold and delicious, its purity filling him, healing his wounds. Going back inside, he got his jug and dunked it in, recharging it.

Tom dressed and ate a big breakfast, deciding again that it was best to do so while he could. Meanwhile, anxiety gnawed at him. Finally, though, unable to think of any other (good) reason to delay, there was nothing else for him to do but go.

Looking at the sun, he estimated the time to be around 9:00. Gathering himself, Tom hefted the backpack. Still too heavy. Walking back outside, he bent himself over while lifting it up. It felt like a bag of bricks. Slowly, he got one arm, then the other in and stood. The pack slumped solidly down, putting an incredible weight on his shoulders. Not only that, something was jabbing him from behind. It wouldn't do. A momentary reprieve.

Reluctantly, he again bent over and slowly got the pack back off. He opened it to see what the problem was. It was the folding shovel. He wrestled it out, then took another look at his pack. When he'd filled it yesterday, he'd thrown supplies in haphazardly. *Stupid.* He dumped everything back out on the ground, then with more care, began to repack it, starting with putting his extra clothing between the inside back and the rest of his gear. An additional buffer. He still could not think of anything that he could leave out. Finally, it was done. The hat now, though, was on his head and gun on his belt. Once more, he struggled to get the pack on, grunting with effort. Then he noticed the padded straps below, dangling from either side. *Oh, a belt.* There was a clip on both ends. Seizing them, he gave a little jump, hoisting the pack higher, and snapped the belt together. Again, it came down to rest, but this time on his hips rather than his shoulders. It made a big difference.

That done, he turned around one last time to say goodbye. Goodbye to the world of man, goodbye to that future. *This* was his world now.

"So long," he said simply, and, turning back around, set his sights on the hill. "This isn't going to be easy," he said aloud. Then off he went, over the stream and up the mountainside.

In short order, Tom was out of breath and had to stop. In fact, he stopped exactly twenty-seven times going up that hill. He was ashamed of his condition. *A man of my age should be able to run up this knoll,* he thought. Eventually, though, he made it, albeit hacking, gasping for air and shaky of leg. He briefly thought about dropping his pack and taking a rest, but scolded himself for his weakness.

Tom looked out again over that skyline. Enchanting. He withdrew the PinPointer, hoping that, if he just turned it on temporarily, Dietrich wouldn't know. He did, and the two blinking dots reappeared, green and red. Withdrawing the estimator, he found their distance had closed. Now it was thirty-two miles, twelve miles closer than yesterday. It made him nervous. Switching on his own beacon, the two dots resolved to the bottom of the little screen while a blue light appeared at the top. He set the two points of the estimator on the blue and the green dots and was horrified to find that the distance between him and Julie had actually increased! Where yesterday it was six hundred and fifty-three miles, today it was six hundred and fifty-nine! While he'd been lounging, she'd been moving, and fast. *Away* from him. But why? Was she being pursued? He shuddered at the thought that she was running away from Jaqzen. It put a fire in his belly. *Be safe,* he willed her.

Looking back at the little forest path he'd seen the day before, he set his foot in that direction and immediately started down, keeping it in his sight. Shortly though, as he dropped below the canopy, it was hidden by the trees. He tried to judge how far away it was, and guessed maybe two, two and a half miles. It was unnerving going this way, as it was completely unfamiliar. Whereas the other side was relatively unobstructed, Tom found this side anything but. There were sundry large, downed trees that blocked his way, which he was forced to climb around, through, or over. His pack caught time after time on branches. Finally, as the last tree had deteriorated enough, having been weakened by the steady work of beetles and ants, Tom was able to push through, sending thin branches snapping off to the ground. That sent a swarm of insects scurrying.

A couple of hours later, he was at the bottom, then paused to get a drink and take his bearings. He looked up. These trees seemed taller, the canopy higher, making the forest floor a little darker and quieter. It was dismaying. Still, he knew it was morning, and thought that, if he persevered, he should be able to make it to the clearing today. He wanted that, to make it out of the forest today. The thought of spending another night in its dark embrace with no protection was too much.

Onward he tramped, step by step, for, it seemed, another hour, until he began to doubt his estimation of the distance to the trail. Then he feared that he'd passed it, some overgrown section perhaps hiding the way. Tom stopped and studied the signs. No, he didn't think he'd passed it, since there'd been no overhead clearing yet, the one he'd seen the trail through. If memory served him, that narrow gap had run north and south for a relatively long distance. He *should* run into it. Evidently, though, he was wrong about it being only two and a half miles away.

As he walked, Tom was again alarmed by the variety of unfamiliar forest sounds around him. Sometimes, something would run quickly by, and, though jerking his head, he'd barely catch sight of it. Unconsciously, he kept a hand on the gun.

Over, under, through and around he went, over, under, through and around, pushing past verdant growth. In the meantime, the sun was making its own slow trek across the sky.

187

Eventually, he came to a stream. Removing his pack, Tom kneeled to get a drink. He needed a rest.

He wasn't sure when he became aware that he wasn't alone. Maybe it was the sound of a twig breaking, or a light rustle of leaves on the ground nearby. He raised his eyes and slowly glanced around. His jaw dropped. Through the dappled light he could see shapes, *lots* of shapes, and they saw him. Fear shot through the man and instantly he dropped his hand to the gun on his belt. None of the animals moved, though. Slowly, Tom stood. There was a nicker. High pitched. The sound vaguely familiar. Between him and the main part of the group was a tree, and right on the other side of it, not ten feet away, was one of the little creatures. Its head was hidden. Tom crept around the other side for a better look. Heads began to pop up, watching him attentively. Finally, the little animal that he was stalking raised its head, too.

Tom frowned. It couldn't be. But it was. Horses. *Little* horses. *A whole herd of them* here in the forest.

Fear melting, Tom spoke. "Hello," he said gently. The little thing jumped, then, keeping a wary eye out, moved away. The others moved off too, though not far. Still, they kept their ears turned toward him. Their coats were spotted, camo style, and the mane on their necks short, upright and stiff-looking. They also had little miniature tails. Tom found them cute. He guessed that there were about twenty of them. After a while, deciding that he posed no threat, they resumed eating. On the menu were leaves from the trees and the understory, he noted.

One horse climbed partly on the back of another. *Ah,* Tom thought, *a little indiscretion.* "Okay, well, I'll leave you in privacy then," he said, turning to tiptoe away. The little horses did not move off this time, but never stopped watching him. When he was out of sight, he resumed a more deliberate gait. Somehow, the knowledge that he wasn't alone in this dark wood gave him comfort.

A half-hour after meeting the horses, Tom finally came to the gap in the forest, and, relieved, immediately turned right and toward the exit. He knew, though, from his view on the mountain earlier, that this stretch would be about twice the distance as from it to the forest path. It worried him greatly. He might not be able to make it out by sundown. On the other hand, the route here was clearer than before and he'd make better time. He picked up his pace, not an easy thing considering the extra weight he was carrying. Every now and then, he would be startled by an abrupt sound of some solitary creature that had spotted him first, then high-tailing it. More often than not, he never saw them. When he did, it was usually too dark to make out what they were.

Tom stopped when he spied a large animal in his way. A great burly beast, it had not seen *him*. He had no idea what it was, but thought it might be a carnivore. There were horns on its head - sharp, pointed and dangerous looking. That made Tom more than a little uneasy. The big brute was standing right in his way. Tom ducked furtively behind a tree, hoping the animal would not be long. But no, it showed no inclination to leave, and, in fact, he surmised, might even be sleeping. When he attempted a walk around it, the sound of dry leaves crunching underfoot unnerved him, and thus, annoyed, he opted to wait. In this way, Tom lost another hour of daylight.

When darkness began to fall, Tom's apprehension rose. Realizing he would not make it out in time, he decided to set up his tent/hammock while there was yet enough light to do so. Choosing two trees close enough to each other to accommodate his sleeping quarters, he then fought to install it high as he could. Maddeningly, though, it kept slipping down, until he tied it so that both ropes rested in notches between the trunks of suitably spaced branches. When he could no longer see, Tom climbed inside to spend an awful night, not only because he was thoroughly terrified, or because the hammock sagged deeply in the middle, but also because it began to rain and water dripped in and on him. Still, after lying awake much of the night, miserable and wet, listening and imagining, his body eventually rebelled and he stole a dash of sleep through sheer exhaustion.

In the morning, Tom woke late, achy and grumpy. He looked a frazzled wreck, but no one was looking. Unzipping the bag, he fell to the ground, then, swearing, stood. Fortunately, below was a thick carpet of soft and springy, if somewhat soggy, leaves. Sullenly, he changed clothes, then pulled down and repacked the hammock, cursing its designers. Within a quarter-hour he was back on his way. As the sun rose, though, Tom found his mood lifting. He didn't think that he was far now from the forest exit.

Here and there were larger openings in the canopy and sunlight would stream in most welcomely. Tom came to one opening that was much larger. A beautiful meadow with a stream flowing out of the forest and right through it. It headed toward the middle where there was a boulder, and under that, a pool of water, then it continued on back into the murky woods. Something was lying close to the pool. Something large and dark. Tom backed up. The animal did not hear him and continued its slumber. Then he noticed at the fringe, other animals, some of the little horses he'd seen before. They were hanging back, seemingly afraid to go to the pool. He also spied some small, deer-like fauna.

Tom looked back at the big beast by the pool, lazily snoozing, its side heaving up and down with breath. It jumped slightly, legs moving. He made to run, but the thing remained where it was, evidently only dreaming. He thought that if the other animals, which were likely well acquainted with the beast, were keeping their distance, maybe he should too. So, slowly, Tom inched his way back toward the dark. When he was nearly there and was stepping around a tree, he happened to tread on a dead branch. It cracked loudly. The beast, alerted, suddenly jumped up. Tom dove behind the tree and stood still, though his heart galloped.

A loud grunt emerged from the meadow. Ever so slowly, not wanting to be surprised, Tom peered around the tree. There, he saw a massive form, a pig/boar looking thing with a huge hump just past its neck, glaring around and sniffing the air. He watched it, amazed. *It* seemed, though, not to have the best of vision; eyes tiny and inky black. Likely, it relied on its sense of smell and hearing, he surmised. Besides various grotesque protuberances on its head, it also had a formidable set of teeth and massive canines. They looked like they could do some real damage. Overall, the creature was unkempt and hideous, monstrous even.

Tom wondered what it was. Then he remembered another device that he'd been given, the *Photo Identifier.* If he could get it out and snap the thing's picture, it would tell him. Curiosity overcoming good sense, Tom, with the greatest caution, wrestled the pack off and set it on the ground, propping it against the tree. Then he tried to remember which pocket contained the P.I. Having determined that, he grasped the zipper and began to pull. It made a characteristic staccato sound. Not too loud, but the pig must have heard, for now it gave an ear-splitting shriek, sending the other creatures at the periphery scattering. Tom cringed, stopped. He peered around the tree again. The pig-thing was sniffing the air in his direction. It shrieked again, *A noise loud enough to wake the dead,* Tom thought, involuntarily sticking his fingers in his ears.

More shrieking. *Holy sh...* Tom let go of the zipper and reached for his gun.

Suddenly, there came a sound of rushing steps, heavy footfalls. He whipped out the gun and pointed, ready.

Crash! Shriek! A ferocious, thundering snarl. The racket was deafening.

Tom jumped out from behind the tree ready to fire, but froze. Another animal, brawny, yet a little smaller than the pig, was now locked in mortal combat with the first. Apparently the pig's shrieking had gotten its attention. The movement was so fast that Tom couldn't make out what it was. All he saw were slashing tusks, and a great brown head, all teeth, grabbing that huge black neck, crunching down. The fight raged on, and blood was flying out in every direction, but Tom couldn't tell whose it was, although it looked like the pig was getting the worst of it. Finally, the big brown dog-like creature gave a mighty shake. The pig squealed. The brown one bit down harder, a sound of crunching. Shook again, then the pig went limp. The other animal held the neck of the pig-thing in its bloody mouth, then dropped it, lifeless. The smaller beast grunted with exhaustion and sat on its haunches, breathing hard. It almost seemed to be smiling. Then it began to lick its other side.

Tom, heart still pounding, thought it would be best to make his exit and started to back away, trying to avoid the dryer leaves so as not to make too much noise, when another shape caught his attention. Small, tawny-red, long fur. A short tail held straight up. Gingerly, it walked over to the other animal, sniffing as it did. At first, Tom feared for the little one, then he noticed a resemblance between them, saw the teats. *Ah, mother and child. This could be dangerous.*

Tom made again to leave, holding the gun firmly. The mother, still panting, moved to get up, to greet her baby with the kill, but immediately faltered and sat down again. Something in the way she did it, ungracefully, caught his notice.

Then she lay down near her prize, puffing heavily. Something wrong. He continued to watch. Her baby walked to her and gently touched her muzzle, then licked its mother's face. Mother closed her eyes, now wheezing, and rolled onto her side. Then Tom saw it: a large, gaping wound, spilling blood, soaking her coat ... and the ground. He drew in a breath. The little one, not understanding, walked to the kill and sniffed at it, mother turning her great head to look, to make sure she ate, then lying it back upon the ground.

Her breath came now in great, drawing gasps. *She's dying,* Tom thought. Her little one, though, continued to eat. Then the mother struggled to get up, a dreadful effort. Finally standing, she wavered, then fell back on her haunches, then up again. Like a drunk, she walked over to the stream of water and bent her head to sip, dehydration coming swiftly. Her muscular legs shook and she stumbled once more, then collapsed, but, now near the water, she was able to drink freely. After a time, she stopped and closed her mouth. Her little one came to her, making soft mewling sounds. It sniffed at its mother's sides. Eyes closed, she held her head up and it rocked with her panting. Loud puffs; yet her breathing was slowing. Her head went down, breath slowing further. Large heaves of her chest, then ... then ... it was still. Her mouth opened, and her head rolled into the stream. She was dead.

The little one made a small, barking sort of sound. Sniffed at its mother's massive head. Barked again. Whimpered. Barked. Then it grabbed a mouthful of the thick fur under mother's ear and pulled. Bravely, it threw its slight weight backwards. *Tug, tug, tug.* It barely rocked the huge head. Bark, *tug, tug, tug.* After a while, spent, it stopped, sat, then, whimpering, it walked next to mother's side and lay down there, absorbing what warmth it could from her. Every now and then, Tom caught the sound of muted whining.

The whole thing had happened so fast. One moment's thundering life followed suddenly by the eerie silence of death. The whole forest silent. It shook him. Tom cast about, not knowing what to do. Finally, he decided it was time to go. Grabbing his pack, he hefted it up, grunting under its weight. Too heavy. Getting it on, he turned and walked away, leaves crunching underfoot. He looked to see if the little one noticed, but if it heard him, it gave no indication. Still it lay there, next to mother's protective side. The smell of her would probably keep other predators away for a while, he reasoned. In the night it would probably slink away and begin its life alone. It would have to grow up fast to survive in this world. Maybe instinct would take over and it would be all right. Tom wished it well.

But, deep down, he knew the little one would die too.

Tom trudged on over the leaves. A smell of tannin in the air, of wet, decomposing humus. A wisp of coolness touching his cheeks. Where the sun made it in, though, he felt warmth. A sudden explosion of wings and birds that had been unseen upon the ground abruptly took flight. He jerked, heart thudding. Cursed. Something was bothering him. He didn't want to think about it. Continued on. The forest menaced; he had to leave it. Make it to the open plains. He didn't know how much farther it was.

Tom, nerves tight, kept a cautious eye out on either side of him as he walked, not wanting to be surprised again. He still held the gun in his hand, then, seeing it, holstered it at his side. The pack dug into his shoulders. He'd forgotten to connect the belt. He stopped, panting. He'd been walking fast, thinking only of getting out of the forest. He bent over to snap the buckle. Still troubled. He was avoiding something. *Click*. Straightening. Looking ahead, he stood. He knew what it was; knew what was nagging him like an old woman. But he couldn't. There was *no way*. It was foolish to even *think* it. Tom stood looking out, southward toward the exit, still a ways off, angry. He shook his head. Cursed again. Then, closing his eyes, he sighed and turned around.

He couldn't leave the little thing to its fate without at least trying to do something. And so he headed back into the dark. A half dozen times he thought of turning back again, but he couldn't. Not Tom.

A quarter-hour later, he was there. Tom looked at the horrible scene. Still lying by its mother's side, was the little animal. The sweet little creature that would grow up to be just as awful as she. *But it wasn't now.* He glanced about to make sure that nothing else unpleasant was hanging around, but there was naught, at least not apparent. Slowly, Tom walked to the two huge mounds. The big black one and the smaller brown one not far from it. Finally, standing between them there, he was awed by their sizes. Much larger than they'd looked from fifty yards away. Monstrous. The air was thick with the smell of iron. Blood from both animals had saturated the ground in iron red, red mixed with red, indistinguishable. *At that level, we're all the same,* Tom thought, *so why do we fight?* A silly question.

The little beastie had not moved, its eyes still closed.

"Hey, little one," Tom said softly. It didn't move. He wondered if it had somehow willed itself to die, but its steady breathing said no. Crouching down, Tom looked at it, wondering if it was safe to touch. Still its eyes were closed.

"Hi," he whispered. Reaching out a hand, Tom lightly patted the coat of the small animal. It opened its eyes and looked at him. Yet it did not seem alarmed and made no other movement. Tom noted a wild look about its eyes. Gray iris surrounded by orange, or was it yellow? Tom brought his hand forward again and slowly stroked its fur, ready to whip

it away if necessary. Clean, brindle-colored fur with black ends. Black mixed with brown below its ears. A black muzzle. The tail bushy and short. A lovely coat, likely kept up by mother. The little one closed its eyes again. Peculiar. No fear. Or was it surrender? He continued to stroke, the fur soft and pleasant to touch.

"I'm sorry about your mother," Tom said sadly. "I'm sure she was a wonderful mom." There was no reply.

"So what happens now, little one?" The little one rolled onto its side while he pet. He judged it to be about a month old, maybe two, though he had no real idea. Looked like it weighed about ten pounds or so.

"Do you want to come with me?" Tom asked, forgetting his previous reticence. Then remembering it, he felt ashamed. How could he think of leaving a baby like this alone in the woods? He crouched down next to little one, then put two hands on it, front and back. When there was no reaction, Tom began to lift. Amazingly, the little beast never opened its eyes. Gently, he set it in his lap and continued to stroke.

"I have go somewhere, a long way, I could use some company. What do you say, come with me?" He waited, and, hearing no objection, stood with the little one in his arms. It made a tiny barking sound and moved as if to jump off. Tom caught it and set it back down by mother. It walked over and again nestled near her.

"You can't stay here, little one. Something will come along and eat you!" Now it looked at Tom, head between its front paws. He reached out and stroked once more.

"What if I cut off a piece of that meat over there?" he asked. With that, he walked over to the pig-thing, and, talking his knife, sliced off a big piece. Then he cut off a smaller one. He took it back to the little one and laid it on the ground before her. He noticed now that it *was* a *her*. She showed no interest, only staring at Tom. He picked up the piece and acted as if to eat it himself.

"Look. Mmm! It's good!" Tom said. To his surprise, the little one began to growl, a small, baby growl that sounded more endearing than threatening. Little one got up, and, walking over to Tom, sniffed at the meat in his hand dangling near his mouth, then, gingerly, while keeping its little wild eyes on Tom's, took it from his fingers. It dropped the meat on the ground, then began to eat. Tom, wondering how long it had been since its last meal, cut off another piece and lay it upon the ground near the animal.

When it finished the first piece, it set to eating the other. So Tom cut another, then another, all the while stroking and quietly talking to her.

He felt good about the beast. It would be nice to have a partner on this trip, then neither would be alone. Still, the little one was so, well, *little*. How would he take care of her? He could barely manage the weight he was carrying now. Maybe she would follow.

When the little one was full, she lay back down, but this time she lay next to Tom's feet, though her tail draped over Mama. She looked into Tom's eyes. Then Tom remembered the P.I. Digging in his pack, he withdrew it, and, standing back, took a picture of the face of the big black pig-looking thing. Words appeared in the viewfinder:

Accessing Database

He waited, and then the assessment came.

Dinohyus

There followed a short description.

Entelodont. Some species up to seven feet in height. Extinct, early Barstovian.

"Seven feet? *Holy* ... so you're only a *small* one?" Tom said, nervously glancing around him. "Crap, I hope I don't meet your parents!" Then, "I think you're supposed to be extinct," he said, looking at the big black mound. Next, he pointed the identifier at little one's mother. Again, the words:

Accessing Database

Aelurodon taxoides. Extinct member of early canine family.

This was followed by additional information.

Something moved in the dark. It sounded big. Maybe something that had caught the scent of blood. Huffing. Apprehensively, Tom looked in that direction, but he couldn't make anything out. His eyes were adjusted to the light in the meadow. Little one barked, a warning yip that said, "Stay away, or I'll have to let you have it!"

"No! Don't!" Tom blurted. Then stepping back over to her, he said, "We gotta go. Say goodbye." Reaching down, he picked up the little beast. The creature in the forest snuffled, moved closer. Tom could barely make out a hulking shape just back of the trees. Little one barked again.

"No, no. Don't do that," Tom whispered anxiously as he hurried the opposite way. Holding her in his arms, he headed in the direction he'd gone before. And on they went, Tom and his little Barstovian beastie.

"I guess it's just you and me, Little One," he said after enough time had passed. "So, what do you think of your name?" Little One just looked at Tom, saying nothing in reply. She was so cute that Tom had to laugh.

"You sure are a beauty!" he said. "How do you stay so clean in these woods?" Though Tom was delighted to have someone to accompany him, it didn't take long before the extra ten pounds felt like twenty. He peered ahead, trying to see if he could spot the opening, but no.

A dark form loomed there, perhaps fifty yards away. It stood to the left of the path he was on, the animal trail that eventually led out of the forest, effectively blocking the way. Same beast as the day before, Tom concluded. He stopped and cursed. When Little One noticed, she let out a loud series of barks.

"Hey! I thought I said not to do that," Tom admonished. "If that thing attacks, you're not the one that's going to have to fight it." Little One paid him no mind, but continued to bark. The big animal stared dully at them, looking slightly bovine, though different. For the life of him, Tom could not remember if this type of animal was carnivorous or not, but again its horns looked menacing. Still, he had no intention of waiting it out again, nor of spending one more night in this forest. Finally, cautiously, Tom began to advance, while cutting a path to the right, giving the thing a wide berth. When they were twenty yards away, the bovine-like animal suddenly stirred, then bolted down the path, but not out of the way.

"Oh great!" Tom said, though now he thought that the animal probably wasn't a carnivore. He likely could have simply gone around it yesterday. Walking back to the path, he pressed on. Each time he got to within twenty yards or so, Little One would bark and the bovine-like thing would run off down the path, then wait for them to catch up again. Tom chuckled. They went on that way another twenty minutes before the animal decided to move off farther to the left and let them by. It stared at them stonily. Its glare was returned.

When he looked back around, Tom was thrilled to see sunlight through the trees far ahead. They were getting closer to the end. It had been a lot longer than he'd thought while looking out from his perch on the mountaintop. He wondered how he'd so miscalculated the distance. As they closed in, the woods gradually became lighter, though still mostly in shadows, and the air decidedly warmer, yet still full of fragrance.

Now he began to notice more flowers. Though they could live in the gloom, they obviously preferred sunlight; he found that the sunnier parts of the forest contained by far the majority of them. The scent was heavenly. Where before there were flowers singly, now they were in bunches. Blues, whites and farther on oranges/reds/yellows.

More shapes near the opening of the path, sun streaming in, making the darks seem darker. Silhouettes. Movement. *Horses.* Tom and Little One continued on, walking among them. The tiny horses moved aside, and it seemed like an official greeting, a proper welcome to the Barstovian earth. He didn't look back.

Fourteen

Tom paused just under the last of the oversized trees and took in the view. It was grand. Lush, green, rolling hills stretched off into the distance, bordered by woodland that receded to either side, and on those hills a variety of animals, browsers and grazers, large and small. Dominating were horses of diverse species, for not only were their sizes and markings different, but they seemed to have separated themselves by clan. And there were others, not horses, but llama/camel and antelope-looking. All standing or walking, lolling or munching the new grass, other little ones frolicking with their mothers. Every one alien to Tom. He also caught sight of smaller, badger-sized animals walking unhurriedly along in a little group over a nearby hillock and larger ones that ambled or loped past singly, the grazers watching and giving them space.

The most stunning of all, though, were the elephants. At least that's what Tom *thought* they were. Near the edges of the forest some distance beyond and to their right, was a herd of large ones, pulling down branches from tall trees and eating the leaves. Unlike modern elephants, however, the upper tusks of these big brutes curved downwards, while another from the bottom jaw stuck out straight or turned slightly upwards. Together they acted as efficient graspers, and indeed, Tom observed, one of the herd was rolling a downed log out of its way. *Elephants, here!* he thought. *Wow!*

Tom suddenly remembered the Photo Identifier. Time to find out what these animals were. And thus they wandered, up the slope, through the wildlife which would lift their heads without apparent alarm and gaze at the stranger and his more familiar, though at present, harmless friend, as they sauntered by. Tom, with Little One on the top of his pack, behind his head, snapping pictures as he went. Not as encyclopedic as Julie's plant-oriented "Case", usually the P.I. only gave the genus name and a general description of the various plants and animals when the species could not be determined exactly by photograph alone, which was much of time. But sometimes the species was also shown. Every now and then, however, it would balk completely with a disappointing *not in database* answer, indicating that the organism was unknown to science.

Breathing hard, Tom attained the slope. Behind him was the high canopy of tall trees. Ahead, the landscape undulated gently to the horizon and thoroughly teemed with life. The quintessential pastoral setting, it captivated Tom. The scent of pure air mixed with the sweet fragrance of wildflowers and trees in bloom. A breeze blowing from his right, from the distant sea, blowing away the heat of the day, ruffling his hair. The clear, blue sky with its voluptuous clouds *cumuli*. Some, far away, promising to unload on the mountains. And the songs of meadow birds. He caught sight of them flitting about joyfully in the tallgrass, chasing each other. Then all at once, a loud rushing, as ten thousand thousand wings, emerging from the green, suddenly lifted to cerulean, taking flight as one. A huge, ever-changing shape. Tom was awestruck. He hadn't known that the earth had ever been like this, this ... *Eden*. Despite his urge to get moving, to find his wife, he couldn't help but smile, then he was laughing. He didn't know why he was laughing, except ... except that it felt good.

This world was so very different from his that he realized just how atrophied his time had become in comparison. How sick and twisted. So strange, so *refreshing* it was to look around, to search, yet find *not one single sign of humanity*, no crushing hordes, not even the tiniest bit of garbage *anywhere*. He threw his arms wide and spun around shouting.

"Yes! Yes! I love it! I love it!"

Little One jumped down into the grass, then sat, mouth open, tongue hanging, watching him. *Just like a regular dog,* Tom thought. He remembered the meat he'd brought, the piece of entelodont he'd sliced, provided kindly by Little's mother. Sloughing his pack off, he laid it in the grass and sat down himself, then opened the top compartment where he'd stored it. Taking it out, he laid it in front of Little One. Raw, blood-soaked, it had made a mess in the compartment. He'd wash it out when he could. Little One set to eating it greedily, giving little growls as she did. Must have been instinctual, for certainly Tom wasn't attempting to take any. Then he grabbed the small collapsible bowl and poured in some water. Little One sniffed, then drank of it. The water turned a bit red. Tom took a few swallows from the bottle.

"We'll have to make sure we stay near water. I only have this one bottle. If the breeze stops, it feels like it could get pretty hot." Little One paid him no mind, but continued feasting. Tom felt hungry himself and dug in his pack for something to eat. Finding a package of freeze-dried "stew", he opened it and, pouring out the water, put it in the bowl. Then he added fresh water. Not wanting to waste time heating it, he stirred and began to eat, then grimaced. It tasted like mildly seasoned, slightly lumpy paper. Experimentally, he set it by Little One. Curious, she put a nose to it, tasted, then curled a lip and let it drip off her tongue. Tom laughed out loud.

"Hey, that's high-tech food there! Took us thousands of years to come up with it. Show a little respect." Then just to show her how good it was, he took another bite. "Yuck! You're right. It sucks." Little One looked at him strangely, turning her head this way and that. Then she slumped into the grass and rolled onto her side, finally closing her eyes.

It'd been a big day for a little one, and it wasn't even noon yet. Soon, tawny fur was asleep. Tom didn't have the heart to wake her. Instead, he got up, and, keeping a watchful eye on her, decided to make an increasingly widening circuit around her, snapping more pics. The camera had a nice zoom feature that allowed him to zero in on the farther beasts. Names and information began to pop up. *Archaeohippus, Desmatippus, Parahippus, Hipparion.* The horses in view. *Aepycamelus, Miolabis, Protolabis, Oxdactylus.* Llama-like fauna apparently related to camels. Camels here in North America! Some rather bizarrely horned deer-like animals. *Dromomeryx, Cranioceras, Bouromeryx.* And the really odd *Prosynthetoceras*, which had forked horns on a tall stalk over its nose like a slingshot. There were also some smaller pig-things, *Cynorca* and a larger version, *Hesperhys*, and a few carnivorans, *Brachypsalis, Leptarctus, Mionictis.* He also snapped some rodent-like creatures, *Petauristodon, Nototamias, Cupidinimus.*

As he walked, he pushed easily through high, knee-level grass. Over this grass, zooming this way and that, were numerous insects. They zipped right by him without pause. Many were beetles. Some alarmingly large. There were others as well. Grasshoppers, colorful butterflies, or *"flutterbys"* to Tom's memory, and huge black wasps with orange and black wings. A beetle landed on his shirt and he quickly brushed it off with a shudder. Most abundant were the bees, small, stingless natives and larger honey and bumblebees, also natives, some with stripes on their abdomens, some without. They mobbed flowers here and there. *It's a bee's world,* he thought. When he caught sight of a shrub covered with lots of the big wasps, he decided to try to get a closer look and hopefully snap a picture. He wanted to know what they were, yet he was also exceedingly wary of being stung. They were shockingly large, with beautiful iridescent black abdomens. When he had gotten as close as he dared, he zoomed in with the camera and took a picture.

Tarantula Hawk, the P.I. stated. *Extremely painful sting.*

Yeow! Tom retreated at the warning, backing away carefully, then turned and walked off, checking behind him every so often. He'd have to give them a wide berth.

Larger and larger his circuit became, farther and farther from Little One, so absorbed was he in his photography. Every now and then he looked back to make sure his she was still there. Finally, a half-hour had gone by, and Tom began to feel anxious to get back to her. Turning around, he headed toward the dark shape in the grass, which would be the little Aelurodon. Then, reaching the spot, he was horrified to find that the dark form he'd been watching was not her after all, nor the pack he left her near. It was a piece of wood. Somehow, he'd lost his bearings. He cast about, then finding his pack, he hurried to it. She was gone. Reaching down, he quickly slung the pack over his shoulders while frantically looking around and calling out to her. Now he was running. Then, off in the distance, heading back toward the forest, he spied a small, tawny-red colored shape moving through the meadow. He ran that way.

"Little One!" he shouted. Not hearing, she continued on her way. "Little One!" he called out again. Now she turned to see him. Tom stopped running so as not to scare her.

"Where are you going?" he asked her. She sat down in the grass on her little haunches. "Probably thought I'd abandoned you." He kneeled down and looked at her. "Were you heading back to Mama?" he asked, stroking her head. He realized that he was already attached to her. Sad that she thought he'd left her.

"I won't leave you," he said. "We're a team now." She lay down by his legs and looked up at him. "Promise you won't leave me?" he asked. They looked deeply each into the other's eyes, Tom and his little Aelurodon, and in that moment a bond formed between them. A bond for life.

As he walked - Little, a warm, furry bundle behind his neck - Tom understood why Julie had been so passionate about prehistory. It was unlike anything he'd ever imagined before. To be honest, he'd never really given it much thought. Had just sort of unconsciously assumed that the way things were in his time was the way they'd *always* been. The way they were *supposed* to be. He realized now how wrong he'd been.

Slowly walking on, he took everything in. A bank of gloriously blue and white flowers on a small rise to his left, yellow and red on his right. Here and there were paths carved in the grass over the long years by so many animals, and he'd walk them for a time, but then found himself again cutting across the green when they'd begin to wander. Often they led to some body of water fed by the rivers flowing from the East, from that gradually rising plain. Well, he *thought* it was the East, but the compass seemed to demur. He wanted to explore up there, but didn't want to be diverted. He was set on making as straight a passage as possible to that blinking green dot on the P.P. That course would force him to climb steeper banks and lower vales than had he simply gone around them. But he didn't care. Except for the weight on his shoulders, Tom felt good.

When he got thirsty, he'd drop the pack, then they'd fill up from the bottle. But it was running low - he knew he'd have to get more. Well, no problem there *per se*, he thought, there seemed to be no lack of it - so far at least. There *was* the issue, though, that a lot of the waterholes he saw were populated by wildlife. As he walked by them, he watched to observe the behavior of these local fauna. He was dismayed to find that, after drinking, they didn't seem to be in any real hurry to be on their way, some just standing and snoozing, others lying down near the water.

The day grew hot when the morning breeze stopped. They finished their water and continued, Tom ever on the lookout for a vacant pool. To be sure, there were available puddles here and there, probably recharged by last night's rain, that he could drink from, but they looked stagnant. No river flowed into them and no animals were drinking from them. A hint, perhaps. But he didn't take it. Bending down at one of these ponds, he noticed there was a film on top, and it stank. Still, he filled the bottle and sipped, then grimacing, spat. *Ug.* He spat again. Wisely, Little One would not partake. Tom looked around and shook his head. What to do? After a while, it became clear that the only way they were going to get a drink would be to walk through these loiterers.

Choosing a largish pool, he began to walk toward it. Heads lifted. Camels, small ones, and a couple of large ones. And some of those peculiar deer-like things. One made a step in his direction. He stopped. It took another.

"Whoa. I'm just after some water, same as you," Tom said. Two more stepped toward him, regarding him curiously. What is this creature that walks on two legs? Little One gave a loud bark. At that, they stepped back suddenly, all heads now on him. She barked again. They trotted off a short ways, not quite seeing the little aelurodon behind Tom's shoulders, perhaps imagining that he was the source of the report, a sound they had learned long ago meant death. Now, Tom saw that some of the deer-like animals were *in* the water as well, probably mucking it up. When Little One gave yet another bark, they began to splash out every which way. Finally, all out, they stood off from Tom and Little One and let them approach the waterhole. Sure enough, the water was brown from agitation. Tom sighed. Should he use the water filter? On water this dirty, there was no telling how long it would last. Little One, though, unlike the last puddle, did not hesitate and began to drink. Tom thought of stopping her, then refrained. He bent down and again took a sip. Not repulsive like last time, but he could feel the grit on his tongue. He needed more than a sip.

When he was about to fetch the filter, he suddenly thought of the stream that must feed this pool. In the tall grass he'd not seen it. Then he discerned an area of turf slightly higher and thicker than the rest. Instinctively, he knew that was where the water flowed. Walking to it, he heard the burbling, the sound increasing as he advanced. And there it was, fresh, clean and flowing. Tom drank deeply, then sighed. From now on, he'd look for moving water first and use the filter only as a last resort.

When he looked up, Little One was walking along the bank of the pond near him, water up to her belly. Ears forward, she was trying to see something in it. Unexpectedly, she pounced. Then again.

"What'cha got there?" Tom asked. Briefly, she glanced at him, the pond weed *Potamogeton* draped across her nose, then back to the job at hand. He strolled over and she looked up at him, now sitting down in the water. Then she barked at whatever it was she'd seen. Something moved there. A fin. It made for deeper water. *Fish. Hmm.* Another bark and something splashed on the other side. A couple more splashes, and Tom looked. Rocks jutted out of the water. On some of them were frogs, throats pulsing rapidly.

Splash! Another one in.

Tom yawned. The sun was hot, and he was sweaty. Maybe he should go in for a wash. He looked at his watch. Wait, he didn't have one now. Squinting up at the sky, he guessed the time to be past noon. He looked around. Still the camels stood looking back at him, waiting for him to leave their waterhole so they could get back to things.

"Oh, all right," he said. "Let's go, Little One." Tom reached down to pick her up, then saw that she was dripping wet. He sighed again. *Maybe she'll follow me,* he thought. He set off walking while looking back at his Aelurodon.

"Come on, Little One. Let's go!" he said encouragingly. She sat and watched him.

"Let's go, Little One! Let's Go!" He walked off a little further. Apparently, she didn't understand the concept yet of following a human being. Tom slapped his hands on his thighs, still calling for her. When she continued to sit there, half in water, Tom said, "Okay, I'll carry you." Walking back, he stooped to pick her up. Water ran off her. He squeezed her fur to get most of it off, then lifted her with a grunt. She helped by stepping behind his head and lying down on top of the pack, paws over it, next to his neck, as if she understood that this was the way they were to travel. Water trickled down his back.

"That's just cold," Tom said. Then to the assembled fauna, "We're going now. Thank you for letting us use your waterhole." They stared back glumly.

Tom walked on for another hour before Little One fell off the pack, lulled by the rhythmic movement of her human's stride. She let out a little cry, though fortunately she was unhurt. Tom took out a shirt, and, tying the arms around the pack, fashioned a sling that was less than ideal. Still, it worked, and Little One didn't object.

By another hour, he was getting hungry and lowered the pack to get some food. Freeze-dried again. And again, Little One turned up her nose at it. This was more concerning. She had to eat, but wouldn't think of eating his simulfood, as he thought of it. Well, eventually she'll get hungry enough and have to. He'd let her wait. Done, Tom was left again with the issue of what to do with the packaging. Earlier, he'd just stuffed it in one of the pockets of his pack. Now he stuffed again. So what was he going to do, haul garbage all across the Miocene world? He could just dump it. He could...

He couldn't. True, it would be a vanishingly small amount, making minuscule difference to the environment, but no, he wouldn't do it. Should he dig a hole and bury it, a miniature landfill, his gift to this pristine world from the future? No, that was out too. His options were dwindling. For now, he'd carry it, until he thought of something better.

About then, he noticed something climbing on the front of his shirt. A tiny insect of some sort. It was headed smartly upwards, up toward his head. He flicked at it, but it remained on him. He flicked again, but this time it clutched on and hunkered down. He didn't know what it was. Grabbing it, he pulled, pulling his shirt away a bit. *Wow, strong little guy,* he thought. Finally, it came loose. Next, he made to shake it off his fingers, but again it managed to hold on. Frowning, he flicked again. At last, it was sent flying. *Tenacious,* Tom reckoned. *Wonder what it is?*

Then he saw another. Up it walked. *Dang!* He seized the P.I.

Deer Tick
Phylum: Arthropoda
Biting insect. Frequents warm, moist areas, dead wood.
Holds onto the ends of tall grass overhanging trails until a
host brushes past, then climbs on.

210

There followed a list of hideous diseases they carried. Tom's eyes widened. He shivered, briskly dropping his pants and checking himself. *Jeez!* There was one on him, on his thigh, *IN HIS SKIN!*

"EIYEE!" he yelled.

He grabbed and pulled, but it held. Panicking, he consulted the P.I., which advised not to slowly pull it, but to do so in one quick movement using a particular tool. Tom, anxious, removed the pack, setting it and Little down, then, unzipping, began hurling equipment onto the ground, finally finding the medical kit. It wasn't there. He had no such tool. Wonderful! He HAD to get that bug out *NOW!* Pinching his skin, Tom carefully lifted the tiny abdomen, then, gripping near the head, gave a swift pull. Out it came. He shook his hand violently. It was gone. A red mark told where it had burrowed in. He consulted the P.I. again. It warned about pulling, said that there was a danger of leaving the head inside, thus causing infection. Lovely. *Too late for that now,* he thought. He looked again. Didn't see anything else there. *Stupid,* he thought, *I got lucky.*

Tom promptly worried that he would catch one of those horrible illnesses. The P.I., though, told him that ticks had to be attached for 24 to 36 hours before they transmitted disease. That relieved him somewhat. Off came the rest of his clothes. Checking, he found another walking on them. He gulped. Then he felt a minute itch on the back of his head at the base of his scalp. He touched it, and sure enough, found a bump that he was pretty certain shouldn't be there. He took hold and pulled. Luckily, it wasn't attached and came out of his hair easily. It immediately set out up his hand. He shook it off.

Dang! Tom thought, *Better watch for them! Nasty little buggers.*

Satisfied that he'd gotten rid of all of them, Tom scanned

his clothes inside and out for others, then put them back on. Then he thought of Little One. She'd been watching Tom from her secure place in the sling. Tom undid it and lifted the little aelurodon onto the ground and began to search through her fur. He found two more, neither attached. *Wait.* There was a large, gray protuberance in her right ear. A big, fat tick. Full of blood, no doubt. Likely from before. Scowling, he got a corner of the shirt and again grasped, paused, and pulled. Little One let out a yelp. And there it was. He threw it far away. A drop of blood formed in Little One's ear.

"Sorry about that. You'll thank me when you don't die tomorrow." Tom fetched the antibiotic cream and applied some. *Disgusting*, he thought, *Ticks*.

On advice of the P.I., Tom tucked his shirt into his pants, and his pants into his socks. Then he thought about what the P.I. had said: "Frequents warm, moist areas, dead wood. Holds onto the ends of tall grass overhanging trails". *OK, that's just about everywhere,* he mused, looking around him. Tom imagined the meadows on every side crawling with ticks. Shuddered. A blemish on paradise.

Happily, that turned out not to be the case. To be sure, there were ticks aplenty, but they were found mostly around the larger waterholes and along the trails leading to and from them. Tom discovered that, if he avoided these areas, the ticks virtually disappeared. He wondered how the wildlife coped with them. Were they covered in ticks? As he walked and observed, he contemplated the situation. *Surely there must be some adaptation, else how could they survive? Some immunity, probably.* Then he noticed something else; something he'd not really noticed before. Birds sitting on the backs of the animals. Hopping about them, even clinging to their sides and legs. Picking at their fur. *Ah*, it dawned on him, *tick pickers!*

Not only that, Tom also noticed that there was an increase in birds around the water holes. Whole flocks flying in and out of the grass. They weren't there just for the water. It was natural pest management; in a world allowed to be in ecological balance, things rarely got out-of-hand.

Tom kept onto the older, wider trails rather than the newer, narrower ones; those where he was able to avoid overhanging brush.

The grass, he now perceived, was not uniformly tall. There were areas where it had been shorn short, areas where grazers had stayed, cut, then moved on. These areas, too, provided respite. Relieved about the pest situation, Tom again allowed himself the luxury of elation.

Abruptly, as if on cue, he observed a dust devil off to his right. Looking that way, Tom saw that one animal was chasing another. He ran to the top of a hillock for a better view. *"Ran"* being a relative word with his heavy backpack; it was more like a clumsy bounding. Panting, he reached the top, maybe ten feet high, and saw that the chase was still in progress. Meanwhile, a whole herd had taken flight, their hooves thundering over the land.

It was clear that the pursued was getting the better of the pursuer. Finally, the latter broke off. Almost immediately, however, one of the other fleeing animals, a small pony-sized horse, strayed too near the larger predator which, making a giant leap, seized it and held on. This greatly slowed down the other, which now kicked madly at its hunter, whinnying loudly. The hunter took a hard kick to the chest, which was enough to dislodge it. But having tasted blood, it refused to be dissuaded and launched again at its prey. Eventually, the horse fell under the other's greater weight. The hunter grabbed it by the back of the neck and bit down hard. At that point the horse stopped moving. It was over.

Tom was sad to have witnessed it. Still, he knew that this was the natural order of things. Everything had to eat. At least it looked like there were *a lot more* herbivores than carnivores. The loss of one would not make a dent in their total numbers. But that would be small consolation to the victim or its family.

The beast sat, panting, while the rest of the herd, now at some distance, regarded it warily. Soon it set to eating. Little One, who had been watching this, decided to check things out and began walking in that direction. Tom jumped up, for he had previously been sitting, and picked up his little beastie.

"No, no, no," he said, "do you want to be the after dinner snack?" Nevertheless, Little One wanted to go. Then she began to whine. Holding her in his lap, he petted, quieting her. On a hunch, he got out the P.I., focused and snapped a picture. He *thought* it looked familiar. *Aelurodon,* it said. *Is that it?* Tom wondered. *She thinks that's Mama.*

"Good call, Little, but that's not your mother," he said. Then a thought occurred to Tom. Little One needed food, and there was food. All they had to do was get it. But how? He thought of the gun, but lost his nerve. What if he only wounded the animal? Seemed to be his new worry. He decided to wait and hope the big aelurodon would finish soon and leave.

So, wait they did. In the meantime, the sun moved farther west and the shadows began to lengthen. After an hour or so, the big aelurodon lazily got to its feet and sauntered off. Tom waited until it had dropped down the other side of a knoll and out of sight, then he rose and walked to the kill. There were other, smaller predators now tearing at the carcass, but seeing Tom, they shrank back. It helped, he supposed, that the backpack made him look larger than he really was. When they reached the kill, Little One was eager to get to the ground and eat. Tom set her down and she speedily set to work. *Poor thing,* he thought.

While she ate, Tom got out more of the rations he'd brought. Even for his time, though, it wasn't great food. Now it was positively repellent. Tom looked at the kill in front of him. A thought passed through his mind: *Maybe I should eat some of this.* Then, *No,* he thought, *I can't.* Still, he knew his rations would only last so long. *I'll have to find another way soon,* he told himself.

He looked at the dead horse on the ground. Again, much smaller than normal, or at least normal for the Anthropocene. When we *had* horses, that is. Though its predator had eaten a large section of the stomach and flank areas, the rest was left untouched. While the body was a solid goldish color, the neck and legs were striped. Then he saw something that took him aback. The feet were different. He thought that horses had hooves, but this one had three hoof-like toes on each foot, a largish one in the middle and two others about half its size on either side. He furrowed his brow. *Strange.* He looked again at the head; certainly *looked* like a horse. Wait! He recalled Julie mentioning this trait in early horses.

Tom spotted something on one of the feet. The rear left foot on the side the horse was lying on. He walked over to it, incurring a small growl from Little One, muzzle already red with blood. "Don't worry, it's all yours," he reassured. He stooped down and peered at the foot. *Ah, I see.* The outside, or farthest away of the three toes, had been ripped nearly off. It must have caught it on a rock in the frenzy, or maybe that kick. In any event, that was likely why the horse was so easily taken down.

Sitting there on the side of the little bank, a warm, comfortable breeze blowing his hair around and tousling the grass, he again pulled out the P.I. It was getting darker, but he paid no mind. He pointed it at the creature. Unfortunately, its savaging by the aelurodon made an exact identification impossible. Several potential names came up, at the top of which was *Scaphohippus,* a member of the horse family. *So, ancient horses,* these *horses, were three-toed,* he marveled. Evolution. Yes, Julie had talked of it, and now he was witness to it: Species adapting to changing environments, themselves changing to fit in, becoming new species. Adapt or die. Life in flux. Where the environment itself was unchanged for relatively long periods, the species therein tended to be as well. But when it was remodeled or reshaped by various processes, often the species that lived there were reworked, too.

Tom glanced up, noticed the sky darkening, then stood and climbed the little hillock that he'd been resting on. He looked out toward the west, toward the sunset. From where he was, he couldn't see the ocean, but knew it was fairly far away. Over it, the sky was shot through with deep ruddy hues interlaced with blues and oranges. A brilliant ruby sundown, courtesy of abundant volcanic gases and ash, and the dust of billions of running hooves. Farther east, the first stars began to show. A wonderful evening. He'd better make camp, he told himself. At least now he wasn't in the middle of a forest at night, but out on the open plain.

Tom turned on the PinPointer. There were all three dots. The distance between him and Julie had shrunk to 644 miles. Not much of an improvement. Tomorrow he'd have to set out in earnest.

He decided to camp where he was, giving Little One the chance to eat freely during the night. Tom worried that his diminutive charge might wander away while he slept, so he tied a string around her neck, not too tightly, but sufficient to hold her. He made the length enough for her to reach her food, about 15 feet away, then tied the other end to a low branch on a small shrub. Little One wasn't too happy with that and pulled mightily, trying to get it off, finally sitting down at the very end of the line with it pulling on her head and looking none too comfortable. Tom laughed at that, then picked her up and lay her next to his sleeping bag. Immediately she went back to pulling on the string.

"*Relax,* Little," he urged, then decided to let her get used to it. Tom got his lantern and journal, blew up the inflatable pillow, then crawled into his sleeping bag.

Night was coming on swiftly, and with it a whole new world, the nocturnal world of the middle Miocene. As the sun had been setting, the occasional random call from this or that beast became more frequent and urgent. Long, low bellows and high, short bleats. Mothers calling their wandering offspring back, to stay nearby for protection. *Mothers are the same all over,* Tom thought, and so, evidently, was fear of the night. There were yips, barks, and howls from some dog-like animals, he guessed. Infrequently, there were sounds of roaring or trumpeting. That unnerved him, and he pushed himself deeper into his bag. Next to him he'd placed the gun, just in case.

When things finally began to quiet down, he peeked out and was stunned by what he saw. Along with the sound of crickets and frogs singing came a new and totally unexpected excitement. One by one, all around him, all around the grass-lands where he bedded, tiny lights began to pop on. Moving lights. Suddenly one would zip by just inches above, then another, and another. Tom sat up and looked out. Indeed, the world was alive with them, lights whizzing by on straight paths or suddenly diving into the grass. While a luminous off-white predominated, other colors accented it, reds, blues, greens and yellows. Next to him in the grass he noticed one tiny speck in motion. Picking up his flashlight, he shined it on the speck hoping to find out what it was. A tiny glow-worm, no more than an eighth inch in length, rhythmically switching its minus-cule lantern on and off, on and off, in its quest for a mate.

As if in reflection of the wonder below, was an amazing

cosmic display above. Most obvious, the huge arm of the Milky Way shone out brightly, and within it, a million stars of varying sizes and hues sparkled and shimmered as if in heavenly song. The rest of the sky, though, seemed to compete for splendor. Numberless points of white, yellow, red, blue, and green. He thought he could even make out the spiral shape of other galaxies and a few colorful nebulae. From time to time, a small dot of light streaked across the heavens, and he would catch his breath when it ended in fiery glory.

At last, the moon decided to make a showing. Full. Large. Closer to the earth by hundreds of miles in the Miocene. On the horizon it looked positively huge. Its warm, cinnamon color fading to a faint rose as it climbed, and then to white when the day's dust settled. Tom was amazed to find that he could actually see individual craters clearly. There it was, the moon, the very same moon that would shine on his own sorry world fifteen million years hence. The same moon that watched over Julie now.

In his time, few or no stars visible at night was the norm, what with all the city lights, the ever-present air pollution, the crowds of communications, spy satellites and weapons systems, the scads of circling space junk, and most annoyingly, the flashing, orbiting advertisements. *Buy This! Buy That!* Political slogans, etcetera. When their diodes failed, they weren't replaced, so one was forced to look at tawdry, flickering ads. Mercifully, a few might burn out altogether, leaving a long, black snake to blot out the stars. They had all the ambience of a cheap motel sign where the heavens should be. It was an obscenity.

Tom turned on the lantern, adjusting it to low.

April 23, Year 1

*My dear Julie, how I wish you were here
to lie beside me now looking at these stars,
at this incredible world of yours. I never
knew. You tried to tell me, but I couldn't
hear you. I hear you now, my love.
Wait for me. I am coming.*

Then, laying the journal down, he turned to see how his little aelurodon was doing. To his surprise, he found her snuggled against the other side of his bag, the string chewed off, leaving only a piece tied around her neck like a collar. Speaking softly, he caressed her fur, then, putting out the light, he turned over and went to sleep.

Fifteen

Tom awoke to fierce barking, his Little One going mad with rage. *"What, what..."* he stammered. Then he heard it, a low, deep, rumbling growl. Menacing. He looked up and beheld a large, dark shape blocking out stars. His eyes went wide. The thing growled again, snarling, snapping. In the bright moonlight, he saw two bared rows of gleaming white teeth and fangs, saliva dripping from them, and eyes fierce and savage. Little One continued her barking. Instinctively, Tom grabbed his companion and was bitten for it. He dropped her and watched in horror as she, ears back, tiny teeth also bared, walked cautiously, but determinedly right up the much larger animal, growling her own small warning.

"NO!" Tom yelled. The eyes of the other looked crazed as it glared down at her, ready to kill. Reaching around, Tom felt for the gun, but it wasn't there. It was clear the other was about to strike.

"GET BACK!" he yelled. Now the brawny creature looked at him, evidently dismissing the little aelurodon as insignificant. It took a step closer, every muscle taut, like a coiled spring. In that moment, two other things happened: Tom found the gun and Little One bit the larger animal on the leg. In a flash, the beast grabbed her and tossed, lunging for Tom, who brought up the gun and fired. The bullet's impact, penetrating the muscle on that great shoulder, threw it off target and it landed on his other side. There followed a blood-curdling howl. Pain and rage. While the shot, even at point-blank range, didn't drop the Aelurodon, for that is what it was, Tom saw, the same one that had killed the horse, it was enough to jolt it. Biting savagely at its shoulder, it stepped back, then again, then turned and loped off around the hillock.

Tom scrambled out of the pack and looked for Little. He found her lying on her side. She looked at him, and he her. Apprehensively, he reached out to feel her, this time without objection. Carefully, he picked her up, and, holding the little bundle in one hand and his flashlight in the other, turned her around, looking for an injury. Searching, but not finding any, he set her down. It appeared that she was only shaken up, never having been treated that way before. He massaged her fur while she looked away. Perhaps she took this treatment from one of her kind as punishment and was dejected? At last she stood and came. Hope rose up in him. Gingerly, she sniffed at his hand, the hand she'd bitten, then licked it. *Is* that *it?* he thought. *She feels bad for having bit me?*

"It's okay, you were very brave," Tom said. "And I'm glad you're not hurt." Suddenly, he realized his mistake, a mistake that almost cost them their lives. Fledgling outdoorsman that he was, he hadn't thought about the consequences of camping out next to fresh meat. *How stupid!* It was a mistake he would not make again.

Gathering their stuff together and repacking it, Tom made for a small grove of trees he saw in the open, maybe a hundred yards away. He would re-attempt utilization of the tent/hammock. Since the moon was now overhead, it provided light enough for him to climb, attaching the rope to one end of a thin, curving specimen. Back on the ground, he threw the one on the other end around the trunk of a nearby tree, then pulled until the hammock was relatively level and tied it off. It was now about eight feet off the ground. Then he attached the strings to hold up the tent, which was sewn onto the hammock. Next, he shoved in the sleeping bag and straightened it out. When that was done, he lifted his pack into another tree, no easy feat, and jammed it between two branches. Now, how to get Little One in there?

"Okay, I'm going to put you in, so don't freak out on me, please," Tom said. Picking her up, he stepped onto a piece of log that lay under the hammock. She was heavy, must have eaten her weight in scaphohippus. He grunted, lifting, trying not to fall. At the entrance, he pushed and she climbed in, then turned to look back.

"You wait there. Don't jump out," Tom ordered. There was one thing left to do. Clearing an area down to dirt and gathering some dry wood, Tom built a fire. He hoped it would ward off the night prowlers. From this point on, an evening fire would become more or less a regular routine.

Finally, he was ready. Climbing the first tree, he pulled the hammock close to him and swung a leg up, scooted, almost fell, then clutched inside. The hammock swung about wildly, the trees bowing a bit, then he was in. Little One jumped on him, licking his face. He lifted her off and turned to zip the flaps shut. Not too comfortable, but it would have to do. At least it wasn't sagging as badly this time. Nerves frazzled, he imagined he wouldn't be sleeping too much that night either.

He was wrong. So tired was he that he was dozing in minutes.

Tom woke to the sound of snuffling, then to a feeling of being jostled. At first, so gentle was it that he continued to sleep, incorporating the movement into a dream.

He was on a boat that rocked back and forth, the sky was blue and a slight breeze blew. He looked down into those waters, wanted to swim there. Clean, unpolluted water, how lovely, *so inviting*. The jostling grew a little rougher, and slowly, consciousness began to return. When an even rougher push came, he awoke and looked down and over to his little aelurodon to see what she was up to, but she was on her back, still fast asleep, head tucked under the folds of his bag. "Hmmm," he sighed.

He was amazed to see how much bigger she looked, just since yesterday. Apparently she'd gorged herself.

Push.

Tom looked around, through the netting, to the outside world, then jumped. Something was just underneath and behind them, a big animal, standing on two legs, it was munching leaves on a thin branch, pulling it down to get to them. It was powerfully built. Involuntarily, Tom yelped.

The big animal stopped eating and simply stood, staring, but not appearing to see them. Perhaps the camouflage design of the T/H fooled the creature into thinking it was a part of the tree. He gulped. When he'd sounded, Little One lifted her head, though her eyes showed she was still partly asleep. He hoped she wouldn't wake and begin barking. The big beast went back to eating, only a quiet munching giving it away. Slowly, Little's eyes began to close again.

Tom decided that the animal was a peaceful vegetarian and began to relax a little. When he saw the massive, sharp claws on its "hands" and feet, he grew concerned anew. Yet its eyes were half closed as it chewed, as if in rapture. It looked to be about eight feet tall. He wondered what it was, but since the P.I. was in his backpack, which was within the branches of another tree, there was no way of knowing.

"Shoo!" Tom whispered. He was eager to rise and hit the trail. "Go away!" Again the big animal stopped chewing and listened, eyes still partly closed. Little lifted her head. "Shoo!" he said again. The big thing turned its head, not knowing where the sound was coming from. Slowly, Tom unzipped a flap and stuck a hand out. "Hey! Come on, get going," he waved. Little One was now standing on him, looking out. *Oh no.* When the big animal went back to chewing, she noticed him. Immediately she began to bark.

The response was sudden. Yowling loudly, the thing swung down on all fours, eyes now fully open. It set to thrashing the shrubbery around it with those muscular arms, sending branchlets flying, apparently trying to scare away the Aelurodon(s). Little One went on barking and Tom put his fingers in his ears. He allowed her to continue, hoping that the noise would scare the animal off, but ready to stop her if it noticed them. Again, he got the idea that its eyesight was not the best. At last, the big creature, exasperated, ran through the brush and into the open about fifty feet off, then, looking back, proceeded to walk away. Little stopped her annoying yapping. "Whew!" Tom shook his head.

Through the netting from his perch in the trees, he looked out at the world. The dawn sky was exquisite. A cool breeze blew. On the grasslands, animals were already at work feeding. Little walked on top of the sleeping bag to her human's face and began to lick.

"Good morning to you, too," Tom replied, petting her. "That was close. Thanks." He lifted her off. "You ready to get going?" His stomach growled. Little looked at it, turning her head in that winsome way of hers. "Yeah, I'm hungry." He thought about that, he'd better be about figuring it out, what he was going to eat. The sooner he was off his rations, the better. Then he remembered the kill from the day before. Not much left of it, probably, with the various scavengers. He looked at Little. "After that feast yesterday, I doubt you're starving." He pat her bulging sides. "Well, let's go," he said.

But when he tried to lift her out while standing on the log, she kept backing up inside the tent, afraid of falling. With some cursing, he finally grabbed her by the scruff and brought her out, but, pushing herself off his chest, she leapt out of his hands and landed in the grass. The force of it caused Tom to lose his balance and he fell backwards off the log, then sat up.

"Okay, thanks for *that*," he retorted. Then putting a hand on her back said, "Look, do you think you could cut me some slack here, I'm on a learning curve." Again, he shook his head.

Tom glanced around, but saw nothing obviously threatening. *Good.* Finally, getting everything out of the trees and packed, he looked around for the girl. He found her back at the kill, again stuffing herself, antagonizing the flies and wasps that buzzed about her. Didn't look like there was much left, maybe the other had come back in the night. In any case, it was now mostly bones. Some of those appeared to have been eaten as well. He gaped at that, wondering about the raw power necessary to crunch through bone.

Errrrr. His stomach. Setting his pack down, he found an energy bar, and, ripping off the foil, devoured it. He wondered if he should have another, then decided to hold off. Today he'd need to look for other food, though he worried that he wouldn't find any. He also needed to refill his bottle with water.

He checked again the PinPointer, a ritual he'd begun and wouldn't stop until Julie was back in his arms, hoping that the few seconds it was on would be undiscovered by Jaqzen. The distance between them had decreased.

Tom stood by while Little ate. Indeed, she did look bigger than yesterday, larger than he'd have thought from one meal. When she was full, she got up, then, to Tom's disgust, defecated on the scaphohippus hindquarters.

"That kind of spoils it for others, doesn't it?" he said, then thought that maybe that was the idea. But if that were the case, if that was the aelurodon way, there should be one from the bigger aelurodon that killed it. There wasn't. *Well then,* he thought, *maybe some* other *bone crusher finished it off while we slept.* He hoped he'd not killed the other one; nevertheless, he felt for the reassuring solidity of the gun at his side.

225

Little One sat and looked at him, perhaps wondering why he'd not partaken of the banquet. Tom bent down to lift her onto the back of his pack. *Wow,* he thought, *I don't know if I can do it!* Then he stooped down, almost sitting himself, and put her on his lap. He huffed, coughed. Grabbing, he lifted, and, bending his head, tried to set her on his pack. She promptly hopped off.

"Come on!" Tom said, "We gotta *go.*" Once more he hefted her up and once more she jumped off.

"Okay, well I'm going with or without you," he said. Then standing, he looked down at her and walked off a few steps, finally turning to glance back; still she sat looking at him. He walked a little farther, but she made no move. Now Tom walked on without looking back, hoping that she'd get the message. After thirty seconds or so, he turned around. To his immense relief, this time she followed, keeping back and to his right about ten feet.

"Good girl!" he exclaimed. Walking over, he patted her on the head, then straightening, continued to walk. While maintaining, she struggled to keep pace with him. Tom slowed a bit to make it easier for her.

After a minute or two, they came across the animal that had awakened them. It was off a ways, under another tree, happily munching. He extracted the P.I. from his shirt pocket, pointed and clicked.

Moropus, a species of Chalicothere, appeared with other information that he could now verify first hand. Yes, indeed, it was a browser that ate leaves from trees. Yet the little computopedia mentioned nothing about its transcendent state when dining on them, or its surly behavior when startled. Whoever put it together could not have known that. Dead bones tell no tales. But *he* knew. It made him feel privileged.

About a quarter-mile behind them, to the northwest, at the edge of a copse of trees, which abutted the larger forest, Tom spied several elephant-types, all males, trying to push two over. They were intent on leaves that remained after the lower branches had been stripped. The biggest one placed its forehead squarely against a sturdy trunk, then shoved, rocking back and forth. The tree, though shaking, held fast, yet the elephant would not quit. After a couple of minutes, it finally gave, to be followed a second later by a sharp sound of cracking. He zeroed in with the P.I., but as there were other trees blocking the view, the device couldn't take a reading.

As yesterday, lots of insects, with birds in hot pursuit, zipped above the waving grasses, many barely missing him, some hitting, falling, then up and flying again. Little One would try to catch them when they got close. Once, succeeding, she spit the bug out, curling her lip at the taste. Tom chuckled.

A wonderful profusion of wildflowers, deliciously scented, spread out before them like a swaying carpet of color. Shooting Stars, Fairy Lanterns, Woolly Bluecurls, Fiddlenecks, Tomcat Clover, Baby Blue Eyes, White Evening Primrose, California Fuchsia, California Spice Bush, Lupines in a variety of delightful hues, Tree and ground Poppies.

Despite the fact that his back hurt from the weight of the pack and from sleeping in the hammock, Tom felt good, actually *better* than he'd felt in a long time. Physically and spiritually. When he reached a stream, he'd partake, then carefully step over it, not wanting to tread therein. He'd begun to feel a reverence for this nature, a respect, and love of it. He knew that he was being unreasonable, that of course he could make no lasting mark upon it, yet, having escaped the ruined world of the future, he could not feel differently.

Escaped. Yes. That is what it was. He'd *escaped*, as from a prison. He thought of Karstens and all those who'd sacrificed for him and felt a love for them. Contrary to our wretched history, the last expression of humanity was a benevolent one. Perhaps in this one small act, the human race had redeemed itself. He was honored - and giddy.

Paradise. He'd always wondered where the idea had sprung from. Some memory deep in our unconscious, buried in psychic antiquity. Relegated to myths and legends. A lie that never happened, the government assured us. A destructive falsehood that needed to be exorcised from our brains. From our very blood. Nothing is free. Endless struggle is the natural order with some meant to toil more than others. Most in fact.

And yet ...

Clouds formed over the southeastern horizon. More rain coming. The day was warming up. It'd be a warm rain. Life-giving water, without being forced from the sky. Sans the chemicals. Minus the radiation. All those nuke tests, bombs, and accidents - they never happened here.

When they got to shorter grass, Little was able to keep up more easily, even running ahead at times. Here and there, they'd come upon the bones of animals that had lived and long since passed, leaving the world to their offspring. *Perhaps in fifteen million years*, Tom mused, turning a large, white object over in his hands, *this skull will be worth something*. Now it was calcium back to the earth. He set it down, stepping over it, and continued on.

A rumble far off, from where silver clouds were gathering, while closer, a few ivory ones drifted by. The rest was wide open sky, sunny and blue. No buildings, no wires, no ads. He looked at them. In one, he thought he saw Julie's face.

My Julie. My love. Oh to live with you in a world like this! To begin anew. Adam and Eve. Oh please, let me find her.

They came to the side of a hill, cut in half by generations of flowing water. Still it flowed. There were rocks, round and smooth, within. How long had it taken them to get that way, almost circular? Likely, they'd rolled along in that stream for ages. Water and sand, sometimes gliding, gushing and cascading, sometimes just trickling over them. Some years, perhaps nothing at all, and they'd patiently wait for the next year. Tom picked one up, felt its mass, passed it from hand to hand. He noticed the direction the stream was flowing: toward him. That's the way the rock was heading. Walking that way twenty feet, he again set it down in the stream.

"There, I just saved you a few years," he said.

They were coming to a bank of trees growing on the side of the hill overtopping the stream, and walked under them. The trees were alive with birdsong, little finches hopping from branch to branch, paying them no mind. No mind at all. The stream now wound to his left and went off that way, gently following the base of the hill, its direction lost to view. Were he to follow it, he would be going off his path, the straight line he'd marked out in his mind to Julie. The other choice was to climb the hillside, and with his heavy pack, that would be difficult at best, especially as the slope was steep. Plus, it wouldn't be easy for his little Aelurodon. He didn't want to push her too much. So they continued along the stream bank.

Miniature fish swam in the many pools; minnows, the P.I. told him. And there were turtles. Little grabbed one, but when it retreated into its carapace, she dropped it. She liked to walk on top of the rocks, though, sometimes slipping, a foot would go in the water and she'd quickly withdraw it. She scanned below, taking occasional dives at the fish, but never catching any.

Tom began to notice trees a short distance off to his left with bright, ruby-red bulbous things hanging from them. At first he didn't think much about them, but when the light hit one just right, he could see that it was some sort of fruit. He made for that way. In a moment, he was there and was stunned to find that they were plums, albeit small ones, not having been bred to the unnatural size of man's taste. The deeper purple ones were very sweet, much better than any he'd had before, when they were still around that is. And this tree was loaded with them. He thought it strange that they would be fruiting in the spring. *Maybe seasons are different here.* Realizing now how hungry he was, he stood and gorged himself, then filled a cloth bag with them. Little One even ate a few, following Tom's lead.

When he was full, he felt much better. The breeze, which had been their companion all morning, became a slight wind, tugged at his shirt. He smelled ozone and looked up to see that clouds were closing in above with patches of blue sky between. *Crud, it's gonna rain,* he reflected. *I'm gonna get soaked.* With that, he felt the first of the drops lightly hit his cheek. He pondered getting under the tree, but then had an idea. *Why not,* he thought. Doffing his pack, he then removed all of his clothes and hurriedly stuffed them in, then put his shoes back on. Fortunately the pack had a rain flap, and he pulled that over, attaching it to the bottom. Then he put it back on. Now he walked naked for all the world to see. Au Naturel. The sky darkened and temperature dropped, yet still it was warm. Then rain began to come down, first lightly, then in sheets, obscuring the mountains in the distance. It felt good. Tom kept his hat on and rain dripped off the brim.

When it began to come down even harder, he saw that the various fauna around him grew still, some turning their backs to it, hanging heads low, perhaps to let the water off more easily. Only he and Little One moved. Several minutes later, the shower abruptly abated, water dripping everywhere. Then it started again. Tom raised his head and, closing his eyes, opened his mouth. *Purest water in the world.*

A flash of white light. He opened his eyes. Shortly thereafter, a booming clap of thunder made him jump. Little One whined and took off at a run.

"Wait!" Tom shouted, running after her. She stopped, ears down, fur soaked, and let him pick her up, shielding her with his hat. Then another flash, and he saw lightning dancing on a hilltop not too far away. It connected with a tree, which exploded in half, one side slipping down the hill. This was followed almost simultaneously by another crash of thunder that reverberated through the valley. Little One struggled to get free and, landing on the ground, again ran off toward a tree. *Okay, I'm with you,* Tom agreed, running after her. Reaching the tree, she slunk under it, then seeing some bushes nearby, crawled beneath them.

"Don't go too far," Tom called out. Fortunately she stayed there, under the boughs of a bush filled with clusters of small red berries, eyes closed, while he sat under the tree. Even with all the leaves, rain made it through, trickling on him from above. *Never mind*, he thought. *It all comes with the package.* As long as Little stayed where he could see her, he could deal with it.

Suddenly, it seemed, the storm was over. Tom waited, then, walking to the edge of the tree-line, looked out and up. Where just before everything had been terrible and foreboding, now rays of sun streaked out hopefully through the clouds, creating patterns of light, surrounded by larger areas still in shadows, upon the ground. From the foliage all around hung a million quivering beads of water, each a tiny sun in itself.

A Miocene storm, he smiled. *Okay*. He heard a sound of shaking and turned to see Little out from the bush, vigorously throwing the water off her body. She walked to him, and he bent to stroke her.

"That was fun," he said, half honestly, looking up at the sky again. It continued to clear. The part of the tree that had been rent in two was now lying on the side of the bank just below. It was on fire, orange flames emerging from the underside portion that had been protected from the rain. After a moment, though, the fire subsided on its own. Tom nodded.

The rain over, they set out once more. Due to thick overgrowth in the area next to the stream, they were obliged to walk off from it a ways. It made a wide arc around the hill. And so, for a while, of necessity, they headed east. Whenever he topped a rise, Tom could see the larger hills in the distance and much farther away, southward he thought, those mountains.

But again, the perplexing issue of why the P.P. compass told him he was headed North while its map, and his gut, told him it was South. He pondered that. *Wait, of course,* he realized, *I am going South, have to be. The sun rises in the East, there's no changing that, and it's on my left, the sea on my right. Then ... there* is *something wrong with the PinPointer.* Suddenly apprehensive, Tom swallowed hard. *What if it's off, way off? I'll never find Julie.* A shudder went through him at that. It was unthinkable. *Oh please, don't be wrong,* he prayed.

The river turned to the right when the hill leveled out. The land ahead was rising. But now they were headed south again. There it rolled before them in gentle, glistening waves of green, framed in blue and white. Tom shot a glance west, back again, then did a double-take. A huge rainbow graced the sky, lingering above the dark of the ocean. It seemed to stretch from north to south. Countless water droplets, each a tiny prism seemingly suspended in air, yet slowly falling to sea as the storm made its westerly way, toward those islands, were capturing the sun and splitting its light into glorious hues. Tom caught his breath. Gaped. Then, unexpectedly, tears formed. *This is what life was supposed to be*, he knew. And with that knowledge came reassurance.

The rainbow reminded him of something. And the flowers. And the stars. And even the insects. Reaching into his pocket, Tom withdrew the color stone. Spherical ... like the earth. But "earth," he knew, is a descriptive, like "land" or "sky."

I shall call you Opal, he thought, *world of many colors.*

As he walked, Tom began again to snap pictures, this time of the plant life. In the water were Willow and Cattail, Horsetail and Potamogeton. There were also huge Laurels and Alders, Aspens and Sycamores. Lovely Maples and Hickory, Hackberry and Yellow-wood, with its long clusters of white, very fragrant flowers. Ash and *Sapindus*, Wingnut and Elm. Also found were Ginkgo and Locust, from which dangled bundles of aromatic, magenta-colored flowers. Below them were Hawthorne and Moonseed, *Nyssa* and *Cordia*, Holly and Barberry, *Meliosma* and blooming *Cedrela*. He also saw *Arbutus* and Wild Rose, though not the gaudy versions of the far future, but delicate, five-petaled blossoms, pink in tone and full of perfume. There were also Sweet Gum and Horsechestnut, aka California Buckeye, Alder and *Karwinskia*. California Bay, whose leaves resembled those of Willow, was a wonderful find. When he pulled a leaf to look, it gave off a strong herbal smell. Maybe he could spice up his food with it.

Then Tom found a real treat. Related to the Bay was Avocado, many of which had the primitive fruit swinging from their branches. At no more than two inches in length, they weren't the big, fleshy, overbred versions of the future, yet they were all the more flavorful for it. Some were hard and still ripening, others softer. These latter would snap off easily to his touch. Under these trees were those that had fallen, and, not being eaten, were merging into dark soil.

Tom reached down and scooped up a handful of the soft, moist earth pushed up by gophers. It felt wonderful, alive, unlike the dry, depleted, poisoned dirt of the Anthropocene. It smelled good, too: strong, rich, *vibrant*. Millions of years of life, death and decomposition had created this wonderful, fertile loam. In the modern era, nothing would be allowed to remain on the ground for long, and leaves that fell were quickly removed as litter.

It seemed to Tom that there was such a glut of fruit here in the Miocene, that the flora virtually competed for the attentions of the fauna, each trying to outdo the others in an attempt to spread their seed. Finding food was an immense relief to his mind. He hoped the abundance would last the entire journey.

As he got away from the rivers and small lakes, other plant forms became more common, especially the Oaks, Poplars and patches of *Taxodium / Nyssa*. Standing like widely spaced sentinels on the savanna were Sabal palms, and under them, an Aloe-like plant.

The day wore on and it began to get hot. The warmth felt delicious on his bare skin. He was walking a broad slope he guessed to be about a thousand feet above sea level, though he had no way of knowing that for sure. There was a lake below, sky-blue and inviting. As they pushed on, the land seemed to be drying out just a bit: the grass not so high and the grazers fewer. Still, all was green.

Tom was drinking more now, and so was Little. When they came to rivers, he made sure to fill up, not wanting to chance running out. Topping a higher rise, Tom paused. His back was hurting from the weight of his pack. Sliding it off, he set it down with a thud. Suddenly he felt *so* much lighter. He stretched and groaned, then looked out. Ahead of him, the thin blue line he'd seen yesterday looked a touch closer, yet still it was a long, long ways off. Apparently, it was an extension of the ocean, perhaps an inland sea. If he continued on this path he'd run right into it. It looked like it cut into the interior, almost to the mountains. He'd have to go around. But not before having a look at it. He figured if he kept up his pace he'd be there in a week's time, maybe two. He'd decide then what had to be done. Putting his hands on his hips, he swung right and left, then reached low to touch his toes - well almost.

Again, hunger gnawed at him, and he found another energy bar and bolted it, stuffing the plastic wrapper in the growing pile in his pack. He ended this with an avocado, cut in two with his knife, which also served as a spoon. Little was hungry too, and Tom looked around for a conveniently abandoned meal. If there was one, though, he didn't see it.

"Let's keep an eye out," he told her. Lying back in the grass now, which almost covered him, Tom rested head in hands. Though the tops were now dry, near the ground it was still dewy wet. The warming grass smelled good, welcome. In a short while, Tom was asleep, dozing under the Miocene sun.

He woke a while later. Judging from the light, he didn't think he'd slept too long. He sat up and looked over to find Little eating. He looked again. Some sort of rodent. A big one. Ground Squirrel, the P.I. told him. *She can hunt!* he thought. *Yay!* After gobbling it down, she set out again, stealthily creeping to a small dome rise on the ground. Arriving, she slunk down, almost catlike, and waited, watching vigilantly. In a minute, a small head popped out looking the other way, and she had it. Crunching down, she quickly dispatched it and brought it back, lying near Tom, but not *too* near. Then, growling, eyes fierce, she consumed it. Finishing, she set out for a third. Or maybe this was her fourth or fifth for that matter. She was probably picking them off while he slept. Though personally repelled by carnivory, Tom was delighted for Little.

"Gotta go, girl!" Tom called out. With that, he picked up his pack and threw it over one shoulder. Instantly, he tossed it off again. *Criminey! I'm sunburned!* He looked at his shoulders. Red.

"Oh, that's just great!" he said aloud. Another accident of his thoughtlessness. Remembering the medical kit, he fetched it and found a small booklet. Under "Sunburn" it advised the application of Aloe Vera. Unfortunately, there was none in the kit. "Lovely," he intoned. Then something jogged his memory. Getting the P.I., he looked at the photos he'd snapped recently. There, Sabal palm, and below them, the Aloe-like plant. *Yes!* A stroke of undeserved luck. Tom hastened to the closest palm and, sure enough, found the plant beneath it. He broke off a thick leaf, which began to ooze a clear, viscous liquid, slathering it on his skin, then sighed. It felt cool, brought relief.

Grabbing more of the leaves, he carried them back to the pack, then found a bag to put them in for safe storage, keeping a couple out to finish covering his skin. His shoulders seemed to have gotten the worst of it. Next, he rummaged out a light, thin, long-sleeved T-shirt, and shorts. It hurt to put the shirt and pack back on, but he had no other choice. Again, he shook his head at his foolishness. Now he remembered Karstens' words: "You're going to have to get tough real fast. There are no rehearsals." *How right you were, Bob,* Tom thought. *Well, it's done, no use kicking yourself over it. Just try not to repeat your mistakes.*

They set out down the other side of the hill. There were still rivers, streams, and ponds here, though they were becoming less frequent. Apparently emboldened by her new-found hunting prowess, Little walked bravely to these pools, and if there happened to be wildlife hanging around, would bark at them until they left. Sometimes the taller camels disagreed and stomped their feet or even chased her, with, Tom noted, a strange pacing gait, one where they moved both legs on the same side of their bodies forwards or backwards at the same time, sending her in retreat. Then, angry, she'd turn around and come right back at them until they vacated. *She's growing up before her time,* he thought. Later, she again relieved herself, though, like before, it was small in size, not in keeping with the size of the meals she'd eaten. The rest apparently going to growth. Yes, her mother was large, very large. Little would be the same. Likely she'd grow rapidly. She'd have to have a lot of food to do it, though.

The land undulated gently here. The sun on his shirt and especially the weight of his pack made his shoulders feel as if on fire. Long about the afternoon, they ran out of water, but stayed their path, ever on the look out for more. After a while, thirst began to gnaw at him. Finally, he spied the edge of a large waterhole on the other side of another hillock. Climbing over it, he immediately stopped. Little began to make her way as usual to roust the wildlife. This time, however, Tom hissed at her.

"Little!" She stopped and turned. *"Come!"* he whispered urgently. She looked at him curiously, then turned back to her task. *"Come here!"* Tom said a little louder. Again she stopped. Tom slapped his thighs and surprisingly, this time Little listened. As she reached him, he grabbed her and lay down on the other side of the knoll out of sight of the two big entelodonts sacked out in the mud by the water's edge. One lifted a dirty head, sniffing the air, then lay it back down. Tom, carrying Little, crouch-ran, making a wide arc around the pool.

He supposed he could try to scare them away with the gun, but with his luck, these great brutes, with their ear-splitting shrieks, would be *attracted* to the noise. They'd have to find water somewhere else.

Another hour went by and Tom was sweating. Not only that, his feet hurt. Apparently they were blistering. He pressed on. When his dogs really began to ache, he stopped and removed his shoes, then socks. There were three, fat, water-filled bubbles on his soles and a few smaller ones between his toes. He wondered if he should drain them, then chickened out when just touching them caused pain. He again got out the booklet from his first-aid kit. It recommended wrapping them in something called "moleskin." This time he had some and, lifting first one foot, then the other, carefully wrapped them. It didn't seem to make much difference. His feet still smarted. To add insult to injury, as soon as he got his shoes back on and stood, the pressure of the lessened space inside them due to the presence of the moleskin caused the larger blisters to pop. Painfully. *Lovely,* he thought, *two injuries in one day.*

A mile on, they came to another water hole, this one not fed by a stream. Little ran and drank heartily while Tom got out the filter, pumped and drank. Then he filled the bottle. Next he took out a plastic bag and filled that with water and tied it to his belt. Soon, though, a tiny hole caused it to begin leaking. He discovered it when his left pant leg wet through.

"I'm just a comedy of errors," he mused.

When the shadows again began to grow long, temps began to drop. Yet it rarely got cold here, just less sultry. Evenings, he discovered, were his favorite time of day - after mornings. It was evidently also the preferred time for other species as well, for that's when they emerged from their forest hideouts to graze, especially the antelope and deer types. The others remained under the midday sun, paying it no mind. It seemed the hottest part of the day was from late morning to mid-afternoon. That's about when the breezes stopped.

They'd not eaten in over four hours, and both were hungry. As they'd trod through the landscape earlier, Little had no energy to hunt. Tom still had some avocados left, but wanted something else. Physically, he was tired as well. Unnaturally so, he thought. And his cough returned, a holdover from his past. His unusual exertions were taking a toll on him. What's more, his fatigue seemed to increase in proportion to the temperature. His shirt, soaked through with perspiration, stuck to his skin.

A happy discovery was the presence of hot springs, wonderfully hued in cyan and gold. He'd not noticed them before, but with the declining light, the steam venting from their surfaces made them obvious. Approaching one, he was taken by a stench of rotten eggs, the smell of sulfur. *Ah,* he thought; he'd been subconsciously registering that stink for miles now, had faintly wondered about it.

His shoulders and feet burned and he was grimy with sweat. He needed a wash. The sun was low, but warm, and the pool perfect. Where the water bubbled to the surface in the center it was undeniably boiling hot, but on the periphery there were areas that felt positively divine. Finding one of his few bars of soap, Tom doffed his pack, stripped and walked to the edge, then slowly went in. Yipping excitedly, Little splashed in as well and jumped around, getting him wetter than he was ready for. *Ah well.* The water came to his knees and he sat down, sighing as he did. Now it was around his chest. Huffing with exhaustion, Tom lay back, leaving his shoulders out of the hot water until he began to feel just a little better. Gradually, then, he eased himself all the way in.

Sleepy. If he were to close his eyes now, he suspected he'd be to sleep in seconds. Tom began to wash the sweat and grime off his aching body. He was spent. After a while, he looked at his feet, to his amazement the blisters had softened and the smaller unpopped ones receded. When the water in them was gone, the skin would harden and begin the formation of calluses. In time, these would cover his feet, protecting them. *Calluses, the original shoe.*

He felt light-headed. *Now what's wrong,* he wondered? Was he getting sick? He tried to think. Did he drink bad water? It alarmed him that everything was happening so soon. He knew he wasn't in the best of shape before, and now he was paying for it. He turned on his side, feeling weak. Something was missing, but what? He wanted to sleep, but felt that he would not be benefited by it. *There's something - something they told me back at the Institute. Something I need.*

Then he remembered. SALT! That was it. He was sweating it out, losing electrolytes and not getting any back. He'd dehydrate without it. His electrical system would stop functioning. Tom rolled over and sat up. Dizzy. He had salt tablets. They'd supplied him with some. He reached over and opened the lower compartment of his pack, again took out the medical kit and unzipped a small pocket on its side. And there they were in a flat container, 200 tablets of sodium chloride with electrolytes. Quickly he opened the container and grabbed two, popping them in his mouth. He chewed since he wanted to make sure they'd dissolve. He followed the tablets with water. A half-hour later, he felt a tad stronger.

There came a rumbling off to his right. Then earth trembled and Tom made to get up, thinking it a quake. The sound increased until suddenly, and seemingly from nowhere, a heavy jet of scalding water and steam shot straight up from a crusty white mound on the ground, rising fifty feet into the air. A geyser. It went wide, then splashed back down in a loud rain of liquid and carbonate minerals. Shortly, however, underground pressure relieved, the show ended when the geyser abruptly stopped. Tom sank back into his pool.

Wow!

He lay back again, relaxing. Maybe they'd spend the night here. Looking at the sky, he figured they had about three hours of sun left. Seemed like a waste of a few hours; still, he needed to recuperate. He glanced over at Little, who sat looking expectantly at him, reached over and ran his palm down her back.

"You're a good girl," he said. Wagging her tail, she approached and licked his face, then lay down, drowsy. He thought how much like a dog from his time she was. Apparently, canine loyalty was innate. He was proud to call her his friend.

Little lay half in and half out of the water, dozing with her head on the bank. Like Tom, she was exhausted. Tom doubted she'd ever travelled this far in her short life. She was caked in mud.

Much as he didn't want to move, he knew they'd have to. They couldn't sleep here. He glanced around for a suitable group of trees to hang the T/H in. There were several candidates. He eyed one such, higher upslope, which not only looked ideal, but would also have a commanding view. He chewed it over, then decided against it, not wanting to drag all their gear that far, settling instead for a knot closer by.

Tom began to push backwards out of the water. Where the water had been, his skin was red. But he felt clean. Then, looking at his arms, he noted something he'd not seen before. Bumps. Little raised swellings were all over them. Pustules. He scratched one. That seemed to make it itch. Scratched another. More itches. Then he saw his legs. Even more, a lot more. "What the...?" He stood and looked down at himself. "What is

THIS?" he said aloud. When his skin color began to return to normal with his withdrawal from the hot spring, the bumps became more apparent. There must have been thousands of them, and they were all itching - *like crazy.* Again, a sense of panic began to take hold. He imagined that some sort of microscopic insects had burrowed into his skin, could think of no other explanation. Then did: a disease, maybe that was it, he'd caught some primitive disease.

Tom gulped, coughed. If these were insects, there was no dislodging them, they were under the skin, eating him from the inside out. He scratched again and again, but with each scratch the itching only seemed to intensify, along with the size of the bumps. He tried to stop scratching, but found it nearly impossible; the tingling of his skin was irresistible. Instinctively, he stepped back into the hot spring and again sat. That seemed to sate the itch, but he knew he couldn't stay here overnight.

Okay, stay calm, Tom told himself. *Somehow you managed to be bitten by ticks, get a sunburn, then heat exhaustion, blisters, a searing jock rash* (which he'd discovered earlier) *and now some strange infestation or disease, all in the space of a single day. Yeah, things are looking* good! *I'll probably be dead by morning.* It was a strange combination of unpleasant sensations, all rolled into one miserable man.

The shadows were blending together as the sun set. *Get up,* Tom told himself, *you can't stay here.* Yet he made no move. Truth was, he couldn't. And that night he slept in the hot spring.

When he woke early the next morning, Tom felt more tired than the day before. There seemed to be no part of him that didn't ache or burn or itch. The red bumps had congealed into angry raised masses. He looked at them dully, then closed his eyes and slept another two hours. In the night he'd slipped, oblivious, into the hot pool up to his neck, a liquid blanket. Fortunately, none of the indigenous life happened by, the foul smell a warning that this was not drinkable water.

When he opened his eyes again, the sun was high behind the small knot of trees he'd intended for the hammock. He felt a mess. And now he was hungry. Famished, actually. He looked around through the fog that filled his brain for Little. She was not to be seen. Sluggish apprehension rose in him, then collapsed again with his consciousness.

He dreamt that he was in a ship headed for the stars. A ship teeming with billions of others, all clamoring and climbing over each other. It was getting hot, and the people wailed. Something had gone wrong. Instead of the galaxy at large, the ship - or was it a sphere - was headed toward the sun, the red orb growing bigger by the minute. Bright, so bright. He shielded his eyes.

And awoke. The sun was beating down hard now. He remembered where he was. Everything seemed hot. Tom spied some shade, the little knot again. Clumsily, he sat up. Groaned. There was Little nearby, just out of the water, watching him, small mounds scattered around her. He looked at them. Squirrels. She'd become an expert squirrel hunter and had collected a dozen of them. No, more than that, as half a dozen were already eaten. Ravenous, dizzy, he stood weakly, then picked some of them up and, dragging his pack, made for the shade. Under the trees, he gathered some wood, and with the magnifying glass managed to make a fire. Then, in his delirium, he skinned, roasted and ate squirrels, something that would have been unthinkable just the day before.

And again he slept, his body hot with temperature.

Sixteen

Julie knew she was in trouble when, after the impact doors shut and communication with control cut off, in the moment just before blackout and launch, Jaqzen smiled at her. Not just any smile, it was a wicked, toothy, unmistakable smirk. A look that said, *Ha! I've got you now!* Then, mouthing the words while pointing at her, he said "Say goodbye to hubby, Bitch! You're mine!" And in the following interval, immediately preceding blackout, he began to laugh.

Those in the control room would not have heard. And in the eternity that was that nanosecond, Julie cringed in fear and regret. She'd allowed herself to be lulled into a dangerous complacency, eager to believe that she'd simply misunderstood the man. She'd never return to Tom. Jaqzen would make sure of that.

Forget silly, far off notions of woman's rights: he had his prize. This would be *his* world. The caveman and his booty. She a slave to the barbarian in a Borroughsesque world of his making. Raping her at his pleasure. On the run, savaging this pristine planet for his insane whims. An orgy of blood. How long had he dreamt of this moment?

She closed her eyes in prayer. Though she was agnostic, not knowing to whom she prayed, she prayed nonetheless. It was all she had.

And then they were out. Psyches obliterated by the vast stretch of time, crushed beneath the weight of millions of years. Nothing could withstand that.

Blackness.

Silence.

And ... then ...

Consciousness. Slowly, slowly, it came back to her. Julie shook her head involuntarily. Rubbed her temples. What happened? She stared blankly, yet seeing nothing. Blinking lights. What were they? Pretty colors.

Fear.

Wake up!

Something moved near her. Casually, she turned to look. Someone lying nearby, sleeping in a chair reclined. Big man. Who was he? She smiled.

Tiny nudgings of memory. Julie rubbed her forehead. The air was thick. She looked around again. Now she could hear small beepings that coincided with the flashing of those lights. A ship. A ... timeship.

The man in the chair stirred again. Absently, she unbuckled herself and made to wake the other. His eyes opened blearily, then closed again. Julie reached out and steadied herself on an arm of her own chair, then, with dull eyes, placed a hand on the clasp of his restraining straps.

Her heart began to beat hard in her chest as if it knew something her brain had forgotten and was shouting it at her. *No! Get out! Now!*

Julie paused, abruptly pulling back. *Enemy!* She didn't know how she knew. She just knew.

Get out! Anxiously she looked around, all the while understanding returned. Julie drew in her breath.

The Miocene! Yes, that was it. She'd arrived! They'd arrived! All at once she remembered Jaqzen. He was looking at her, consciousness slowly returning. He smiled now, though without comprehension. She drew back in horror. *Look for a way out!* Then she remembered the door, darted that way and pushed the button she knew would open it. Open it to a new world.

Nothing. *Oh no. Oh no.* Swallowing, Julie pushed again. There was a sound as of great internal strain. The door was sticking. Stuck. Or jammed against something. What if the Strong Box came to rest with the door against a boulder or the trunk of a tree? She'd die in here.

Then, suddenly, unsealing itself with a ripping-tape-like sound as if it had been shut for a very long time, it slowly pivoted and warm air rushed in. Julie looked out and gasped. Though she'd known what to expect, still, the sight of a new world, a world so unlike her own, startled her. Sights, and now sounds and smells. Julie's mind raced. With Jaqzen still in a stupor, she could make a dash for it. In a month, she would return and take the Strong Box back again to Tom. All she needed to do was stay alive for thirty days. Then she realized that she'd need food and supplies to get by for a month. Suddenly torn, she thought about a quick grab of essentials, but even now Jaqzen was almost out of it.

"Hey ... uh ... hey," he uttered, his voice low, deep.

Julie smiled at him, then dashed back in and opened one of the drawers with supplies, finding the knife. Briefly, a thought crossed her mind. *No.* Instead she grabbed the belts that had been holding her just before and cut them off. Jumping over to Jaqzen, she smiled again, then began to lace the belt around each hand, tying it to the arm of his chair as tightly as she could. The last piece she tied around his legs at the ankles. Jaqzen stared at her. Then he began to move. Grunting, he pulled at the lashings, stopped again to peer at Julie, mouth beginning to open in awareness, eyes narrowing.

"What, what're you doing?" he asked. He struggled again.

Looked around, then out of the door. All of a sudden he was back. Scowling at Julie, he began to wrestle in earnest. "AH! AHHH!" Jaqzen exclaimed. "Let me out, Pine! Let me out!" Now he yanked on the straps. "Let me out right now, or I'll..." With that, he began to heave his considerable weight this way and that. Soon he would be loose and upon her. He roared. The sound terrified her. *"I'LL KILL YOU!"* he thundered. Jaqzen pulled, wrenching with one arm, gritting his teeth, tendons bulging in his massive neck. His face, red with effort and rage, was a mask of ferocity. The strap, under great stress, slipped a bit. Julie cast about fearfully, opening drawers quickly, looking for something that might help her. Jaqzen's eyes, wide with fury, followed her gaze, realizing her plan. A horrible sound of tearing now struck her ears. She looked to see that he was physically ripping through the belt tied around his hands, space-age material designed to hold the weight of two men. In another moment he'd be free.

In that brief span of time Julie had managed to get a number of things into her pack. In a panic, she found the flashlight, a heavy metal thing, and ran behind Jaqzen, swinging it madly at his head. Though still tied, he was able to move out of the way, and she missed. Again she swung and again missed. Jaqzen now freed his hands. He got up, but immediately fell, thanks to his ankle lashings. As he tumbled, arms flailing for something to grab hold of, one hand knocked the flashlight out of Julie's and it crashed to the floor. The sound of it breaking apart masked another sound, it was the side of Jaqzen's head cracking against the solid arm of her chair.

He lay now, silently, while blood slowly pooled on the floor of the Strong Box. Julie stood, breathing heavily, not knowing what to do.

A nausea came upon her then, and, overcome by revulsion, she gagged, suppressing an urge to vomit. After a moment, though, the feeling past, she reached down and tentatively felt Jaqzen's neck for a pulse.

It throbbed there. Rapidly. Just knocked out, then. She felt oddly relieved. At least she wasn't going to be responsible for the first killing in this new world. Confident he would eventually escape, she cut another piece of strap and retied it around Jaqzen's wrists, then set to gathering supplies and loading them into her pack.

With one flashlight now gone, she took the other, Jaqzen's, leaving the big man with nothing to use at night. *All the better,* she thought. Then another thought struck her: *The pistol.* Yes. She found it, and dropped it into the bottom of her pack. "No killing for you, least not with that," she said. If he was so tough, let him meet the wildlife on their terms. Then, *wait.* She looked in his storage area. Ah, two sizable rifles. There were also six cases of ammunition, a thousand shells each. Looked like he was either planning a killing spree galore or to be here a long time. Quickly, she grabbed the guns and set them by the door, then dragged the ammo out and over. She'd hide or bury them.

Something else nagged at her. She walked back over to the unconscious giant. Looking at him, she felt his pockets. A knife. *Let him keep it.* Then she remembered the heavy-looking object in that leg pocket she'd first seen in Karstens' office. *Let's see what this is,* she thought, opening it. Sure enough, a gleaming, ivory-handled six-shooter. A treasured favorite, probably. *Okay, how do you undo this thing?* She fumbled, careful not to touch the trigger. Finally, the side fell open, and there she saw the six bullets. Lifting the gun end up, they fell out into her hand. She closed the barrel again and put the gun back, then refastened Jaqzen's pocket. *Let him think he forgot the bullets.*

Having loaded her pack, Julie lifted, dropped it. *Wow,*

heavy, she thought. It was never meant to hold so much at a time. Well, it'd have to last her thirty days. Then she remembered where ... *when* she was. Despite her fears, her heart leapt. She turned around to gaze at the shafts of light streaming in through the open door. Tiny particles of dust from the outside hovered there, slowly churning in the waft of air that brought them in. She could feel the gentle flush of breeze on her skin.

Lifting her pack, Julie grit her teeth, and, taking a breath, pushed the door open wider with her foot. It swung easier this time, revealing a familiar scene - that wonderful, magnificent view from Karstens' recording.

Light and warmth fell fully upon her now, which made her realize how cool the inside the Strong Box was. *Cold, actually.* She wanted out.

Julie took a step, then another, transfixed by that exquisite scene. There was birdsong all around her - in trees living and green. The air smelled wonderfully fresh and fragrant. The sky was a pure, sweet blue. A warm breeze ruffled her hair, while distantly, an animal called.

No time for that now! She set the pack against the side, then reentered to drag out the ammo, case by case, hiding them within a large, dense shrub behind the Strong Box.

There was one last thing to do. Julie found some of her extra clothes, and, outside, doffed her green jumpsuit, dressing in attire much more comfortable and suitable for the exertions ahead. She stored the suit inside.

She glanced back at Jaqzen; still unconscious, though the movement of his chest was normal. She wondered how long he'd be out. How much of a head start she'd have. *Better get a move on.* She straightened and made to depart. Then a thought occurred to her. What if Jaqzen couldn't get out this time, perhaps too weak from the knock he'd suffered? He'd slowly starve to death and she'd come back in thirty days to the decomposed body of the man still lying there. Then what would she do? Julie decided to even the odds a bit. She took the knife she'd earlier found in his pocket and set it on a small, raised bank in the control wall, perhaps five feet away. When Jaqzen came to, he'd see it, and, with effort, could make his way over to it and perhaps kick it down with his legs. Eventually, he'd cut himself free. By then Julie hoped to be long gone and out of range. In a twisted sort of way, she was actually glad for this turn of events; she'd never really wanted to travel with him, anyway.

Out again, Julie tied the rifles loosely to the top of her pack, then lifted, struggled and fought to get it on. God, it was *heavy!* She wouldn't be able to carry this load for long. But she had to lose them, for her sake, as well as the safety of the indigenous wildlife.

Which way, then? She'd have to decide now. Looking south was a long, somewhat broad ridge, mostly open, but with patches of low growth and trees. It appeared to run for miles in that direction. Behind her, the forest thickened. To her right, in the distance, was the sea and that long, sloping prairie leading to it. It tempted her. Finally, though, she decided to follow the ridge south where she would have a good view all the way around.

A noise. She turned to look. Jaqzen, still out, making a slight grunting. Fear washed over her, fear and unease. She wondered if she'd made the right choice. Maybe she should have done him in, then she wouldn't have to live the next thirty days wondering if he was lurking nearby, ready to strike. *No,* she thought, *I'm not a killer. Best to go, then.* With her foot, she closed the door of the Strong Box. It shut with a decisive *click.* She meant it as a message. *Stay away. You do not belong here. You are not welcome here.*

Then turning around, and bending slightly under the load, she set out.

Julie walked in rapture. *Eden, surely this is it.* Soon as she was out of sight of the box, her fears, and even thoughts of Jaqzen, evaporated. The warmth of the sun felt so good on her skin. It had been a long time since she'd felt it unfiltered by dirty air. She was walking through knee-high grass. She studied it. It was grass, she was sure, yet it was also somehow different. There were tiny flowers on the top and sides of the blades, fuchsia and white in color. A zephyr of sea air blew continually and they responded in waves that ran up the slope and stretched out on over the top. Her hair, too, blew out to her left. Julie thought she could smell it now, the sea, that certain salty flavor that spoke of the tide, of waves crashing and gulls crying, of hot sand and slumber. How she wished Tom was here.

Though she shifted the rifles periodically from one shoulder to the other, she was tiring rapidly under their weight. They were sapping her energy. She had to unload them soon. Twenty minutes out from the Strong Box, Julie decided the time had come. Looking around instinctively to make sure she wasn't being followed, she sat down on the ground, then, with the weight of the pack resting there, she slipped her arms out of the straps and stood. A feeling of lightness made her steps springy.

To her left and down the ridge on that side, the vegetal growth was tight. Chaparral. She knew it was evolving, adapting to the coming change in climate. In time it would cover so much of California's landscape as to typify the state in the minds of non-Californians. But that was a long, long way off, as far as she was concerned. A lovely, sage-like fragrance, typical of the chaparral community after a balmy summer's day, wafted to her nose. *Ah, Salvia clevelandii,* she thought, *Musk Sage, with its peculiar, ball-shaped flowerheads and splendid blue florets.* Hummingbirds were zooming around them, competing for a taste of its nectar.

Reaching out, she touched it, felt it, loved it. *You'll have a long, noble history here*, she thought.

There were other plants below, too. Lots of Coyote Brush, and here and there, familiar Yuccas stood out with tall loads of creamy white flowers that people would later call *Our Lord's Candle*. And unfamiliar plants. Flowering in crimson, violets, and yellows. *What are they*, she wondered? Even to her specialized scientific mind they were new. One, a delicate vine that crept over the other, harder-edged plants, had tiny orange flowers. Bees large and small zipped in and out among them, thrilling to the variety of choice, eager to gather as much of the precious nectar as their diminutive bodies could carry. To pollinate. Julie thrilled.

Surely a world like this will last forever. It has to, it felt so right. A brief memory from the far future threatened to mar her reverie, a world so horribly different as to be almost alien. The memory didn't last. *This is now. This is real. This is truth.*

She remembered why she stopped, walked back to the pack and untied the rifles. Heading to the overhang that swept down the left side of the ridge, she hefted one, gauged the trajectory, leaned back, then swung hard. Silently the rifle flew over the tight, tangled wood, turning in a quiet counterclockwise as if in slow motion. It seemed to take minutes to sail outwards, then down, down it went, never to be recovered. Maybe one day, one day in the far future, someone would find the barely discernible impression of what looked like a gun in a rock. It would be brought to the attention of authorities, then stuck in a category with many others. An *"Oopart"* they'd label it. An Out Of Place Artifact. A convenient place to store - and forget - disturbing anomalies. *Perchance my footprints will be there too*, she thought.

Seizing the other, she hurled it as well. Soundlessly it went over the side, until it, too, was out of sight. This was followed by the pistol. Lastly went the lead she'd removed from Jaqzen's revolver. With its disappearance went her anxiety about the senseless slaughter he had schemed. Every bullet gone was a life saved.

An eagle glided over the area, perhaps attracted by the unusual sight. She drew in her breath, held it, watching. A whisper of breeze ruffled its feathers. There were shadows from the sun on the pines below. And warmth. A squirrel running across the ground, then up a tree. The scent of pine, of ... impossibly clean air. The oxygen here, she recalled, is richer, exceptional. She exhaled, a feeling almost of intoxication.

Julie turned and headed back to her pack. With the extra weight gone, it was substantially lighter. Still heavy, but welcome. When she shouldered it now, she wasn't bent. *I can handle this.* Looking around her again, just to take in the sights, she smiled, then set out once more on her path along the ridge, which undulated into remoteness.

As she walked, Julie picked out the names of animals. As expected, there were numerous horses about, downslope to her right. Herds of them of various sizes, mostly abiding with their own, but, she observed, there was also some co-mingling. At this distance, she could only guess the species, soon giving that up. It was strange that fossils were more recognizable than the real thing.

Closest to her, browsing in the shade of some large oaks, were *Protohippus* and *Archaeohippus,* diminutive horses of two hundred fifty and a hundred thirty pounds respectively. Farther on, near the lee of a large pond, was a small herd of *Desmatippus.* Down a side flank of the mountain and spreading out a long way was a large herd of *Scaphohippus,* an abundant, small, three-toed horse, standing three feet at the shoulder. They seemed to be less group oriented than the others. Within their throngs grazed *Acritohippus*. At the edges and within the forested areas was *Hypohippus*. It weighed in at five hundred plus pounds.

She searched, but failed to find *Miohippus*. And that would be as expected, since it would have recently become extinct. *You never know, though,* Julie thought, *one could still turn up.*

She topped a little rise, then descended through a saddle. She noticed that the ridge was gradually lowering, with other ridges branching off at perpendicular angles, each a temptation to follow, to explore. After a few minutes, she topped the other side of the saddle and saw spread before her a spectacular panorama of ocean and cliffs, perhaps five miles away. A wide, shallow bay, fed by a river, cut several miles back into the land. It was bordered by low, green hills that seemed to run to the horizon. Above it were enchanting, cottonball clouds set in a deep blue sky, the bluest sky she had ever seen, and just below were large birds gliding in graceful arcs. Julie sighed. Then she looked closer, paused, and removed her pack. She was after her binoculars. Finding them, she focused on the gliders. Her heart sped up. She adjusted the glasses, and her jaw dropped. She let out a loud whoop now and laughed.

The birds were indeed very large. White chest and head, with bicolored, gray wings, to a non-expert they would have appeared to be merely some sort of jumbo pelican or gull. Julie knew better. This was *Osteodontornis*. With a wingspan of twenty feet from tip to tip and a standing height of four feet, it was one of the largest birds ever. And there it was, sailing above the blue of the sea as if it had always been and would always be. Julie clapped her hands and danced around a bit then, there on the ridge, in the middle of the Miocene.

Those horses closest to her lifted their heads to stare at the strange sight. *What is this biped? What is it doing?* After a moment, though, sensing no danger, they went back to grazing, but kept a wary eye out all the same.

Julie snapped a button on the binocs and it became a camera. Again she zoomed in on the osteodonts and began to photograph. *What a job I've got!* she thought.

As the day wore on, the temps rose, and Julie unscrewed the cap to her water bottle and began to drink the last from it, then stopped herself. Why was she drinking water from her time? True, it was the best you could buy, but... she poured the rest on the ground, then headed toward a spring she'd noticed. Cold, clear water bubbled up from below. Tentatively, she bent and sampled it. It tasted of earth. Fresh. Delicious. Forgetting the filter, she drank, and drank more, she then flushed and refilled her bottle. Tiny bits of dirt and organic matter swirled around. Its clarity was not to code. But this was *clean* dirt. She remembered as a child her father had explained the difference: there was clean dirt: natural soil, which contained minerals we needed and organic matter that, for the most part, we had evolved with. That's why you could drink spring water and not get sick. Then there was dirty dirt. That was anything polluted, usually by man. Oily, chemically, radiologically, you wouldn't drink it unless your life depended upon it, and even then maybe not.

To be sure, there would be plenty of instances, she knew, where she'd use the filter. A standing pool of water could be stagnant. Even flowing streams could be havens for bacteria like Giardia if infected wildlife had eliminated into them. But springs could be counted on. Generally streams, too, were fine. One could create a makeshift filter in a stream by digging a path for some of the water to flow into, and within that, two or three little bowls in succession. Each would act as traps to catch debris, etc. By the time the water was out of the last one, it was generally cleaner.

Julie removed her shirt and bra. The warm air felt cool on her breasts, which were wet with perspiration. With no cover though, the sweat would quickly evaporate and she knew better than to hike bare in this sun. She did not need a sunburn, so after hanging the bra on the top of her pack to dry, she re-donned the outer long-sleeved shirt, but left it unbuttoned. It felt freeing to allow her breasts to bounce and sway with the motion of her gait.

Although she estimated the height of the ridge upon which she walked to be no more than perhaps a thousand feet, she could clearly see the land around her on all sides. For the most part, it was lower, flatlands and foothills, with some mountainous terrain near the coast: the ancestral Santa Anas, she assumed. Far to the northeast, though, it rose again to a lovely grandeur: the nascent Sierras. At 8,000 feet, give or take, they stood at roughly half the height of her time. With sustained uplift, they'd continue their ascent to the sky. Yet, with the Pleistocene glaciations still millions of years away, Yosemite's famous domes and prominences weren't there yet.

She could guess the plant life there: at no higher than 1,500 feet grew oaks, and reaching to 2,500 feet would be Cypress, Big Cone Spruce, Douglas Fir, and Tanbark Oak. These would spread down the central west Sierran slope. Within this community would be Madrone, Ironwood, Pacific Wax Myrtle, some fan palms, *Sapotaceae,* Pinon pine with their edible, highly nutritious nuts, and the lovely Rhododendron. Also found would be good old avocado, a luxury she'd not enjoyed in many years. She wondered about them, hopefully she'd find out soon. On the eastern side of the Sierras at the lower margin of mixed conifer forest would be a live oak woodland savanna. Species of oak found there would include Canyon Live, Mesa, and Interior Live Oaks. There would be a number of Poplars as well, including *alexanderii*, a small-leaved cottonwood; *subwashoensis,* aka Verdi poplar, and *payettensis.* In the northern Sierras would be Sequoias, of course, and Arborvitae, Fir, and growing below them, masses of Red Huckleberries, and on and on. No doubt she'd also run across many species still undiscovered by modern man. The prospect of uninhibited exploration excited her scientific mind.

By an hour later, the ridge had lowered considerably and along with horses, she began to see myriad camel species. There was *Nothotylopus,* and *Australocamelus,* a specimen she recalled that weighed in at 320 pounds. *Pliauchenia* and *Michenia mudhillsensis,* which ran to 500 pounds. And there was *Rakomylus.* Most abundantly were the big *Aepycamelus,* which stood ten feet tall and weighed up to 1,800 pounds.

Finally, she saw the huge *Zygolophodon.* Herds of the mammoth, five and a half ton proboscidean were lingering around a large mud hole, playing, spraying, and rolling in it. Others were pulling bark from some yellow-flowered acacia trees exactly like their distant descendants, the elephants, would do. The Zygolophodon, like their, at his point, rarer proboscidean cousins, the *Gomphotheres,* in fact aided the spread of grasses and the evolution of horses and other cursorial fauna by their stripping of bark and felling of trees. At one time, their arrival in North America was used as a marker of the beginning of the Barstovian age. Before their entry, all was dark, dense, closed jungle and forest.

Julie sat now, lower down on the western slope of the ridge, tall grass blowing around her, concealing her, and listened. This is what a *natural* world sounds like. Smells like. Feels like. All sensation. Scents and fragrances. Visual and aural. Nothing harsh, abrasive or offensive.

A large, clumsy beetle buzzed past her nose and she jerked back, startled, then laughed. It felt good to do. It'd been too long since she had. She lay back in the grass, her shirt falling open, the sun caressing her skin. All kinds of insect sounds were around her. In fact, Julie now noticed that very fast flyers zipped here and there just over the tops of the grass. Sometimes one would collide with a blade taller than normal and instantly be down. In a minute, it would climb back to the top, lift its wings and be off again on its mission of urgency.

Spying through her binocs a hidden canyon covered in sycamores and shadows to the left of bay, she momentarily thought that it could make a good camp. Still, she was only about three hours from the Strong Box - and Jaqzen. Probably too close. She wanted to see it, though. But first, the bay itself called to her. The sea marked the long line of a transform fault that would later become the San Andreas fault system, the demarcation between the North American plate, which was moving southeast, and the Pacific Plate, which was moving northwest. The future coast ranges were still under water or emerging as islands.

She sat up, got a drink from her bottle, then stood and hefted the pack on her shoulders again. Then she set her feet in the direction of the part of the bay closest to the canyon.

It took her two hours to get there. She followed faunal paths that twisted and turned, bent and curved, zigzagged and meandered.

Rarely were they straight for long, except when she finally got to level ground. She could have saved half the time just cutting across the waving grasses, but was interested in these trails. Eventually, though, she reached the bay, a graceful sweep of sand and surf.

To stand here, she thought, *and see nothing but blue expanse, hear nothing but seabirds and the lap and pound of waves on the shore is otherworldly.*

There was a large, roundish boulder to the right of the upland and its shaded ravine, and, as Julie approached, a dozen turtles slipped off it and into the water with a dozen soft splashes. She removed her shoes and walked with them in her hands, stopping when she saw the giant leatherback turtle, *Psephophorus californiensis*, on the far side. A huge thing, it was three times the size of modern leatherbacks. It turned its head to regard her, probably wondering what she was, then made its sluggish way back to the water. Soon it was gone.

Julie decided to go for a swim, too, and removed her clothes, setting them down on one side of the boulder. Then she stuck a speculative toe in and found, to her surprise, that the water was warm. She didn't know why she was surprised as she knew it *would* be. Gently, she launched and loved the feel of Miocene water on her skin. Under the surface, sounds disappeared, only pearly beads of air, both from her and gases from the decomposing detritus buried below, made any note. It was ethereal.

> *O Land, O Earth, O Sea, O Skies,*
> *how beautiful you are to my eyes.*

Julie swam there for the better part of an hour. Finally, she reached down and took some sediment and began to scrub the oils from her skin. A Miocene sea bath.

> *O the water falling from my hands, through my open fingers,*
> *like a cascade of stars, sparkling, twinkling, glittering, back*
> *home to the sea.*

Overhead the osteodonts glided, landed on prominences, and walked awkwardly near their grassy nests. Their call was not what she'd expected. Julie had assumed it would be loud and raucous; instead it was more like quiet chatter, reminiscent of sea gulls. This, though, could be punctuated with sudden shrill exclamations if another flew too close. But that was the exception.

Julie walked out now, dripping water, Rachel Welch-like. Only this was *15 million years B.C.* She lay down on the warm sand, in the shelter of a low cliff. Closed her eyes. Fell asleep.

By and by, she awoke to find a group of very strange creatures nearby. They were ambling out of the water and looking uncertainly at her. They looked almost like sea hippos. Julie sat up, amazed. *Desmostylus.* Apparently, she'd appropriated their resting area. She stared back, smiled.

"Hello, Desi," she said softly.

The Desmostylus moved their bulk from one foot to the other, eyes anxious, not knowing what to do. Should they flee or should they stay? Their genetic memories contained no hint of her species.

So comfortable was Julie that she hesitated to get up, and yet she did not want to upset these great creatures who likely had called this very spot home for who knew how long.

"Okay, I'll go," she said at long last, and in regret. "Nice to meet you." Slowly, she stood, then walked over to her clothes. The beasts began to make loud barking noises and she nearly had to cover her ears.

When she was dressed, she turned to say goodbye, but something caught her eye. Movement. *Different.* She looked, looked again, focused. Then froze. On the ridge above was a figure. Upright. Quickly going to her pack she dug out the binocs, then crouched behind the boulder, carefully pointing them at the figure and zeroed in. He stood there with his own binoculars looking down, down in her direction. Jaqzen. A big bulk of a man. He'd seen her, surely. Julie's heart began to beat hard in her chest. She'd forgotten he was an expert tracker. Then an arm went up ... a wave? No, it was a rifle, pointing at the sky. *How?* A shot in the air, barely audible. A way of saying, *I see you.* Julie swallowed. Crouching back behind the boulder, she looked again in the direction of the hidden canyon. If she ran that way he would undoubtedly note it. There was in fact, she surmised, *nowhere* she could go and not be seen. Still, she had to try.

God, why hadn't she done him in when she had the chance? Instead, like a trusting schoolgirl, she'd walked along the ridge, an obvious route, probably leaving a path anyone could follow. She glanced around the corner of the rock again. Gone. Not there - then - *Yes, there he is! Running downhill!* Hastily, Julie hoisted the pack onto her back and raced toward the canyon.

Seventeen

For two days Tom slept in a temperature-driven stupor, unaware that several interesting things were occurring. One, was the fact that Little had assumed the position of sentry. For such a small aelurodon, she had a very loud bark, which sent most of the large beasts packing. Fortunately, those that didn't were harmless herbivores, which would dully eye the yapper and continue chewing, seemingly in a stupor of their own. If Tom had been aware and well, he'd have found Little's frustrated attempts to scare these huge sluggards away hilarious.

Another interesting thing had to do with Tom himself. Though in an unconscious, muttering, oneiric state, he had gotten up several times to find water, chew bitter willow bark and relieve himself, each time returning to sleep on his bed of grass under the trees. He would remember none of it.

After the two days were up, strength returned, and with it, cognizance. Opening his eyes, he gazed up at the light filtering through the leaves above. A glorious sunrise. Turning his head, Tom briefly wondered about that, then remembered. He'd been sick. Now, though, he felt better. *Much* better. Instantly, there was Little by his face, grinning, if ever a dog could be said to grin, her entire body wagging in tune with her tail. Then, strangely, she decided to climb over and stand with her feet on either side of his head, warm, fluffy belly covering his eyes and tickling his nose. He laughed.

Lifting her, Tom sat up and rested her in his lap. *My, she is getting bigger,* he thought. Then he looked around himself, amazed. The carcasses of a dozen ground squirrels were scattered about him. Perhaps she'd left them in hopes that he'd eat and get better. And indeed, he *was* hungry, mighty hungry. Then an odd thought, a wisp of memory. In his previous ailing condition *he'd eaten them too.* Surprise and revulsion followed. Then practicality: they'd likely aided his recovery. He just hoped he'd cooked them first.

Okay, I can eat ground squirrels. He looked around at those lying on the ground. How long had they been there? He did not want to get sick again.

Setting Little down, he stood and looked at the bounty. While some had flies or wasps on them, others did not. Fresh kills? Tom reached down and felt one. Still warm and soft. Then another. The same. Then another. And another. In all, he found seven good, obviously recent kills, and so, after building a fire, he set to skinning them one by one with his knife, then skewering, roasting and eating them. They were good, there was no denying it. Though there were some initial dull pangs of conscience, they were outweighed by the sharp pangs of hunger that gnawed at his stomach. Still, Tom was glad that he wasn't the one doing the actual killing.

Physically, he looked a wreck. His clothes were dirty and he stunk, a combination of body odor and sulfur from the hot spring. The rash was still there, but not nearly as itchy as it had been. Apparently, his insistent, though unconscious, scratching had actually sped up the healing process. Rather than the sensitive light pink swellings of two days prior, now it was a deeper and slightly hardened, rufous color. He wondered and worried what it was. Then he had an idea. Finding the P.I., he aimed it at his left thigh where a large patch was and snapped.

Accessing Database

Then came back the diagnosis and description:

Toxicodendron diversilobum
Poison Oak

Contact Hazard

A small to medium-sized shrub generally 2 to 6 feet high.
Identified by its characteristic "leaves of three."
Capable of causing a miserable, itchy rash
which can last days or weeks.
Not to be confused with non-toxic lookalikes
Blackberry (*Rubus ursinus*) or "Squaw Bush" (*Rhus trilobata*).
After exposure, wipe affected area with alcohol
within 3 to 4 hours to remove or lessen effect.

Tom clicked on the icon indicating that there were photos available. These he studied. Now he remembered having pushed his way through the stuff back in the forest when he was coming down the hill from the Strong Box. He'd thought it was quite lovely then, and certainly it was, but it was one plant he would not make the mistake of *touching* again.

Sitting down, he glanced at his feet. Ah yes, another of his recent misfortunes. Pulling a bare foot up to his lap, he studied it. Gone were the puffy swellings. They were replaced by flattened, hardened skin. *Good,* he thought. It was the same with his other maladies. The jock rash had passed, likely also helped by the sulfur. The tick bites had receded to tiny pinpricks of red. The sunburn had darkened his shoulders. There the skin was just beginning to peel. All in all, things were improving. And they would improve, of that Tom was determined - determined, that is, where he could help it, not to make the same mistakes again.

Suddenly he thought of Julie. Getting up, he ran to his pack, still lying by the hot spring. Tom flushed with gratitude when he saw it. Unmolested. It could easily have been ripped and pilfered or snatched and carried off by some curious creature attracted by the lingering smell of food. And it did smell, bits of the entelodont he'd collected for Little still within.

Brushing all of that aside, though, he found the PinPointer and hurriedly switched it on, eager to see where his wife was now. In the time he'd been out, she could be even farther away then she was before. He held his breath. There was a pause, then a beep. *A* beep. *One* beep. One light, the red one. The green was not there. Slowly his mouth opened in fear. *No. Please no.* Almost in answer the green beacon abruptly popped on and began to beep too. Tom let out his breath and said another thank you, a lopsided smile cutting raggedly across his face. *Thank God.*

Happily, rather than farther away this time, Julie had actually closed the distance between them. At twelve miles, however, it wasn't much. The red light representing Jaqzen had closed as well. He was now nineteen miles from Julie. Alarming.

Then the green light went out. *What the...?* It stayed out. Tom suddenly worried that something was wrong with his Pin-Pointer. He gave it a shake, tapped on the crystal. It made no difference. The green light was gone. Tom gulped and tried to figure out what it might mean. Had he just witnessed Julie's death? Had she perhaps fallen over a cliff or been attacked by a wild beast? Or maybe, maybe it was something more benign, but just as worrying: maybe her PinPointer was malfunctioning, caused possibly by an inadvertent bump on a hard surface? Or could it be losing power, the solar cell batteries that fueled the device finally past their normal life? To be sure, her trip was only supposed to last thirty days.

The chance that any of these scenarios might be true sent icy cold shafts of fear through his psyche. He tried to think of other possibilities. Could there be another reason why was the green light was out, then on, then out again, while the other remained on the whole time? Why, in fact, had the two lights been separated by so much distance? He knew why that was, but had not wanted to acknowledge it to himself before: Julie was on the run. She was being chased. It was the only logical explanation.

Then... Tom thought, maybe what was happening with the green light was *something else.* Maybe she was *intentionally* switching it off so as not to give her position away to Jaqzen, only turning it on when she noticed the blue light, his own light, blinking at the top of her screen. That would mean that she knew someone else was here, likely to try to rescue her. Of course, it would mean that Jaqzen was also aware that somebody else had arrived. He'd probably been watching his own screen, not only to seek and find Julie, but also to monitor this newcomer, this threat to his plans, whoever he might be. Tom switched his beacon off.

He wondered if Julie had been on the run from the start, thinking it only about five weeks since her launch. Had he known that, in actuality, it was more like four months since she'd arrived, he would have been horrified. Yet, somehow she had managed to elude Jaqzen, a trained tracker, all that time.

Tom's breathing was rapid and again he felt the need for speed. But now he knew that would be foolhardy. If he was going to reach her at all he had to be smart about it. Running wasn't an option; not only would he exhaust himself again, he could attract the attention of a pursuit predator. No, he'd go as fast as he could and still get there in one piece. In the meantime, Julie would have to take care of herself. There was no other way. But he had confidence in her: she had an uncommon intelligence and strength of character. *She could do it.* And he hoped the discovery that someone else was here and headed toward her would give her courage.

Something puzzled him, though. *How did she know that my beacon was on and was then able to respond to it if hers was turned off so as not to give away her position?* Tom scratched his head, then, frowning, he looked at his PinPointer, turning it over in his hands. He'd been given only a brief orientation to the technical equipment before he left. There was only one switch on the device that he could see: On / Off. He turned it over again; that's when he saw the seam, an almost invisible line around the two-inch screen. *Hmm.*

He picked at it, careful not to use too much force. *Snap!* The screen lifted on an internal hinge revealing other controls beneath. *Ah!* Tom nodded. There was a focusing dial, a brightness display, along with a "Filter" button, which was a mystery. At the bottom were "Tone On / Off" and "Beacon On / Off" switches. He smiled. So she wasn't turning it completely off then, only the wristband beacon part, the tone she kept on. When she heard that second beep and knew someone else was "online", she'd switch her beacon on briefly to alert him to her presence, then would switch it off again. *Clever.*

He wanted to test it out. She might not respond this time seeing as she'd just done so moments before. On the other hand, she could realize that it was a test, an attempt at communication. Tom turned his own beacon and tone off, clicked the screen shut, then switched PinPointer back on. Instantly came Jaqzen's beep and his red light. He waited for several minutes. No green. Then he reopened the lid and turned his beacon and tone on and waited again. Ten seconds later, he heard it, *"Beep!"* and there was her green light. It stayed on momentarily, then was off again. That confirmed it; she did know someone else was here, and they had just communicated. This pittance of contact was almost as good as a telephone call. His heart soared!

Now if only they could think of a way to make these communications exclusive to themselves. The Focus button? He switched on again. There was Jaqzen, and then, seconds later, Julie. He adjusted the dial. It brought the area where the red and green dots were closer to the center of the screen, making them appear larger. This was accompanied by a long string of rapidly changing digits that increased or decreased as the resolution did. Green switched off again and so did he. Okay, give it a rest, she was probably getting antsy about this.

So Focus was not going to work as he'd hoped. Again he studied the device, but could find no way to limit it to one person. *Crud.* Tom sighed. He hoped for Julie's sake that Jaqzen hadn't been paying attention, that he hadn't caught on to their little breakthrough.

Tom wanted to set out immediately, but he needed to wash himself and get the filth out of his clothing. Not only would dirt and grime weaken the fibers and thus the lifespan of his garments, it would be an irritant and possible health issue for him. He did have another scrubbed pair in the pack, but wanted a clean backup. Roughly cramming his gear, they headed over to a clean water pool. A few *Dromomeryx* that had been standing nearby sauntered off. It wasn't fast enough for Little's liking, though, and she set to barking and chasing. They hightailed it, and the little rabble-rouser trotted back triumphantly.

Stripping again and getting the soap bar, Tom waded into the pool. It was shallow and warm. He remained standing and set to washing, the soap and water that splashed off clothes and him turning the water opaque. The mud he kicked up quickly enveloped that bit of pollution.

"Sorry guys," Tom apologized to the blithely watching *Cranioceras.* When he was clean, he walked out, got the towel from his pack, dried and dressed. Indeed, he felt great. Strangely better than he had in a long time. Now he reloaded everything with care.

"Well, Little, are you about ready?" The scruffy aelurodon looked up at her human expectantly. "Let's try to do it better this time, shall we?" Staring at him now with closed mouth, she turned her head this way and that. Tom paused, then corrected himself, "Okay, *I'll* try to do it better this time!" He reached down to pet his growing companion. "You could use a bath, too, you know," he snorted. She stood, grinning again, ready to be underway. Tom gazed at his decided upon route, off toward the hills to the South. They would be heading in that direction, up a low, grassy rise dotted with a few trees and scattered with small herds of grazing animals. He knew from his previous observations that eventually they would come to an inland part of the sea that was surrounded by gentle hills, and to the far west of it, what looked like a large island.

"Well then, my friend, let's be going!" Tom said. Pointing a finger stiffly toward the horizon, he shouted, *"Ho!"*

Along the way, Tom often veered from the path to inspect the glossy fruit growing from a particular tree or shrub. If it looked appealing, and if the wildlife seemed to favor it, he would pick and taste it, testing for edibility. Anything bitter was spit out. Everything else he consumed. After thinking about this strategy further, he decided to use the added precaution of prior identification with the P.I. No sense poisoning himself on a lark.

As now usual, Little would run off whenever she heard the shrill calls of ground squirrels. The sound seemed to excite her at an instinctual level, and occasionally one would be caught off guard. Then, rather than retreat into the hole where she stood guard, it would take off at a run, and the chase would be on. Little was quick in the short-term, but if the pursuit was long, her growing weight began to slow her down. Some day, he surmised, she might not be able to rely on speed. He wondered what she'd do then.

A couple of hours later, the land began to get softer and slightly mushy, interspersed with a more normal, solid feel. He trudged on without giving it much thought. When it became mushy again, his feet sinking slightly, he looked down wonderingly. The ground was wet. His shoes were wet. He glanced around for Little and discovered her keeping pace off to his left on higher terrain about fifty yards away. He headed that way.

After a few minutes, climbing to another rise, Tom looked back toward the lowland and now noticed that it was scattered with lots of pools of water, but few animals. Of course, he'd seen these pools pretty much the whole way so far, but now there were more of them. They were also larger, and farther down the hill, some had coalesced into small lakes. Indeed the whole area had a saturated feel about it. Better stick to higher ground.

Up ahead, half a mile or so, he noticed that a large river cut across their path. He watched it as they closed in. At two hundred yards, the sound of its rushing became noticeable, seeming to increase with every few steps. Little eyed it too, looking unsure, perhaps afraid. She began to slow, then trail Tom, getting farther and farther behind. He turned and called, but she held back, still following, but cautious and uncertain, taking tentative steps now.

At twenty yards, the sound of surging waters loud, Tom stopped and examined the situation. Where the water ran downhill, it seemed gradually to spread out, cascading over small boulders and toppled trees, falling over itself in a mad rush to oblivion far off. Uphill, the scene was more serene. The river there, though swift, was much reduced in width, probably because, he assumed, time and flow had carved a deep gorge. Still, it looked to be no less than maybe fifteen feet wide at its narrowest. He decided that if they were going to get across, that way was the way to go. Tom turned to find Little again by his side. While he stood, she'd crept up. She was looking at him and glancing around as if trying to find another way altogether. Tom bent down and smiled, stroking her head.

"Don't worry, Little," he said, raising his voice to be heard above the tumult, *"It'll be okay. But we do have to get across."* He looked uphill again. It was fairly steep, but open country. With his eyes, he followed the course of the river distantly to where it seemed to originate in the space between two high hilly ranges. On either side was thick vegetal growth, short trees and shrubs, growing in the perpetual moisture.

They began their ascent. In a minute's time, Tom was huffing, but he felt good. He stuck his thumbs under the shoulder straps of his pack and took it one slow step at a time. All the while, the sound of the river and its swirling mists charmed him. Tiny droplets of water clung to them. Once, he surprised a small grazer of unknown derivation hidden in the dark, tangled growth next to the torrent. Evidently, his clumsy steps were unheard. It jerked, then quickly bounded away. Little gave no chase, letting it go free and unmolested. She was tiring a bit from the hike, or saving her energy for wiser pursuits, something more her size and which she had a better chance of catching. *Good,* thought Tom.

Up they climbed, Little showing less fear of the river now. They came to a small rivulet that had carved its own tiny canyon, three feet across and as deep. Tom stopped, then walked to the edge and jumped, easily clearing the ditch. Little held back, though. Tom called, but she wouldn't jump; instead she walked along it a way until she found a narrower gap. This she jumped and ran back to Tom's side.

"Good girl!" he complimented. There were other such rivulets and offshoots to cross, each which added their waters to the whole, and she became more daring in her negotiations of them. On one particularly deep gully, however, having jumped, she slipped on the other side, and then was hanging onto the bank with her front paws, crying and trying desperately to pull herself over. Tom dove and grabbed her by the scruff, drawing her up. She cried piteously at that, perhaps reminded of punishment she received from mother when she'd done something wrong. Grab and toss. No real harm was meant of course, or incurred, but she'd learned its significance all the same. Tom held her close, his face buried in that thick, tawny-red fluff. *Silly girl.*

Still higher they climbed, Tom inhaling and exhaling rhythmically with each step, every so often stopping for a rest. At those times, he'd turn to look at the land, now far below, and, taking it all in, reveled in its phenomenal beauty. Upwards were areas of flatness, and he noticed that there the river would slow. At the third such flat patch, there was a large tree that had fallen across from one bank to the other. Between was a gulf of eighteen or twenty feet with rushing, foaming water just below. He'd spotted it because the growth on either side had been cleared and scores of hoof steps in soft mud converged on it. Plainly, it was being used as a bridge by other Barstovian fauna. There was a problem, though. Poison oak, for now Tom was well familiar with its look, was growing from the descending sides of the steep banks. It had grown up and partially around the log on both ends, tossing about in wind and spray being generated by the force of the river.

"*This is where we cross,*" Tom shouted. Little looked dubious. He turned to consider the P.O. again. He couldn't get across as it was, and that left him with no other choice than to try to remove it. Then he remembered that he had some cutters in his pack. He dropped it and dug into the small side pocket where they were, then walked nervously out onto the log a ways. A long stem of the green misery whipped menacingly in front of him. He grabbed it with a gloved hand and pulled toward him. It smacked his face, the drops of water on it running coldly down his neck.

"Oh that's lovely," he muttered, shaking his head. Fitting the cutters around the stem, he snipped it and dropped. In a second, it was out of sight downstream. This, Tom continued to do, bit by bit, until he was past this first load. He knew he'd have to wash his face, hands, and gloves when he was through.

He began walking across to the other side. In the middle, though, the deafening roar, the wind and wet, gave him a case of vertigo. Though broad, the wood was slick and he slipped, his heart leaping in fear, but he was just able to catch his balance before going over.

"Jeez!" he exclaimed, cursing. *"Be careful!"*.

Tom continued to the other side and repeated his pruning of the poison oak there, enjoying several more personal encounters. He turned then to go get Little. There she was, sitting at the end of the tree by his pack, waiting for him to return. Tom thought about calling her to come, but loathed the idea of her falling in, so he headed back to fetch her. Reunited, he surveyed his handy work. A nice, clear path, he hoped the other animals appreciated it. He slid the pack on, then stooped to pick up Little, groaning under her weight.

"This is where we go across, and you don't give me any trouble, all right?" he asked her. Little's eyes were wide with apprehension, which didn't help Tom's confidence any. Holding her tightly, he began to walk. Almost immediately she squirmed. Tom tried to hold on, but she wasn't having any of it.

"Be still!" he shouted, but holding a wriggling aelurodon while trying to cross a raging river on a slippery log was too much for him. Soon she was out and on the ground. Tom let out a volley of expletives. He reached to scoop her up again, but she jumped back and hustled just out of reach.

"Okay then, you want to stay here, be my guest!" Tom bellowed, his voice barely audible above the thundering din. He

turned and walked slowly back across to the other side, feeling bad for having shouted at her. Reaching it, he looked back, hoping to encourage Little across. She wasn't there. *Oh no,* he thought. He called out, but she failed to appear. Angry and frustrated, Tom made to head back once more. He supposed they'd have to find another way. Stepping out onto the log again, he walked most of the way across, when something caught his eye. He looked down and behind himself. There was Little, following him. She'd already come across hard on his heels and had made it to the other side. Probably she was wondering why he wanted to go back yet again. *"Oh my god!"* Tom said, exasperated. Then, rolling his eyes, he turned around. Little pivoted and walked deftly across. On the other side he shook his head, smiled, then laughed. Probably she'd seen his close call before and was not about to let him carry her.

Emerging from the trees, Tom saw a pond a hundred yards off, walked over, stripped and scrubbed his clothes with sand, then wrung them out and tied them to the back of his pack. After that, he stepped in and gave himself a sand scrubbing as well. Hopefully it would be enough to remove P.O. oils. His other clothes from earlier were dry by now, so he donned them, thinking what a lot of trouble all of this was. Truth was, though, he was loving this journey, every delightful, miserable minute of it. And he never forgot what and who it was for. Julie. She was ever in his mind.

A cascade of miniature butterflies, like empyrean glitter, suddenly spilled over the trees and danced above the meadow. Tom gaped, grinned, laughed again.

He could see that there would be other rivers to cross. Most of the large ones seemed to run down, then south, eventually ending in faraway deltas, bays and estuaries around the top of that huge inland sea. He still wondered about it.

Eighteen

For days they walked. Days on days. And the days became weeks. Over hill and dell they went. They forded rivers and streams, always brimming with fish. Picked their way along the sun-dappled shores and inlets of lakes and tarns. Scooted timidly across the sheer face of towering cliffs when the alternatives were worse. Pushed through tall grass and stiff thicket - lush, verdant growth that half-buried trees - and drier lands. If not for the journal, he'd have lost track completely. As the weeks dropped away, each of them was changing. Tom had stopped shaving his beard and combing his hair. It now ranged wild as the land around them, constantly tousled by the wind. He was also growing stronger, his breathing easier. His cough had vanished. The skin on his face darkened and his confidence increased, the set of his eyes now a little less fearful, a little more sure. He'd never felt better.

Little, too, was changing, and the rate amazed Tom. She had trebled her weight, constantly on the chase after ground squirrels. He suspected, though, that, with her increasing mass, she would soon lose her acrobatic edge and would have to begin hunting larger prey. Still, like her human, she was growing surer and more serious. When she barked at the large herbivores blocking their path, it now seemed to be less of a playful request and more of a warning. It alarmed Tom when she began to bite the running flanks of much larger beasts, and he worried about the possibility of a kick.

There was something else that Little began to do which annoyed him. As each day wore on and grew hotter, she would simply stop at some point under the shade of a large tree and refuse to go on. The first time this happened, Tom did not notice until he heard her bark and turned to find that she was sitting down a hundred yards away, ears pointed forward toward him. Her first two barks he'd missed, having gotten into a bit of a walking trance in the dripping heat. He called her, but she wouldn't budge. He wondered if something was wrong and tread back, but, having inspected her, found nothing. So he turned to continue and called her, checking to see that she was following. Still she sat, unmoving.

"Oh, for crying out loud!" Tom exclaimed. *"What is it?"* At this, Little lay down, mouth opening in a wide grin. Actually though, it was more of a pant, her sides heaving rapidly. Tom wiped the sweat from his face with his forearm, unknowingly smearing dirt across it. *Ah, so that's it,* he thought, *she needs a break.* He looked out under the boughs of the massive oak. Waves of heat were radiating upwards from the ground in the exposed areas. The cooling breezes of the morning had changed to hot gusts. *Okay,* he thought, *let's take one.* At this, he brought out the water and gave some to Little. They both drank readily.

Ten minutes or so later, he said, "OK, all rested?" He reached over and pat her on the head. She was still panting, but he was impatient to continue. Tom stood and re-donned his backpack. "Let's go, girl," he said. Still, she lay immobile. He frowned and repeated himself. Little's reaction was to roll over on her side, eyes half open, but still watching him. Tom shook his head. He knew that trying to carry her was out of the question. "Hey, who's the master here?" he said aloud. Her eyes closed.

Tom sighed. Then he swung his pack back off and again sat down. "Alright, I suppose you know this world better than I do." He plumped the pack like a pillow and lay down next to her. In a minute, he was out.

When he woke, the sun was high in the sky and hot. Little was still snoozing, now laying on Tom's other side. He drifted off again.

In all, they slept on and off under that tree for four hours. When finally he roused, Little was standing at the edge of the great oak's shade, looking out. It didn't seem quite so hot now and Tom sat up, to be greeted by a wagging aelurodon. She licked his face, adding to the smears of dirt that were accumulating there. His hair, too, was dirty and stood out in all directions. He felt hungry and thirsty. Then he noticed that there was a furry form lying in the grass nearby. Little bringing home the bacon. *Home,* he thought. *Home is where the heart is.*

He walked over to it. It was larger than a squirrel by several times. A rabbit. *Good*, Tom thought. He cleared the ground bare of grass and leaves, things that might catch fire, and then built one. When it was going, he set to skinning the animal, an unpleasant job. Finding a dropped branchlet, he speared and roasted it in the blaze. Fortunately, the boughs of the tree were high, so no spark alighted. Ten minutes later, the hare was cooked and they ate it eagerly. Little finished up by easily crunching and swallowing the bones. Nothing was wasted. When they were done, they headed to a stream of water and drank deeply. At least the *water* was still cool.

With the drift of time, Tom and Little fell into a routine: a couple of hours before noon, Little would decide that they'd gone far enough and would sit under a tree and bark until Tom noticed, then he'd walk back and there they slept or hung out until the stifling, tropical heat dissipated somewhat. They made up a bit for this loss by hiking on into the evenings when there was enough moonlight to see the plains ahead.

A couple of incidents along this stretch of the journey marked it indelibly on Tom's mind. The first was as they were walking through a dry canyon, its steep sides closing in, then falling back as they went. From the walls he sometimes saw fossils jutting out, strange skulls, leg bones, etcetera, and sometimes pieces of petrified trees, ferns or other plant life. At one point, in a pile of rubble near the bottom, were a bunch of them all jumbled up. A portion of the hill had slid off and with it went the fossils. What animal they once belonged to he couldn't tell, but it reminded him of Julie, and how thrilled she would have been to find them were they still back in the future. That's not what made the canyon walk so memorable though. It was the rattlesnake bite.

As they were moving down the path, suddenly he heard an odd, unfamiliar, clattering sound, not unlike a maracas. Tom continued on without giving it much attention, dulling thinking that it was pebbles dislodged from the embankment above spilling down. Then he felt a swift jab at his foot. Immediately he looked down to see a large snake recoiling. It had struck hard and was readying itself for another go. Tom jumped and danced away just as it struck again, hitting only air. He almost lost his balance on a rock. Little made to lunge at the thing, but he grabbed her just in time. When they were a safe distance away, he examined his shoe. Two puncture holes near his ankle. Luckily, they'd not penetrated to his skin. But as his shoes were low topped, he thought about what a close call it was.

The other incident, which he *less* fortunately experienced the full brunt of, was after they had made their way out of the canyon. They'd been running low on water and needed a refill. Spying a spring and large pool, they made straight for it. It was perhaps two hundred feet from the mouth of the ravine. Milk-weed plants were growing in the area around the pool and were being visited by butterflies. There was another, less cordial in-sect, however, that made calls on the plant; they were big, iridescent black with orange wings. Tarantula Hawks; wasps a good three inches in length. The same wasp he'd photographed that day when he first emerged from the forest. This time he did not see them. Little did, though, and kept her distance, woofing lowly.

Walking to the spring, Tom bent down and began to drink from the cool water bubbling up from below. On a hot day, it was so refreshing. He slaked his thirst, but wanted more. Moving to a better angle, he again rested on his hands and bent to drink. Alas, this time one hand, his left, came down directly on top of one of the big black wasps. It, too, had been drinking. He felt a little lump there, but gave it no mind. A second later, there came a hard, sharp, electric pain of such intensity that Tom jumped backwards, falling on his rear. Reflexively, he leaped up and ran fifty feet away, then stopping, looked at his hand. A sizable red swelling in the center of his palm throbbed. He held onto the stung hand by the wrist with his other and bent over double, placing both hands between his knees, all the while howling in agony. It hurt like nothing he'd ever experienced. A few minutes later, the pain was mostly gone. Still, he'd never forget it.

They were making about ten miles a day walking the rocky foothills, the broad slopes and the shallow canyons that made up this long, low range that ran to the South. When the going got too rough due to choking growth, steepness or cliffs, they'd head back down to the valley. If there had been a single discernible trail the whole way Tom thought they could have done more, but often the one they were on would either peter out or begin a gradual swerve one way or the other. More often than not, Tom discovered that they had gotten off track and had to find another route. Finally, he decided that it might be best to climb to the top of that hilly range where he could get a good view of the way forward.

That little diversion cost them three more days, as what appeared insignificant from a distance, ravines, bluffs, over and undergrowth, usually turned out to be full-fledged obstacles. Halfway up, Tom cursed his decision to do it and almost decided to head back down to the valley. Then, gritting his teeth, he'd look at the top of the rise, still miles of hard hiking distant, but seeming closer than it was, and push his doubts back down. Once they made it to the top, the way ahead looked like it would be fairly clear and level, at least that was his *impression* from there at the bottom.

Yet, unlike the valley, the vegetation on the upper slopes was tighter and in many places, rampant, even impenetrable. Still, in the areas where the trees opened up, he could see much farther than he could down in the vale.

The nights, though, were something else. Soon as the sun began to go down in the West, the shadows would blend together and the forest close in. In the forest the darks were darker, the sounds closer, and Tom discovered that it frightened him. It wasn't like sleeping on the open prairie at night bathed in moonlight, voices dissipated rather than concentrated. Though the plain could be hair-raising as well.

Just a week previous, he awoke to a slight noise, perhaps a twig being stepped on, and discovered a herd of Zygos quietly browsing the leaves from acacia trees nearby, the small copse of arbors he'd chosen for his hammock attracting them. The closest of the group was no more than twenty feet away. They were enormous, powerful brutes, yet, in the wan moonlight, he saw that they were also capable of the most delicate of proboscidean maneuvers, picking just the leaves they desired. They were also extremely adoring of their young, indulging and enduring their mischievousness with aplomb. Fortunately, so quiet were they that Little, lying next to him, slumbered on. And so, Tom watched them, gray in lunar lamplight, until finally sleep overtook him. In the morning, they were gone.

Here, on the other hand, the forest was dense and there

were all kinds of creepy sounds around. Most unnerving was the stealthy note of nocturnal prowlers. Sometimes Little would begin to growl at the darkness, at something Tom couldn't see, and he'd reach out to try to calm her, whispering, fearful of attracting a carnivore looking for an easy meal. Occasionally, there'd come a sudden crashing through brush racket that sent his heart racing. He did not sleep well.

Yet, when the dawn sun rose, and birds sang out, Tom often found his fears evaporating. At times during the daylight hours, Little would slip away, which forced him to wait, as he didn't want to lose her. So he'd explore a bit. Invariably, five or ten minutes later, she'd return with lunch in her mouth.

On the third day of climbing, toward the late afternoon, they finally made it through the forest. Now they stood on a grassy mountainside that swept up at an angle to the top. Tom figured it would take half an hour to reach it, about how long he thought they had until nightfall. All the same, he was worn out and debated spending the night here. It was pleasant, extremely so, he thought, with a warm breeze and a commanding view of the valley below, all the way to the sea and the islands beyond. A large, white moon had risen early, and in spite of his ever-present sense of urgency and worry for Julie, Tom felt an elation he'd not known before. Maybe it was his relief at finally being out of the foreboding forest. Maybe it was his increasing sense of confidence and accomplishment, that he was actually surviving, and, in fact, doing reasonably well, so far at least, in this most wild of worlds.

There, spread out before them, beneath the mountain range on which they stood, was a scene of profound beauty. Even Little seemed awed as she stood on a boulder jutting out over the drop, her fur wind-blown, a look of serenity on her face, of maturity and utter confidence. To be sure, she was still a pup, but she had put on weight rapidly in the last three months, having gained perhaps thirty pounds from constant hunting. He guessed her weight now to be about forty or fifty, and it looked like pure muscle. He walked toward her and she turned her head to regard him with a look of somberness approaching the wolfish. The inherent nobility of the canine clan. He thought, as he began to stroke her, that she was growing up fast, seemed to understand the nature of the journey they were on, though he realized that that couldn't be the case. She's going to be formidable, he knew, the best companion he could possibly have asked for. She returned her gaze to the valley.

Tom sat next to her on that boulder jutting out over the drop, his legs dangling. Though it was grassland to the rise behind, here and there were still areas of forest, and above that, the stars were beginning to show. Below, as the night wore on, the moon was making its own showing, reflecting off the waters of a large lake, its end dammed up by *Umbogaulus*, a Barstovian beaver. Around them a chorus of crickets sang, and Tom, on his board piano, played in soft accompaniment. In spite of his troubles, Tom felt at ease. Laying his instrument aside, he withdrew the opal to look at it. Beautiful. Muted colors scintillating there. Benevolent. Mysterious.

My dearest Julie. How do I write this? How do I describe the indescribable? You were so right (of course!) about this world, about this time. And I am captured! It fills me, fills every part of my being. Every sense. Every day that goes by, I love it more.
I never knew. Never knew how wrong our world was. How enslaved we were. Never knew there could be such beauty, such joy. Such freedom, such peace.

It's not complete, though. There is something missing. You. Where are you, my love? Please be safe and know that I am coming. Your husband is coming.

July 20, Year 1.

Tom awoke expecting to find that Little had supplied him his usual warm fare, and indeed there were several small mounds in the grass nearby. He walked to look at them and frowned with disapproval, then took out the P.I. and snapped a picture. "Wood rat," it said. "Unknown species." Tom grimaced. Even with his newfound omnivory, he couldn't bring himself to eat a rat.

He looked around for his aelurodon, but she was nowhere in sight. "Little," Tom called out. "Little One." Still no show. Oh well, he knew that she was likely around somewhere, checking out the place. Tom arose, stretched, and rolled up his sleeping bag, finally tying it to the top of his pack. There was a cool, crisp breeze, something he'd noticed nearly every morning, and it carried a lovely scent of pine, redwood and other evergreen foliage. He walked naked to the promontory he and Little had spent the last evening upon, looking out at that moonlit landscape. Now it was brightly lit with warming sun. A new day. Gorgeous. Inviting. The wreckage of the future an eternity away. He couldn't decide which view was better, evening or morning.

Tom became aware of another fragrance now. He looked around and found the usual abundance of flowers in the grass. Little bees were already hard at work, buzzing from floret to floret. He bent to smell them, walking about, investigating here and there, sticking nose into this or that blossom, each with a subtly different hue of scent. And yet, though sweet, none of them was the source of the delicious aroma he now sensed.

A liquid sound nearby, a faint babbling, gurgling, within the trees. Water running over rocks, *the rill*, though now only a fraction of the mighty river it would become. A few arbors with sun shining through them, barely concealing the vista far down in the great valley. He approached happily, the scent increasing until he was upon it. Small native pollinators were already busy insuring the continuance of both species, plant and bee. A symbiotic relationship. It was a shrub with thick leaves and delicate pink-white bell-shaped flowers. Manzanita. Others, already pollinated, had grown red berries. Irresistibly, he picked one and popped it into his mouth. Without chewing, he rolled it around upon his tongue. An apple cider tang, light and tart, touched his taste buds. He bit down gently and found a seed within. The tangy portion was the thin outer shell around it. Tom got an idea and picked bunches of them.

He carried them back, retrieved his collapsible pot, then sat on the grass and began to crack the skins from off the berries. They flaked off readily. These he put in the pot. When he had enough, Tom added fresh water from the stream. Then, clearing a small site and gathering some stones, he started a fire and placed the pot on top of the stones. In short order the water began to boil. He removed the pot and set it on the ground to cool.

Something rustled in the bushes a short distance away. Tom looked, expecting to see Little. Instead, a tall form walked tentatively out through the growth, small head held high and proud. He drew in his breath. The animal's ears were forward, but sometimes turned to the various notes of the glen, the chirp of songbirds, the plash of water, the whisper of pine. Though there were bits of dry leaves clinging to its thick, wavy fur, it had an air almost of aristocracy. But not the haughty nobility of human invention. Tom recognized it as the splendid camel

Aepycamelus, and guessed it stood maybe ten feet in height. It looked heavy and strong. Its fur was a creamy white with brown tinting.

Out it walked, sniffing the air. It strut a few paces, then bowed its head to eat some grass, as if sampling it for fitness. Tom wasn't sure it saw him, if so, it gave no indication. When it had emerged perhaps twenty paces into the glen, other forms appeared behind it. Two more Aepys, smaller by half than the first. Its young. They stepped out hesitantly, carefully. Finally, out came mother, smaller than dad, but just as noble, all four now sniffing the air.

When they were all out, a strange thing happened. The father began to walk toward Tom. It stopped to within four paces. Tom's heart beat hard in his chest. He wondered if he should jump up, shouting, and send them packing. But he didn't; instead he simply stayed put. Father now bent down to sniff at the pot where the berry tea was cooling, then walked two more steps and sniffed Tom, first his head, then shoulder. He felt the large animal's soft, moist muzzle touching his skin. Then the camel lifted its head as if in thought, or perhaps it heard something, but with eyes on either side it was hard to tell what he might be looking at.

Little, carrying another animal, walked out of the brush and paused. She dropped the catch on the ground and surveyed the situation. Tom was afraid that she would burst into a run, causing a general panic that might get him trampled. Instead she sat, mouth closed, and gazed at the huge beast with, he thought, respect. Unusual for her. The big male again dropped its head, touching Tom's cheek. Then it softly nibbled with its thick lips. A quivering feel that tickled. The human was afraid that he was about to be chomped, but no. Maybe it only wanted to taste the salt on Tom's skin. Little was on alert, but made no move, merely staring solemnly.

After a bit, the Aepy simply walked off in a measured, dignified manner, followed by the rest of the family. They disappeared into the brush and were gone. Tom let out his breath. It was an experience that he would not soon forget.

Little picked up her kill and came to her master, dropping the carcass in his lap, and proceeded to sniff his face and body as well.

"What am I..." Tom said, pushing Little's bristly muzzle aside, "the local olfactory delight?" He stuck his nose near an armpit, sniffed and withdrew. "Whew! What's the attraction anyway?"

He looked now at the kill, another rat. "Where are you finding all these things?" he asked her. "No offense, but I'm going to go ahead and abstain for now. You can have it." Tom lifted the creature from his lap by the tip of its bare tail and held it our for his aelurodon. She looked at it, then at him, without comprehension. Finally, ever so delicately, she took the rodent from his hand, backed up a couple of paces, then lay it on the ground, glancing at her human once again as if to make sure that he was indeed allowing her this exquisite treat. When he didn't object, she set to its rapid disposal. Tom grimaced. Looked like he'd be eating vegetarian this morning. Fortunately, he had a supply of plums and avocados from below that he'd been carrying tied to his belt. It added to the overall weight, but it was a necessary addition.

He thought of Julie. "She'd love you, too," he said to Little. At that, his smile disappeared and he got up and retrieved the P.P., found a shady spot so he could see the screen clearly, and switched it on. Each time he did this, he worried that his signal would be picked up by Jaqzen as well. Tom was loath to give away the fact that there was another human present, knowing that, without the element of surprise, he might not be able to catch the big man off guard should it come to that. Forewarned is forearmed.

The screen resolved, and he turned up the resolution as usual, and as usual, he fretted during the moments it took for Julie to hear the beeping and turn on her PinPointer likewise. As expected, Jaqzen's red dot flashed his location, now 637 miles away.

Beep. A green flash.

Beep. Beep. His heart leapt. She was 609 miles from him, as the crow flies. With all the stops and starts it was a paltry improvement. The problem was that, while in actuality they'd travelled much farther, it hadn't been a direct route. They'd been heading east, south-east to attain the rise and there'd been a lot of backtracking and detours. But they were closing the distance. He knew that she must also see his blue dot on her screen, was, even now, looking at it. How he longed to reach through the void and touch her, how maddening that he couldn't.

Green switched off, and so did he. Twenty-eight miles were all that there was between Julie and Jaqzen, between her and who knew what. Again, Tom wished for her safety.

He strode to his pack and loaded everything in, careful to make sure that nothing would jab. Yesterday he'd apparently been less careful and some item dug in his back for an hour before he took the pack back off in frustration and found that the shovel had again gotten wedged between his water bottle and the inside of the pack, next to his back. Though this part of the ruck did have thick padding, yet, even with that, the hard rubbing was irritating.

After tying on the bag of fruit, he lifted with strain, bending over to heft the whole thing up and on. He pondered afresh if there might be anything he could do without, but could think of nothing. He guessed that to a *real* backpacker he'd look a sight, carrying all this weight around. They'd probably laugh at his impracticality. In the Miocene world, though, he didn't have the luxury of having his supplies delivered to him at strategic points along the way.

Looking off through the trees, he could make out the ridge top not more than a half-hour distant, followed it with his eyes. He wanted to see the other side of this high-ground; thus, that was the way they'd go. And so, off they set.

They walked at a gentle angle that would bring them to the rise. It was easy enough to simply step over the little stream now. He realized, as they climbed, that the temps at this altitude were cooler than those below. But that would make sense, he supposed.

When he reached the crest, Tom gasped. The land on the other side was much more elevated than that to the west; after a short dip past the rise on which they wandered, it then sloped gradually upwards in modest undulations, random hills and isolated volcanic peaks all the way to the horizon, East, North and South. An angled highland, lush, green and grassy, dotted with small groves of deciduous trees and larger areas of evergreen forest. In barer locales, here and there, were vents and geysers pumping steam into the sky, and pockets of hardened, black crusts where lava had flowed in years past. If enough time elapsed between flows, however, the land was reclaimed by luxurious mounds of grass. He consulted the PinPointer. This was the Mehrten Volcanic Plain, it said. Southeast, a rare prominence jutted from this more or less smooth highland: Sierra Buttes, 6,000 ft. That made it double the height here on the crest, according to the altimeter.

Not just the occasional lava, sundry rivers flowed here as well, down the highland's long, flattened length, then, abutting the rise, formed pools and small lakes with stunning views of the bottomlands.

"A Mio-scene!" Tom declared.

On the other side of these, streams continued through gaps in the bank, then down the long route westward to again form lakes, larger now, or join together into wide rivers. From there, it was on to the Temblor, the name the P.P., and he now remembered, Julie, had called that inland sea.

The areas of deciduous and evergreen trees on the uplands surrounded bodies of water, as if there had once been lots more here, but then they'd receded to these oases when the climate, or maybe the land itself began to change. Or maybe it was overbrowsing. Besides grass and patches of forest, there was not much shrubbery in the majority of the open expanse between oases. A precursor to a dry future? Later, as the northern Sierras rose, land eastward would become a full-fledged desert, adding to the Great Basin. But for now, the land was high and he could see from where he was that these lochs were large. They'd be here a good while longer.

Lingering in the general periphery of the lakes was a variety of mammal fauna, especially horses, but camelids looked abundant as well, and, slowly plodding in small herds near the forest margins, the mammut, Zygolophodon. Yet, as he scanned, he saw what looked like another kind of elephant, similar, though not exactly the same. The tusks were different. He'd seen them just once before, at the beginning, hauling down branches and rolling trees. Now, they were standing ankle-deep in water exuberant with growth.

Tom swung the P.I. to his eyes from where it hung around his neck and zoomed in on one. He snapped the pic and back came the reply: Gomphothere. They seemed to be keeping their distance from the comparably sized Zygos. The one he focused on was pulling at a tough bunch of sedge-like plants, or maybe it was vine, half as tall as the elephant itself. Whatever it was, it had a solid grip. Even so, the Gompho finally ripped it out, banged it on the ground to remove the dirt and shoved it in to its open mouth. Then, noticing movement, Tom saw that there were other Gompho heads protruding just above the tall grass. *They're fairly well disguised in there,* he thought. He counted seven of them.

There was yet another surprise. A group of primitive Rhinoceros. Tom could tell by the general body shape, and of course the horn, although it wasn't very big. Still, there was no mistaking. The P.I. called them *Teleoceras,* and there were a lot of them. They seemed to like hanging out in the rivers and their inlets to the lakes. Except for the elephants and the smaller, faster animals, the other fauna were giving them space. A little off to the right of the group of Teleos though, was another kind of rhino. Long-legged. At first Tom thought they were more Teleos, but then noticed the lack of a horn. *Aphelops.* Perhaps shyer, they apparently preferred the cover of the woodland edge, but were drawn by the company of their braver cousins. Tom wondered why he hadn't seen these rhinos on the seaside of the range.

Something loping along, bounding south, toward the forest, through wary herds that moved out of its way. Tom zeroed in. A carnivore. *Ursavus,* an early bear. Three species names popped up - the P.I. couldn't determine which it was - *brevirhinus, pawniensis* and *primaevus.* Evidently the beast was too remote to make a precise identification.

It was an immense pastureland, Tom concluded, reflecting on the tranquil vista. Ideal for the animals living there.

To the South now, the prominence of the true mountains was more apparent. These were purple with distance and height, looking both foreboding and majestic. Just below them, on the seaside, dark clouds clung as if caught in the mountainous grip. It was raining. Quick, jagged flashes of light met the earth, while great slanting curtains of water fell from those clouds in motion so slow he could barely see them moving, to the waiting land beneath. Again he wondered about them. The map indicated that they were the Sierras. The northern corner of the inland sea didn't look more than maybe fifty miles away from them, if that.

On the left side of the mountain range, the land looked mostly bare and dry. True desert. Then he noticed something else, something he'd not discerned before. On the very tops of those mountains, there was white. He looked again, refocusing the binocs, followed the ridge as far as he could see. For a good long way, yes, there was white capping it. His creeping smile broke into a broad grin. SNOW!

"Ha, haa!" Tom shouted. "Look at that, Little. *SNOW!"* Little looked in the direction her human pointed, but seemed not to understand. Tom tried to do a bit of a jig, but with all his gear it was awkward. *"What a world!"* he shouted.

He looked down again, southward, and, visually following the range to sea level, saw that there would be hills and vales, grassland and woodlands, numerous deep canyons and great rivers to cross. Many flowed to that inland sea, a huge marine embayment, which, from this height, looked not too far away. So then, he conjectured, it must be a mixed salt/freshwater body. Brackish. What kinds of animals live in water like that?

Tom studied the scene as they walked, trying to think of the best path to take. Much as he wanted to see the snow, he knew that would be a foolhardy plan, costly in time and effort. There were no roads, and it would probably be hard going, with many ravines, boulders, thick vegetation, and a lot of ups and downs. Generally difficult land. No, not now at least. Someday, maybe someday. With Julie.

On the other hand, it looked like he *could* stay on this rise for a long way, relatively speaking, before he'd have to descend again back into the valley on the seaside. Assuming that the rivers would be slowest closest to that sea, he wondered if it would be better to try to cross them there. Of course, they'd also be widest there too. Or, maybe when they reached it, they should try to skirt that mountain range so as to cross the rivers at the narrowest point possible. Still, it looked steep and rugged, and he'd already learned that things that look easy at a distance were often not when one was upon them. Well, he had time to decide. In the meantime, he'd stick to the rise with its superlative view.

A cool morning breeze caressed his skin. The sun shone gaily, a million points of light on the sea, twinkling, shimmering, coalescing into one. He'd enjoy it while he could. By the look of things, a shower was headed their way.

Nineteen

Julie ran for a week. Ran until she was exhausted. She'd used the PinPointer to keep track of Jaqzen, always turning it on just for the moment it took to locate him, then switching off again. She hoped that he didn't notice the beeping sound on his own PinPointer that indicated she was signaling.

He must have, though, for it was obvious he was definitely pursuing, each day making more or less progress. She wondered why he hadn't found her yet, seeing as he was such an experienced tracker, though she was certainly not trying to make it easy for him - sticking to areas of moisture, places like grasslands and marshlands whose foliage bounced back soon after it was stepped upon. She walked the coast at night, the waves advancing and retreating, erasing her footsteps for all time. And she hid among herds of grazers, nervously walking through them, while they parted for her, then closed again after she passed, their heavy footmarks soon obliterating her own.

Somehow, though, Jaqzen was able to keep up, albeit miles back. She had hoped he would tire of the chase and would quit. That, unfortunately, did not happen. More likely, she knew, he was instead enjoying the challenge. Perhaps he already knew where she was and was just toying with her, toying the way a cat plays with its prey before finishing it.

All this while, Julie was simultaneously exploring her new world. She confirmed that the magnetic poles were indeed shifted, as positive now pointed South on her compass. She also spent time looking for and gathering wild edible plants. Avocados made up a large part of her diet, but with it, she supplemented the sweet fruit of various *prunus* species. She also loved prickly pear cactus, burning the needles off after impaling them with a stick. *Claytonia,* or "Miner's Lettuce," which she found on moist forest hillsides, reminded her of the store-bought lettuce she used to eat as a child, only tangier.

In her "salads", she variously included, when available, Wild Onion, Chaparral Current, Gooseberries, *Calandrinia ciliata,* aka Red Maids, Golden Chinquapin, Madrone berries, Black Walnuts (though their shells were enormously difficult to open) and pine nuts, particularly Pinon pine nuts with their much easier to crack shells. She seasoned and spiced these with Yerba Buena and California Bay leaves. Another find was a species of *Sapotaceae,* which had edible fruits.

Near fresh water, she used the roots of Cattail, while, near the sea, she used kelps. Also available were delicious and sweet Blackberry, Serviceberries, Lemonadeberries, Thimbleberries and tiny Strawberries. She used California Goldenrod, Squawbush, Mint and Manzanita berries for tea.

Julie also stored a supply of bright red rose hips for their vitamin C content from the pretty ancestral wild roses she found near bodies of water. No sense getting scurvy. The small, pink and white, five-petaled blossoms betrayed their genetic potential. A potential that would be exploited by humans to beautiful, but also sometimes extreme and garish extents far in the future.

For proteins and healthy fats, she used avocados and acorns, which had plenty. Red oaks, the evergreens, tended to accumulate tannins that had to be leached from the nuts before one could eat them. The tannin was bad for kidneys. Native Americans usually leached them by setting them in a stream of water until the acids were slowly carried away. It was a process, though, that might take days, or even weeks. White oaks, on the other hand, did not accumulate the same amount of tannin and could, within reason, be eaten raw. One could tell the difference between them because red oak acorns were smaller than whites, had fine hairs on the inside of the shells and the nutmeat was darker, while white oaks with their larger fruits had no hairs, and the meat was lighter and less bitter. Thus, she avoided the reds and ate the whites. It was said that battles were fought by Native Americans over good oak land.

Julie was a vegetarian, not a vegan, so when she happened upon a partially uncovered nest of turtle eggs one day, she quickly heated water and ate a delicious hard-boiled breakfast, dousing the round, white orbs with some sea salt she found in a large, crusty block just up from the shore and had ground a bit of.

Most of all, though, Julie exulted in the stunning abundance and variety of wildlife, counting, for example, over a dozen species of horse and camels respectively, and nearly twice that many of dog so far.

When she knew that she could not go on without a rest, Julie looked for a place where she could hide. She found it in the form of a cave high up the side of a sedimentary cliff. It was fortuity that she even saw it, as it was hidden by the long, drooping branches of a huge overhanging oak, which leaned well over the edge. Another decade or two of weathering, one final lizard scurry across its crumbling face, dislodging yet another bit of gravel, and that oak would be at the bottom a hundred feet below, having fallen in a clatter of rock and debris, the haze of dust rising up afterward its only eulogy.

The cliff face was composed of ancient stratified layers laid one upon the other, and she wondered about its age. Even while hunted, the scientist in her was never far away, and every moment was still a glorious one. She kept a small paper notebook in her breast pocket and was often taking it out to register some new or confirmed finding.

When she found the cave, she had just come around the corner of a lower sedimentary mound deep in a forest, following a small stream choked with growth on its banks, though here and there showing itself and permitting a drink to forest fauna. She stood, noting something unusual about a particular flower, while wiping the sweat off her brow, creating a long stain on her right sleeve. Was it the same genus that she knew? She observed and recorded the features of its leaves. Ovate, pinnate. Thinking deeply, trying to remember, she glanced up and saw a dark spot high on the side. Looking closer, she squinted, as the sun was in her eyes. Shielding them, she lifted her binocs. A cave. Sizable, it looked. And hidden.

A ray of hope. Julie gazed around the prominence; it seemed to descend on the other side. The stream cut to the right, but a dry streambed on the left said that, in times of heavy rain, the water wound both ways. In it were long, colorless, uprooted Cattail reed stems plastered in masses against the broken trunk of a fallen sycamore, telling of a big storm last winter, or the winter before that. Winter during the Miocene was, of course, nothing like it was during the Anthropocene. The temperatures here were nearly uniform year round, almost tropical, with a slight dip when the sun was lowest.

Julie walked the path to the right, through the water. She thought of pushing through the brush, which was past the stream banks, but besides looking too overgrown generally, it was also overrun with poison oak. She could have taken the easier way to the left, but the soft ground might leave prints, giving her away. Besides, at this point, Julie wasn't thinking prim and proper. She was thinking survival.

It was longer going around than she thought at first, but after perhaps two hundred feet, the cliff met the bank. It looked to be about a forty-degree incline to the top and was covered in oak saplings struggling to grow in the dense shade and thick blanket of leaves created by their parents. There was plenty of poison oak - she'd have to use caution on the ascent. Filling her water containers, she fixed her sights uphill and set out.

As she trudged on, one step in front of the other, oak leaves crunching underfoot, Julie realized that the forest scent she'd been subconsciously noting was tannin. Leaves and acorns accumulating and breaking down in water - the regular rains of this tropical/temperate era. Good ol' oaks. Stubborn, resilient, strong. Pretty much the same now as they would be far in the future. Living fossils. No wonder they were a symbol of strength and endurance.

Huffing, Julie at last reached the top, again wiping her brow. She was hungry, but had gathered an assortment of edibles from the flora she'd been passing through. Still, she was tired and knew that she needed protein. She looked at the big oak which was disguising her new home. A white oak, a Valley Oak. There were acorns on it, and some newly fallen; they looked ripe. Julie thought about that. In her time the acorns didn't ripen until autumn, and yet here things were different. With no discernible winter to speak of, she'd suspected that fruiting was a more than once a year occurrence. There were now likely two, or even three fruitings, though she thought that two was probable; the energy required for three would be extraordinary. If that were so, then this might not be fall. She'd become convinced, too, that it wasn't by the simultaneous occurrence of normal *spring* traits, such as the persistence of an annual rye-like grass. Additionally, the sun was not where it would be in her time during an acorn drop.

Yesterday when she pondered this dual fruitingness, she remembered something that had been written once by a famous French explorer to the Americas, Pierre Esprit Radisson, circa 1652. It was a beloved quote that she'd committed to memory.

When describing his journey through what would later become the United States, before his fellow white men began to arrive in earnest, he said:

"The further we sojourned the delightfuller the land was to us. I can say that in my lifetime I never saw a more incomparable country....The country was so pleasant, so beautiful and fruitful that it grieved me to see the world could not discover such enticing countries to live in. This I say because the europeans fight for a rock in the sea against each other, or for a sterile and horrid country. Contrariwise, these kingdoms are so delicious and under so temperate a climate, plentiful of all things, the earth bringing forth its fruit twice a year, the people live long and lusty and wise in their way."

Twice a year. *Hmm.* Julie set to gathering a load of the oak nuts, placing them in a bag. There was something *else* peculiar that she'd noticed, at first unconsciously, then with startling awareness, since she'd arrived in the Miocene. The vegetation - trees, shrubs, *everything* - were *larger* than they should have been, at least than they *were* during the Anthropocene. In fact, the majority of the trees here were truly gigantic in size, towering high and wide, lofty branches spreading a hundred feet or more on either side of the massive trunks. Under them she felt tiny and humbled. Julie thought about it for a while, then finally decided that it was the much higher quantities of carbon from volcanic sources, coupled with extra nitrogen fixation from the atmosphere due to the frequent lightning strikes, that was the likely cause. The vegetation was making evolutionary use of the extra carbon, as it ought to, since higher CO_2 had been a fact of life for millions of years. That, plus the longer growing season, contributed to the increased growth.

Julie walked to the edge of the cliff and looked down. The cavern was maybe five feet from the top. Too far for her to just swing into. There was a thick bough though, the branch, whose branchlets and leaves blocked the entrance from easy view. If she could just climb down far enough, maybe she could jump into it. If she didn't make it, though, the fall would do her in. The old oak itself barely clung to the top. Conceivably her added weight might bring it - and her - down. Like that sycamore at the bottom. And that would be that. The end of all her hopes and dreams. Of humanity's, for surely she represented the last hope of the race.

As she thought about things, now that there was the time to think, she began to worry that perhaps this whole episode was about more than just random discovery. Maybe they had thought that she could be the mother of the next human race with their fittest male, Jaqzen, the father. The thought made her reel with revulsion. Jaqzen as the father that is.

But, if true, it meant that they knew that the spaceship idea was hopeless, doomed to failure. A technocratic pipe dream sold to the public. Were they, or some of them, instead staking all of their hopes on her, on she and Jaqzen? If so, then it was a wasted dream, for she'd never join with him, the ape-man. He represented all that she despised in her species. And she was in love with another.

Julie grabbed a branch that hung low, the one she'd be using to climb into the cave, and tugged at it, testing the tree's stability. No movement. She now positioned herself away from the rim, just in case, and pulled harder, it didn't budge. *Okay,* she thought, *that's good, it looks like you still have some hold.* She removed her backpack and lay down on the edge of the cliff looking inside of the cavern. There was rubble on the floor and old, dried and broken roots from the oak coming through the ceiling. Probably what was holding the tree up.

Anxiously clutching the branch, Julie took hold of her pack and hefted it over the side. The weight almost made it rip from her grasp, bits of rock crumbling down, sending a jolt of fear through her. But she and the tree held fast. Pausing a moment to collect herself, she began to swing her arm, backwards and forwards, in toward the cave, then out, and again, until she had the swing as right as she could make it, then let go. *Thud,* it fell on the floor about a foot from the brink.

It was with an odd feeling of irony, and disgust, that at the very moment that the pack hit the floor, Julie remembered that she had a rope in it. It was quite long enough to have tied to another oak or to a crop of rock nearby. She shook her head. She was tired. There was nothing for it now, though, but to climb down holding onto the branch of this precariously positioned tree. While it was only five feet to the cave, that was to *its ceiling.* The floor looked another six feet below that. Eleven feet, that's how far down she'd have to climb.

She studied the branch now, looking for strong branchlets that could hold her weight. A couple of minutes later, Julie grabbed onto two of them and, swallowing, carefully turned around and began to descend. Almost immediately, gravel broke loose and fell in a clattering rain below. Halfway down she felt the tree itself shake, move just a bit. Her nerves jumped and she paused until all was still, then she continued, heart beating hard in her chest. Finally, she was at a level where she could climb around and step onto the floor of the cave. She did so without further ado and was in.

Her shirt was soaked with sweat from the climb up, and down, but she was too tired even to remove it. She sat heavily, breathing hard, then rose again to sweep some painful rubble out from under her.

After a minute of rest, Julie opened her pack, withdrew the water container, and took a long drink. Then, seeing an area of soft, dry sand, and demurring a deeper investigation of the cavern, she grabbed the thermal blanket and lay down on her side, closed her eyes, and slept.

Julie awoke abruptly, hours later, at twilight. There was a high-pitched sound of whistling and a muffled rush of wings. At first she jumped, then, realizing what they were, lay back down and let them out. Bats. She'd be sharing her home with bats. The thought sent an involuntary shudder up her spine. Then she remembered that this was *their* home and she *a guest*. It would be a thrill actually: though she'd seen them flying about her in the Barstovian evenings, from the little mosquito eaters that saved her from pests which had designs on her blood, to the big *Antrozous pallidus*, or pallid bats, that fed on larger insects, now she could observe them at close hand. In her time, bats were long gone, having succumbed to white nose syndrome and other maladies related to man's encroachment and mismanagement. Yet, even though as a scientist and ecologist she loved bats, she couldn't quite get past the creep out factor of naked, nervous, flying mammals winging above her head.

Unlike the pallid bats, these were a small, mosquito eating species, she recognized, as they flew almost soundlessly over her, silhouetted by the orange, red and indigo of the gathering night. A common species in California, now and to the end. Long may they live, she thought sadly.

Looking out now through a gap in the leaves, Julie could see other groups of bats from other areas merging with her troop. Somehow they knew the exact time to leave their caves and trees to meet up like this. Before long, they were a huge party, diving through the air in epic waves and spirals like

301

swimming sardines, before finally dispersing into the darkness on their insect hunting mission. What a pity that people would learn to fear and destroy them because of silly superstitions and old movies, leaving themselves vulnerable to diseases they might otherwise not have encountered.

It was a hot night and Julie removed her dirty clothing, leaving it in a pile on one side. Tomorrow she'd wash them in the river with sand, sans detergent. She drank, then poured some water into her collapsible bowl. Finding the Ceanothus blooms she'd gathered, she stuck them into the water, then out, and rubbed them together in her hands. In a few seconds, a suds-like foam appeared, and with the water, she spread it on her body, rinsing as she went. It wasn't perfect, she could have used more water, but when she was done she felt much better. Smelled better, too. Then she put on a pair of shorts, got some food and sat by the entrance of the cave.

Through the oak, she could see, in the fading light, the ocean, five miles or so distant. It was a lovely, charming sight, and again made her yearn for the company of her husband. Ache and hope for his companionship. Julie prayed that wherever he was, *whenever* he was, he would not give up until they were reunited, impossible odds though they were.

This was the first real rest she'd had in a week and already she was getting sleepy again. She ate Luisian fruit and acorns. The latter definitely needed something, maybe if she pounded it into a flour and added some honey to make bread - if she could find it. *Apis nearctica*, the only species of honeybee ever known to be indigenous to North America, *just happened to live during the middle Miocene* and should be hereabouts. She'd have to keep on the lookout for a hive, but she knew the proteins and fats from the acorns would do her good. She guessed that she'd lost about ten pounds since she left the Strong Box.

It had been a tough week. Luckily, she'd not personally met any of the larger predators, though on the third day, as she was coming down a dark, overgrown path to get a drink from a river, just as she stepped out of the vegetation, she noticed an animal previously invisible to her searches, lapping at the water. In point of fact, they noticed each other pretty much simultaneously, each yanking a head in the other's direction. There followed a brief moment, which seemed to last ages. It had a wild, distant, almost crazed look in its burnt orange eyes, giving no indication of its much later importance to her own species, no recognition of her form. And why should it? Instead it hissed, quickly turned its head, then darted into the undergrowth, never to be seen by her again.

Julie shivered with excitement. *Oh my God!* she thought, *Pseudaelaurus*, considered one of the first, true, primitive cats! A huge smile spread over her face. It looked between a bobcat and mountain lion in size. Its fur was a mottled brown base, incorporating darker, leopard-like circles, while its rear legs were striped with black. Though its fur was rough, it looked clean, as if it bathed often. Like a lynx, it also had a tuft of black fur on the tip of its ears. Mottled black fur also framed its face. Unusually, a long stripe ran lengthwise down the top of its tail, ending in a black tip. It was the eyes that struck her though, fierce and no-nonsense, an animal very much at home here in this raw wilderness. Raw wildness. It, and its descendants, would play a large role in shaping it.

Even in her day, there were still cats, and though he tried, never had man been able to tame its savage heart. Feral cats were just as prehistoric at the end as now, at their beginning, nature's Miocene programming apparently just too strong to break.

Are you the first? Julie thought wistfully after it, realizing that it was a nonsense question.

Still.

Now as she sat in her cave, its entrance suffused with moonlight, she drew the cat from memory, not having had the opportunity to photograph it. She dearly hoped she'd see more of them.

For an hour, Julie recorded, struggling to keep her eyes open, but it was too much. Having almost finished the cat, her hand dropped the pencil, while slowly she lay down in the soft sand, unconsciously hoping that she wouldn't sleepwalk.

When she awoke, morning light was streaming in. Julie stretched and grunted. The sand had been a perfect bed, she found, conforming itself to her shape, the trapped air in between the grains holding warmth next to her body. If it had been solid ground, though, the effect would have been reversed: warmth drained and muscles aching.

Through the opening in the cave, she could hear the river below. Birds were also active, singing and alighting at the entrance of her new home, seemingly to get a glance at this new wonder. One, two or three would land on the branchlets outside, jot in and dance about, chirping loudly, then zip out, only to do it again soon thereafter. It made her laugh.

"Hello there," she called to them sweetly, "and who are you?" One hopped a few paces in her direction, but when she moved, they all dashed out in a flurry. Seconds later, they were back. The closest one regarded her with quick, appraising looks, as if trying to understand what she *was*. Julie rummaged around in her pack for something to give them, then found some small red berries and rolled them toward the aves. The bravest hopped toward it, hopped back, then forward again and grabbed one, taking to wing in the same instant right out the cave, followed by the others twittering noisily.

Now that there was some light, Julie looked around inside.

The cave appeared sizable, stretching back into the darkness beyond. She got some food and drink for herself, then went to its mouth and sat, legs dangling over the side. A cool breeze brushed her bare skin, for she was still shirtless. Julie looked down; she needed a bath. In spite of her earlier rinse, long stains of old sweat and dirt nonetheless stuck to her usually immaculate body. She felt embarrassed, yet also foolish for her embarrassment.

Through gaps in the oak bough, she scanned the horizon. It was forest, and beyond, mixed wood and grassland. It called her from her sanctuary to *come* and *investigate*. Indeed, the urge to explore was strong. She could do it and use the cave as her base camp.

Something moving slowly out at sea, but not too far out, caught her attention. A wisp of something dark, curling up into the air, then dissipating. She studied it, wonderingly, at first thinking there might be fire somewhere, possibly caused by a lightning strike. Something about it nagged at her though. Then, squinting, the answer began to dawn on her. Quickly she rose and found her binocs, then sat back down and looked out while making adjustments. There was a small rise in the water where the wisp originated. A bit of red. Red, flaring up a short way and oozing down. Julie caught her breath. A VOLCANO!

She thought hard now, trying to recall. "Volcano. I know I'm in southern California. So what was there here...?" She scratched her head, frowning, then suddenly remembered. *Yes! How stupid of me to forget. There were volcanoes here. In the areas that later became the Los Angeles and Orange Counties. In Palos Verdes, Pomona, Glendora, El Modeno and other places, flows of basalt, andesite and rhyolite were deposited. In fact, they continued there until the end of the Luisian.* She thought about that, "There? I mean here!" she said aloud.

305

With nary a thought about safety, she could barely contain her joy. It was wonderful to be living through everything she had learned about this special time, from the literature and in the field, to see all that hard-earned research come to life before her eyes. There were - *are* - lots of other volcanic episodes in this general period, she reflected, the largest being the Columbia River Flood Basalts, when very large, hot, fluid and fast-moving basaltic lava flows, rich in magnesium and iron, spilled from tears in the earth's surface and flowed through Washington, Oregon, Idaho and possibly even California. One of the largest to ever appear on the surface of the earth, the lava fronts will be up to 100 feet high! In time, at some locations, the lava will grow to two and three miles thick! Eventually, it will cover 63,000 square miles! With a total of 300 flows, there should be major eruptions there occurring every 13,500 or so years, and smaller ones roughly every 75 years. *One could be happening there right now*, she thought excitedly.

Julie tried to further narrow things down. "The Wanapum Basalt, Roza member specifically, should be current, that lava flowing from 15.5 to 14.5 million years ago... I mean, about *now*," she corrected again. "It will only account for 5% of the total Columbia flow though, while the earlier Grande Ronde accounts for 90%. If only I could see it.

"There are other volcanics occurring as well. There's arc volcanoes in Nevada, and the Mehrtens in the northern Sierras. *Wow!*" She gazed at the smoke again. There wasn't a real explosive threat from many of these flows. Though large, their lavas mostly exuded from fissures in the ground, oozing out like toothpaste from a tube. Julie knew she was going to have to get a closer look at that volcano.

She peeked down at the river now, so tantalizing, a hundred feet below. Then she remembered that she'd have to climb the eleven feet on that shaky branch to the top again. The prospect made her spirit sink. But there was no other choice, and realizing that, she was able to put self-recrimination and other distractions out of her mind. It was a trait that Tom admired.

Julie put on her shoes, then dug in her pack and found the rope, slinging its loops over her head and one shoulder. She did the same with her camputer. Then she walked back to the rim and looked down. It was a long way. She gripped the branch in front of her and pulled. It held tight as yesterday. She retested the side branchlets she'd climbed down on. The same. And so, mumbling a quick prayer, she grabbed two of them and began to hoist herself up. Branch by branch she went, always trying to make sure that she had at least three contacts on the tree at any one time so as to more evenly distribute her weight.

The rope caught a few times and she had to carefully disentangle it. When finally her head was at the level of the ledge, she stretched out a hand, somewhat impatiently, to clutch at a branch a little too far away, simultaneously lifting her right foot. This placed most of her weight on the branch under her left foot.

It snapped and she dropped, shrieking, holding on by one hand. Her feet dangling in the air, Julie screamed and flailed about, trying to reach another branch. Then, abruptly, the tree itself moved, sending an electric jolt of fear through her. Dirt and gravel cascaded to the ground, the bigger rocks bouncing off a boulder at the bottom, ringing out in the riverine canyon.

"Oh no!" Julie yelled involuntarily, panic in her voice. The tree moved again, sending more gravel hurtling downward. Heart racing and pulse pounding in her ears, she willed herself to stop thrashing, then grabbed another branch, gripping gently, but firmly. She hung on now, trying to still her movement, while glancing below. The tree held. Gulping, she wondered what she should do: continue the climb, or try to toss the rope one-handed around something and hold on. Uncharacteristical-

ly, she cursed her lack of foresight the day before in not using the rope. That slight oversight might cost her her life. She again submerged the thought and scrutinized the tree. It barely held, yet there was nothing close by enough to toss the rope to, and even if there were, the very act of hurling might be enough to bring the tree, and her, down. She had no choice but to continue.

Studying each branch she would use, mentally discarding some, she ever-so-carefully grasped a branch above her head without putting too much weight on it. It complained anyway. Pressing on, she again ever-so-carefully lifted a foot and placed it on the branch just above. There was no reciprocal movement from the tree. Two more feet up, until her waist was now level with the top. One more and she leaned over, laying her weight upon the ground, legs hanging. This took most of it off the tree, the cliff edge, though, responded by crumbling, sending another shower of rocks down. Julie stretched out her hands and painfully inched herself forward, scooting again and again until finally she was there. Her stomach hurt from the rocks, having gained a handful of cuts, but she had made it!

Julie sat now and scooted back yet further, then dubiously standing, wiped herself off, breathing hard.

"That was close," she breathed in shaky understatement, a tremor in her voice. She looked around now for something to tie the rope to. There were other trees that she could use, and that big boulder off to the right. She decided on another tree, as the possibility of the rope slipping off the boulder, slim though it might be, made her too nervous. There was a smaller oak, about seven inches in diameter, which stood back about ten feet from the edge that should work though. Tying the rope around it with several square knots, she pulled tight. It was strong. Then she tied loops down its length, spacing them a

couple of feet apart. Done, she walked near the edge and coiled the rope there, ready for use.

Nerves still a-flight, Julie turned now and headed downhill, oak leaves crunching underfoot, stepping around rocks and being careful not to touch the poison oak. When she got to the bottom, she stopped still. A group of seven tapir-like animals were eating from the stream. *Miotapirus.* They were medium-sized and roughly pig shaped, with stripes diagonally across their sides and on their short tails which now stood erect. Typical of tapirs, they also had an elongated snout, like a mini proboscis. Seeing her, a few of the closest ones lowered their heads and grunted. This, she surmised, was apparently meant as a warning. Others, snouts flexing with surprising elasticity, dug into the stream bank with their front feet, pulling up plants. The rest, though, just stood and gazed, mouths in mid-munch of some river vegetation. After a few seconds, they began to back away.

"It's okay," she whispered, fascinated, "Don't be afraid." Silently she lifted the camputer and snapped some pictures. Later she would add comments.

After the Miotapirs disappeared, Julie decided to follow the stream a bit. Dappled light shone in from above, moving with the motion of the leaves and branches high overhead. As usual, there was a nippy morning breeze. Later, the day would grow hot, she knew, but, if she stayed near water and shade, temps should remain pleasant. Microscopic droplets of water, sightlessly, soundlessly evaporating from a billion leaves fluttering in the gentle winds, cooled the air, keeping it fresh and fine.

With care, Julie stepped on boulders in the stream, trying not to slip. After a while, she could hear a sound of rushing beyond, which spoke of a waterfall; it increasing in resonance as she grew closer.

It was a lovely one, eight feet high. When finally she stepped around and below the place where it fell, past the obscuring leaves of a maple, the sight took her breath away, for even more lovely than the waterfall was the pool it splashed into. Large, perhaps twenty feet across, and deep, with overhanging ferns.

These were *Woodwardia*, the giant chain fern, ten feet tall and as wide. Their fronds moved gracefully in the mists and breezes of the falls. There were plenty of other shrubs too, that, except for the chain ferns, seemed to be staged smaller toward the front and larger back including Madrone, Holly, Barberry and Horsechestnut with its characteristic large, smooth seeds. Mexican Buckeye, *Karwinskia* and Moonseed too. On the right side grew mounds of wild rose.

Trees of sundry varieties also lay claim to a place near the sacred pool, their thinner branches and leaves likewise moving in and out with the cool gusts. Maples, green leaves faintly tinged with red/orange foliage near the upper part of the fall, Hickory, Hackberry and Yellow-wood, Ash, Sycamores and Wingnuts, Poplar, Elm and lovely Locust with their deliciously scented wisteria-like flowers in bloom. To Julie's left was a Madrone with its almost Manzanita smooth, red bark. A large specimen of California Laurel, Alder and Liquidambar also jostled for space.

In the pool, Julie saw scores of small fish and a few large ones. They darted in and out of obscurity. Ocher and burnt umber salamanders just inside the waterline moved with the ripples, perhaps lulled to sleep by the tender current. There were turtles as well. Seeing her, two dove into the water with a splash that sounded like a musical note. On the back and left side of the pond from where she stood was a bank of sand, dry with the sunlight and shadow that bounced in and out of it. A nice place to lie down.

Colorful finches were flitting in and out here, singing loud as they could, their tiny voices, barely heard above the rush of the water, yet a melodious compliment to it.

Julie beamed, then wept. She didn't know why she was crying. They weren't unhappy tears. That is, until she thought of Tom.

Come to me, my love..., she prayed, saltiness wending to the corners of her mouth. Her words ephemeral, evanescent on the wind.

Julie walked to the sandbar, removed her shorts and stepped lightly into the pool. She drew in her breath, its coolness making her skin prickle. Slowly, she stepped forward, soft sand under her feet. When she was up to her knees, she launched herself, creating a small wave that went before her. Then she turned on her back and floated there, sunlight checkering her face, her closed eyes.

This is heaven, she thought, *better than heaven.* She felt a tiny tickling on her thigh, looked down to see a small fish sampling her, tasting her. It made her laugh. On the bank, at eye level, a turtle watched her stoically. *It'll be this way forever,* she thought. A familiar tune of Tom's played in her mind. Something from his board piano. *La la la. La la la.*

La la la. Julie took handfuls of sand and rubbed it on her body, washing away a week's worth of grime. When she was clean, she gazed at her form in the water. It was turquoise/blue/white. Full, sensual.

She swam slowly to the other side. Something she wanted to see. Was it? Closing in, she saw that it was. *Vitis californica... Grapes!* There were wild grapes growing here, both at ground level and high into the trees above! Thirty feet up she saw them, clusters of the small, green and purple orbs. She wondered how they would taste when they'd not yet been "improved" by man. They certainly *looked* good.

A light passed through, making each translucent, a promise of sweetness within. Stepping out of the water and onto the opposite bank, she walked a few steps to a poplar, its leaves spinning, turning in the now warm breeze, its branches supporting loads of the fruit. Reaching out her hand, she held a bunch, caressing them, squeezing one. It was firm, yet also gave. *But just a little.* Smiling, Julie picked it, held it up to the sun. Inside she beheld a tiny seed, the assurance of more to come, of future betoken. Seeds, little miracles, precious gifts of nature, later made sterile by selfish men with profit motives. But that was far off.

She placed it on her tongue and rolled it around. Spherical, like the earth. It reminded her of something the Russian Astronaut, Aleksei Leonov, had once said about viewing the earth from space:

> The Earth was small, light blue, and
> so touchingly alone, our home
> that must be defended like a holy relic.
> The Earth was absolutely
> round. I believe I never knew what the
> word round meant until I saw
> Earth from space.

She bit down. The world exploded, though this was an explosion of flavor, of tang. It was better than she had hoped, the small size concentrating the sugars. In her day, when there were still grapes available, the large size they were bred to tended to dilute the sweetness with extra water. *What was our issue with size, anyway?* she wondered, then laughed at that.

Julie snapped off several bunches, thanking the vine for so kindly providing them. She would do her best to repay it by distributing its seeds far and wide. Another laugh erupted from her throat. *Crude, enough of that.*

She swam back to the other side then climbed out, lying down in the sand. It was warm, soothing, embracing. There she indulged her palate. A minute later, she was out.

Twenty

In her idyll, Julie lived undiscovered for another week, eating, drinking, swimming, and learning, taking a couple of days off to travel to the coast halfway through. That turned out to be quite an adventure in itself.

First, she caught the attention of a rather large predator, *Plithocyon*, a huge bear-like animal that looked to be at least a half ton in weight. Father of the bears. Seeing her walk freely across the grasslands it began to follow, stalking her. When she turned and noticed it, it stopped, then began swinging its head from side to side, raising its nose to the air to catch a whiff. It appeared to be straining to see her. Evidently it had poor vision and wasn't all too sure what the heck she was. Seemed to depend more on smell than sight. Certainly she *smelled* edible, but she looked biggish. There was nothing in its genetic registry to account for her.

For her part, Julie, while alarmed, couldn't help but snap pictures, keeping some trees in sight that she hoped to run to and climb should the bear get too feisty. When it noticed her noticing it, the beast growled churlishly, curling its lips, then began a waddle-like stalk toward her. Julie put her camputer back down on her chest, where it hung from a lanyard, and began to back up. The trees were a good hundred and fifty feet away. A thin stand of poplars.

Seeing her retreat, the ursid grew emboldened and uttered a deep, sonorous snarl, thunderous in magnitude, and began to trot. At this, Julie yelped - for Plithocyon was a agile runner - dropped her backpack, turned and fled. The ursid pursued, galloping to the ruck, then stopping, while Julie made it to the trees and began to climb the first one. Ten feet up, she turned to see the beast sniffing at the pack. It put one foot on top, then turned it over, clawing at it. Julie yelled, shooing. She wasn't too convincing, for the beast ignored the pesky sound. It could smell food inside and bit at a pocket. Julie yelled louder, trying to make her voice sound more authoritative. She contemplated climbing back down to hurl rocks at it. A stray thought occurred to her, *Could it be that this chance encounter will plant a deep-seated memory within the beast, such that its kind would forevermore be interested in what people were carrying? Forever harassing us for scraps and being shot for it?* Just as suddenly as the thought popped into her head, though, she dismissed it as illogical.

There came a sound of ripping as the plith, foot on top of the pack, attempted to pull the mysterious covering apart. At that, Julie howled in protest, then started to climb down. She had to try to save her equipment. A small pile of rocks nearby would serve as ammo.

At the bottom, she looked nervously at the bear, hoping that it wouldn't decide to abandon the pack for her. It took no notice, however. Julie chose a rock, leaned back and hurled it. A very lucky shot, it bounced right off Mr. Ursid's skull. Plith jumped and looked around, but seeing nothing nearby, went back to trying to open the pack. So she tried again with another, which bounced off the ground near its face. Plith paused now, making that terrifying growl of his, but did not look up.

That's when a group of Zygolophodon happened into the clearing. While perhaps not as tall as Gomphotherium, they were still extremely stocky, looking like gray, walking boulders, she thought. The Plithocyon now swung its head to look at them. Soon as they saw him, the herd charged, trumpeting noisily. Julie jumped behind a tree and stuck her fingers in her ears. The plith turned and ran off at a gallop.

Thank you! Julie thought.

Unfortunately, however, this developed into a new problem, for the elephants *also* took an interest in her pack, first touching it everywhere with their trunks, then turning it over, and again. At least they weren't trying to open it, she mused. When the old ones got bored, they walked off, but now a young one with more pep decided to have a go. It grabbed the pack by one strap and began to drag, then swing it around. *Oh no,* Julie worried. It seemed interested in a smell on the inside back, likely her sweat. It pushed at the pack with its head, putting what looked like considerable pressure on it. Julie thought of resuming her rock throwing tactic, but doubted it would work as she hoped. Finally, the young Zygo carefully placed a foot squarely in the middle of the pack and stood on it, rocking back and forth until a loud crack was heard coming from it.

"NO!" Julie shouted. The herd turned to look at her, stared, then gratefully, turned back and sauntered off. Julie waited, giving them a margin of distance, then sprinted to her pack, grabbing it and dashing, or more like dragging the heavy thing, back toward the trees.

She opened it to survey the damage and let out an expletive. *"Not the pot!"* she wailed. Though it was supposed to be collapsible, it had a bad habit of opening while she walked, and she'd had to remove the pack and close it many times. Now it was smashed flat.

"Well, guess I won't have *that* problem anymore!" Julie said to herself. "Damn!" She decided that it might be best to leave before the plith returned, so she stuck the pot back in her pack and headed out.

Julie began to wonder if maybe she should have kept one of the firearms, if at least to scare off those brutes that needed scaring off. Another regret.

After a jaunt through open birch forest, which offered up wonderful views of sky and sea, the way before her was gradually downhill, with expansive grassy plains reaching all the way to the hazy shoreline. On her left, the last of the birch forest broke off sharply down and away from her, while on her right were low hills and, closer by, strange outcroppings of rock. Ahead looked like miles of parkland and the usual groupings of beasts scattered about. With ample space between them, there was no real danger of too close an encounter.

The sky was darkening now, a scent of petrichor in the air. Julie looked up to find that it was filling with thick, ebony clouds, which undulated in characteristic waves. Mammatus. A heavy rain was likely coming. The clouds had the benefit of blocking the sun, bringing the temperature back to a more comfortable feel.

She thought about those birches. With the coming change in global climate toward the dry, they would slowly begin to recede eastward, toward the Atlantic, as would other hardwoods like Maple, Plum, Pecan, Elm, Hickory, Alder, Bald Cypress, Liquidambar, and Nyssa, eventually ending up in the northeast. Animals that depended on these flora would also begin to go away, such as some families of borophagine canids, oreodonts, dromomeryicids and chalicotheres. On the other hand, there would be an increase in plants that do well in dry conditions such as Juniper, Mountain Mahogany, Palm, Oak, Pine, Fir, Spruce, grassland, chaparral and desert. In the Great Basin, the mixed conifer forest would retreat northward and into the mountains to be replaced by a dominance of oak-pinyon-juniper woodland and hard-leaved shrubs.

The world would continue to dry, peaking at around six million years before the Anthropocene, in what science would call the Messinian Salinity Crisis, a time when the climate became seriously arid.

Sadly, coinciding with this drying crisis and sharp increase in seasonality, a faunal crisis would occur wherein over five dozen mammal genera would become extinct, the worst in the record of North American land mammal genera, till the age of man. Most browsing taxa would disappear, along with the decimation of grazing and mixed feeders as well, thus ending this special event on the earth, the Clarendonian Chronofauna. But that was still a long, long way off as far as she was concerned, and she could enjoy this paradise as long as she wanted.

The cool breeze was welcome, and the tall grass tossed about in waves all around her. Off in the distance, Julie eyed that which she was going to investigate: that thin trail of smoke climbing high into the sky with a glowing ember at its base. As the sun receded westward and clouds to gather, the progressively darkening sky made that ember burn brighter, offering an appealing contrast to the blues and violets.

A light patter of rain started softly falling, the *pit, pit, pit* of drops hitting the tops of the grass and the tiny purple, green and white flowers near their tips. The sprinkles increased until they blended together in a hushed melody, accented by the occasional whistle of a ground squirrel calling others of its clan in from the wet. She'd earlier observed that, at variance to the single, sharp note of their later descendants, these squirrels made more of a quick, melodic trilling. It was not unpleasant.

When the rain began to come down just a little harder, the grass bowed over to let the drops off, wetting her bare legs. Like the grass, a herd of *Protohippus* hung their heads and ears low, dripping and snoozing. Even though the shower was not a strong one, the total mass of drops between her and it blurred the horizon, and the glowing ember that was the volcano dimmed.

Droplets of clean water ran down her cheeks. Julie inhaled deeply; the smell of wet grass was heady, intoxicating.

Other animals called out, but their voices were muted, obscured in the rising aural timbre of the rain. Her feet were, by now, thoroughly soaked in her socks and shoes, and she decided to remove them rather than risk the blisters that would result if she continued on in them. Sitting in the wet grass, she pulled them off, then tied them to her pack by the laces. Then she decided to disrobe entirely, to peel off her saturated clothing and go au naturel. And why not, the weather was certainly balmy enough. She laughed at herself, a sight she must be.

Unlike in the future, there was no need to fear this rain. Thus, standing and re-donning her pack, she recommenced her walk, delighting in the feel of wet grass under her feet, between her toes. It was a freeing, liberating sensation. Where she met bare earth, her toes would squish through the cool mud, sometimes sinking to the ankle. In these places, she wove a zigzag path through ground squirrel communities, their denizens, tight, warm bundles of fur, fluffy tails covering their noses, now safely nestled in their underground dens, dozing away the trauma of the shower. Julie laughed again. Then she began to sing.

A favorite vocalist, it was Enya's *It's In the Rain*.

Now that it was almost night, she needed to find a place to sleep, though she wasn't sure she'd be able to in the rain. The sky was, by now, evenly veiled in clouds, the water coming down in sheets. Julie looked around for some way to escape the squall. There were trees she could hide under, yet there were other creatures standing beneath them. She came across a small, shallow cave that she could probably squeeze into, but, alas, the ground inside looked wet, gritty and uncomfortable.

After another minute of searching, she found a large, heavy-looking overhang of ancient sandstone and embedded river rocks. Below it, on a raised platform of eroded sand, was a nice, thick tuft of green grass. The overhang impeded most of the rain and the turf beneath was largely dry. Still, thanks to the breeze, some made it in anyway. Julie took off her pack, groaning with relief, and set it down resting against the boulder, then she surveyed the area, looking for something. There were a couple of old, fallen trees thirty yards away, and she headed for them. It was dark now and hard to see, but she could still make out dry branches lying on the ground and set to gathering them. Back and forth she went, until she had made a leaning wall of tree limbs firmly positioned against the open side, which checked the further encroachment of the rain. After this, Julie dried herself, spread her sleeping bag on the soft grass, and, gathering some food, lie on top of it.

Thunder sounded in the distance, and she wondered if it was the storm or the volcano. Minutes later, she was asleep.

When she woke, the sun was peeking through tall cumulus clouds, while water *drip, drip, dripped* off the face of the overhang above and around her onto the saturated grass. Birds sang brightly, calling out the new day. Another day of wonder and joy. In no hurry, Julie went back to sleep.

She was awakened an hour later by a violent tremor. She'd been dreaming and heard the rumble of some gargantuan beast coming to mash her into the soil. Julie jumped up, and, bleary eyed, looked around for the raving devil. There was none about, yet the ground continued to roll, dislodging some of her lean-to branches.

Earthquake!

Pebbles spilled off the underside of the overhang, peppering her head and shoulders painfully. Julie staggered into the open and tried to brace herself. The ground continued to roll beneath her. Then there was a terrific explosion. It came from the direction of the ocean, and she looked that way, eyes wide with fear. The volcano. A plume of gas and dust was rolling out the top, below which a bright layer of lava flowed.

Herds of animals went racing by, she could see them through gaps in the trees, the sound of their hooves creating a thunder of their own. There was another explosion and quickly Julie plugged her ears. The next one knocked her off her feet, but she was up again in an instant, ready to move. With that last display of raw power, however, the stentorian rumbling stopped, the earth ceased shaking, and, plume billowing, the crisis passed.

When she was satisfied it was over, Julie straightened and summoned her nerve. A Miocene alarm clock. *Never much cared for alarm clocks,* she thought. She turned to look at the plume. It darkened the southwest quarter of the sky, but was dissipating. Steam boiled up from the area where the hot lava connected with water. The future Los Angeles was under construction. She had to see it.

The temps were already climbing. Julie gathered her clothing and walked to a stream to wash them, pounding with rocks and wringing them out. Wrinkle-free they would not be. She got into them wet, reflecting amusedly about why it was so hard to get wet clothes *on.* But she'd decided that it was a good idea, as the wet would help to keep her cool in the baking sun.

She wanted to check on Jaqzen's progress and switched on the PinPointer. There he was, seventeen miles back. Uncomfortably close. Too close for her. Julie slipped into her pack and headed out.

The ground grumbled and moved continually as she closed in on the volcano, but it was only a shadow of its earlier activity. Occasionally, however, these fairly quiescent times were interrupted by more violent phases. In the intervals between noisy eruptions, an eerie quiet dominated, for by now she was alone, everything else that had any sense having long run off for safer environs. If the quiet held long enough, though, she knew they'd be back.

As she walked, Julie began to encounter splatterings of hardened pyroclastic lava that had ejected from the volcano in the past and landed on this far side. The closer she got, the more frequent their occurrence. Rather than being alarmed about it, though, she was reassured, for she surmised that these extra violent expulsions were uncommon, as there was plenty of vegetal growth within. Walking on the hardened lava was something else. Though technically the volcano was putting out a fluid, low silica basaltic lava called Pahoehoe, which is generally smooth, the action of launching and landing at distance, it partially cooling in flight, made it sharp and dangerous like the more high silica-content of Aa. Julie put on her gloves for fear of slipping and gashing her hands into one of the sharp projections. She tread carefully.

Julie was thrilled to find within these solid lava mounds seams of translucent Olivine, an exquisite, olive-green crystal, called Peridot when of gemstone quality. She stooped down to study them, then found a nice specimen lying in olivine sands around the mounds and pocketed it.

The tension mounted in her as closer she came, step by halting step, until, finally, she was there, standing on a rise above the agitated sea, waves pounding the cliffs below. The Miocene Pacific. As beautiful as it was vast. To fall there, a hundred feet down, would be certain death. Then, ironically, as she thought about the prospect, another sudden movement of the earth almost pitched her into the waves and she jumped back in fright, subsequently deciding that it might be safer to lie down on her stomach to watch the show. She wedged herself between two thin trees near the edge, an arm wrapped around each.

The actual volcano was less than a quarter-mile away, but huge gobs of bright red lava spilled from it into the raging sea as from a giant soda that had been shaken. Steam sizzled audibly, and an acrid, burning, sulfuric odor filled the air. Julie tied a wet cloth around her head, covering her face below the eyes. Another rumble that she felt to her very core sent a thrill of excitement through her, but she was safe. After each, more of the red-hot lava would belch out and roll down the side. This was not a peaked volcano though, but a lower level plateau version. Rather than height, breadth would be the end product as more and more land was gradually being added to the future state.

Julie knew that a tectonic rift ran right through here that would become known as the San Andreas Fault system, a system notorious for its many devastating earthquakes and the resulting billions of dollars in damages it would cause. She knew that the sliver of land on the west side of that fault, land that would contain the Santa Lucia, Gabilan, and Santa Cruz Ranges, Point Reyes Peninsula and all the cities around them, in short, most of coastal California, was on the Salinian block which was sliding inexorably northward. The highest tips of those later ranges were either still under the sea or islands jutting out from the mainland, anxious for their day in the sun. In fifteen million years, the spot where these lands were would be 150 plus miles north of here. Meanwhile, the rest of California would be pushed and pulled, sliced and diced.

Presently, Yosemite's domes and prominences are still embedded in soil. The Grand Canyon is developing, as are the Andes. North America is detached from Central and South America and would be so for another 12 million years. On the other hand, Antarctica, while attached to Gondwanaland, is drifting away from it. With summer temps there reaching up to 45 degrees Fahrenheit, tundral plants, and small trees grow on its coast and well inland. In Alaska, temperate forests of Oak and Beech, Hickory, Walnut, Sweet gum, Basswood, Elm, Wingnut and Katsura are common.

However, this situation was soon to change, geologically and climatologically speaking, when Antarctica's separation from South America forming the Drake Passage, and the Tasman Gateway's opening between Antarctica and Australia, will create a strong circumpolar current around the southern continent, thus concentrating the cold there. This will re-establish the Eocene glaciations and ice caps that will characterize the South Pole ever afterwards and lead to the coming worldwide change in climate. Already, Julie suspected, that the process was in motion - the coolness of the mornings suggested it. At 13 million years before the Anthropocene, the process will accelerate.

That night at dusk, Julie enjoyed the spectacle of the reddest sunset she'd ever seen, the volcanic ash coloring the sky just for her. Then, at twilight, she reveled in the brilliant contrast of reds, yellows, purples, blues, and a hundred variations in between, close up. Of lava as it poured into the ocean. She wondered if there were a more beautiful sight and snapped several pictures. Later, she lay on her sleeping bag in the open, well back from the cliff, having no fear of being eaten by anything, as there was nothing around to do the eating. The show was *magnificent*. The low-level rumblings, along with the glow and occasional ejection of lava, was better than any fireworks display she'd ever experienced as a child. Still, tired as she was, she slept soundly, volcano and all.

The next morning, Julie headed up coast for some further exploration, then back toward her cave camp when her chronometer alarm began to sound, reminding her that it was time to return to the Strong Box. Over the last couple of days she had thought more about what she had to do. She would hang out at her den a spell longer, then make her way back to the box, praying that she didn't come across Jaqzen heading in her direction while en route. On the last day, she would make a dash inside, bolt the door and wait for transference.

The plan made her feel guilty, though. Could she really do that, just leave the ape-man here to fend for himself all alone? On the other hand, he was probably in his element here, she thought, with targets aplenty, shooting anything that moved. Shouldn't leave him here then, to wreak his havoc on this virgin land. But if she invited him into the box he'd probably grab her and that would be that. So what to do? It seemed an unsolvable problem.

Julie lounged for the next several days at her secret hideaway. It was a good thing she headed back when she did, for it rained hard the first two of those days and she spent the time confined inside. The sound of the rain, though, was soothing, and she caught up on some much needed rest. Her waking time was filled with observing and recording the eruption, but also with writing in her scientific and personal journals. There would be a wealth of plant DNA specimens to take back and analyze and videos to study. She could fill an encyclopedia with the data she had gathered.

Topping her list were all the new species she'd cataloged, and in just two weeks time! Species that, for one reason or another, never fossilized or were never discovered in the fossil record, including a number of dry land Dromomerycidae, antelope types with fantastic horn structure, and who seemingly never drank, instead getting their water from the plants around them. One of the most bizarre species had two horns that completely encircled its head. Another had nine to eleven sharp horns that protruded straight out from the sides of its face, starting at one side of the bottom jaw clear around to the other with a gap at the throat. Another had antlers that, instead of on top of its head, wore them obliquely on the bottom jaw. Still another had horns that began at the shoulder and, increasing in size, went to the top of the head.

There were also some new species of horse and camel. One of the former she at first misidentified as a totally new animal, it looked and behaved so differently from the norm. For one thing, it was a loner, at least as far as its own kind was concerned, preferring either its own company or that of the dry land Dromos which it seemed to fancy, even sleeping with them under the boughs of giant oaks. Two, it actually had a small horn of its own, centered unicorn-style in the middle of its forehead, and a narrow, but thick rim of fur that ran the length of its spine like a Rhodesian Ridgeback's. Another version of horse had even stranger behavior. These actually competed aggressively against other species of horse for good grazing territory, but they did it as a group, pack-like. Roaming, then charging as one, routing all others. Another interesting thing about them was that they had an almost lion-like mane that covered much of their necks. Finally, and quite surprisingly, they were apparently somewhat omnivorous, preferring to graze, but also sometimes scavenging from the kills of satiated carnivores. Julie watched these ones for a long time, captivated.

She was thrilled, too, when she'd discovered a species of pygmy rhino while spying an overgrown island close to the mainland a few miles north of the volcano. As it happened, she was only shooting some random pictures of the isle to be looked at later. When she did get to it though, and increased the resolution for a closer look, the group was unmistakable. Rhinos, except that they were all pygmies. She could tell by their size as they browsed next to some osteodontorns, which, fearing no threat, freely walked among them.

Lastly, were the animal types that were totally new to science. Rare individuals that usually lived solitary lives, like the furred thing she barely caught a glimpse of hovering on the edge of the forest before, seeing her, it receded back into the shadows. This one unnerved her, for her first impression was that it was almost primate in appearance.

In her treks so far, Julie had also come upon many objects that in her time would have been big news among the paleontological community. Bones of all kinds, shells and fossils, though these were from even older times, perhaps early Miocene or Oligocene. One, a Titanothere, jutted halfway out of solid rock, a shoulder blade stove in, and its left side rib cage smashed. Its head still raised in a look of defiance at whatever had been strong enough to do it in. *A find like this,* Julie thought as she caressed the skull, *would be the highlight of anyone's career, yet here it is, exposed to the elements.* As such, it probably wouldn't last another thousand years before finally succumbing to sun and rain, then back to the soil it would go.

The rain ended in the early morning hours of the third day. When the sun came up, it shone inside the cavern, driving a shaft of light into Julie's closed eyes. Instinctively, she covered them with the crook of her arm, rolled over and tried to go back to sleep. The sound of an abrupt crack got her up. The old oak finally going? Though she did have a rope securely tied above, with loops for her hands and feet, still the possibility that the falling tree might rip it down as it went worried her. She looked out at the tree expecting to see it go, but except for a few dried leaves falling from it into the canyon, it made no move.

CRACK!

The sound was unmistakable. It was not the tree. It was a gun. Blast and ricochet. *Jaqzen!* Julie rolled into the shadows, her heart suddenly thumping. *OH NO!* She panicked. *He's here! He's found me!*

CRACK!

It didn't sound like he was immediately nearby, but was also not too far away. She judged the distance to be about an eighth mile. It was coming from the midst of thick woods straight out from the river below. He was following it. She strained her eyes, but saw nothing moving. After a few minutes, there was another report of the rifle. Julie jumped. Jaqzen was getting closer, but why was he shooting? Was he so confident that he could give her this notice of his arrival, give her another chance to get away?

She didn't know what to do. She had no weapon. Additionally, she was stuck in the cave, like a mouse in a hole without another way out. She wondered if she should try to make a break for it, but decided against it, then thought that if Jaqzen was going to get her he'd have to climb down to do it. She would make it hard for him. Course, he could just wait her out. Starve her out. No, she'd die of thirst long before hunger. Julie looked around for some rocks that she could throw. He wouldn't get her without a fight.

Another blast, this one very close by. Then something moved within her view. Big. It was him, emerging from an edge of the forest just upstream and walking in her direction. He held the rifle at the ready in both hands, advancing slowly. His pants were soaked from the waist down, having obviously waded through the stream, now a swift running river thanks to the rain. His hair was wild and his face unshaven and bronzed.

He had a ragged tear on one arm of his dirty, long-sleeved camo shirt, which was encrusted with dried blood. Crazily, Julie felt an instant pity for the man and an involuntary urge to call out, to summon one of her kind. The only other human in this world. Then, *no*. She quickly suppressed the thought.

Jaqzen stopped, noticing something in the soil in front of him. He bent down, examining it, feeling as if for freshness, then lifted his head and looked around him. What was it, Julie wondered? Had he found some clue to her whereabouts? She never walked in the soft, wet sand near the hill, loath to leave footprints. It couldn't be that. Looking down again, Jaqzen then stood and carefully glanced all around him. Had he found her? He looked up in the trees.

Julie ducked back into the shadows, then drew in her breath. *Oh God!* Julie realized, *The rope! He'll see the rope!* Though it hung behind the oak branch, still, it was likely visible with the sun upon it. Indeed, Jaqzen's gaze settled on the cliff face, looking keenly in her direction, eyes squinting, and a scowl on his face. He seemed to be looking for a long time.

I'm done for, she thought. Jaqzen turned his head and looked past the cliff into the trees on the other side, then back around again. Maybe he didn't see her! He lifted his rifle into the air and pulled the trigger. BOOM!

Julie jumped. Then Jaqzen yelled out.

"I KNOW YOU'RE HERE, PINE. YOU CAN'T RUN FOREVER. I'LL FIND YOU! BETTER TO JUST COME OUT NOW!" He shot again, then continued his slow way down the river, soon passing out of sight.

He hadn't seen the rope! Julie exalted. She was safe for the moment. But what if he spotted some clue that she was climbing the hillside? He didn't though. Somehow.

Opalescence

Julie stayed until the next morning, hoping to give Jaqzen some distance before launching hard for the Strong Box. There was no more time to waste. Alas, it wasn't to be. After walking on for the rest of that day toward the coast, Jaqzen suddenly turned and began to head back in earnest. Julie knew it from the PinPointer. He must have known that that was her plan, too. Of course, it's what she'd do. So now it was a race to the box. Even if she made it days ahead of time, she planned to lock herself in and wait, hoping that Jaqzen wouldn't be able to destroy it before retrieval time. To that end, she drove herself relentlessly, day and night, crashing through brush and leaving a very noticeable trail.

By the time she reached the ridge and Strong Box days later, Julie was utterly exhausted. Standing within the wooded shadows at the edge of a clearing, checking to see if Jaqzen was there, Julie was shocked to find him lounging against it, near the entrance, waiting for her, cigarette hanging out the side of his mouth, apparently having just eaten. In front of him, lying atop a bloody rock, was a hunk of flesh with his knife sticking into it. The front of his shirt was doused in gore. He'd eaten it raw. Julie suppressed a gag. Jaqzen's rifle leaned on the wall beside him. There was a Gomphotherium tusk lying on the ground ahead that had been savagely cut out. The heads and pelts of other species were scattered around as well. Too, garbage was strewn everywhere, casually discarded. Broken glass and plastic obscenity from the future.

The bastard! Julie seethed, gritting her teeth. She wanted to do him some harm, but lacked the means. She glanced around her for something to use, then snapped out of it. She had to get into that box. Slinking back into the trees, she decided to wait until he slept, then race in.

He had that covered too. Julie stepped on a twig and it snapped. Jaqzen immediately took hold of his gun, glancing around him, laughing as he did.

"So you're back, are you?" he yelled. "Heh, I knew you'd be! Well, COME ON, THEN!" He began to shoot randomly, a wild look of gleeful rage on his face. Then, standing, he lowered his pants and flung himself out. "Here I am. *COME AND GET IT, BITCH!*" he laughed roughly.

Julie turned away in revulsion. Jaqzen pulled his pants back up, then yelled, "If you want in here you're going to have to go through me!" Laughing again. "IF you ask *nicely,* MAYBE I'll let you in, otherwise you're stuck here, baby, for the rest of your freaking life!" He fired a few more times, looking around, trying to see her.

"You made a mistake taking my guns, Bitch. Nobody, but *NOBODY* messes with my guns!" he continued. "But you didn't get 'em all, did ya?" Jaqzen shot again. "I'm gonna get 'em back, Bitch. One way or the other." He paused, then remembering something, pulled out a small black device from his pocket. "Hey! But I got something of yours. Yeah!" The EMP weapon Karstens had given her. She'd forgotten about it. "What were you planning on doin' with *this* I wonder? Well, it's in safe keeping now!" he laughed.

He looked around himself, at the gore. "Yeah, I've been having some *fun.* Guess I just like slaughterin' little bunnies! But I'll tell ya, if you wanna put a stop to all this *madness,* all you gotta do is just come on out!" He waited, but she remained where she was.

Then he said something that shocked her. Shocked her to her very core.

"Got news for you, Bitch. You're mine." Laughing again. "That's right, you belong to *good ol' Deet.* See, you were never *meant* to return. Nooo. No, no, no." Jaqzen looked around again, peering into the growth, trying to find her, ready to spring at the first hint of movement. "You think you were chosen because of your supposed 'superior' intellect, do you? Just shows how *dumb* you really are!"

Julie listened solemnly, apprehension rising in her throat.

Now Jaqzen thrust out his head, arms behind him, bellowing. "Let me fill you in on a few things, Bitch! They don't wantcha back! Probably kill you if you showed up. Can't have you *blabbing* now can we? So, you wanna know why you were picked? It's not because Jim Hodges is you're friend, that's for sure. Naw, you were picked for the same reason I was, we have the right *blood type!* Ever wonder why you rarely got sick while your *loser* of a husband caught everything? We were gifted with some sort of immunity, you and I. But don't think we're the only ones. Naw. They discovered that about a tenth of a percent of the population has it. That's actually lot of people! So you should be grateful! I could have had *any number* of females. Now on top of that, they ran tests on you, found out that you've got something called 'super-fertility.' Great genes. *Yeah!* And you'll pass on those gifts on to future generations. When they went looking for candidates, it was just a coincidence that they found someone who is knowledgeable about this time period, and that would be an obvious step up in survivability." Jaqzen paused to scan the forest again. "I told 'em though, I don't *need* no help. But what can you do? Guess it was just meant to be!

"You see, me and you, baby, we were *meant* to be together. Me, the King, and you, *my bitch.* Anyway, that's the natural order right? Just look around you at your beloved animals. Male's always stronger, isn't he, makes the rules, doesn't he? *Ain't no women's liberation in nature!*" Jaqzen shouted, laughing again. "So you see, you're here to stay, and I'm the only game in town, so maybe it's time you get off your *high* horse, forget that reject of a 'husband' and got some common sense into your pretty little head 'cause *you ain't going nowhere, and*

I never lose, and I never quit till I get what I want." He ended his words with more laughing.

Stunned, Julie slunk back into the woods, vomiting behind a tree. Her mind reeled. No, it couldn't be true. Karstens seemed such a good man. Honest. He wouldn't do something like this. In the back of her mind, though, Jaqzen's words confirmed a nagging suspicion. If all they wanted was a leaf gatherer, they could have picked anyone. Still, how could they have chosen someone like *him*, even if he had some special genetics, the man was a barbarian. He used to work for the government, though. Maybe he had connections. Or maybe he was lying.

Whatever the facts were, though, there was one thing that was clear: she had to get back, try at least. For much as she loved the Miocene, the Anthropocene, her stinking, wretched, dying world of the future, was where her husband, her heart was. Once back, maybe they could find a way here again.

Julie contemplated looking for the rifles. But the day was closing, and even if she could remember where she threw them, the actual chances of finding one in the dark and returning to the Strong Box in time tomorrow morning were slim. Thus, the rest of the evening she simply watched through the trees and waited. Jaqzen made no attempt to find her, lest she dash past him and into the box. He just stayed there near the door, stuffing himself with his Gompho, belching satisfaction, blood dripping down the front of his shirt, not moving, except to urinate, which he did as vulgarly as possible.

There was no other way, she finally realized. She'd have to surprise and attack him somehow, maybe kill him, and she had to do it before tomorrow. It was the only way she'd ever see Tom again. Right now, though, overcome by extreme tiredness, she knew she had to get some shut-eye.

Julie crept off a way and found a hollow under a fallen tree layered with a thick blanket of white oak leaves. It was hidden well. She crawled inside, covering herself with them and fell immediately to sleep.

Julie slept through the next day. When she woke later that evening, she dashed to the forest clearing, heedless, frantic.

The Strong Box was gone, and so was Jaqzen.

Twenty One

It rained on and off for the next week as Tom and Little closed in on those purple peaks shrouded in clouds. Some days the showers fell hard and Tom would retreat under a tree or inside his T/H to wait it out. Disappointingly, it seemed that precipitation drove the squirrels, which were such a staple of their diet, back underground, forcing the aelurodon to find and catch larger game. Further, they were unquestionably diminishing in number here at altitude. Now she brought things like *Leptarctus*, *Plionictis* and *Sthenictis*, larger animals that could fight back. Indeed, she showed up at one point carrying one of these in her mouth while limping, a bloody gash in her left front leg. Tom was moved by her dedication to their pack, their survival, and washed, then treated the wound as best he could. Little, though, refused to accept the bandage.

Tom also found that he could not walk in wet feet for too long, otherwise the rubbing and chaffing in his shoes incurred more blisters, making it painful to continue. When he could, where he could, usually soft, unrocky grassland, Tom would go shoeless. His feet, though, were hardening, as calluses built upon each other, forming a solid mat which, while not a particularly attractive feature, were useful. Perhaps given enough time, he speculated, he wouldn't need shoes at all.

The first morning of the next week, the high snowy heights were above them. Tom, once again worried that they were headed in the wrong direction, remembered the "Map" on the PinPointer. He flipped it on. Instantly an outline of the state of California appeared with its future counties and cities. And there was the long chain labeled "Sierra Nevada Mtns." He'd have to turn on his beacon to place himself. He did this quickly and looked. There was the red light as usual. Seconds later, the green popped on. He looked at his own, the blue, and there he was, at the head of the mountain chain. They were indeed the Sierras. According to the PinPointer, he was just south of the Sonora Pass, or what would later be called that. The section of Sierras north of it, not having developed yet, was a long, gently sloping highland dotted with volcanic peaks. The map also showed that they were still within the Mehrten Formation. Yet, the compass needle pointing south continued to confuse him.

The way was progressively getting harder. To avoid the rocks and keep to the grass, Tom decided to begin heading back down and toward the inland sea, their path describing a slow arc. The going was pleasant. He could not have known how fateful the next week would prove to be.

Past mid-afternoon the following day, while they were descending one side of a long ravine that ran from the peaks above, Little began to whine and act strangely. She seemed to sense something that Tom could not see, running in short sprints to a lower ridge edge, looking down repeatedly. Expecting to perhaps find a large beast keeping pace just below, Tom nervously peeked over the side, but there was nothing that should cause such alarm: a herd of Hipparion half a mile lower galloping north.

After a while, Little ran down the bank toward the flatland far below, then ran back up, now yelping loudly. It was most unsettling, and Tom began to worry that perhaps his aelurodon had caught some Miocene disease or other. He watched her closely, hoping this wasn't the case. Then he thought about the wound in her leg. Calling her over, he inspected it, while she licked his face, still whining. Though rough, it seemed to be healing. He knew that didn't necessarily mean anything, however. He checked her over, running hands through her fur, but again discovered nothing wrong. Maybe she was sick. If so, he dearly hoped that it wasn't fatal. Without her, he would be in real trouble in this prehistoric world. Could he even provide for himself adequately, he wondered? Besides that, he loved her.

A loud rumble sounded from the direction of the mountain peaks and Tom jerked his head that way, eyes wide. The rumble continued, distant, but growing louder, approaching. It sounded like a closing freight train. Then the ground under him began to shake, at first just a bit, then increasing. *An earthquake!* Instinctively, he threw himself on the ground and held on. The ground rolled under him while Little barked in fear. Tom too feared, feared that the earth might open to swallow them up. He tried to stand, but his balance was knocked out and he fell back hard on his rear.

The rumbling and shaking stopped. He waited there, hoping that it was over. When it seemed to be, he looked around for Little. She was nowhere in sight. Suddenly she barked behind him and he jumped.

"HOLY CRAP...!" he stammered, *"Don't do that!"* Tom yelled, angry. She did not stop. Instead, she ran ahead a ways, then back again in a panic, now barking furiously. Her actions scared him. Was she rabid? Would she attack? She had grown a lot and was now at least sixty pounds of muscle and ferocity. He gulped.

"It's okay! It's over," Tom tried to reassure. She dove straight for him. Tom glanced around for a stick or something to fend her off with. "NO, LITTLE!" he shouted, throwing up his arms to protect himself.

Another rumble. Tom looked back uphill. Something happening there. Then Little had him. She was pulling him down. He looked at her in horror. She had seized him by the sleeve and was wrenching him with all her might, growling in anger. The rumbling was increasing. He looked back up the mountain; something was coming. Little let go of his sleeve and barked at him.

Now he saw it: a dark wave growing into view, moving fast.

"LET'S GO!" Tom bellowed. And down they shot, while a lahar, an avalanche of snow, rock, mud and volcanic ash, dislodged by the earthquake, roared down after them. It was hard running with the pack on and Tom thought of jettisoning it, but knew he would regret it later, so he didn't. Little was much faster and kept turning around barking at him to hurry up. It was getting hard to stay upright, then he came to a cliff, a short, but steep drop before him. Little had gone around it. Tom was about to jump and turned to see how much time they had. Not much. A wall of mud as high as he slammed into and swept him over the side and down, then covered him, while it continued on. Another two hundred yards and it was over.

Tom lay there, unconscious, buried almost to his neck in alluvium from the mountain. While he still breathed, it was an effort, for not only had his breath been knocked out of him, but the pressure of the mud was a weight on his chest. His heart thumped laboriously, struggling to hold on.

Julie. She was calling, reaching out toward him and he her. Their fingers almost touching, then she began to pull back, to recede. She yelled his name, but no sound came. Slowly, pain in her eyes, she was fading.

Beat, beat .. beat, beat .. beat ... beat ... beat ... beat .... beat ...

Yanking. Digging. Pulling.

It was Little. She had dove in after him and was now using all of her power, all of that savage Barstovian aggression to get him out. Insensibly, Tom opened his eyes, his vision foggy, his thought nonexistent. Something, moving slowly, so slowly, covered in filth. Eyes fierce, red. Teeth bared. *Snarling. Digging. Digging.*

Leaves drifting by. Hovering, hanging, suspended in the air. Nothing moving. All is still, silent and black.

Sleep.

Pulling. Yanking. Dragging. He was out, now sliding down the slippery surface of the mudflow, finally stopping face up. He opened his eyes again. Breath. Something caked in mud barking quietly at him.

Sleep.

Consciousness returned and so did sound. He was not where he was before. Now he was on solid ground. Next to him lay Little. Absently, he stretched out a hand to pet her. Immediately she jumped up and barked at him, then began to lick his face. His head ached. Tom reached up and found a painful swelling over his left temple, winced, looked at his hand and saw blood. He groaned, lay back down, then, a moment later, fought to sit up. Little was all over him, jumping over his legs, racing around and licking him.

"Okay, okay," Tom said, reaching out a hand to her. He looked back at the river of mud that had washed over him, it ran almost from the top of the mountain, miles distant. A brown scar of dislodged boulders and downed trees, snow and mud, it filled the ravine they'd been in. Water from that snow now melting, running down over and under the mud. Over him. He gingerly touched the lump again. A big one. Probably got clobbered by a rock.

Tom got on all fours, then slowly to his feet. He stumbled back to the ground, then sat, head down until the spinning stopped. Then he tried again. He felt wobbly and remained bent over at the waist until he was steady. Finally, he stood and exhaled. Inhaled and exhaled. His heart rhythm was returning to normal. He looked at himself: *what a sight!* Then at Little and laughed weakly. A stab of pain in his head stopped him. "Yeow!" Tom exclaimed, "Take it easy."

He eyed his aelurodon again, "You should see yourself!" he said. Then he remembered, her warnings, warnings that he'd been deaf to, and that she had saved him. Tears began to flow, and on his knees he went, throwing his arms around her and hugging.

"Thank you," he whispered and kissed her head. "You're the best." Little wagged her tail, looking much at that moment like a regular dog. Albeit a big one for her age.

Tom thought of something then. Something was missing. *Oh no,* he thought, *my backpack!* Casting about, but not seeing it, he looked at the trail Little had made when she dragged him out of the muck. Fifteen feet in he saw a strap sticking out. There it was!

"I gotta get my pack, Little. Don't panic, okay?" Her mouth wide and tail wagging, she barked. Tom waded into the mud one big step at a time until it was about waist-high. Little barked again, then again, a note of concern in her voice. Tom shooed her, then turned back to the job at hand. It was thick and took him a minute to reach. At last, feeling down in the slop, he grabbed hold of his pack and pulled. It was amazing how strongly mud could hold onto something; he thought about how hard it must have been for Little to get *him* out. Tom dug down and around, then straining with effort, freed the pack. The exertion made his swelling throb. If it was heavy before, it was double that now. He dragged it across the face of the slide.

When he got it out, he lay it on dry ground and began to wipe the sludge off. Tom worried what he would find when he opened it up, some of it he could clean, but some of it was delicate instrumentation.

The PinPointer!

Fright gripped him. As quickly as he could, he pulled the muddy straps out of their holders and lifted the flap. Mire poured out of the main compartment. He began to feel around in it and withdraw the various items. Water filter, medical kit, fire starters, handsaw, etc. He unloaded until the main was empty. *Where is it?!* He thought he remembered putting it in the main compartment after the last time he used it. There were other compartments. *Maybe in one of them.* One by one he opened and emptied each pocket without finding the P.P. When he got to the last one, his face screwed up in fear, he already had plans to get the small hand shovel and dig through every bit of that slide, Sisyphean style, until he found it, no matter how long it took. But when he ripped open the last pocket, there it was. Not even wet, the zipper had kept it clean and dry. Such a sense of relief washed over him that Tom began to shake and had to lie down.

He needed to test it. Carefully opening, he switched it on, and on popped the red light, pulsing like a heart. The green, however, did not come on. Tom waited patiently. But only the red beat. Another five minutes, but there was no change. No green light. No Julie. His welt throbbed like that red light. *If you've done something to her Jaqzen, I'll find you. I'll get you.* He couldn't have known that Julie was only asleep.

Praying that she was okay, Tom reloaded the pack and dragged it to a stream. There, in succession, he cleaned each item and finally the pack itself, setting them all out to dry in the sun while he lay in the shade. Little had jumped in the current and cleaned herself off, though cleaning was not her intention.

Instead, she had noticed some large trout and was making a splash trying to catch them, but having no more luck than when she tried the first time.

Something caught Tom's eye. A bright gleam of light coming from back up the slide, reflecting off something not noticed until clouds had wandered by and the earth had rotated just enough to catch the angle of the sun. He stared at it wonderingly. Then, one by one, other tiny reflections appeared, sparkling like day stars. He sat up, resting himself on his elbows. *What is this*, he wondered, *something dislodged by the flow?* The lights now shone from a thousand points all the way up the slide, an amazing spectacle.

Tom determined to have a look, and stood. The dazzling brilliance from a large object sixty feet away made him cover his eyes. Through the gaps between his fingers, he kept it in sight while approaching. Amber light from the thing was actually hot on his skin, so well did it express the sun's rays. Once again, Tom waded into the muck, wanting to decipher the mystery, but unable to see through the radiance. Moving off to the side of the object dimmed it just enough that he could now make out a shape. Large, blocky, smooth.

GOLD! Tom let out a loud, triumphant shout.

Waist high in mud, he pushed through and clamored over it with difficulty until he reached the giant nugget. It was partially buried in a pile of rocky debris, and was hot to the touch. Having grasped it, he quickly withdrew his hand. Except for gentle undulations in its surface, it was flawless. Breathlessly, he began to scoop away the rubble and detritus until the solid hunk was revealed. Slowly, Tom shook his head. It was magnificent. It was *unbelievable*. He looked around him now, at the other shining objects. Here and there were other chunks of the yellow fire. Who knew how much was still buried.

"Ho-ly crap!" he said to Little. "HOLY CRAP! *Look at this!*" Little had partially gone in after her human, but not farther than chest high. Still, she kept a keen eye on him, wondering what it was all about.

Tom remembered now that, in the far future, this would be gold country. Here the precious metal would be discovered, triggering a mad rush of panners and prospectors from across the young United States, eager to cash in. Claims would be made and towns flung up, while villains and heroes would fight legendary gun battles in the streets. A whole western lore would be created. Native Americans would be massacred or shoved onto reservations, while homesteaders settled their ancient lands. Meanwhile, buffalo, which used to number in the millions, were all but exterminated. The railroad followed, sealing the deal. Not far behind, of course, came the establishment of a new state: California, the Golden State.

Gold would be the backbone and standard of currency for the country, until eventually changed into paper money. Sadly, greed would be institutionalized in the new capitalist system, and the rich would begin their usual rise to the top, trampling the poor and their paper rights along the way.

Tom looked at the glimmering chunk of metal, so beautiful before him, and recoiled. Death comes as an angel of light.

He soon thought better of it. Precious metals and gems, whether that be gold, silver, diamonds, rubies, or *whatever*, were not evil in and of themselves. Until *Homo sapiens*, they were merely natural expressions of a wondrous planet, delightful and diverse like life itself. No, it was their *misuse* by us that was evil. Beauty alone cannot be evil.

Tom reached out now and dug in the cool, moist soil under the huge nugget. He wanted to get the heft of it. He lifted, strained, yet it barely moved. *Wow.* He lowered himself down to get partially below it and lifted again. It moved upwards an inch or two. Continuing to heave, Tom put all of his power into it, the knob on his temple throbbing with the exertion. He grunted loudly through gritted teeth. Finally, panting, the giant golden rock was on his shoulder, weighing him down, the side that had been away from the sun cool on his cheek. *It must weigh almost fifty pounds,* he thought. *What would it be worth in* my *time?* He knew though. The monetary value of it could see him and Julie, their children, and possibly grandchildren through lives of luxury. Now, though, it was *just a rock,* a beautiful burden forcing him down.

He tossed it back into the muck, and it sank. In a second, it was gone. With time, it would be ground into smaller chunks and even into dust, and reburied. People would kill for a tiny piece of it. A little later it would be recombined into bricks and stored in secret repositories by secret agencies. *Ah well.*

Tom climbed out of the mud bath. As a souvenir, he found a much smaller, though equally beautiful, nugget, weighing no more than a pound. A gift for Julie, fitting payment for the knob on his head. He smiled and thanked the lahar.

Days later, they were still quite high on the Sierran slopes, and in fact, in an effort to avoid a sharper drop off to the west than Tom wanted, had been walking along an elevated, secondary ridge toward the South. Unfortunately, due to rises, falls and curves in the way, not to mention massive sequoias, big cone spruce and cypress, he wasn't able to clearly plot his course. If he had, he surely would have chosen to descend earlier, for now, after days of hard work, they stood on the edge of a massive V-shaped cliff and canyon that dropped steeply into misty shadows far below. The place had a feel verging on the tropical. Here, a deep river, coming from the east, through towering evergreen forest, fell, becoming a colossal waterfall. Within and around those falls, on either side, was a hodgepodge of wet boulders and dripping vegetation that would be much too difficult, and dangerous, to negotiate.

"Wonderful," he remarked sardonically, though his word betrayed the trepidation he felt.

They stood looking down, pondering their options, none of which were particularly attractive. Tom shook his head. "Okay, so do we go back?" he asked aloud. The prospect was daunting; it would require hours of mostly uphill travel, re-pushing through areas of thick growth. But what was before them was equally, if not more, daunting. It appeared doable, but *just*. If one were prone to pathological optimism. Since the way straight below was clearly nonviable, he scanned the terrain around it. To the right, the land, though with much less vegetation, was quite steep and strewn with rocky outcroppings of all sizes. Were they to fall there, they could be dashed upon them. On the left, beyond the river, the side facing the West and the sun, were mostly pines, oaks, and under them, giant ferns. From what he could see, while there was the occasional large rock between trees, it was less congested, less steep. Yet, even here it was about a 40 degree angle all the way to the bottom, and that looked a long, long way down.

"WHY?" Tom shouted into the air. His question came back to him as a series of abrupt echoes, voice ricocheting off huge slabs of granite half a mile away.

Tom looked up. The ridge he was on continued around both sides of the canyon, but then each also dropped eventually into the chasm. Past it was more mountain. Now he seriously considered going back, but when he looked to the bottom, through the mists of the waterfall and paralleling the rushing river it became, he thought he could make out a narrow clearing, a trail that twisted around to the right and possibly out to the plains beyond. And, in fact, when he looked horizontally through the trees southwestward, he believed he could see the large embayment.

He considered the options again. If they went back, there was nothing to guarantee that they wouldn't meet the same or other issues farther on, things he hadn't seen from his angle, other chasms, other pitfalls. Tom sighed. Down it was then, to the left, through the oaks and pines.

First, though, they had to get over that river. Tom spotted a broad, fallen tree, and like previous crossings, it would be their bridge. The water, calm here at the top, made this crossing painless. Then it was an eighth mile walk to the point of descent. They did it in five minutes, continually scanning their chosen path for the best entry site. Another five minutes, and they were at the clearest section. The way was still occluded by trees, and it was steep, Tom worried.

He looked around for a walking stick, something to help keep him from falling forward, and found one in a bare, narrow branch of about the right length lying on the ground. With his knife, he whittled the end to a point so as to penetrate the leafy mass and bite into the soil, thus maintaining his balance.

He glanced around again, hoping that this spot was their best choice. *Well,* he thought at last, *there's no way around it, I've stalled long enough. Might as well get on with it.*

"Probably going to take a while," he said to Little. "Are you ready?" His hiking companion stared at him, mouth closed, waiting for the word. "Then let's go," he said. Tom set one foot shakily in front of the other on a carpet of oak leaves and pine needles, simultaneously resting heavily upon his staff. In a bit, he was descending sideways, staff, foot, foot - staff, foot, foot. Little, being on four feet, wasn't having any problem at all and jounced ahead, then back again. *This is going to take all day, at this rate,* Tom thought. He almost slipped a couple of times. It was amazing how slick oak leaves on a steep bank were. *Don't fall.*

He fell, stick hurtling out of his hand, high and away, and instantly was sliding, feet first, down the hill. In a second, he was flying.

"WHOA!" Tom yelled out, afraid. He tried to stop himself, but could not, his momentum too great. Then, with the pressure on his heels, he felt himself begin to lift forwards, threatening to hurl him head first. Instinctively, he tried to lay, luge style, on his back. He'd forgotten about the pack and sleeping bag. The bag disengaged and bounced by him down the hill. *"OH, YEAH!"* Tom shouted, quickly lying back. That increased his velocity. There was a tree rapidly coming his way. He was going to slam into it. Innately, Tom, legs straight, feet held stiffly together, moved them to the right and he swerved out of the way. Easily. Relief washed through him, but, all too soon, there was another. This time he moved his legs to the left and again he was around the tree. Hope washed through him.

He was fairly hurtling along now, Little racing beside, barking excitedly. Around trees and down straightaways he continued. When he saw a large obstacle from a distance, like a boulder, he moved in time to avoid it. *I must be going twenty, thirty miles an hour,* Tom thought jubilantly. Still, there was an edge of fear at his speed. He looked back and saw that he had already come quite a distance. Now he had passed Little, who, dodging and jumping trees, was struggling to stay with him. He tried to break by jamming his feet harder into the ground, but that threatened to upend him and he gave it up.

"Come on, Little!" he yelled, *"Keep up!"* She barked in return. A deer, startled, jumped out of his path. Quail exploded noisily from some low-growing manzanita. Then he plowed through a monster pile of leaves. Still, he flew.

Tom was halfway now and tearing down the hillside. He looked back to see Little far behind. He yelled to her again to keep up, looked forward to see a yawning gorge ahead. Fear shot through him and he turned his legs to the left. It was a big one, in a few seconds, he'd be upon it and over. His jubilation instantly turned to terror.

Tom tried to pull his legs harder to the left, but almost toppled sideways. Quickly, he studied his trajectory. He wouldn't make it. No, he could. No. He screamed.

At what seemed blinding speed, he was around it and continuing on. *I have to get control*, he thought. But the way ahead was now open and, except for a few ferns, he could see nothing else in his path. He turned his head around again to find Little, but she was nowhere to be seen.

"LITTLE!" Tom called.

The ground began to level out a bit now and his pace to flag. He looked ahead, judging that there was still a half-mile to the bottom. To keep his speed up, Tom began to push some with his hands. He tried to see what would be the best stopping point, finally deciding upon one which was farthest to his left and closer to the exit of this deep canyon. Then he saw his sleeping bag. It had opened and was flopped in the branches of a tree near the river. The ground continued to level out now, and after a certain point, a particular degree at which gravity, velocity and friction all concurred, he came to a stop.

Well, that was fun, Tom thought, *and convenient!* He paused to gather himself. The sound of the river he'd seen from above was loud now. He turned around again to look for Little and saw a shape bounding straight down at him, barking furiously. Not an angry bark, mind you, an excited bark. Excited by the romp, thrilled to find her master. She barreled at him. Tom ducked and she jumped right over him, then stopped herself and ran back, now whining, climbing over and licking his face, as if she'd not seen him *in ages*.

"Okay, okay!" Tom laughed, shouting to be heard above the din of the water, equally happy to see her. *"What a good girl!"* When she was calm, he looked back at the top of the ridge high above them, at all the trees and rocks in their way, and marveled at their good fortune.

Still a hundred feet up on the bank, he could see the trail he'd glimpsed from the top that wound around and out. *Naturally,* however, there was a problem. In his single-minded concentration on getting down the mountainside he'd overlooked one important fact: the trail out was on the *other side* of the river, and that river looked *a lot bigger* at the bottom than it did from the top. In fact, it was more like a rapid, as water roared, boiled, and churned tumultuously, throwing spray outwards. The mammoth waterfall and subterranean streams that emerged here fed the river with an endless supply.

Tom thought about trying to make it out on his side of the rapids, but promptly dismissed it. Not a chance. The vegetation was simply too thick. He'd have to fight for every inch. Not only that, but poison oak grew riotously over everything. The trail on the other side, though, was clear and obviously animal made. He tsked, and laughed at his turn of luck.

There was a pile of large, smooth boulders next to the torrent, which had crashed down from above sometime in the remote past. As they were close by and would offer a better view of the other side, he headed for them. Little followed. First, though, was to collect his sleeping bag from the tree, which was on the way. Having pulled it down, he checked for damage, but amazingly found only a small tear. He rolled it up and reattached it to the top of his pack. Climbing the boulders would not be especially easy, he noted, since, what started out hard-edged ages ago had been slickened nearly to a polish with water, weathering and time. Additionally, algae grew on its surface, likely making it extra slippery.

"Wait here," Tom yelled. He then turned and began his ascent. Out from behind his granitic protection, water sprayed him eagerly, and in seconds, his clothes were wet through. They flapped behind him in the gale. If his hat hadn't been fastened he'd have lost it. But he smiled broadly, for on the other side of this rock pile was a line of smaller boulders most of the way across, which he believed they *could* get over. He whooped.

Looking back over to call Little, Tom discovered that she was already next to him, dense fur also doused, having climbed lesser rocks to get there. "Good girl!" he said approvingly. It looked like she had gotten over her earlier fear of water. That would make this *much* easier for him.

In the cacophony, he couldn't hear her whine.

Now they had to ease down to a lower boulder, then carefully make it across. Though the rocks seemed adequately spaced, there might be some jumping involved. That could be *tricky* seeing as all of them were wet.

"We have to get across!" Tom shouted. Little, her eyes partly closed due to spray, was looking at the rocks and the water and seemed to understand. *"I'll go first. Stay with me!"* With that, he slid down and touched foot onto a rock. Immediately his foot skidded. He lifted and repositioned. *Maybe this won't be so easy after all.* Spume slashed at his face and he glanced down into the maelström, then back again.

Pushing himself off the boulder, Tom stood precariously, trying not to slip, and walked a few steps. He went a few more, then turned back to call Little. She bobbed her head, nervous, then carefully jumped down. Tom saw that her claws were gripping the rock-face strongly. He turned back to the job ahead, determined to be extra careful, to plant each step with thought and precision. The jumps were nerve wracking, and once, Tom slipped and landed painfully on his shins, skinning his palms, but he did not go over. He gulped.

In the middle, water crashed mightily against two rocks, and he lowered himself down to get a better center of balance. A big, booming breaker slapped him hard and Tom reached down just in time to dig fingernails into a tiny crevice and hold on. He turned around to make sure that Little was okay.

She wasn't there.

With a jerk, Tom looked at the downstream rapids. His heart sank. A head pointing toward him was swiftly being carried away. She yelped, but he couldn't hear. Without a thought, he jumped in, banging a shin on another rock. Then all the world was turmoil. He was under and being pushed down and around. Water, dirt and gravel roiled all about him. Tom swam hard trying to get to the top. His pack, though, was weighing him down. He fought to right himself, but was helpless against the powerful current. His head went under, then up, and he gulped air and water, then down again. *Must get the pack off.* He wrestled with it, panic in his blood. It wouldn't release. He had to have air.

When people are afraid they stop thinking.

Tom willed himself to think. He grabbed one strap with the opposite hand and pushed. The pack swung off, hanging on by the other strap. A brief hesitation, he can't lose it, can't lose this pack, then it was off and ripped from his hands. It was all a matter of seconds.

Tom forced himself up and gulped air. Hard to do. Water in his face. He righted himself again and looked back. He was already a hundred yards downstream. Turning around again, Tom looked for Little, lifting his head up to try to see over the churning waves. Farther on he saw a small knob that could have been a branch being carried away. With all his might,

Tom swam forward, adding his strength to the river's. When he closed within forty yards, the water being less agitated here, he could hear Little's yelping. She was fighting to get to the side, paddling hard as she could. She did not see Tom. He yelled, but his voice was weak. Still, he thrust his arms for her.

Her head went under. Then up again. Then under. A swell crashed over him, forcing him down. He fought back. Rose again. He did not see her. Did not see her. Then again. She'd stopped yelping. Tom screamed at the top of his voice and paddled harder than he should have been able. He closed in on her, breath coming in agonizing gasps. Now, though, he could see that she had stopped swimming and was simply being carried along.

"NO!" he yelled out.

As before, time seemed to slow and sound to disappear. The universe resolved to a pinpoint. NO!

Ten seconds later, he had her. Instinctively he grabbed and pulled, but the river was transporting them both. A fallen log ahead. They were going to hit it. Tom put out his hand and turned a bit to allow his back to absorb the impact, while holding Little with the other.

Crash! They hit. Pain shot through his arm. The surge was pushing them under. He could not let that happen. Tom turned his back to the log, while holding his aelurodon's head out of the water. He held onto a branch.

"LITTLE!!" he yelled. Her head bobbed. Tears flowed and were quickly added to the river. Tom let the water push her against him, while he endeavored to pull them over to the side. He'd never in his life done anything so physically arduous and felt utterly spent. Still, he would not give up. Then he felt rocks under his feet. Slipped. Felt again. Bellowing like an angry Zygo, he pulled them over to the side - lifted Little out, then, struggling, himself. He pulled her higher up the rocky bank.

She lay limp. Tom, finding more strength, picked her up, her head lolling, and carried her up the side on shaky legs, then rest her on some grass. He heard gurgling. Picking her up again, he turned her upside down. Water began to flow out of her mouth. She was heavy, and he so tired, but he held on. It seemed she'd inhaled the river. Then the water stopped. He laid her back down. She wasn't breathing.

"LITTLE!" he yelled. No response. *Think.* Tom put his mouth to hers and cupped the side of her muzzle. He blew, blew, blew. Tears ran down his cheeks. He blew again, again and again.

She coughed. Water in his face. Coughed again. Thrashed. Her eyes rolled down. Opened. She coughed once more. Saw him, made to get up, but he pushed her down, smiling a smile so wide his face hurt. *"No. Rest,"* he commanded. Little began whine like a puppy, chastised, stricken that she had done something wrong. She struggled to get up again and he allowed her to roll from her side to her chest.

"That makes us even, I guess" Tom quipped. Again, she cried like a baby, and this time Tom, his arms around her, cried too.

Twenty Two

When Tom awoke, the sun was rising. It was the next morning. He did not remember having gone to sleep. His clothes were still wet and he felt like he'd been run over by a Barstovian elephant.

Water was rushing by, reeds on the bank tossed about in the river wind, the air cool.

Little was gone.

Tom looked at the wet sand of the trail and saw tracks. They were recent, for some of them overlaid his from the previous day. Sometime during the night an animal had come and gone, right by them. The prints were small. Antelope type. He looked around again for Little; saw her tracks headed downpath. Then he stood and stretched, muscles protesting. There was a deep red and purple bruise on his shin where he'd banged it when jumping in the water. He touched it and winced. Painful. His left arm too; it had been yanked back and hurt.

Walking to the river, he bent and cupped his hands, bringing water to his mouth, and drank. Then he remembered something: his backpack, *it was gone!* Without it, he'd never see Julie again. He'd be lost in this wild world, all alone, for the rest of his life. The prospect of it filled him with anxiety. It was the belief, the expectation that they would be rejoined, that had given his life hope and meaning. No, he had, *had* to find that pack!

Suddenly cold, Tom removed his clothing. He had nothing dry to replace them with. Shafts of light were streaming through openings in the otherwise closed canopy of the riverine environment. He lifted a hand to it. Warm. Finding an overhanging branch, Tom hung his clothes and shoes to dry, discovering in the process that the bang on his shin had torn a hole in his pants. Not large, but he knew how these things were. With use, it would slowly widen. Remarkably, the seat of his pants were unscathed even though he'd used them to descend a mountainside. There were still leaves in the pockets. His shirt, though, somehow, in spite of the pack, had a sizable rip in the back.

Tom walked to the edge of the water near the downed log he'd climbed out by yesterday, and scanned the embankment on both sides for his pack. Nothing. Yet, it was hard to know for sure, since these plants grew thick and could be hiding it. He tried to keep the growing dread that he'd never find it out of his mind, but failed. That pack could be anywhere. Perhaps it was snagged on an underwater limb. Maybe it was miles down river. It could be *anywhere*. Maybe in the tumult it opened, its contents now spread far and wide, buried in liquid muck. He shook his head.

A sound behind him made him jump. Something coming around the corner, climbing over a fallen bough. He watched apprehensively.

It was Little, his faithful companion. Fatigued as she must be, still, she had gone on her regular morning hunting jaunt and was now bringing back breakfast. It was thick-furred, muscled, and bloody; probably not easy to get. Tom bent to hug his Aelurodon, then inspected her for injuries, finding a tear on her right ear and a bleeding scratch on her muzzle. Nothing else. She dropped the animal at his feet. Deprived of the P.I., he was unable to identify it, but it was nothing he'd seen before. Well, it looked enough to get them by.

Wait a minute - crud - no way to cook it, he recalled. Tom looked again at the animal. It was an unappetizing mess.

"I'm sorry, girl, I'm not eating that raw," Tom said. Little angled her head right and left, not comprehending. "It's all yours, girl," he added, gesturing with his hands. She looked down at her kill, then back at him. *"Ooh,"* he sighed exasperatedly. "You eat Little, I don't want any." He leaned down and pushed the kill back toward her, then he thought, *Maybe she's gotten used to the taste of cooked meat.* Lately, she didn't eat until he did and he always ate his food thoroughly heated. He decided it might be best to show no interest and walk away. Little sat, watching him.

"We have to find the pack," he told her, slapping his back to help her understand. Little turned her head toward the river, then back at him. Maybe she gets it, he hoped. Even though he wasn't going to eat raw meat, he was still hungry and looked around for something else. Then he noticed that the trees and bushes around them were alive with berries of all kinds, singly and in bunches. He knew he was taking a chance, but decided to rate their edibility based on taste. Some he liked, others he rejected. One he quickly spit out was bitter, a small, white berry that would later be called Creeping Snowberry. He also refused another that was indeed edible, it just wasn't sweet: Toyon.

On the other hand, he found many to his liking. Without knowing exactly what he was eating, Tom enjoyed the delights of thimbleberry, serviceberry, chokecherry and golden currant. Grapes grew high up in the trees and down below. He had to reach up to get any though, since, like the other fruits, the easiest ones to reach had already been taken. *Ah! The reason for this path,* Tom discerned.

Then, spying a petite, red berry, Tom did a double take. Tiny, triangular-shaped, seeds *on the outside.* Could it be? Tom picked a few and popped them into his mouth. A rush of familiar taste filled his palate and he hooted. *Strawberry!*

Farther down the path, he saw a viney type plant with darker colored, bulbous berries. They looked familiar, something from his childhood, perhaps. The leaves, though, gave him great pause. Grouped in three, they looked very much like poison oak and he certainly *did not* want to mess with *that* again. Nevertheless, something was different, but he couldn't tell what it was. Where was the P.I. when he needed it? Like poison oak, this was a vine with long, thin branches. Gingerly, he took hold of a branchlet to have a closer look and immediately let go. Tiny thorns hurt his fingers, some embedding themselves in his skin. He pulled them out one by one while studying the plant once more, not wanting to give up on so tasty looking a fruit. Tom tried to remember what he'd read about poison oak. He didn't recollect anything about big black berries or thorns.

Feeling that he was taking a stupid risk, Tom decided to give one a taste, picked, and bit ever so tenderly into it, ready to spew every atom of it out at the slightest question. Instead, the berry fairly popped in his mouth, and purple juice, the very definition of sweetness, flooded his tongue. He knew what it was! *Blackberry*, succulent, flavorful blackberry! When he was a child of ten, when every good thing was disappearing, including his father who'd died the year before, his mother had spent a small fortune to buy them some blackberries. Donning her old apron, she whipped up some cake, placing the berries and cream on top. Now he remembered the two of them sitting at the little table in their kitchen. Walls, yellow with age, or was it the lighting, soft, gentle lighting, like her. They had two baskets of berries, one for the cake and an extra. Together they ate every last one. It was one of his happiest memories. The next year mom died. Died of a broken heart, his aunt had told him.

"I love you, Mom," Tom said.

Mist swirled. Wiping his eyes, Tom turned back to the task at hand. He thought about how far they'd traveled, but knew that he could find the area where they'd went in the water. Best to start at the beginning. Little had already devoured her breakfast and was sitting next to the path keeping an eye on her human. He put on his shoes, but left the rest of his clothes hanging; no sense in getting them wet again. Then together they walked back, while he continued to feast on berries. Delicious food, free for the taking. *What an odd, alien concept,* he pondered, not for the first time since arriving here. Free food. Free *anything*.

As they slogged, he kept a look out along the embankments for his pack, or anything from it, shaking his head at the seeming impossibility of the undertaking. Every sweet he'd savored this morning had been doused in a bitter seasoning of doubt and dread.

It was impossible to see much of the embankment on either side, for thick growth obscured his view. The clamor of water increased as they grew closer to the falls. Like yesterday, it was almost deafening. Approaching the place where they went over, Tom looked back to find Little falling behind. He understood and would not force her to come. She barked a warning at him, but he barely heard. Mist swirled around him, tiny droplets that wet his skin. His hair blew out behind. Cautiously, Tom climbed a dripping boulder and stood looking out, yet with all the mist and roiling water it was hard to see. Even if it *was* here he might never notice it. He swallowed hard.

He could not go into the water to find it. *Way* too dangerous. Besides that, Little might jump in after him. All he could do was walk back down the path as far as he could, and in the areas where shrubbery blocked his sight, push through it to have a better look.

They set out again, Tom keen to spot anything unusual, stopping long enough to get dressed. An hour later, after having gone a long ways, they were almost out of the canyon, yet, no sign of the pack. Tom was very discouraged. But he was *not* going to leave without it. They'd have to go back and look again. Then a thought occurred to him: what if he could find something of relatively equal weight and buoyancy, something he could toss in the water about where he lost the pack and then follow to see where it eventually landed? It might work - or it might lead him on another wild goose chase. On the other hand, from where he stood, his options were rather limited. He'd give it a try. Now, what to use? The first requirement, of course, was that it *float*. He grimaced. What could he find that would float? And what if his pack *didn't* float? What if it just *sank?* He decided not to think about that.

Back up the canyon they trekked, Little faithfully following, but possibly wondering what silly human game this was. *Back and forth.* Tom figured that it would be about noon by the time they'd backtracked to the falls. He studied every opening along the stream, even climbing trees, rocks and the hillside when he could. Still no luck.

In due course, they were almost there. He'd been thinking what to use that could float and had hit on an idea. Perhaps a couple dozen yards from the cascade, he'd seen a termite-ridden chunk of log that had broken off the main trunk of an old dead tree when it finally fell years ago. He bet *that* would float. Walking to it now, he surveyed it critically, then lifted. Thanks to termite action, its original mass, and thus weight, was greatly reduced, its load felt similar to the pack's. Sharp pieces were on the ends, however, edges that could catch on something and stop its progress down river. He'd have to break those off. As much as possible, this piece of trunk had to model his pack.

Tom found a blunt, palm-sized rock, and began to work on the log. Breaking off the protruding parts was not as hard as he'd thought it would be. The termites, though, were not amused and swarmed out. Hundreds teemed over the wood, and then onto the ground in an effort to find this haughty vandal. Any other time, the vandal would have been an insectivore, a bear perhaps, who would have greedily lapped up the moving mounds of protein. Now, however, their assailant, after shaking off the few that made it to his arms, merely kicked the log away from them and continued chipping. They'd soon find another piece of wood.

Nevertheless, Tom felt a twinge of conscience at his casual, all-too-human usurping of the termite's home. His calloused dismissal of *their* rights.

In ten minute's time, the big pieces were gone and he set to working on the little ones. When he thought he'd cleaned it up enough, Tom walked back to the mad river to consider his next move. He realized that trying to get the large chunk onto the boulder was unlikely. Even though the rocks that went across were roughly lined up, the first one on this side was back from the bank a little too far to climb with something in his hands. Not only that, but with the constant slap of water against its north face it was wet and slick. Yet, looking down the river from the side and noting that the water swirled away here toward the middle, he thought that if he tossed it in it should soon find the same course. But he'd only have one chance at it.

Tom walked back to the log piece, picked it up and hoisted to his right shoulder, again feeling its heft, then turned back to the river. There he set it down, then peered at Little who was lying comfortably on her side, watching him. She came awake at his word.

"Okay girl, I'm going to put this in the water, then we are going to follow it. Be ready to move." Little sat up.

Tom bent down and heaved the log up again, then maneuvered close to the edge as he dared. Water pelted his legs.

Eyeing his target, he took a breath, then tossed. The log splashed in, then went down. *"Crap!"* Tom said. Then it was up again, farther down the river, and moving fast.

"YI!" Tom cried out. He ran past Little and down the trail, keeping an eye best he could on the moving wood. In a flash, Little was romping past him, tail up, barking her unique Aelurodon bark. It was hard to keep the wood in sight as it was frequently hidden by the waves, bright with solar reflection, and he thought he'd lost it a few times. He decided, though, to keep himself jogging at the same pace as the log, and that paid off. Passing a long patch of tall cattails which obstructed his view of the river, he was delighted to see that the log was exactly opposite him and still bobbing along with the current. There were, of course, objects like fallen branches and boulders in the river and he worried that it would catch on one of those. But approaching them, the log would then be zipped around their sides before making contact.

This went on for, what seemed to Tom, a long time, and he thought that they must have traveled the better part of a mile. *Could it have gone this far?* Now he wondered if one of the straps from his pack might have snared on something and be behind him. A small antelope with crazy horns appeared on the trail before them as they careened around a corner and Little lit out after it. Tom knew that it would be much too fast for her to catch, so he didn't bother calling her back.

After what seemed a very long time indeed, Tom was getting winded and breathing hard. Maybe he made the log so water worthy that it would float all the way to the sea! It seemed that nothing could stop it. Little was again at his side and running parallel. They startled a flock of quail, which startled him in return, bursting from their secret place and into the air. The river was slowing and widening. It began to describe a long curve to the right, then left. They were nearing the exit.

Grassland was visible beyond the high canopy of trees. Maybe another quarter-mile. By now, Tom was convinced that they'd passed the pack up. They'd have to turn back and try yet again. It looked like he'd have to actually travel down the river itself somehow. He shook his head at that, wondering how he'd do it.

Another mass of growth to block his view. They trotted past and as usual Tom glanced to his side to make sure he was on track. The log did not reappear this time. Tom did a double-take. He looked downriver, but didn't see it. *Where is it? Did it finally sink?* He jotted to the edge for a look back upriver, straining to find the wood, slowly casting his gaze inch by inch. The river having slackened at this point, vegetal growth was free to venture farther from the bank-side and in toward the middle. It was hard to see around.

Though still flowing with some strength, the river had lost much of it with its expansion. Tom thought that he could slog up his side of it if he held onto the various branches and reeds, then he could try to find out what happened to the log. To be sure, there was a lot of debris here that he could hold onto, a variety of detritus that, having fallen into the current, had finally found a resting place at this wide bend in the waterway.

"Wait here!" Tom commanded Little. She sat and looked at him sternly. "I'll be back in a minute. Promise." Then, turning, he waded into the river. It pushed at him as he made his way forward along the side. Soon he was waist-high, then it was just below his chest. He held onto each of the branches firmly as he pulled himself along. One dislodged and almost dislodged *him*. He grasped another and chose with more care. Little barked.

Slowly, handhold by handhold, Tom made his way. He was now in water deeper than he was tall. Little barked again. She could not see him and that worried her. Tom yelled reassurances. After five slow minutes, he came to a little nook, a slight clearing in the flotsam. And there, *there was the log bobbing in and out.* At last it was at rest.

"Ha!" Tom said triumphantly, "Found you!" he smiled. A small victory. "Guess I did a pretty good job," he said. Then, floating it out with one hand while still holding onto something with the other, he sent it downriver again, watching as it disappeared from sight. Tom sighed with resignation. Once more upriver.

Something blue, unnaturally blue, caught his eye. It was just past the open midpoint in the river, lodged in some reeds. He looked at it as it too bobbed in the ceaseless flow. Seconds passed, then his eyes gradually widened and a huge smile spread across his face. *My backpack!!!*

Tom let out a whoop that resounded under the riparian canopy. Whooped once more. Little bayed, ran to the other side of the cattails, then jumped in after her human.

If ever he'd had a happy moment, this was it! The pack floated half out of the water, one strap snagged by a submerged branch. Carefully, holding onto the far end of that branch, Tom drew himself across. The current increased in force the closer he came to the middle, but keeping himself on the upstream side of the branch, there was no danger of being swept downriver. When he reached the pack, he removed it, and thanked whatever gods had occasioned such a miracle. Loath to lose it again, he slung it over one, then switching hands, the other shoulder. *He had his pack back again!*

As he hauled himself across, Little was just coming around to meet him, whining and dog-paddling. Tom met her with a kiss to her head.

"Look what I found!" he exclaimed jubilantly. Then he thought that he should get them out of the river. "Okay, let's go," he said. Going downriver was much easier than up, and he only needed to hold onto the wedged debris to keep from being pushed into the middle, though, at this point, he didn't think the river was nearly the threat it was before. In a short minute he was bank-side, then hauled himself out. Little also climbed out and promptly shook herself free of the water, sending droplets flying every which way. Again, Tom hooted and did a little jig. Little yelped in joy and jumped on her human, nearly knocking him back in. Tom laughed.

Okay let's see how everything is. There was one item, however, only one, that he was truly concerned about. The PinPointer. Sitting, Tom carefully unzipped the pack, then began to withdraw the enclosed objects one-by-one, setting them on the ground beside him, then around him. The PinPointer he'd put in a special cushioned inner pouch. Now he opened that pouch gently with his thumb and index finger. There it was. Sleek, wet, but, he hoped, undamaged. Removing it, he set the pack on the ground and opened the P.P. Instantly the display came alive. It worked! Yet another whoop. Tom clicked on the map, and seconds later, there was the red blip, pulsing as usual. But no green blip. Tom swallowed. He remembered that the last time he'd turned it on Julie hadn't register then either.

"Come on! Come on!" he implored. "Where are you!" Still, only red showed. "Shit, *COME ON!*" Tom yelled. He shook off a rising fear that maybe she really was gone, killed by Jaqzen. His hands began to tremble. Then he thought that maybe she'd lost or broken her PinPointer. In that case, he'd still never find her. Or could it be that, he, still being part way in the canyon, that, well, maybe her signal simply could not reach him? Maybe that was it, he reasoned, though he knew the illogic of it. If he could pick up Jaqzen, he ought to be able to pick up Julie. Or maybe *she* was in a temporary location that blocked her signal. He'd try again when he was out of the canyon.

Grimly, Tom began to close the P.P. when he heard another blip, this one a slightly different aural hue than the other. He raised the lid again and looked. The green light. *Julie! She's still alive!* Again, Tom shouted for joy. His anxiety lifted, his life restored.

Everything he had been through, *everything*, the worry, the fear, the pain, was worth this moment.

It was truly a great day.

Twenty Three

At the mouth of the canyon where the tree line ended, Tom decided to rest. Even though he'd slept the night before, still, he felt bone tired. All the activity of the past several days had left him feeling wiped out. He badly needed a good rejuvenating sleep.

He couldn't have picked a lovelier place. From this point out was an undulating plain of tallgrass, only just yellowing as the year advanced. It was hot out there, but under the high riparian canopy, the river flowing nearby, the weather was extremely pleasant.

Places like this wouldn't last long in modern times, he knew. First they'd be claimed by someone and fenced off. "Private Property" and "No Trespassing" signs would be strategically positioned around the periphery, with violators to be prosecuted by law. Later, when the press of humanity increased and all the good available land confiscated, their value would shoot up. At that point, the temptation to sell would be too great. Most of the real estate would then be parceled out in 40 acre increments and streets laid down. Later still, these would be further subdivided into one acre fractions. Cookie cutter houses would be wedged in, each fenced off from the others. Additional blocks of land within would be sold to commercial interests, and up would go shopping centers and parking lots, auto repair yards and schools, city government buildings and landfills.

As the population increased, the pressure to capitalize would lead to a further reduction in lot sizes to half and even a tenth acre. Towns would become cities. Apartments followed, then high-rises, joined by monster freeways jammed with legions of cars. As the floors ran up, the whole ran down. There'd be seedy precincts and pot holes in the streets. Empty, litter-filled lots behind eight foot high chain link, and graffiti defaced billboards. Smelly gas stations and liquor stores on every corner. There'd be stories of secret dumping of toxic wastes in the creeks, the ones which hadn't already been diverted to ag land or paved over. In the more "rural" areas, giant lots crammed with thousands of cattle, pigs and chickens living in miserable conditions would be ignored by a meat-eating commons. Technology outpacing wisdom, all of this would coincide with a general drop in the public morale and a rise in disrespect. Yet, *still* the population surged.

~ Meanwhile, a delicate balance was quietly passing, a precarious tipping point in which faces blurred and names became numbers ~

There'd be battles over resources locally. The farmers wanted all the fresh water and cared not that other species would suffer. In return they'd drench their mass produce in poisons and send a chemical-laden stew downstream. In time, country would fight country, then state, state over water, timber and food, employing all the devious legal devices in their toolkits. "Rare earth" minerals, vital for many technologies, would be hoarded, and then fought over. A man could be an enemy simply by virtue of birth in another place, and horrifying weapons would be released for petty differences in doctrine. To give every new mouth its due, whole forests would fall and entire species disappear, little noticed. Cities would become Megacities, which spread, then merged until it seemed all the world was covered in asphalt and concrete, skyscrapers and slums. Over all, a shroud of smog and pollution, air, land and oceanic, would creep ever on like an unstoppable malignancy. With ingenuity, we'd hold on for a while. Nevertheless, a horrific end was not far behind.

Now, Tom felt like he owned the world. He could go anywhere, no questions asked, no papers to show, no rules to follow, no lines to stand in or crowds to fight through.

In the shade on the edge of the forest, he folded down some green and made it into a soft bed. And though it was just past midday, he reclined there, hidden like a baby fawn in the grass around him. The soothing sound of water at his head and cool puffs of air tickling his cheeks, he slept soundly until morning.

Tom dreamt of many things that night, snippets of cliffs and gold, of racing and swimming. Lastly he dreamt of gun shots. A fierce battle in the control room of the Institute. The shots got louder and more intense.

He awoke, yet the sound of guns continued. Alarmed, he jumped to his knees to peer over the top of the lea and see where it was coming from. His vision resolved slowly and he rubbed his eyes. Then he saw what it was. There were two antelopes fighting and crashing horns on the plains. A whole herd of them were grazing farther off, apparently wanting nothing to do with the quarrel. Then he spied another group, clearly females, for they were slightly smaller than the males, standing disinterestedly off to one side of the brawl, grooming each other.

Ah, he thought, relaxing, *the reason for the skirmish. Always a woman involved.* Sighing, Tom lay back down and listened to the sound of it. Through the tall, yellowing grass, he gazed at the sky, so blue in contrast. He looked at the underside of the canopy of broad-leaved deciduous trees a hundred feet above him. Birds were flying there, twittering and jotting excitedly from branch to branch. The elegant sound of water burbling over rocks on its course to join the great inland sea somewhere out there was delightful.

Something evidently startled the antelope, for the fracas ended in a sound of hundreds of hooves sprinting away. Away from him. He didn't get up. He wondered what time it was. Mid-morning it looked. Again it was heating up in the open. Along with the cool breezes of the forest, an occasional gust of hot air made its way to him. Yes, it was going to be really hot today.

Tom thought about his route. South of course. Should he then stick to the edge of the forest canopy since it ran roughly in that direction, or should he head west out there, in the blazing sun, toward other forests he could see patches of? It seemed a no-brainer. Yet, just past the scattered areas of trees, he'd seen a line of blue when he was on the mountain, and it pulled at him. What was it like, he wondered, that pristine pre-historic sea? Tom was seriously tempted to go that way. Still, it was essential that he to get to Julie as quickly as possible.

He'd tried yesterday, before bedding down, to judge the distance to the blue. Hard to do. Heat waves radiating from the ground in between didn't help. His stomach growled. Oh. Yeah.

"Girl? You here?" Tom called out softly. There was no re-ply, of course. She'd be out hunting. He wondered what break-fast would be this morning. Now that he had his stove back, he supposed that he could return to his new-found carnivorous diet. Still, even though he wasn't doing the actual killing, he felt guilty about it. On the other hand, he was not yet quite as adept at providing for himself as Little was by nature. Until he was more familiar about which foods contained protein, he'd continue to eat her catches.

His stomach growled again. He looked over to the forest. *Maybe I'll go gather some fruit,* he thought. Indeed, he'd discovered some delicious additions to his diet. As he was about to get up, Tom suddenly heard a sound of growling.

Vicious, and it was coming his way. Again startled, he got up and looked to see the grass being pushed aside by something approaching. Eyes wide, he instantly began to back up, not stopping to gather his things. What was it? He searched for a visual clue while continuing his retreat. Then, in the opening he'd made yesterday, she appeared. Little. Eyes ablaze in ferocity, she was dragging a large animal in her mouth, one of the antelopes. Too distracted by its scrap with the other, it failed to notice the powerful predator that crept up on it in the tallgrass. Now it was limp, its neck snapped in the powerful jaws of the Aelurodon.

She dropped it there, in the opening, and stood panting. There was blood around her muzzle, but no obvious signs of injury.

"Well, you're first big kill!" Tom congratulated. He walked over to take a closer look, but immediately stopped when, hackles raised, she began to growl at him. His heart leapt.

"Easy, girl," he said. Little continued to growl, still flush from the battle, reluctant to give up her first real trophy. *"Easy."* It had been the first time she had displayed any kind of real aggression toward him and it unsettled him. Even though he'd gotten comfortable with her, he mustn't forget that she was a powerful wild beast and was only going to get stronger. But soon as he'd thought it she immediately began to show contrition and flattened her ears back while walking over to him, tail wagging. Tentatively, Tom reached a hand out and stroked her, she sniffed, then licked it, hackles now lowered. She was clearly excited by her exploit and Tom wondered what he should do, try to cut himself off a piece of the kill first or wait for her. He sensed that as Alpha male of this little clan he was supposed to grab some of it first, not doing so might upset the balance - and her, yet he was understandably reluctant to incur her wrath again.

As if in answer, Little walked a few yards away and lay down while watching him. "Okay," Tom said to himself lowly, "get some of it." Reaching into his pack, Tom found his knife, then approached the kill. He judged its weight to be about 70 pounds. Its legs were solidly muscled. Surely, if it had been aware of her, this antelope could have easily dashed away. But Little was discovering that, while fast, she wasn't as fast as some the bigger game, so she had to learn the strategy of ambush hunting. Tom cut off a leg, not an easy or pleasant chore, then carried it, and his portable stove, away from the kill so that Little could eat as well. She rose immediately, then lay down next to the animal and began to feast.

There was no way, Tom knew, that they'd be able to eat the entire thing now, but maybe he could cook some of it and bring it along for later consumption. On the other hand, that might attract other carnivores. Well, he'd see how it went.

It went. Halfway into the cooking process, Little began to growl again. Tom looked up swiftly, but saw nothing. Nothing besides Little now making snapping motions toward the grass on the other side. He stood. *"Uh oh,"* he said lowly. It was a pack of some other kind of dog thing slowly approaching them. They had a rough, scruffy, savage look about them, as if they were used to squabbling with Aelurodons. When they saw *him*, they immediately checked their advance, unsure of what this new, tall animal was. But they snarled defiance. It was hard to tell how many there were in the tallgrass, but he guessed at least five. Little was now standing and snarling back fiercely. Tom couldn't have known it, but Aelurodons and these beasts had a long history of disagreement, an intra-family feud going back a million years.

"GO AWAY!" Tom yelled. The lead one, the one he could see, a big brawny male, snapped back at him, froth and foam dripping from his mouth. Tom remembered the gun. It was in his backpack. The pack was lying on the ground between them. It looked like there was going to be a fight, and he suspected that Little would get the worst of it, for even though she was growing robust herself, she was just one against five. Tom made a step in their direction, toward his pack. Little, seeing him, did as well. Fortunately, the leader of the pack took a step backwards. It had thought that Tom was rising to the challenge and that its bluff wasn't quite working. Tom took another step forward, then another. Little was at his side, hackles also standing on end, a ruse that made her appear larger.

Then the pack did something unexpected, they began to circle about and behind them. Little's head swung around. Tom sensed that were he to touch her now he would be severely bitten. He didn't. Instead, he took another step, and was almost to his pack, when the lead animal jumped at him, flashing teeth and rage. He was grabbed mid-lunge by Little. Instantly the world was a blur. The two beasts fought ferociously, roaring horrifically. The rugged Alpha tore at Little's face, but Little, though a bit smaller, soon began to dominate. She was on the other's back. Just then, another rushed in from behind and jumped on her. Little turned to deal with it, then another came at her.

Tom dove for the pack and yanked it open. Something ripped. He reached in toward the bottom, where he stored the gun, found it, took it out - then dropped it. Swiftly, another of the brutes sprang at him. He stood and instinctively spun sideways to avoid the main assault, catching a fang across his shoulder, which ripped open painfully. He wobbled. Again the animal came at him. Tom turned, this time kicking hard, catching it in the chest, which knocked it off-balance, yet slowing it down very little.

The girl, for her part, fought valiantly. But there were now *three* of them on her. Tom again jumped for the gun, got it, and, pulling back the trigger, took aim and fired.

One of the pack fell dead on the spot. The report was so loud that the others fled posthaste. Except for the one in Little's mouth. She wasn't through with him, and, shaking vigorously, chomped down on his neck, finishing him off. The pack would be leaderless.

Why Little hadn't run from the sound of the gun was a mystery. He looked at her. There was blood everywhere. She sat then, panting and exhausted, having acquitted herself admirably. Tom went to have a look, and she lay on her back. Most of the blood appeared to belong to the other dog-like beasts. But she had a nasty rip in her side, a hunk of flesh torn down and hanging. He could see muscle underneath. She also had several deep gashes on her muzzle. Those would likely scar and become a permanent feature. Additionally, there was a chomp on her tail, but it didn't look too serious.

Tom shook his head. Although he'd been reveling in this paradise-like world, if he needed a reminder that this was, in actuality, a wild, and could be, a very dangerous place, he just got it. It was a lesson he would not have to learn twice. From now on, the gun would be at his side.

Tom rummaged around for the medical kit. Finding some iodine, he opened it. He intended to pour it into Little's wound, and then bandage it up. He hoped it wouldn't sting. He contemplated using the alcohol, but thought better of it. Gently, he poured some iodine into and around the wound. She whimpered. The next part would be tricky. Retrieving a surgical needle and thread, while talking gently to her, Tom began to sew the flap of skin to the attached sides. Little made no motion or sound, which he was immensely grateful for. Finally, persuading her to stand, he got some gauze out and began to wrap it around her. He used every bit of it, though he doubted that it would stay there.

Little looked at something on Tom's shoulder and he

glanced that way. His shirt was ripped, and he had a deep gash of his own. Blood flowed down his arm, his upper sleeve red with it. She stood now, shakily, and sniffed at the wound, then began to clean it by lightly licking. Surprised, Tom allowed her this strange behavior. Perhaps an Aelurodon thing? Finally, he thanked her and made her lie back down, then walking to the river with soap, proceeded to wash the laceration until the bleeding stopped. Afterwards, he took needle and thread and sewed his own unanesthetized skin together and bandaged it up. It hurt like the devil, and he'd have a scar, but he was getting tougher.

Turning to the attacking animal, Tom took out his P.I. and, laying the beast on its least destroyed side, took a picture to find out what it was. *Carpocyon* was the answer.

"Hmm. According to this, Carpocyon was mostly found on the other side of the Sierras. Maybe you were emigrating," Tom speculated, sorry that it ended up the way it did. Then, stooping, he noticed that it had acquired some ticks, mostly around its head, including a few in its ears, but also on its chest and the anal area. *I'd be temperamental too if I had that on me,* he thought. Likewise, Tom snapped a photo of the head of the antelope-like animal with the two oddly asymmetrical horns: *Ramoceros.*

He decided that they should remain where they were for another few days to convalesce, and dragged the carcasses of the two Carpocyon out far as he could onto the plain. If something was hungry, he hoped they would keep it, or them, occupied. Obediently, Little stayed behind. As they were near the water, he brought some to her often, which she lapped up. She also ate a lot of her antelope kill. At midday, she rose to relieve herself, ate again, then slept.

Tying a rope around the Ramoceros just forward of the rear legs, Tom tossed it over a high, bare branch, then hoisted it up a into tree and tied it off. Next, he built a fire below to smoke it. He'd planned to try to keep watch through the night in case the Carpocyon, or some other threat, chose to make a return visit.

Tom wanted another walking stick; not only would it be useful for going up and down hills, it would also be an aid in quick defense. He found an attractive tree with smooth, reddish, peeling bark and nearly straight limbs that he thought should work nicely. Madrone. He snapped off a good section and, sitting on a log under the cover of sheltering trees, the fire crackling in front of them, cleaned up the small side branchlets, then whittled the end to a point.

That night, the stars were magnificent. Somewhere out on the plain an owl hooted rhythmically, calm restored, and once again, this land was an Eden. Tom reflected upon the strange juxtaposition of life and death here. He knew that without death there could *be* no life. Yet, it was hard for his human mind to reconcile such brutality in an otherwise perfect world.

He finally accepted, reluctantly, that this stark incongruity was a necessary fact of life, a law of nature as impossible to separate as the front of a coin from its back, and as light is from darkness.

My dear Julie,
What a strange world, this Miocene of
yours. Beautiful, yet deadly. Enrapturing,
yet frightening. You were right, though.
This is real life, and I am in love with it.

He included no date this time, for he'd lost track of the days.

The week that followed was the opposite of the previous day's electrification. At dawn on the third morning after the big battle, while it was still dark, Tom resolved to get an early start. He'd decided to head out west/southwest, following the course of the river toward the line of blue, feeling irresistibly drawn toward it. He knew that it was going to be another sweltering day and hoped to reach it before noon. By noon, however, they were still quite a ways from it, though they had reached the line of trees. Evidently from his position high on the mountain, he'd misjudged the thalassic proximity. Had he realized it was so far away he would have stayed the foothill path. Additionally, unknown to him, the main forest river had broken off to the south and he was now following a smaller arm. He'd been unable to discern the change as the riparian areas were protected by thick walls of impenetrable growth. While forested, the country was now flat, and no hills afforded him a chance for a better look. Climbing the trees was fruitless since their branches, and those of other trees around them, veiled his view out. Nevertheless, on the pair continued.

The land baked. Waves of heat shimmered upwards from the plains, whilst the fauna stood motionless in small groups to the west and north, dozing. Tom, too, was getting torpid and paused for a rest. He knew that Little would appreciate it as well since she had been lagging behind for some while.

When he stopped, he gave her the remainder of the meat, which he'd smoked before, taking only a fist-sized chunk for himself. She devoured it in less than a minute. Then they lay down, side-by-side, and slept. After a while, Tom began to snore and Little, disturbed, got up to relocate a dozen feet away.

When he awoke, it was twilight and frogs were beginning their evening chorus. Woodland nightbirds of various species were sounding in piercing whistles and weird, spooky chatter. Mosquitos hummed about his face and he swatted them away.

The tops of these trees were lower than in the mountains, and he could see the first stars beginning to shine through. Tom now regretted having chosen this way, but deplored the idea of turning back. Onward it would be then. Tomorrow.

He stood, and with his flashlight, found some wood to make a fire. Its glow reflected, dancing orange from the closest trees. He was famished and played his torch around looking for something he could eat. Fortunately, there was fruit, a delicious, purple, but sometimes red, star-shaped thing, which the P.I. had no name for. It had a juicy red/orange/yellow center and grew abundantly on yellow/green vines flecked with splashes of purple. It tasted like grape candy. Silky smooth. He hoped they were okay to eat for he wolfed down a dozen of them, the sweet nectar running down his arms. Then, full, he drank liberally from a rivulet that wound its way under the climbing plants.

A cooling breeze lifted his hair. Tom strode back to his pack, arms loaded with more of the purple star fruits, and to Little, still sleeping. She awoke, bleary-eyed, at his approach and woofed, then seeing him, lay back down. As he had no more of the Ramoceros left to give her, he brought her some of the tasty new produce he'd found. To his amazement, after sniffing it, she too "wolfed" it down, which was all the testimony he needed. If anyone should know, it would be her. He ate another. Then Tom lay back, board piano in hand, and, lightly playing, gazed at the stars through the slowly swaying branches above. Now and then, one shot across the heavens leaving a long white trace, which soon faded. Tom watched until his head nodded and eyes refused to stay open. He'd wanted to write something in his journal for Julie, but by then the fire had dimmed, and so, after a few more moments, he put the board down and turned on his side once more to sleep.

At daybreak, Tom was awakened by the sound of a jay-like bird cawing loudly above them. It appeared annoyed by their presence, which it had somehow missed the day before. He rubbed his face and discovered that there were little itchy bumps above his beard line as well as on his arms. The mosquitos had had their way with him while he slept. He grumbled. There was a cost to following the river, especially where it slowed.

He rose and bathed in a pool of cold water while Little hunted. It was good to know that she was back to normal. The rest had done them both good. Further, the mystery fruit hadn't killed them. He again stuffed himself. Little arrived with one small animal, which again the P.I. had no knowledge of. He let her have it, but filled a bag that he hung from his belt chocka-block with the fruit. Then they set out.

In an hour, the bag began to drip purple juice from the bottom and they were forced to eat as much as they could, then discard the rest. Though he'd not seen any more of the strange star fruit since they'd left camp, he did not think that lack of food would be a problem. His repertoire of edibles was increasing daily.

Around mid-morning, the river began a long, gradual curve to the south, which made Tom happy. They continued under the line of trees that grew reliably around it in case the day turned hot again. Some time later, they dropped into a bottomland of cool, soft sand, in which were the prints of numerous animals. The way was slower here and sand often filled Tom's shoes, which he'd have to stop and dump. Finally, he took them off and tied them to the top of his pack - securely. He did not want to find later on that he'd lost one. While this move did not necessarily make the going easier, it was im-mensely more pleasurable. The feel of sand under his feet was luxurious.

Then he thought, *As long as I'm staying under the trees, I might as well wear as little as possible.* And so, removing everything but his shorts, from which the gun hung, and of course the backpack, he carried on.

An hour later, they came to an open area, thick with Cattails. The river here, Tom noticed, further slowed and began to spread out. No, not the river they'd been following, this was a shallow arm of it. There were Cattails far as he could see, bordering, and within that arm. He walked to the right, over a little rise. Still, the Cattails continued. Tom sighed. *Always the obstacles*, he moaned. Heading back a bit for perspective, he pivoted and looked again at the way forward. It was choked. Shaking his head, he walked the other way, then saw a thin trail through the reeds. Following it visually, he could see where it came out a quarter-mile or so distant. An animal route. Who knew how long it had been here. Anyway, since it was open, shoulder width at least, they decided to take it.

The ground here was mushy, like a shallow bog, and they picked and sloshed their way through. Funny thing about Cattails, they have these tight, sausage-shaped things at the tops of the plant that are packed full of tiny seeds. When the time is right, and the wind blowing, they release these seeds, which then float on parachute-like filaments in the air, drifting upwards and out, sometimes for miles, hopefully coming to rest in another riparian environment. There, they can begin life anew. But the seeds can *also* be released by the slightest brush of something rubbing against the sausage-shaped thing - something like a shoulder, which is exactly what Tom and his aelurodon companion provided as they strolled through the shallow marsh. Suddenly there were tiny white seeds aloft *everywhere*. Thousands of them. Tens of thousands. They floated high, carried to the sky by the subtlest of whispers. In short order, Tom and Little were covered. At first startled, Tom laughed. Laughed at the sight of Little speckled white, laughed at yet another wonder he'd never known about until now. *What a world!* On the other side, they shook clothes, hair and fur free, sending hundreds more seeds flying, then recommenced their journey.

After a while, Tom started to note, subconsciously, that the river was beginning another incremental turn to the right, to the west. They continued on, but he felt a slight nagging about something, something *not quite right,* although he couldn't put his finger on it. Then he discovered that, except for the wayward compass, the PinPointer map did not work in this forest. It apparently needed at least two reference points to function, yet the trees were blocking both Julie and Jaqzen's signal. What's more, with no hills around to climb, he couldn't even ascertain his general position. It was dispiriting. Hoping for clearance, Tom continued his walk southwest.

Yet, days passed, and it seemed that they would never reach the sea. The way just seemed to go on and on.

One afternoon, Little took off after something through a thicket of brambles and understory which climbed a low hill. Seconds later, there was a kerfuffle, loud squawking and the sound of brush being violently disturbed. Then silence. Tom waited. After a minute, out came Little with a large turkey-like bird in her mouth, obviously expired. Lunchtime.

He hadn't the slightest idea how to deal with the feathers and just began to pluck. Keenly interested, Little wanted to help, but Tom kept her back. Then, done, he cleared a suitably sized area, built a small fire and roasted the avian on a willow spit. Turkey indeed! He'd remembered the other time he'd had one, again with his mother. Thanksgiving. She said, *You always need to be thankful for what you have.* They had nothing, nothing but each other. He was thankful.

Little ate with passion and Tom watched her, noticing just how big she was getting. He guessed she must weigh close to eighty pounds now. Meanwhile, *he* was getting slimmer and leaner. He wondered if she was moonlighting, eating while he slept. Perhaps. But he was happy for it. He needed her as large and strong as she could be. After lunch, they upped and continued on their way.

Eating so much made Tom sluggish. When he was tired again, he sat down for a rest under a giant maple. It, in turn, was shaded by an even larger sycamore. Puffing, Tom held his staff at arm's length, hand at the top and casually glanced at it, though without really seeing. He hummed, turning it around, admiring the smoothness of the bark. His humming stopped. He frowned now, shocked. There was a long, wide crack in it.

"What?" he said, appalled. *"Already?* Humph! Guess they don't make walking sticks like they used to!"* Tom put his fingers in the rift; the madrone stick was weak. In the hot air it had soon dried out and expanded. He'd need another. Still, he liked its smooth texture and ruddy color and wished he could find one like it. One that wouldn't split that is. At any rate, he'd hold onto this one until he could find a suitable replacement.

The following afternoon, after hiking all morning, Tom noticed off to his left, on the riverside, some huge puffy things hanging in the trees, occasionally engulfing them entirely. Subconsciously, while noting their presence, he'd avoided changing course to walk over and investigate. If he did that every time something new and interesting happened by, his progress would be considerably slowed. Tom continued on, but the numbers of strange puffballs increased. With another mile, the giant lacy puffs were growing further away from the riverbank and closer to their footpath. He regarded them with puzzlement. They had an airy, almost ethereal texture. Another mile on and their numbers began to decline, and then, finally, they were gone. When he'd not seen any for a quarter-hour and had forgotten about them, suddenly there was one more. A big puff of the wispy stuff in a ball shape, hanging from a branch.

Curiosity got the better of him, and, as it was only a hundred feet away or so, he decided to go have a look after all. Tom strode over.

When he was within twenty feet, however, he slowed down. There was *movement* within that mass. It was *alive* with movement. Still, he came closer. Presently, his earlier look of hopeful interest was replaced with a look of horrified disgust. He shuddered. Spiders! Thousands of them. It was a giant web, and these tiny arachnids, generally solitary, were functioning in some macabre cooperation. But why? Was it so that they could catch large prey?

The thought reeled him. Tom backed up. While he found their alien design fascinating, all those legs and eyes, there was also something about spiders that had always given him the creeps. He had an almost genetic repulsion to them, and this nest amplified that instinctive arachnophobia infinitely. Tom turned and trotted out fast as he could with his heavy pack.

On the edge of the forest, he looked back and around, but didn't see any more nests. He thought about that long swath of them he'd walked by. All those spiders. Must have been millions, no, *billions* of them. Involuntarily, he shuddered again, a queasy feeling in his gut.

They walked on for hours, having seen no more spider nests before Tom felt safe enough to take another rest under the canopy. Yet, during that time, he could not stop thinking about them. He'd have nightmares. Thankfully though, having not noticed any of their nests before that afternoon, nor after the last one, it appeared that this was just a bizarre, localized oddity of nature, an isolated pocket of creepiness in an otherwise delightful forest.

What he didn't know was that, if occasionally a species became overly abundant, it was temporary, an aid in natural selection. Tomorrow the flocks of pest control aves would arrive.

The river began another modest swing west and Tom decided to cross it next chance he could to get to the other side before they got too far off track. He'd look for an opening in the trees made by the wildlife, some pathway that likely went all the way through. Why blaze a new trail when they could just use one others had already made? He perceived that the river was again slowing. Now it just burbled along gently. The ground under his feet was getting wetter. Evidently, the river was broadening some. They might have to walk across a knee-high section.

As they progressed, Tom would grab a bite from the various fruits he had now learned were good to eat. Nothing was saved of the turkey; whatever Tom had left, quite a lot, Little had eaten with rapidity, bones and all. She was a proficient bone eater, as a matter of fact. It accounted for a goodly percentage of her diet. Before they'd left the foothills, he watched as she'd crunched her way through the Ramoceros, including the sturdy thigh bones. She was growing and her jaws were becoming heavy and powerful. Teeth large and sharp. Muscles working dramatically. Small pieces of bone would show up in her stool, he noted.

Though beefier, Little was active and still liked to chase things. Unfortunately, ground squirrels, always her favorite, were, these days, too agile for her, and, frustrated, she would set to digging madly at their dwellings, destroying in seconds what had taken them hours to build. Then, unsuccessful at the hunt, she'd give up and walk away nonchalantly as if she'd never actually *meant* to catch one. Tom pet her as they strolled. Her back was now to his fingertips. She had the same thick red-brown hair with black tips as did her mother. Unlike the Carpocyon, her fur was always clean, or if it got dirty, say by walking through mud, soon as it dried the dirt would simply fall off, leaving her unsullied.

Whenever he started to get too cozy in his assumptions about her endearing qualities, however, she would blow them away in a display of raw, barbarous violence. Now that she had to take down slower, and bigger, game, she was coming into her own. It disturbed him, but he had to accept it as a part of the natural order. All the same, he would turn away in sadness from the cries and carnage of her victims.

Even her play now was getting too rough, though she didn't know it. When he rested, she would sometimes amble over to him, pushing with her weight and knocking him off the log or rock he sat on. She would then escalate with more pushing, and even growling and mouthing him, placing an arm or leg in her chops and biting down - though mildly. But it unnerved him. She was a wild animal. Perhaps she didn't have an "off" button if pushed too far. He thought now of the irony of her name: Little. *Might have to change that.*

Peering up at a dull, humming resonance, a large, slowly moving swarm of bees, not an uncommon spectacle in the middle Miocene, was abuzz over the tree tops, making their leisurely way to a new home. Tom gaped until they passed from view.

At evening, they bedded down under the sky, sans fire, still no sea in sight. He'd also not seen any sign of a path through the waterlogged land to their left. He wanted a wide one, not trusting an extended walk on a narrow trail through deep forest that might end at nothing. He thought that there had to be one, and tried to push down an indefinable feeling of foreboding that creased his brow. Too, no signal from Julie for this long was worrying, but he consoled himself with the conviction that he was traveling in the right direction.

The mosquitos were merciless that night, as were his dreams.

The next morning was exquisite, cool breezes blowing away

his fears. Bright blue sky framed by springgreen leaves and bright bird song. Were they meadowlarks or some extinct version? Tom wondered, smiling.

The trees around them he photographed. Names came up that meant nothing to him. Lawson Cypress, Arborvitae, Fir, Malosma, Poplar, Bald Cypress and Sour Gum. Tom put the P.I. away when he found food. Sweet fruit, and farther out, avocados. Little was not happy about it, but she ate them anyway. Fasting was patently not in the Aelurodon vocabulary.

He found a possible replacement for the split madrone. Manzanita was also attractively smooth-barked and ruddy colored, perhaps more so, and it appeared to be very hard. Problem was, unlike madrone, it was usually twisted and crooked. Finally, he found one that was passably linear. He took it with the handsaw and fashioned it, while they sat under an avocado tree in an open space.

A woodpecker sounded. Tom, glancing up, happened to notice movement out of the corner of his eye. Casually, he looked that way to see a huge beast walking ponderously down a grassy bank on the far edge of the meadow. His eyes went wide. More than huge, it was gigantic. Another Aelurodon? Maybe. But this seemed bigger. Fetching the P.I. Tom stealthily snapped a picture. *Amphicyon* it said. Bear-dog. With its long legs he imagined that it could easily run down any potential prey. It looked to be made of solid muscle, and they rippled with its every burly step. Its mouth, open to aid in cooling and capturing scent, displayed four huge canine teeth. A born killer. It had to be four or five hundred pounds. Probably a male. Truly awe-inspiring. Thank goodness it hadn't seen *them*. But then Little saw it. Her ears pricked, hackles raised and body stiffened. At first, simply staring, she then began to growl, a deep sonorous rumble from her chest. It was a vibration he felt. Tom dropped his food and threw his arms around her in case she was thinking to go after it. Surely if she were to fight such a giant she would be torn to pieces.

"*Easy, girl,*" he whispered, swallowing hard. "*Shhh.*" He was fairly sure that his pistol wouldn't stop that thing, should it charge.

Little ceased growling, seemingly aware of the extreme danger, but kept her attention fully on the other. Tom knew that were he to give the word, or if she were to misunderstand a word, she would be off. Off to her death, that is. That couldn't happen. He held on tighter, and together they watched the beast, as, lumbering, it disappeared into the far forest.

An hour afterwards, though, an even more awe-inspiring, even more frightening sight met his eyes. He knew something was changing when he could see sky through the forest in front of him. When he could hear a sound of distant roaring and a wind began to penetrate and blow their way. Finally, coming out of that Miocene forest, he stepped back, staggered at the sight.

The inland sea! They'd made it! It was incredible! It was beauteous! He'd never, *ever* seen anything like it before, even in his dreams. There was nothing, nothing in his life that had ever, *could* ever prepare him for this, this immense expanse of blue water, which Julie variously called the San Joachin and Temblor Seas. Waves lapped gently on the shore in a soft lullaby. Birds dived into the waters, then reemerged and took flight again. Shearwaters and auks, gannets and albatrosses, avocets and a seagull-like bird, *Fulmarus miocaenus*. Another flock of these latter squabbled in high notes on the beach to his right over a dead sand crab.

High in the sky, though, was a *true* wonder. Soaring slowly in wide, graceful circles, there were three of them, *Osteodontornis*, the Miocene king of birds. Tom shielded his eyes from the sun as he watched them, then they welled up and he dropped to his knees in the soft, warm sand. Little just stood, eyes half closed in the wind, and stared, solemnly, out at that giant ocean of blue.

If anything could be described as beautiful, this was it, and in that moment something happened. The place struck a chord in him so deep he didn't know it existed. An ancient, primeval note, one that said, *This is home. This is where you were meant to be.* And it all came together, everything he'd been feeling subconsciously. This world. This time. *This is real. This is home. The lovely and the fearful. The easy and the hard.*

The hard. There was a problem. As ever. That quiet, meandering river on his left, he now discovered, was, in truth quite, quite wide - and deep, for it had, unknown to him as they'd trekked through the forest, been joined by others coming from those high Sierran mountains. Now it flowed heavily into that prehistoric inland sea, whitecaps on its tips.

They were at a dead-end. They'd have to turn back.

Turn back. He shook his head at the thought.

Or ...

Or ....

Or...

They could go across.

387

Twenty Four

After the departure of the Strong Box, Julie stayed in the area for another two days, perhaps hoping that, finding her missing, the scientists fifteen million years away would send it back for her. Meanwhile, she busied herself picking up and burning debris. There was no return of the box, however. She wondered what Jaqzen told them, and if they would buy it. The third day, she decided to head back to her home in the hill.

On the way, she discovered, to her dismay, that she was not alone after all. Jaqzen was apparently still there. The sound of gunshot betrayed him. Hearing it in the distance, she climbed a tree on top of a hill and looked out. More gunfire, but he couldn't be seen, too many trees in the way, though she could tell *about* where he was. She guessed a mile to the northwest, in a less dense woodland. The report of gun carried far in a world virgin to abrupt human noise. She continued on her way southwest, to her hideaway, grateful that he hadn't seen the smoke from her fire.

Julie remained there for another three months or so, undiscovered, soon remembering the PinPointer. She checked it everyday in case they finally sent someone back to fetch her. As discreet about it as she could be, Julie only checked it when she was away from the cave. Jaqzen could be watching.

In the meantime, she explored her new world as much as possible, reveling in old wonders long lost to people and discovering many more new species, all of them completely unknown to science. Flora and fauna. Scores of new foods, too. She learned how to wash when the soap was gone. How to mend clothing when it began to fall apart. And later, how to make new garments from scavenged animal skins and make new shoes from the toughest parts of these hides.

She found a marvelous grassy hill, with a stunning view, and a certain, *feel,* that drew her, and each evening she sat and watched the island volcano, and the sun as it sank to the West. Then she would sing. Sing for Tom. Now it was Enya's *If I Could Be Where You Are.*

Afterwards she would pray, pray for her husband, for her heart, to come to her, to come home; its impossibility never occurring to her.

During her time at the cave, Julie was evolving, becoming stronger, more confident in her abilities. Yet she never lost what it was that made her *who* she was. Julie Pine, scientist, wife, woman. Everywhere she went, Julie studied and took notes, cogitated and drew tentative conclusions. She also kept a daily journal, a diary of sorts, and added memorable experiences.

One that stood out was an extraordinary migration of small, brilliant yellow, canary-like songbirds with purple and red striped wings. She didn't know what kind of bird they were. The day before, there had been a virtual plague of pesky flies attracted to the abundant fertilizer on the prairie. She holed up in her den the whole time in an attempt to escape them.

Julie woke the following morning to find the flies gone. Instead, there were dozens of the birds, all singing and chattering gaily on the branches of her overhanging oak and thousands in the trees around. They also fluttered through the sky in lively clouds, diving in and out over the forest and in waves from tree to tree. Sensing that this was a happening of grand proportions, Julie climbed her hill, and sat on the far side looking out toward the open west. Scattered oaks and kopjes dotted the countryside here, but mostly it was grass, grass and grazers. Horses, camels, antelope, some proboscideans, a scattered variety of carnivorans, both large and small - the usual. It turned out, though, that the hordes of yellow birds she'd seen from the cave was but a tiny representation of their actual numbers.

Down on the grasslands and stretching out for miles toward the North, South, and West, the birds flew in truly epic waves, going after the numberless flies, which rose up in flight. But not only were there the yellow birds, including several other previously unknown Miocene species, there were more familiar perching birds, or their ancestors, too. Vermilion Flycatchers, Scarlet Tanagers, Orioles, Bluebirds, stunning Indigo and Painted Buntings and a variety of plainer songbirds. Wrens, Warblers, Vireos, Thrushes and Sparrows. A virtual orchestra. But it was the yellow that dominated. Though they kept to their own feather, still, the effect was of cooperation in this feast. The air was practically electric with all the mad excitement and so much chirping, trilling, twittering, pipping and peeping. Most of the grazers tried to ignore them and continue with their eating, grateful for the diminishing of the flies. A few, however, convenient landing pads for throngs of merry songbirds, would run off a ways, then stop and go back to their feeding.

Julie wondered about the migration. In this tropical/temperate world, it wouldn't be one based on a need to escape foul or freezing weather. No, this migration was simply a pursuit of one of the bird's favorite foods. The insects had hatched in their billions and the birds, timing it precisely, descended upon them as they took to wing. In a couple of days, when the fly numbers no longer justified it, the birds would disband and disperse. Still, even with this many birds, she knew that they would only devour about half the number of flies. Many more would fall to other predators, reptile and insect. In all, maybe ten percent would survive to breed and continue the line. She had no fear for the flies. The numbers of songbirds, though, were simply stunning, dwarfing anything she'd ever read about the migrations of old.

Some days later, she was witness to a different, yet equally remarkable, event. Walking through a dark, pathless forest on her way to another scientific adventure, Julie thought she heard faint cries and stopped. She listened now, waiting in silence. The sounds did not return until she was about to leave, then there they were again - small whimperings off to her left a bit. She looked that way. It was even darker there, shadowed by heavy vegetal undergrowth. Julie strained to hear the sound again, and it came. Barely audible, something in pain, a cry, yet muted, as if it were trying to be inconspicuous. A flush of concern came over her and she approached the area she thought the cries were coming from and stared into the dark, trying to see. Another whimper, so faint, it was coming regularly now, with each breath of the animal.

Julie dropped to her haunches trying to adjust her eyes, unsure what to expect.

"Hello," she whispered, "are you okay?"

Slowly, the indistinct outline of an animal shape lying on the ground began to form. It was small and spotted. Julie was tempted to get her flashlight, but thought somehow that this would be a violation, and she withheld.

The animal was lying on its side, breathing rapidly. She could hear that now. The sun moved imperceptibly. A note of slightly brighter light appeared, and then she saw it. A small horse. Hipparion. Unknown species. She drew in her breath.

"Are you okay?" she asked again in a soft voice. Still the animal breathed hard. Its side bulged, moved. Julie swallowed. Then she reached out a hand and lightly, ever so lightly, touched her, touched the side where her baby was. There was a dampness to her fur.

"Oh, you're going to be a mom!" she said in hushed tones. The cries got a little louder and quicker. The animal might be reacting to her presence negatively. She did not want to disturb it. Yet the scientist - and the nurturer in her, impelled her to stay.

There was more movement, vibrational waves rolling along the little horse's abdomen. More whimpering. Suddenly, something from the back end appeared. Little dark hooves, one set of them, then quickly following, long, thin legs. The next part though, the foal's head, did not show immediately. Naturally, it would be larger and would require more effort on the part of mom. However, she lay same as before and seemed to make no extra attempt. How long had she been lying here, Julie wondered, trying to deliver her baby? She was probably exhausted.

More cries then, and the Hipparion mother lifted her head to look at her side. She heaved, but nothing more emerged. She laid her head back on the ground.

After several more tries, Julie said, "Can I help?" This was followed by another move, a big convulsion, and louder cries. She drew back her hand. Nothing more came. The little horse's breathing became rasps. *Oh no,* she thought, her heart breaking. Then she hit on a plan.

The next time the horse heaved, Julie grabbed the legs of her young and pulled. There was resistance and mom cried, then all of a sudden the baby shot out, followed by a wash of fluid. A big foal. All she'd needed was a little help.

Baby lay there, as did mom, not moving for a few moments, then it lurched. Still, mom lay, too tired to do anything more. The foal lurched again now, and tried to get up. Mom looked over, then once more lay her head down in rest, gathering her strength. After another moment, she lifted her head to look at her offspring, a deep genetic urge overcoming her other requirements. Julie sensed that she was too close and edged back a bit, then stood and tiptoed several more feet away. Mom, not seeming disturbed by Julie's presence now, stood herself, then turned around and began to lick at the membrane around the face of her baby. The touch stimulated it and immediately it lurched again and tried to stand, making a small cry of its own. It fell, but it did not give up. As Julie watched, tears in her eyes, it tried again and again. She wanted to reach out and steady it, but withheld.

"Come on, little guy!" she said encouragingly in low undertones. Though obviously drained, mom continued to clean her baby. Finally, after five strenuous minutes, the foal stood, shakily, a dark, wet form and sought out its mother. She was there, and after a few failed attempts at location, found her teats and began to drink. Mom's mouth hung open, panting, and Julie worried that she was too tired. Yet, bravely she remained and fed her new foal, while casting uneasy looks at Julie.

Julie wondered if there was anything else she could do, feeling almost like a mother to the little horse herself, but could think of nothing. She decided, then, that her presence might be more of a hindrance than a help, so she began to back out. The little Hipparion mother watched her, and Julie thought she intuited gratitude for the assistance from this stranger.

"You're welcome," she whispered, wiping her eyes. Julie stood and watched them a minute longer, then said, "Take care of each other," turned, and walked away. She hoped fervently that both would be safe. Feeling spent emotionally after that, she decided to cut her day short and head back home. There, she wrote in her journal about the happening. She'd not taken any photographs, feeling that would have been an intrusion, so her words alone would have to suffice.

Yea! Witnessed the birth of a Hipparion!
May he run like the wind
and live a long and happy life.

Julie spent the night on her hill, and slept under the stars.

Then, one day it happened. She was sitting on her hill experimenting in making alcohol when there came a pulsing tone, a steady beep issuing from her backpack. *Jaqzen*, Julie thought in fear. He'd tried to contact her many times after she'd first left the Strong Box, then stopped when she didn't reply. Now, here he was doing it again. For her part, she'd not turned on her own device in sometime, except on rare occasions to place him, so as not to give herself away. She'd know when he tried to find her, but if she left hers off he wouldn't know where *she* was.

Still, she needed to know his location, always hoping that he'd gone off on a false trail and was now somewhere far away. She *had* to know. With serious misgivings, she opened her pack and took out the PinPointer. Then, pausing, she flipped it open, turning it on.

There he was, Jaqzen, the red light. She smiled. He was about fifty miles away - no, it was forty-four. Not as good, but good enough.

She was about to switch off when she noticed the "resolve" light was on. Julie squinted, then shielded the face of the PinPointer from solar glare to make sure. Yes, it was lit. She remembered that there was something, something she'd been taught about the device and this light back at the Institute. Quickly, she felt for the little round button on the side and pushed it. Immediately the two dots that represented she and Jaqzen shrank and dropped to the bottom of the screen. Then at the top another appeared. Blue. It pulsed, as did her own. She stared, incredulous, then let out a little yelp of surprise and covered her mouth. Someone else was here! *They'd sent someone!*

She continued to gape wide-eyed at the screen for minutes, her heart and mind racing. She knew she should switch off, but couldn't. Then the blue light went out. She waited another minute, then, afraid of alerting Jaqzen, switched off herself. She sat heavily on the ground and puzzled over it. The Institute had sent someone, either that or there was some sort of malfunction. If they did send somebody, why did they put them so far away? It didn't make any sense! She flipped her PinPointer on once more to look, but this time there was no blue light. She switched off again when she noticed Jaqzen's red light blinking. Certainly, he'd been alerted. If he was watching just now he knew her general location. His light was pulsing; he *must* have been looking. She swallowed. She couldn't stay now. She'd go to meet that blue light.

Jaqzen, in the midst of skinning the Barstovian sow, *Dyseohyus*, heard the beeping. A little late. He ran to his pack and threw it open, removing the P.P. There was nothing. He scratched his head. A minute later, the green light appeared. It remained on. He made a rapid calculation. Ha, ha! he grinned, *I've got you, Julie Pine!* He did not stop to wonder why she might be beeping him. He knew only one thing: his prey, his opponent, that which through cunning and stealth had eluded him too long, was inadvertently signaling him. He smiled while packing, tearing off a raw chunk of flesh to eat on the way.

"It was only a matter of time, Pine," he said confidently.

Early the next morning, Julie loaded her pack and climbed one last time out of her cavern home, saying goodbye to it as she did. Altogether, she'd lived in the cave for four months.

Four months of sunrises and sunsets. Four months of study and leisure. Four months of happy memories. It had become her home. She hated leaving.

She'd also be leaving her hill and the wonderful pond. Filled with sadness, Julie wept. It was a soft cry, like a gentle rain. She could have lived here the rest of her life. Even if she never saw Tom again, she could be happy. There was a lifetime's worth of things to see and learn. Many lifetime's worth.

Suspecting that Jaqzen could be on her trail after yesterday, Julie switched her PinPointer on. She gasped. *He was!* In the night, while she slept, he'd made twelve miles! Twelve miles closer to her. He knew where she was and at this rate would be here by tomorrow. If he had taken note of the other, the blue light, he'd know that she'd likely be heading that way and would try to cut her off. A cunning tracker, she knew that she'd have to outwit him to get by him. Thus, mistake or not, Julie chose to make a long detour and head south, switching on her PinPointer at a few locations along the way to give him the false impression that she was going in that direction. Then, at the end, turn it off, make a U-turn and arc around west, then north. If she was lucky, he would keep south. And thus she went, following well used animal trails, hoping that other prints would erase her own.

It worked for a while, too. Not long though. In a day he was on to her. It was her too frequent checking of his position which raised his suspicions. Suddenly, her signals stopped. Her last beacon, he'd noticed, was moving off laterally toward the ocean. Between she and it was thick forest, and a long, semi-wide strip of open land. No doubt, that was the route she'd return by. He checked his progress behind an abutment of rock halfway in and turned off his beacon, while waiting for hers. Darkness fell.

At dawn, she sent one more. A last inquiry - and a mistake. She was indeed a fraction closer now and heading his way. He was right! He had her! Jaqzen figured her probable speed, had breakfast and sat tight. Mid-morning, he climbed the highest hill around him and took out his scope, scanning the horizon from which she was coming. A lot of animals, as usual. He sat there for hours, smoking, flicking butts and watching.

Julie was fairly certain that she had fooled Jaqzen. In her checks, it was clear that he *was* following her. That afternoon, she decided to begin her about-face, first veering off westward for a ways, just under cover of the trees that juxtaposed a wide and lush grassy plain enclosed by low hills a mile or so distant. When the sun went down, she made camp. In the morning she would continue north, leaving her PinPointer off. By then, she thought he should be many miles south of her.

When daybreak came, however, she felt she had to know for certain and switched on briefly. There was no signal from him. She switched off again, pondering that.

In the broad meadows next to which she walked, was a large herd of mixed grazers. Camels, antelopes, horses, peccaries. She took note of these last, *Hesperhys*, *Cynorca* and *Prosthenops*. She remembered that it was a tooth from Prosthenops, found by rancher and geologist Harold Cook in 1917, and described by Henry Fairfield Osborn in 1922, that led to the mistaken notion of a so-called Nebraska Man, which Creationists used as evidence of the supposed fraud of evolution theory.

"You rabble-rouser you!" Julie tsked.

Other prehistoric fauna roamed the pastureland, the oreodonts *Ticholeptus* and *Merychyus,* a 200 pound, plant-eating cud-chewer with a short face, tusk like canine teeth, a long tail, short feet, and four-toed hooves. And there was *Brachycrus*, a rare, hippo-like oreodont which weighed in at over 700 pounds. Its hanging half-trunk was quite nimble, and able, Julie noted, to both pull a snout full of *Potamogeton* or pick up a scampering beetle and put it in its mouth.

With fascination, she also observed the hornless ruminant, *Longirostromeryx*, a saber-tooth deer and its chevrotain-like relative, *Pseudoblastomeryx*.

When she finally spied her first chalicothere close up, *Moropus merriami*, Julie was ecstatic. It was a strange creature, which looked like a cross between a horse and a sloth, with sloping hindquarters and back legs shorter than the front. It stood on those powerful rear legs and pulled down branches from trees to browse. It also used its formidable sharp claws for defense. This one she guessed weighed about 300 to 400 pounds.

There was a thunderous bellow some distance away. A zygo. It was followed by similar bellows in answer, dispersed out to the far reaches of the plain. There were other calls as well, different tonalities, vibrations, pitches. Soon, all the plain was alive with sound. A quarter-mile away, a herd of *Scaphohippus* galloped south. There came a booming behind her and Julie jumped. *Tapiravus*, another tapir like animal. It stood at the border of the field. *What a deep voice you have,* Julie thought.

There was yet another sound now, a high-pitched howling of sorts. It too was joined by other howlings from locales unseen. When it began, the bellowers went silent. Julie climbed a small hummock and pulled out her binocs to have a look.

"Osbornodon!" she exclaimed. It was a pack of three. They belonged to an ancient family related to canines, the *Hesperocyoninae* and, in fact, were its last members. Soon they would be gone. Averaging forty to fifty pounds, they lived by scavenging the kills of other animals. Julie photographed the living fossils, then looked around at the other sources of canine

howling. These sounds were similar, yet different. Barking, baying, yowling and yelping. Staccato cries and long, low timbres. Adjusting the focus, she found variously: two tomarctus species, canines which resembled coyotes, and tiny *Cynarctoides*, a mink like ground squirrel hunter of no more than two or three pounds. Loping by in the mid-distance was *Protepicyon*, a 75 pounder and ancestor to *Epicyon*, which should be arriving in another half million years. One of its species, *Haydeni*, will stand three feet at the shoulder and be the largest dog to ever live.

Another canine, *Euoplocyon,* was a pure carnivore, weighing around 20 pounds, and there was *Phlaocyon,* a fox to coyote sized omnivore with raccoon like markings on its face. These latter she spotted high on horizontal branches in some pecan trees. They were attempting to liberate honey from a hanging hive of angry bees, which swirled around them. Julie rejoiced in her discoveries, then did something a little wild and crazy; she began to howl herself, and together they sang, Julie and her Barstovian family.

When finally the howling began to wane, then the plains were silent once more - silent, that is, except for the light, colorful notes of bird song, and the whisper of the breeze through the grass and trees. A quiet world.

Under the wide, blue sky, she lay. In the sacred pasture. Her arms and legs spread out to embrace it all. She'd never let it go. Thin blades of green waved above her head and softened the ground beneath her. A huge beetle zoomed by a few inches above. It hit a tall shaft and somersaulted into the green. Julie flinched, then laughed. Finding it, she saw it struggle to right itself, then slowly begin walking along. Choosing a certain blade it climbed, or tried to, but the grass kept bending down to the ground under the beetle's greater weight. Again and again it tried, but failed to climb. Then Julie picked it up in her hand.

"Hello there! Did you want to fly?" she asked sweetly. She lifted her hand above her head. The beetle walked to the end of her fingers, stopped, then lifted its shell-like carapace, exposing the delicate wings. A moment later, these began to flutter, and, after a bit of a drop, it took to the air and zoomed off into obscurity.

"Bye!" she sang after it, waving and giggling again at the sight of the big bumbling bug.

Julie walked down the knoll and toward a small stream. It was getting hot, and she was thirsty. Better fill up her water pouch too. While at her camp and sitting on the hill one day, her metal bottle had fallen, rolled and dropped off the side before she could catch it. It landed in a rocky patch a hundred feet below. Now there was a deep dent, and centered within that dent was a tiny puncture, a pinhole really. Yet, although tiny, it was enough to cause the leaking out of most of her water. She'd panicked at first, then figured that she would be better served by thinking. She could plug it with pine sap. It was only a temporary solution, though.

And so, following the orbit of a group of vultures, she found the remains of a *Prosynthetoceras*, a strangely horned deer-like creature about the size of a wapiti. She searched, then, with no small amount of repulsion, cut out the stomach. There was no other choice. Carrying it to the nearest stream, with her fingertips she washed it inside - by stretching the stomach opening and putting in her hand - and out with sand, water and crushed oak leaves. Then she allowed it to dry. A new water bottle!

Her pouch filled, Julie stood and re-hefted the pack onto her back. She was about to leave when she happened to look to her right. Something was moving there, among the various herds of grazers, trotting, seemingly heading in her direction. It looked a long ways from her, perhaps half a mile. A camel with a long, thin neck. She turned back and started out. Her pace was slow, but steady; she knew the cost of haste was depletion.

Silence. A minute went by when the usual cacophony of songbird suddenly stopped. It was like an alarm. She glanced again at the dark thing coming from her right, frowned. It was closer now and seemed to be moving straight for her. Instinctively, she took hold of her scope, which swung from the lanyard around her neck and brought it to her eye. She dropped it in a shriek. *It was Jaqzen!* He was racing at full speed and carrying his rifle.

Terror overtook her, and Julie immediately set off at a run toward the north. Jaqzen adjusted his trajectory to match, calculating when he would intercept her. He'd left his supplies on the hill while she was still carrying hers. *She's slow as a wounded skunk, while I'm fast as an antelope,* he mused. *Let her run. It won't be long now.*

In near hysteria, Julie hurried, crying in fright. She could hear Jaqzen's roaring, laughing, the triumph in his voice. He was now about an eighth mile away. Animals in his path moved off and away from the madman. *This is it then,* Julie thought in anguish. Too late, she realized that her pack had been hampering her, but she dropped it anyway. Ran faster now.

She was coming up on a large herd of *Hypohippus*, an edgy, quarter-ton horse that preferred the forest margins. As well, within their ranks were a few of the similarly sized *Megahippus*. They were between her and Jaqzen. Maybe if she ran around them and kept low. But he was closing fast. Then a thought occurred to her. She looked across the backs of the primitive horses, which, already nervous, were milling about in antsy circles at the running two-leggers. She headed straight for them, flailing her arms and yelling for all she was worth. That was all it took. Like a flash, they were off and thundering toward Jaqzen in a panicked flurry of hooves and dust. She last saw his head above the herd, but that was soon hidden by the hazy veil.

There were two gunshots, seconds apart, one which whizzed by her, then nothing else but the sound of hundreds of galloping feet. She didn't wait around to discover the outcome. Racing back to retrieve her pack, she then lit out again through the forest.

Twenty Five

Tom stared out at the open sea southeast and into the distance. The *Temblor*. The Sierras projected high, gauzy blue and faraway. In between was this expanse of deep, dark water, though how deep he had no idea. How could he do it? He looked around at the "supplies", a variety of trees of various sizes. No, it was impossible! He had no axe or hatchet, no hammer or nails, no rope or glue. He did have a handsaw, but what could he do with that? A depression came over him then, and he sat once again in the warm sand, head in hands. How stupid that he hadn't thought about the fact that the river they followed from the mountains was *between* them and the mainland. That it might grow in size. When he was at his lowest and feeling good and sorry for himself, Little came over and nuzzled his neck with her cold, wet nose. Her timing was just right, and he smiled.

"Thanks, old friend," he said, stroking her thick fur. "Got any suggestions?" She sat and looked expectantly at him, tongue lolling to one side. Tom sighed. "Me neither."

The mid-Miocene Temblor Sea extended inland from the Pacific all the way to the future Bakersfield, in places its waters almost lapping at the foothills of the Sierras. Vertically, it ran from Fresno in the North to the San Emigdio range in the South, or roughly 150 miles. Compared to the Pacific, it was shallow and warm, generally varying between 200 and 600 feet deep, with areas of both shallower and deeper waters. It was enclosed on the West by the Diablo Range, but still connected by inlets, and seaways; one, through a slender strait from the future Monterey area to Coalinga, and another wider passage from Santa Maria, north.

With time and weathering, California's topography would erode. By the late Hemphillian it would wear down to its granitic roots. By the end of the Pliocene, though, 2.2 million years before the Anthropocene, the North American Plate would rise thanks to subduction by the Pacific Plate, and the waters would begin to drain. Meanwhile, the global climate would grow colder. A lot of oceanic water was being sequestered at the poles and frozen into ice. All this would cause a gradual lowering of the Temblor sea level and closure of the inlets. Eventually, the seas would be driven out of the interior.

By the Pleistocene, however, about 700,000 years B.A., the former Temblor, now called the Corcoran or Lake Clyde, would become a larger, 225 mile long by 50 wide, fresh water lake, fed by glaciers. But that was fourteen million years away.

Something jumped out there in the blue. A dolphin. No, two. No, three. Then more. *Kentriodon*, the Miocene version. There was a whistle; it was similar to the sounds he remembered hearing on the old nature programs his mother had secretly stored. She'd made him promise not to reveal them. He never did.

Now watching the Kentriodon, Tom thought about how easy it would be to get across this inland sea - if he had flippers. But of course, he didn't. He gazed at the mountains again, trying to see the shore.

"Wait a minute." He remembered something, something he was told back at the Institute about his binoculars. He got them, remembering now. Tom set them on a boulder at eye level. They focused automatically. Then he adjusted them until the level gage indicated that they were perfectly inline. Finishing that, he pushed a small black button on the side. Instantly an invisible laser shot out and back again. In that fraction of a second, it travelled to the foothills and returned. A figure popped back, blinking in red: 12.4 miles. That's how far it was to that point on the hill. He nodded to himself, readjusted and focused on the shoreline. 7.9 miles. Okay, from where they stood it was roughly eight miles to land. He thought about that: *It really isn't that far ... is it?*

Tom looked anew at his surroundings. Maybe. Maybe. Then he began to sketch in the sand.

His first idea was to make a canoe. It occurred to him after he chanced upon a fallen log with an already partially hollowed out center. Could it be beaver work, he wondered? He decided that it wasn't, as neither end appeared chewed. Perhaps insects then, or simply rot. Anyway, it was a convenient find. All he'd need to do was clean out the middle better and taper the ends.

How did the Native Americans do it? With sharp implements, of which he had none - of the right kind at least. The inside of the log, though, was soft and shouldn't take too much work. He looked around and found a hard piece of glassy rock, chert, and banging the sides with another rock, created a sharp edge. A hand axe of sorts. He believed he could carve out the core with it. The ends would be harder. So Tom set to, chopping and flinging chunks behind him and whistling.

Little lay down on the other side of the log near the waves and watched him as he worked. Tom thought about her. Seeing that Amphicyon before got him thinking. The huge beast seemed to lumber more than walk. He doubted that it was made for long migrations. Probably it stayed within a certain territory. Was he asking Little to do something not in her nature to take this long, cross-country, one-way trek? What if she finally balked? But she wasn't an Amphicyon. Still, the thought worried him.

Tom stopped every now and then to sit and rest. Fresh water ran in a rivulet nearby and he drank liberally. Little, at times, fetched some crab walking on the beach, risking a good pinching when she did. She bit down on them, easily crunching through the carapace. Tom found eggs from some kind of sea turtle and cooked them. Some of the lovely purple star fruit also grew here, the sun shining beautifully through its semi-translucent skin, and he sated his need for sugar therefrom.

A couple of hours after beginning, Tom felt that he'd carved enough from the center of the log to comfortably fit he, Little, and their supplies. He tested it by loading everyone and everything in. Little had to be pushed, but, finally, ponderously, got inside, lying down in the middle, thereby taking up most of the room. Tom shoved from behind to move her, but she resisted, then, with a grump, gave in and sat in the front of the carving. There was room for all. He carved some from the ends now with his handsaw. The result was not smooth, but it was an improvement. Then, with everything out, he got behind it and pushed to get it into the water. It wouldn't budge.

"Oh lovely!" he said. All this work and he wouldn't be able to get the thing in the water. Tom now began to dig some of the sand from underneath the canoe. Water ran into the cavity. Glancing up, he noticed that the tide was now a little higher. He gazed around and deduced that tidewater regularly overtook much of this beach. Ah, he had only to wait.

They spent the next hour exploring the coast, west. Pebbles in the moist sand were small and smooth, like little jewels, polished to a shine by ages of tossing in the tide. It was a pleasant feel on bare feet. Oyster and other shells lay open among the stones, iridescent mother-of-pearl gorgeously reflecting the solar light. Tom collected several.

As they'd closed on the Temblor earlier, aloft in the trees he spotted massive stick and reed nests and their tall, slender, blue/gray residents. The heron-like birds were elegant fliers, but their call was a rough croak. He glanced up now to see one peering over nest-side down at them. A few hundred yards away, in another grouping of trees, was a large flock of cormorants. He noticed that many of the trunks, branches and the ground beneath them were white with guano. The stuff was thick and mushy to walk in. Smelled too. It was probably a great fertilizer, though. About half of their trees had been defoliated thanks to who knew how many generations of the birds idling there.

They continued on, then came upon a band of Giant Leatherback Turtles laying eggs in a wide area of sand. Little wanted to go after one, but Tom restrained her and to his amazement she listened. Then they sat and watched as the turtles dug holes with their rear flippers and dropped big eggs in them, carefully burying them afterwards and heading back to sea. It was all very serene.

The tide had risen further, and when he thought they'd waited long enough, they stood, turned and went back. The water was at about the halfway mark on the canoe now. Tom removed his shoes and pants and dug out more sand, then pushed from behind. When the tide had climbed higher, the log began to move. He got the rope from his pack and attached it to a knob on the log, walked up and around a palm, then back again. He didn't want to chance losing his boat. He continued pushing and the canoe began to rock. Finally, with one large wave and strenuous pushing, it was in and floating. It bobbed admirably.

"YEAH!" Tom shouted, scaring a gang of avocets, which flew off noisily down the beach. He held onto one end of the rope while the other end tugged gently. He tied it off and contemplated a paddle. *A modified frond from the palm might do nicely,* he thought. First, though, he wanted to test the craft's watertightness.

With some difficulty, he climbed aboard and sat, or *tried*

to sit. Soon as he was on, however, the log began to list, spinning slowly to the right. His mouth went a-gape. The canoe continued to roll, while Tom held on with white knuckles, yowling. With him on, it was finding a new center of gravity, rotating until finally the hatch he'd carved out was pointing downwards, unloading him in the process. Soaked, Tom, swam out from underneath, then stood in the semi-shallows wondering what went wrong. Slowly, the log rolled back to upright, so he tried again, and again the log went south, dumping him in the water. Tom tried several more times, hoping that perhaps a different sitting configuration might work. It made no difference, each time he ended up face down underwater.

Swimming out again, Tom stood and smacked his head with his hand while roaring expletives, then, still cursing, stamped out and picked up rocks to throw at the "canoe." For good measure, he threw a few as far out to sea as he could. He couldn't believe it! In truth, though, he was madder at himself, at his lack of expertise. Finally, ashamed and dejected, Tom sat down. Back to the drawing board.

The sun was past the halfway point in the sky now. If not for the continual sea breeze, he'd be baking. He would not give up, so Tom went to look for another log, then ditched the canoe idea altogether when another began to form in his mind. If not a canoe, then what about *a raft?* He'd try it before going all the way back to the mountains.

Now he thought about how to construct a raft. It shouldn't be too hard, he reasoned. As a youngster, he'd once read a picture book about it. He'd need logs, long, thin and straight, tied together. A lot of them. For rope, he'd try vines and hope they held. Thus, Tom roamed the forest and edges, dragging likely candidates back to their temporary camp. That took several hours more, as he had to wander farther and farther away to locate suitable subjects. Fortunately, willow cut easily.

When he had his pile of logs, Tom grabbed onto old vines hanging from trees and pulled. They were stiff and resisted, before snapping off. *No.* Next he thought about the green ones and tried them. They were supple, flexible and did not break. *Okay.* With apologies to the starfruit, he climbed the trees and severed lengths of vine that varied between ten and fifty feet long, letting them drop to the ground. Then, down, he carried them back and went about trimming the ends of the logs with his handsaw to make them all of similar length.

When twilight came and the sky turned violet, he stopped. He was amazed with what he'd been able to do in a few hour's time. The stars shone brightly and the milky way reflected from the sea. Waves lapped rhythmically like the heartbeat of the earth, and windy gusts blew, as was usual here. The forest looked especially dark in contrast, even seeming to spook Little, who, sensing something there, gave a sudden loud, strange bark that startled Tom. He jumped.

"Holy ... *Don't do that!*" he chastised. Still, she looked into the ebony jungle behind and to his right, growling deeply, ears pricked at a certain point. Tom strained to see and hear, but saw nothing. It wasn't the first time she'd scared the bejeezus out of him, and it probably wouldn't be the last. All the same, he was glad he had her. He thought that he would not sleep that night, yet, soon as he lay upon the soft, warm sand he was gone.

He slept deeply until Little woke him up with her nervous growling. She lay with her body pressed against his as if for protection, and when she growled he could feel it. He decided to get the flashlight and have a look, but, shining it toward the forest, still saw nothing. When she continued her performance he turned irritably on his side and, grumbling, went back to sleep.

409

In the morning, Tom found that Little was now on his other side, placing him between her and whatever it was that had been upsetting her. "Thank you," he said disgustedly. He decided that before he did anything else, he wanted to go have a look and see if he could find out what it was that had so disturbed her. He got the gun, not wanting to be unprepared, just in case, then made his way toward the river. They had to push their way through and around various trees and understory, finally scooting across a narrow wedge of sand past a sharp corner of granitic rock that angled to the sea. The last remnant of an ancient mountain, its sides were covered in ferns and lichen. Waves broke at their feet, tossing eel grass to and fro, then it was over to the other side.

For the first time, he saw the full width of the river. But it wasn't the waterway that most interested him. Standing as he was just the other side of the sill, Tom looked upriver to a rather amazing sight. Lining the banks on both sides and within the wide river itself were hundreds, perhaps *thousands* of huge creatures, animals he'd not seen before. Now on the other side of the old mountain, he could also hear them, *gronking*, for that is how the noise they made appeared to him. There were gronks all up and down the two banks, and it was loud. He marveled that he'd not heard them before. There was also fighting within, thrashing so severe that he could not see the participants for all the whitewater. The flow that ran beyond them was red. Little stayed behind him.

Intrigued, Tom took out his trusty P.I. and snapped a picture of the closest specimen, a mighty beast that slept on the bank not a hundred feet away. *Paleoparadoxia*, it said. Gazing at a safe distance through the binocs, he first noted their bodies, gray on top, fading to whitish with gray circles beneath. This animal had countless deep gashes on its sides. When it opened an eye, he noted that it appeared cloudy. Probably blind, at least in *that* eye. Doubtless from fighting. On its far side were numerous smaller Paleos, which, Tom guessed, were its harem, and some young.

Judging their size to be too heavy to be very quick, Tom thought he should go and take a closer look. Firmly, he told Little to sit and stay put, but he didn't think she would be hard to convince. She wasn't, though she *was* agitated at his departure, eyes staring hard at him, ears attentive.

Tom turned and walked toward the big Paleo, camera at the ready. He did not think the gun would be needed. Little commenced an annoying whine, and Tom turned and shushed her quietly as he could. He noticed, as he advanced on the creature, that it had a large square head with short, but sharp tusks. As it breathed, a whitish sort of bubbly foam came and went from its nostrils. It also had enormous, inward turned front feet with individuated digits. In between was webbing, which likely turned its feet into effective paddles in the water. Behind was a tiny tail, for which he could see no practical purpose.

When he was almost upon the snoozing clan and looking down at the camera to set it for some pictures, one of the brood opened an eye. Maybe it was the snap of a twig under Tom's foot, or maybe simply chance. Immediately, it began to make little gronking sounds. Tom looked up. Then others in the group started to call out. In rapid succession, the clamor moved down the bank, as more of the Paleos opened their eyes and began to gronk. Tom stuck his fingers in his ears. He still wanted to get his picture, and fumbled with the camera with one hand while plugging his ears with a finger and an upraised shoulder.

The monstrous brute that he'd been sneaking upon lifted its massive head, not knowing what was causing all the commotion. Blind in its right eye, it had not seen Tom walking slowly up to photograph it. It looked out across the river, then swung its head left. Seeing nothing to warrant such an uproar, it looked casually to the right. It was not blind in its left eye and now it saw Tom.

"Hey!" Tom said with a wave, then he snapped a picture. For a moment, the brute did nothing, taking in this unknown form standing before him. "You're a big boy, aren't you?" the biped offered. In reply, the brute blasted Tom with a gronk so loud that it almost knocked him backwards. *"Whoa..."* he said, stunned. That's when it happened.

In a flash, the animal lifted its immense bulk from the ground and was *running* at him.

"Yikes!" Tom yelled and ran in reverse, almost falling. Nevertheless, the creature was very fast and would soon have him. Losing a second to turn, Tom ran for all he was worth. It wasn't easy on the sand though, and the animal gained on him. When it was about to crush him under its locomotive-like momentum, Little flew by in the opposite direction, coming up behind the Paleo. Viciously she bit at the brute's hindquarters, barely penetrating the thick skin. It was enough, though, to halt its progress. It turned to face the Aelurodon, but seeing Tom sprinting to the point, she jumped over the Paleo's head, across its back, and tore off after her human.

At the corner, Tom shot a glance backwards. Little was right behind him, while the big Paleo had ceased its pursuit and stood looking in their direction, mouth open and drool spilling onto the ground. Its sides heaving from the exertion, it remained where it was to make sure the intruders were going. Quickly, yet gingerly, so as not to jab himself, Tom stepped past the rock, followed by Little, then swiveled to peek around the corner once again. The brute stood, still looking around him, then turned and strut-waddled back to its place near the females, tiny tail in the air, triumphant. Reunited with them, it let out another loud *Gronk*.

The sight of that huge butt wagging back and forth suddenly struck Tom, in his adrenaline charged state, as funny. No, it was *hysterically funny*, and retreating safely to his side of the point, he began to laugh out loud. He laughed long. He laughed away his tension, and when he was done, wiping the tears from his eyes, Tom felt better. He'd needed that.

"Well, one thing's for sure," he said to Little, "we can't go across the river. Out to sea it is, then!"

Having gathered the necessities for building a raft, Tom was eager to get started. Wisely, though, he knew that they should eat first and did just that, downing a variety of fruit and eggs. Little wandered off to find her own breakfast.

Now, placing all of the thin logs side by side, Tom decided which should go where. From the first, he laid them butt end to head to try to keep the whole as square and even as possible. No one layer cheapie this, he would make two layers for extra floatation potential.

It went fairly quickly. The first set of logs he cut to roughly 7 x 7 feet. These he lashed firmly together with the vine, weaving it in, out and around each log. When he ran out of "rope" he'd get more and continue from a couple feet inside the previous tied section. As there was no dearth of vines, he attached continuous lengths from one end to the other. Then he pulled on the logs to test their strength. They held fast. He lifted one end to check its overall sturdiness; it was solid. So he started another group of logs next to the first and tied them the same way. In a short while, it too was done, then, struggling, he lifted it and lay this group in the opposite direction to the first, looping vine through the ample gaps between logs to secure them. Again he lifted from a corner. It was heavy, but sound. Tom thought about putting on a third and final floor, but then decided against it, reasoning that any more, and the bulk might be an impediment to easy sailing. *Ah, yes, the sail,* he thought. What could he use? He remembered the thermal blanket. He'd not employed it since arriving, as the nights here were not cold enough require it. Now he opened it and stretched it out upon the ground to check its size. Coincidentally, it was also 7 X 7 feet, thin and light, yet tough. He wondered what it was made of. Surely its designers never imagined that their blanket would serve instead as a Miocene sailcloth. Choosing a thin, straight log, three inches in diameter, Tom grabbed the chert piece he'd used earlier and scraped the trunk clean of bark until only the smooth wood beneath showed. This he jammed in a space between the two layers all the way through to the ground beneath. He pushed it a bit further, then straining, lifted one corner and rested it almost upright on another timber. He tied the bottom of his mast pole to those around it tightly as he could, threading braided vine through the gaps, attaching it strongly and pulling the rest through the floor. He then set the raft back down and again tied the pole off topside. It was firm.

He found another pole, straight, but that angled in at six feet, cutting off the end just past a bend where a large, sturdy knot had formed. This he hewed to a long sharp point. Tom then carved a corresponding hole in the mast pole that he could set the point in. It balanced there. He lifted and banged it down a few times to test for solidity. It was sound. Removing it, he now found a couple of thinner poles and joined the three at their ends, thus forming a triangle. This part was not nearly as strong as the rest and Tom swore as he tied and retied, again and again, trying to make it stronger. Still it flexed too much, but there was nothing else he could think of to do. He didn't think the pieces would come undone, but he still did not like the feeling of instability. Finally, he found a bunch of straightish branchlets, and with more vines, tied them at the corners. That made it stronger. Lastly, he tied a piece of rope at the bottom of the mobile pole, above a cut-off branch and circled the mast with it, wrapping it below another cut-off branch on the mast's opposite side, then tied again. He heaved now up and down. Solid. *Good.* He swung the mast frame around and was satisfied that it would move freely, but not come easily loose. He hoped it would be sufficient.

Next, Tom got the sail and tied it (or tried to, for the wind threatened several times to blow it into the trees where he'd never be able to reach) first to the top of the movable pole at a juncture of a small trimmed off branch, then to the bottom at a similar juncture. The sail flapped madly in the wind and he wrapped it around the pole, tying it temporarily there for safe keeping, lest it be torn to shreds. He'd wait to attach the sail to the other poles when they were on the water.

It was time to devise the rudder. He chose from among piles of driftwood at the margins of the river and the sea on their side of the jut of rock, old wood that had been planed by the pulse of the tide and time. Finding a suitable subject with a broad bottom - the rudder, and long, narrow handle - the tiller, he attached it just loose enough that it could turn either way and thus help to steer the craft.

The last thing he needed to do was to make himself an oar in case the sail was lost. It would have to be stouter than the palm frond. For this he selected a comparable piece of driftwood. Even so, it would be a last, but lame resort, for he knew it wouldn't work well on the raft. He lashed it, and his backpack, securely to the deck.

The sun had advanced across the morning sky and now stood at ten degrees from perpendicular. Tom sat in the warm sand and looked at his creation with satisfaction. He was hungry and wolfed down more star fruit, then decided to gather as much as he could for the voyage. He hoped it would be uneventful.

Now that all that was left to do was to launch, Tom began to feel a disquiet about it. He looked out to gauge the calmness of the surface waters. Thanks to the wind, there were small white-caps far as he could see. Not good sailing weather, he intuited, especially for a greenhorn like himself. Should he wait to see if it quieted down some more? He thought about it, then resolved to wait another hour.

Twenty Six

In an hour, the water had indeed calmed a bit, and, heart pounding, Tom determined that it was time to go. He figured that they had a good eight hours until dark. Surely with a nice aft wind they would be at the other side in no time. And so, again loosely tying their craft to the palm, he pushed it into the surf. She floated and rocked nicely with the waves. Tom flushed with involuntary pride, then, up to his waist in water, clambered up and on. There was no overturning as with the "canoe" previous. He sat, and, as there were two layers, the top of the raft stayed dry. Tom smiled and nodded to himself.

"Not bad, eh?" he said to Little. She stood back, up to her chest in the tide, and watched without reply. "Well ..." Tom said, looking around again at the raft, "let's go!" The girl splashed out to him, now swimming at his feet. "Come on!" her human urged. Yet, though she tried to climb up, she could not; instead she dog-paddled and whined. "Oh, do I have to lift you up here?" Tom asked. He slid back into the water while still holding onto the mooring rope with one hand. Bending down, he got his other hand and arm under her and lifted. *"Sheesh!"* he said. She was heavy! "You're going to have to help me now." Little got her front feet on the deck and tried vigorously to pull herself up. Meanwhile, Tom boosted, struggled and grunted with effort. "What the heck have you been eating, girl, rocks?" he said.

Finally topside, she was a happier girl and her tail stood upright in joy. Then she barked and shook, sending ten thousand droplets to the four corners. Tom, tired from the strain, climbed aboard with difficulty. He rested on his back a minute, then sat and looked once more at the craft. Except for being slightly lower now, it looked none the worse for their combined weight. *Okay.*

Releasing the rope, Tom carefully stood and unfurled the sail. Again the wind wrenched it out of his hands, but he quickly seized it, and, with a small piece of vine, tied it at the bottom outward point of the triangle. They had their sail! He then attached another length there for control, which he held on to. It worked; almost immediately she began to push back onto the shore. Hurriedly perching behind, Tom pulled on the vine. The entire raft turned with it - the wrong way, though. He let loose some vine, the mast swiveled and the sail filled, turned the tiller the opposite way, and like a miracle she was heading out to sea. Tom beamed.

"What a super job you did, Little!" he said, facetiously. Little stood stiff, but excited and barked her unique aelurodon bark. She barked, and then barked some more. Tom laughed.

They were moving at a spanking fine pace, now a couple of hundred feet from shore. Presently, he saw where the great river flowed into the sea, and its numerous denizens, still cavorting and fighting. Looking down the far side of the river, an area earlier shielded from his eyes by rocky outgrowth and vegetation, he saw that the numbers of Paleos increased along the bay and into the distance, a remarkable sight! He also discovered, now that he could see it, that their sanctuary was actually part of a huge, semi-deep estuary, as abundant sand was obvious below the surface, having been transported by the river all the way from the mountains. That same flow was now helping to speed their voyage.

Tom played the rudder right and left to get a grasp of how to maneuver the thing, found that turning it too far was not a good idea, the sailcloth threatened to tear and the craft to upend in the waves. However, if he turned *just enough* he could go right or left. So moving the tiller gently to the right pushed the whole raft left at an equally gentle pace. It was like having a steering wheel! He thought that the best thing, then, was to make a long swing, an arc, toward the far shore, now probably *more* than eight miles distant.

He looked back again to find, with amazement, that the land they'd left was now probably a half-mile behind them. It wrapped around a peninsula, then receded northwest. A thin stretch of beach and breakers was still visible, and behind it, a long bank of trees that appeared impenetrable. Tom marveled that they'd come through such a deep forest. Framed as it was by the blue of sea and sky, it was a lovely tropical vista.

"Hot dang!" he said, remembering a phrase from an old television program, circa 1950s, far in the future.

A side effect of the wind was a constant spray of water on them, he could taste the salt in it. Knowing that much of this water was fresh, coming from the mountains, the presence of salt betrayed another source as well, and he looked west, following the land to their right with his eyes. From his low perspective, he could not see the Pacific, especially as there was a nebulous, ill-defined, snowy white mist that shrouded it in secrecy.

"Fog!" Tom said in delight. In the world of man, fog increasingly became smog. An ever-present, disgusting brown haze that held pollution close to the lungs.

When their pace began to slow a bit, Tom judged that the great river was losing its energy. Soon they'd be going wholly on wind power. He thought that they'd now gone about a mile. Looking south, Tom had a new idea. Instead of simply making a beeline for the far shore he'd seen before, why not just continue on in this way? They certainly were making good time!

A shadow fell across them and the water about, and Tom jumped. He looked up to see a colossal form circling above looking down at them. *Osteodontornis.* What could this new thing be, it must have wondered? Tying the sail to one side while working the tiller every so often to maintain their direction, Tom lay back and returned its gaze. It was like a giant seagull, only its head was sort of pelican-like and its beak had tooth-like projections around the edge. The tips of its feathers fluttered lightly. When the bird swooped over he could just make out a whooshing sound. Mostly it glided, but when it flew, it flapped in slow up and down motions. There weren't gangs of them; evidently they preferred groups of two or three. He wondered how they ate fish. It would seem that take off from water would be an arduous affair. In a minute, he got his answer.

The osteodonts indeed never landed in the water, least not that Tom observed. What they did was to fly in big, lazy looking circles, scanning the subsurface for fish, then suddenly they'd sweep down upon them. But these were not just *any* fish. He'd not noticed them before, but did when he carefully watched one of the great birds. It swooped low, then rose, swooped and rose. The others followed its lead, again, never actually touching the water itself.

He thought he saw something else there, then got out the binocs and looked. That's when he saw them, *flying fish,* they were jetting from the water, gliding high over the surface, then dropping back in some distance away. *Fantastic,* Tom mused, *fish that fly!* If one didn't see them with his own eyes, one could, quite understandably, doubt their existence. Yet, what would make these fish jump to their deaths, he wondered. That answer came when a kentriodon jumped out after them. Then others did. Ah, it was a feeding frenzy.

On the outskirts was yet another dolphin-like mammal, this one having a long, narrow, beak-like mouth full of teeth, and tiny eyes. When a fish flew in its direction, it would suddenly reach up with those scissor-like jaws and snatch it from the air. *Pomatodelphis,* the P.I. said when he focused on one that exposed its upper body. They were supposedly near blind as they generally lived on muddy river bottoms where sight was of little use. Using their superior echolocation however, they were obviously able to calculate the fish's trajectory. He watched for a few minutes longer, noting that, even with the triple threat, there seemed to be no lack of flying fish, most of them evading the trap.

Tom put the binocs away and continued to navigate toward land, though now he was aiming farther down the coast. They glided along smoothly, the raft taking very little effort to steer. Tom began to whistle. Little still stood at the head of their craft watching everything with keen interest. It went this way for a time.

Then something unsettling happened. A large, gray shape *went under them*. It continued for what seemed a long time, then it was gone. Tom's eyes went wide.

"What-the-hell-was-*that?*" he asked aloud, frightened. Little stood back from the edge and barked at the form. He quickly shushed her. Next to them, then, on their left, or port side, another form slid by, quiet as a whisper. Then another on the right. Tom wracked his brain to remember. His mother had told him about them he was sure, but he could not recall. Giants in the ocean. He gulped. He wanted to snap a picture, but could not as they were submerged. How could he forget?

In a minute, they were gone and the threat passed. It was odd that they appeared to be trying get as close to the raft as possible without actually *touching* it. He wondered why they hadn't simply knocked he and Little into the water and eaten them. It would have been easy enough to do. But they hadn't. Still, the idea that there were creatures that big here scared him; they completely dwarfed the Paleos. Tom decided that maybe it would be best to head to land after all. Turning the rudder slightly, he made for it, now ten miles distant. Once again, he had let his assumptions put them in danger.

Now he kept his eyes peeled on the water below them as much as on the horizon. To his astonishment, he discovered that there was a host of strange sea life all around them. Though he did not know what they were, he saw in the clear blue waters, Manta rays, Diamond Back Stingrays, Butterfly rays, Eagle Bat rays, Giant herring, Giant Sea basses, Mackerel, Surgeonfish, Tuna, Pufferfish, Sunfish, Guitarfish, Sawfish and Skates.

All was not serenity, however, as the Temblor also swarmed with sharks, including the Tope shark, Requiem shark, Tiger shark, Sand Tiger shark, Angel shark, Bramble shark, Lemon shark, Blacktip shark, Sharpnose shark, Gray shark, Hound shark and Smooth-Hound shark, Catshark, Swellshark, Basking shark, Bullhead or "Horn" shark, Dogfish shark, Thresher shark, Six and Seven Gilled sharks, Mega-Mouth shark, Snaggletooth shark, and Hammerhead shark. The shark that dominated by sheer numbers though was the Mako and variations thereof (Hook-Tooth Mako, Longfin Mako, Shortfin Mako and Giant Mako). Had Tom known the potential for danger should they fall in, he would have opted for the long trek back to the mountains. As it was, he'd never heard of a shark before. Important sea scavengers, they were gone by the late Anthropocene (along with dolphins, whales and most fish), victims of pollution and ruthless human predation. When he saw their telltale dorsal fins moving about above water he scratched his head as to what they could be. Then he saw one up close and recoiled at the teeth. When he had to stop at one point to reattach the sail at the bottom corner, they were soon inundated with curious Blacktips swimming circles around them. Fortunately, they showed no inclination to follow once the raft got moving again.

Notwithstanding the unknowns and the fears, still, sitting

on the deck of his craft while holding onto the tiller, crystalline blue waters below, salt spray in his face and the cry of gulls in his ears, Tom could not help but exult, and ripping along, he laughed with joy.

Miles past the sharks, he began again to reconsider his decision to make speedy landfall. So long as there was no apparent or immediate threat, why not *coast the coast?* If he stayed close they should be able to make the beach quickly, if necessary. Thus, a quarter-mile from land, Tom turned the tiller slightly left and began to parallel the shore.

Not only was the sea full of life, the beach was too, he noted. There were basking sea lions by the hundreds, *Neotherium* they were, and the big dugong, *Metaxytherium.* Around another juncture he saw *Pelagiarctos,* a ten foot middle Miocene walrus and fearsome carnivore with fangs instead of tusks. As he watched, a gang of three was attacking a large group of *Allodesmus.* Evidently they both claimed the same territory. The Allos, though smaller in size, defended themselves by charging the Pelas in numbers. It seemed a fair fight, although the Allos looked to be taking a beating. Tom did not want to hang around to see the end.

Around the mouths of the larger deltas were more of the river dolphins, *Pomatodelphis,* and the dugongs *Dusisiren* and *Dioplotherium,* while onshore lay dozens of *Thecachampsia*, a marine crocodile. They were drinking in the sun, some with mouths open wide as if hoping something would land within.

Besides *Aglaocetus*, the baleen whales he'd seen earlier, many other whales also swam this warm, semi-shallow sea. Maxing out at 25-30 feet, however, most were but modest versions of the Leviathans to come. There was *Parietobalaena*, another baleen whale, *Scaldicetus*, and *Aulophyseter*, extinct sperm whales, *Tiphyocetus, Peripolocetus,* and still other whales roamed these fertile waters. Rounding a headland, he drifted past the skeletal remains of a *Herpetocetus* that had washed ashore.

Not counting the Kentriodon and Pomatodelphis, other dolphin/whale like cetaceans were here as well, like the toothed *Oedolithax, Nannolithax, Platylithax, Liolithax, Grypolithax, Lamprolithax* and *Loxolithax.*

Sky, beaches and hillsides also teemed with avifauna, all squawking, jousting or cavorting, while white sandy banks that rose ever so gradually to grassy meadowland drifted silently by. The gentle sound of water running along the sides of the raft, leaving a soft wake in its passing was hypnotic. It was all so peaceful and the sun so delicious that Tom's eyelids began to droop. He successfully fought the urge to sleep for another hour, jerking his head up several times, but, inevitably, lying back 'just for a moment', Tom fell asleep.

He woke abruptly to the sound of Little barking. A bump under the raft lifted it slightly and pushed him over. He opened his eyes.

"What're you..." he began, squinting around him. There was another bump, harder this time. Tom blinked, rubbed his eyes and looked out to land. It was a long way off. While he slept, the boat had followed its own course, the way of the wind. He stumbled to his feet, holding onto the mast pole for support. There was a large, dark hump in the water ahead of them, something with an enormous dorsal fin attached. It continued there for a moment, then soundlessly dove, barely making a ripple. Next came a long pause, then ... *Thud!* This one lifted the raft up a foot on one side, and both scrambled to remain on deck.

Tom's heart began to beat hard in his chest. It beat so hard that he thought it might burst. He gulped, saying nothing, trying to get a gauge on what was happening. Again, the huge, dark form was in front of them. Some animal, a type of the finned kind he'd seen earlier, but much, *much* larger. It was toying with them, coolly trying to toss them into the water.

"Oh no!" Tom yelled. Immediately he grabbed hold of the tiller, and, hands trembling, turned it. The raft turned too, though now, as the wind had died down some, it seemed incredibly slow to respond.

"Oh please," Tom said anxiously, *"please."* Slowly they picked up speed. Intrigued, the monstrous shark easily kept up, swimming apace on the right, then surfacing to catch a glimpse of them. It stayed nearby for another minute before it dove yet again just below the surface. The animal was a dark gray/black, which alternated in vague, diagonal, ribbon-like waves across its sides. The effect was clearly camouflage, helping it to blend into moving water. A creature its size would be rather obvious if not disguised, and that would make the catching of prey difficult.

Little did Tom know, this was *Carcharocles megalodon*, Meg for short, at sixty feet, it was the largest shark ever to roam earth's seas. And it was the marine terror of the Miocene.

Tom looked around for the beast, sensing that it might be coming up behind them. Glare from the sun there blinded him. When a moment went by and nothing else happened, he hoped that the creature, curiosity satisfied, had left. They were picking up speed now as the wind began blowing onshore. Not seeing any more sign of the animal, he tried to relax. Little, drool spilling out the side of her maw onto her coat, watched for the Meg from her spot at the front of the craft. Tom noticed ahead of them now, as they got closer to shore, that more of the sea lion-like creatures they'd seen earlier were swimming and leaping in the water towards land, as were some of its larger denizens. *Moving fast,* he thought. He scanned the waters around them as they headed in the same direction. Still no sign of the big shark.

Tom was midway into self-congratulation when, out of nowhere, the pair were flying from the raft and into the air with raft flying after them. Tom looked over to Little. She seemed to hang there for a long time, turning in a slow aerial somersault. He closed his eyes as he hit the water, heels first, in a mute somersault of his own. Then he was under.

He'd been here before, under water, the only sound, that of bubbles of air forced in with him. So sudden. Down, down. Then he was rising and at the surface once more, gasping and sucking in air.

A wave crashed against his face, and he swallowed. Up and down he went on the breakers, instinctually dog paddling. He tried to see what was happening. There was the raft twenty feet away, mast gone. Tom swam toward it, but it was hard in the choppy water. Finally, he reached it. With an arm on the side, he looked around for Little, but couldn't see her. A terrifying thought went through his head, *What if she was taken by that giant?* He climbed onboard laboriously, then stood, dripping, shaking, and looked out. There was a knob on the rollers. It was her. She too was dog paddling.

"LITTLE!" Tom cried out. She turned toward him and barked. It was a fearful bark that sounded like, *Help!* *"Come on, girl!"* he yelled, and obeying, she began to swim toward him. The waves were weakening now as the commotion abated. In a minute, the raft merely rocked on the declining surf, going nowhere without a sail. Still, it was a solid place. Thinking of the Meg again, Tom shot a glance around him. Nothing obvious. He wondered where it had gone. Maybe it was even now rising in another swift attack.

Little closed the distance, still swimming toward him. Tom worried that something would seize her from below. Then she was there at the side. Try as she might though, she could not climb aboard. Tom, as before, jumped in and held onto the raft with one hand while pushing her up with the other. Finally, she was on. Then he struggled up as well. He looked out again to find the Meg, and saw movement farther out toward the southwest, away from land. Another big form was swimming by. Whale. It looked about an eighth-mile away. And now he saw the fin moving toward it, cutting through the water like a giant knife. Their Meg. It had foregone them for larger prey. A second later, the fin was gone. Meg was diving. Where before it was merely toying with them the way a cat might a mouse, now was serious business. A whale had happened along too close for its own good.

Tom felt a pity for the other beast. Three of them had come and gone without so much as a bump, while the evil-toothed Meg had intended to kill and eat them, perhaps flossing with their bones. He watched in morbid fascination. The whale was evidently unaware it was being stalked, the Meg having shut off all sonar. When the smaller of the two, the whale, discovered the Meg, it moved swiftly, quicker than Tom would have thought possible for such a large animal. It turned to head west, to deeper water, flapping its tail. Then, suddenly there was another big splash and all was chaos. The two fought there for minutes, the whale fighting back with everything it had. It beat the Meg with its tail and rammed it with its head, all the while it was calling out for help from others of its kind. Shortly other whales charged in, and they too rammed the Meg.

It was not enough. The Meg had bitten its prey on the rear, a deep, tearing gash, and blood was spilling into the sea. Tom could see the red now in the churning water. Still, the whales fought, even chasing the big Meg for a ways. The shark headed off a bit to recover from its beating, but remained in the vicinity, waiting. It was only a matter of time. The other whales stayed near the first, protecting it from another assault. But it was too late. In fifteen minutes, the stricken whale was turning sideways. Soon it would be dead. After the Meg was done, dozens of smaller sharks would come in to finish up. By tomorrow, there would be no sign that the battle of a lifetime had happened here.

Tom wanted out of the water, onto the safety of land. He'd had no idea the sea harbored such fearful creatures. Problem was, the mast was gone. *Or was it?* Now he saw the bottom of the mast sticking through the center of the raft, and the rudder at the end. She was upside down! He stuck his head in the water to look. Yes, the mast was still there, though pointing in the wrong direction. And there was his backpack still tied to the deck, hanging down. That frightened him. He thought about trying to turn her over, but soon gave that up as impossible. What if he could take the mast off and bring it around to the new top side? No, he didn't think that would work either. He looked at the shore; it didn't look that far away; he thought that he could do it, but doubted if Little could swim that distance. Then he remembered the oar he'd made. He stuck his head in again. Luckily, it, too, was still lashed there.

Tom took a gulp of air, and, holding on with his hands, slipped over the side. From there he swam to his pack, opened a wing pocket and found his knife, carefully extracting it and resealing to keep other items from falling out. Then looping a strap around one arm, cut it loose and brought it topside, laying it on deck. Then it was back under to cut the oar loose. Then the thermal blanket. At last it was time to cut the mast loose. He severed the under-ties, then holding the knife in his teeth, made back for the side and up again. Little was there with her face almost in his, whining.

"Back up, girl," Tom told her, hoisting himself on. Restored to the craft, albeit on its underside now, Tom cut away the remaining straps holding the mast. That loosened it, and when he stood and stomped, the mast went through and out, then rose and bobbed next to them.

After folding and storing the blanket, he set his sights for the nearest shore, and began to paddle. It wasn't easy. What he really needed were *two* paddles, and a way to attach them to the raft, but he hadn't realized that before. So he stood and paddled, first off one side, then the other. Incrementally they made progress, and after a long time, his arms painful with strain, they reached the first undulations, budding waves forming when the seabed beneath began to rise and force the water onto land. He paddled some more, and then they were moving on the tops of low breakers, advancing toward the beach. Tom tried to steady his raft, but finally just sat, holding onto Little while the swell carried them on. Soon, sea lions moving out of their way, they were there, beached fifteen feet from dry sand.

Tom grabbed the pack and jumped off with Little following. They sloshed the rest of the way in. Fortunately these animals were shy, and, making "urching" sounds, galumphed out of their way. Perhaps it was the sight of the Aelurodon. Whatever, Tom thanked them. Then he lay down. Little too was drained, and, barking a warning at the sea lions, lay down next to him.

And there, on the warm Miocene sands, encircled by a troop of lions, they slept.

Twenty Seven

Walking, walking, walking. I am so tired. So tired. How far have I walked in the past few days? Losing a lot of weight. Maybe not such a bad thing. Ha! I'm dirty, my clothes, torn, ragged, my hair filthy. Saw a reflection of myself in water and laughed. This pack no longer feels so heavy. Physically I am getting stronger. But mentally...

Such beauty around me, it's exhilarating. I forget why I am walking, where I am going, and sit under a tree on a hill, simply looking, simply being.

I'm tired of the chase. I need to rest. Need to sleep.

Julie had continued heading north, toward the blue light. She'd seen no sign of Jaqzen for days and hoped that he was no longer on her trail. On the third day, in the afternoon, leaving her things lying on the ground where she'd dropped them, she strode into a large pool of steaming water, heated by the earth, by a magmas hot spot far below, for a bath. There she sat in thermal water up to her shoulders, head resting against a big rock in the middle, and promptly fell asleep.

When she awoke an hour later, it was to the sound of growling and agitation. Turning her head to her left, she there saw one, no, two, no, three *Cynelos*, a species of Amphicyon, or "bear-dog", all males weighing about 200 pounds each, pacing the bank not twenty feet away, glaring at her hungrily. They were not put off by the water, *per se,* but by the *heat* in the water. Now they growled and then hurled strange, muffled, throaty sounding barks. They also salivated, drooled, slavered and slobbered their desire to partake of her person. If she would be so kind as to make her exit from the pool, they could begin the feast. Julie though, as the potential *feastee*, was not *quite* as enthused about the prospect and stayed put, keeping a careful eye on the trio. So, stubbornly they patrolled, refusing to leave. A couple of times, one of them, bored with the wait, provisionally stuck in a foot, only to quickly withdraw it again. They walked clear around the pool, inspecting every inch for possible access, but found none.

To be sure, after another hour, Julie wanted to leave, but the big beasts decided to lay down just outside of the water's reach and wait her out. In a while, they were lying on their sides happily snoozing, and she stood, intending to head in the opposite direction, creeping out stealthily.

Not stealthily enough, however. She stepped on a sharp rock and let out a yowl that woke them. In no time, they were running to that side and barking their strange, muffled bark. And thus, Julie retreated once more to the center of the thermal pool and sat, wrinkling skin and all. She tried her trick of throwing rocks at them from the boulder she sat at, but that proved to be ineffectual.

Julie observed that they appeared to be none too bright, occasionally walking or turning into each other, which would set off a row of snarling and snapping. Each, in fact, had scarring across their backs and necks she observed, having first misinterpreted them as random stripes. She suspected that they were inflicted by the others. Were these a group of brothers that simply failed by chance to go their separate ways after weaning like most other animals, or was this groupism of older offspring a species trait of Cynelos?

Another hour, and Julie was getting thirsty and tired of

sitting. She knew there was a stream of fresh water nearby in a narrow, tree-lined couloir, for she'd drank from it earlier. Funny that when denied something, a person wants it that much more, and as time drifted by, she found that she was positively parched. The Cynelos had no such restrictions, and one or two at a time would head off to lap his fill, then come back to lie by the side of her pool once again. Julie, irritable, shouted at them. They replied. When she thought she'd have to sit there for the rest of the night, maybe the rest of *her life,* she was rescued when a family of oreodonts, *Merychyus elegans*, herbivorous cud-chewers, happened by. Their heavy bodies of between 150 to 250 pounds were striped tan and black. They were walking in a line along the high edge of the bank, not having seen the Cynelos.

One of the Cys, hearing something, turned its head and stared at them a moment, closing its mouth as it registered these brazen party crashers. What it saw was food. It barked, and, forgetting all about Julie, loped after the Oreodonts. Its brothers followed suit, and the Oreos took off at a run, heading for the forest. In a moment, they were gone in a cloud of dust and Julie quickly stepped out of the pool, skin red, dried and dressed, then headed for the stream with her water skin. She drank and filled the pouch, then looking around her, went back to her things.

Gathering them, she made her departure, lest her tormentors should happen to come back. It was another time when she wished that she'd kept one of the guns, not to kill the Cys, but to scare them off. On the other hand, she realized, that might bring worse, bipedal danger.

It was with mixed feelings that she watched the Cynelos going after the Oreodonts. The latter were definitely on their way out by this time in the Miocene. An endangered species in paradise, but they had had their day. Nothing lasts forever. In time, the Cynelos, too, would be gone.

On the afternoon of the fourth day, the stretch of forest she'd been walking along ended and the land cleared ahead of her. Now it was rolling hills with only a few scattered groves and shrubbery here and there. Coming upon an abutment of grass-covered sandstone that rose gradually to highlands to her right, to the east, she spied the telltale shimmering that bespoke a body of water. Circling the mound, the lake, contained within a grassy, shallow-sided bowl, opened out before her. Julie, who had stopped to catch her breath, exclaimed in astonishment. Enchanting and elegant, it was better than comeliest park she'd ever seen in any book.

The lake was small, as lakes go, maybe a half mile in circumference, but ever so lovely and inviting. A couple hundred yards from her, on the right, there was a small grouping of tall, broad trees, valley oaks, bowing over it. Curtains of lace lichen hanging from their branches waved gently in the cool zephyrs that whispered across the water's surface, the moss barely touching it, but leaving tiny ripples when it did. There was a similar grouping on the lake's other side as well, and bordering those, some large sandstone boulders. Shadows there were deep, enigmatic. In areas around the pond's margin grew a low evergreen flora, which she could not make out exactly, except that there was an abundance of red berries. Farther toward the west were some low hills and oaks that tempted her explorer's mind, and just the other side of them, the blue of the Pacific.

Near the stand of trees on her right, a herd of giant Zygos were drinking and snoozing. There were seven of them. Behind the Zygos was a small band of horses; she couldn't tell which they were though. Beyond them, the land rose and fell in gentle undulations. The grass was still green here. Green, but yellowing as the year wore on. Nonetheless, wildflowers were rife in a variety of colors; there were masses of small white flowerets, checkered by tall blue blossoms, sprinkled with red filaree and golden dandelion florets. Buzzing and fluttering over them all were bees and butterflies, both large and small. A river flowed into the lake at the far end from somewhere in the east and flowed out again not far from the sandstone abutment. It made a pleasant burbling, tinkling sound, not unlike wind chimes. On either side of the outflow was Cattail, Willow, Laurel and bunches of *Mentha arvensis*, or Wild Mint. From somewhere else came a sound of waterfall. Complementing these was the sunny trilling of field songbirds of an indeterminate class.

Past the western side of the lake, on the open, lower meadowlands, were gatherings of a variety of fauna. Camelids - *Procamelus, Cuyamacamelus* and *Protolabis*. Each species keeping a discreet distance from the others. There were the usual peccaries including *Cynorca* and *Hesperhys*. Also drinking, lying and grazing a little farther out on the plains were Dromomerycidae, Barstovian antelope of the family with crazy, ornate antlers. She saw *Subdromomeryx, Plioceros* and lots of *Merycodus*.

Hearing something over her right shoulder, Julie turned to see walking down the other side of the abutment toward her, a large Mustelid, *Brachypsalis*, an animal about twice the size of a wolverine and twice as fierce. She recognized it right away and backed up behind the mound, peeking around a corner to watch it. She didn't think it was fast enough to run down its prey, perhaps relying more on the hide and pounce method. Fortunately, the animal did not spot her. As she watched, it walked along the face of the abutment, then disappeared through some unseen opening. A cave! From its hideaway, it had a good view of the entire lake and, after dusk, would sneak out, using its superior night vision to find and catch prey. Why it was out during the day, Julie could not guess.

It was a mother. In a few seconds, it emerged from its den with a young one in its mouth. Not having seen Julie, it again walked around the rock face, up the hill, and was gone. Julie doffed her pack and climbed the mound on her side to follow its progression. The mustelid doddered on toward a grouping of trees and understory in the near distance until she did not see it anymore. It was vacating, likely because it worried its home had been discovered, probably by a male. If found, the male might kill the offspring of other males so as to bring the female back into estrus and thus sire his own.

Tiptoeing back down the hill, Julie wanted to have a look at the babies. Digging out her flashlight, she hoped that she was right and wouldn't be confronted by another adult inside. Carefully, she crept to the entrance. It was concealed by a tough manzanita and some weeds that grew through it. There was an opening that had been made by the comings and goings of Brachys, and possibly other animals that had called the cave home before them. The ground below was a smooth, shallow depression, worn by years of use.

Julie called out softly. "Hello..." There was a sound of movement inside. She waited, ready to spring to her feet if need be, but nothing appeared at the opening. So Julie stuck in her head and flashlight arm, then flicked the light on. The cave fell silent. Steadily she played the beam around the walls and floor, looking for the animals. Then she saw them. There were two cubs with short, tan-colored fur, looking quite young. They lifted their heads and still closed eyes in her direction. A whimpering note came from one. *Maybe it thinks I'm mom,* she thought.

"Hi," Julie whispered. At the sound of her unfamiliar voice, the whimpering stopped and the little bundles knitted together in an even tighter bundle. Julie smiled. *Babies are so cute, even when they are going to grow up into fearsome predators.* She shone the light above now and was surprised to see that the ceiling was high and the walls wide. The cave was spacious and deep, with shadows at a bend in the rear. Who knew how far it went? A person could stand up in it if she wanted to. An idea came to her. *Better get out before the mother returns.* Backing out, she stood and looked upslope. No sign of her yet. She walked the other way and again up the side of the mound. *Ah! There she is now, doddering this way.*

Julie ducked down quickly and hastened to her pack. Taking it, she ran, half crouching to the small stand of trees near the river and hid there, turning around to watch the mustelid mother. Right on time, mom rounded the corner and ambled to the entrance of the cave. Mother then stopped and began to sniff the ground at the opening. She smelled Julie! Now she ran/doddered to the side where Julie had come down, sniffed some more, then back to the cave and went in. Momentarily she came out, now with two babies in her mouth. She wasn't taking any chances. Looking around, the mother Brachy hurried off back upslope and to her new den.

That left the cave free for a new tenant - *Julie!* The opening was wide enough for her to slip in if she crawled on her stomach and the inside was surprisingly clean. Apparently, Brachypsalis was a tidy house keeper, removing offal and uneaten foodstuffs so as not to attract predators, insect or beast. Like the other cave, this one had a thick, sandy floor. Shining her flashlight around, she spotted a couple of bats, miniature ones, their heads shaking nervously at her presence. She could put up with them if they could her.

The cave could not have come at a better time. Bone tired and ready to drop, Julie propped her pack in the opening to block it and smoothed out the sand. Then she lay down and slept.

When she woke, it was night. Switching on her light, she saw that the bats were gone. Oops, the pack! She'd used it to block the entrance. Then how had they gotten out? Julie looked the other way; must be an alternate exit. Moving the heavy thing, she wriggled out of the cave and stood, looking at the lake. A full moon reflected from its tranquil surface, yet occasional ripples there bespoke tiny water nymphs. Down its center, a gauzy mist rose, wispy like a chimera. Frogs croaked in tenors and altos. She went to an area behind the willows and relieved herself, then walked to the top of the grassy mound, which was her cave and sat, feet dangling over the side. In the meadows to the right were zippings of luminescence: whites, off-whites, reds and blues. The trees nearby also flickered with their colors. Julie smiled and breathed deeply.

The eastern mountains were high and dark. In the long canyons below the summits was darker forest, while in the cold, fragile air above, still darker clouds drifted. A flash of light within. There would be another rain soon. Perhaps that was why it was still mostly green here. Tall mountains held onto clouds longer than low ones.

A star shot across the sky, and she made a wish.

The dawn air was crisp, and, outside the entrance of her new apartment, Julie stretched lazily. Again, the morning coolness bespoke the coming cold. Antarctica already had an ice sheet, but in a million years or so, with the opening of the Drake Passage and the establishment of a circumpolar current which concentrated the frigid temperatures at the South Pole, eastern ice would begin spread west. Other currents would then carry cold water north and world would begin to cool.

Though clouds continued to gather on this side of the mountains, the sky was still mostly blue. Sunlight shone down from behind the grassy mound and glistened off the water. It reflected back in her eyes, which she blocked with a hand. An ensemble of damselflies, like dwarf dragonflies, only slighter and more delicate, alighted on rocks being lapped at by the waters of the lake. They were blue of body. When one lifted off, another would too, then they would joust in the air a foot above, and land again. They seemed to favor these particular rocks, and even when gone for a minute or two, would return repeatedly to them. A big orange-bodied dragonfly now came by, hovered motionless in the air, then was off in a flash after a bee.

Julie noticed something - whitish - sticking, half-buried, out of the face of the abutment that she'd not seen before. Walking to it, she saw that it was a fossil, a skull, an unusual one - carnivoran, *with horns.* Her mouth opened in wonder. Although her focus was the Barstovian, she was somewhat familiar with animals from other eras too. This one was unknown to her, and probably unknown to science.

She stepped back and looked anew at the grassy mound, then strode forward and brushed away the surface dust. Strata, layers of sedimentary rock laid down horizontally in ages past, were now slanted at a 30 degree angle. An angular unconformity, it spoke of a time when some geologic process, such as an earthquake, had shoved the land up. The tilted strata would continue below ground for who knew how far. She looked along the plane of the abutment and now observed other similar mounds stretching out for some ways, perhaps half a mile, and nodded. At one time they'd made up a single unit, perhaps an imposing mountain range, dignified and majestic, but now eroded to these humble above ground remnants. Yet, through it all, this skull had survived, bone slowly replaced by rock. In another hundred thousand years, any sign of the previous range would be gone.

She could not guess the age of the skull, but knew it must be old - as must the cave whose wall it was in, for it had taken a very long time for water to carve it. A familiar urge now arose in her. The urge to uncover and discover. To learn and know. To understand the secrets of the earth. To give body to this beast and remember it. To honor it and the earth from which it sprang. A wondrous planet. As her old icon, Stephan J. Gould, said, a Wonderful Life.

On the other hand, she was on a journey; charming as this place was, she couldn't stay. She'd have to let it go. The thought made her sad.

The sound of running hooves made her look up. Horses. Julie went and got her binocs. Focused. *Parapliohippus!* In a cloud they ran, creating a rumbling that sounded like thunder. It was a solid, yet, soft-edged sound, which she found agreeable. As a prey animal, horses were easily spooked and were running all the time. It could be something as small as a wasp sting. Once one was off, the rest were as well.

In a minute, the dust was clearing. One of the horses was still there, however, just standing. She thought that strange and continued to watch, then realized that this was a different horse. Not a Parapliohippus at all, this was a larger *Hypohippus,* a browser. On its rump were diagonal stripes of black on semi-shaggy chestnut fur. Slowly, the Hypo began to walk. The stride was irregular and jerky. It was limping. Julie exclaimed in sadness. A wounded prey animal would not last long in the wild.

Without a thought, Julie set out to see if she could get a closer look. Maybe there was something she could do. When she climbed upslope of the lake, the animal turned its head to look at her. It stared for a while, then gazed back at the herd of Paras, by now several hundred yards distant. They'd stopped to graze once more. The Hypo again turned to regard Julie's approach, then began to walk, painfully, toward the herd of Paraplios. It was hard for Julie to watch. Step after agonizing step it went, getting slower with each footfall. Finally it could not go on and ceased its halting gait, turning to see Julie, distress in its eyes. As she advanced, Julie could see the wound. Dried blood encrusted its left flank and ran all the way to its three-toed hoof. The leg did not look broken, though, or like a predator attack. She wondered what could have caused it. A puncture? Additionally, the Hypo's hooves were seriously worn and cracked, the result of having run a long way. The sweat of exhaustion, of fear, wet its coat.

Closing slowly, Julie began to talk to the horse. "Hi, sweetie. What happened to you?" she said as she approached. Its eyes wide with apprehension, the horse uttered a warning that it could not back up. It tried once again to walk, but stopped, unable to go on. As she moved toward it, it turned its head forward again, making no move against her. Then, ears drooping, it dropped its head. It was giving up. As she approached, it closed its eyes.

When she realized what had happened, Julie began to cry, to weep for this innocent made victim by a thoughtless act of cruelty. Inwardly, though, she was red with rage. In shock, the horse made no move as she probed its hip, looking inside. Seeing the bullet, she at first startled in disbelief. Then she knew. When she had used the herd as a shield against Jaqzen, days prior, she'd heard gunfire. This poor animal had been his victim. He'd taken the bullet meant for Julie. In fear he ran, through waves of pain, ran to keep up with his clan, then beyond when the pain didn't stop. How many miles, she didn't know. A lot though. Julie, her arm around the dying horse, cried, her tears mixing with his blood.

"*I am so sorry*," she wept. "*Please forgive me.*"

The horse was going into a pre-death state of non-feeling. It fell to its knees, then lay down on its side, head on the ground, as if surrendering to a bear-dog. Julie stroked it and said a prayer. Prayed that the earth would give this animal another chance.

An idea occurred to her. *What if ... what if she could get the bullet out? What if she could fix it?* She stood now and raced to fetch her pack. When she was there, she hefted it onto her shoulders and dashed back again fast as she could with the heavy thing. At the horse, she dropped it and got out the medical kit. Inside was a surgical knife and other tools. One was a slim pair of forceps. She had no real medical training, but she did have common sense.

Donning gloves and finding a small pair of scissors, Julie first trimmed the fur around the wound close to the skin. Next she got the flashlight and, holding it in her mouth, pulled back on the opening of the intrusion with the fingers of one hand while fishing around inside the wound for the bullet. The flesh inside wanted to close, and she had to maneuver in a certain way before she could see it again. It was lodged in bone. Julie pushed the forceps in and felt around, trying not to cause any more damage than necessary. Then she felt it, a hard protuberance. It was jammed tight. Carefully, Julie opened the pincers and slipped them around the projectile. She pulled, but it did not budge. Pulled again, and again no movement. Now, holding firmly, she began to rock her arm right and left, up and down. In a minute, she felt a shift. Hope sprung up in her, and she continued to rock her arm. Gradually, it began to loosen, moving a little more. Julie put her weight into it. Meanwhile, the horse lay with eyes closed. In a few minutes that seemed an eternity, the bullet released and she pulled back and out, dropping it on the ground.

A smile spread over her face. She needed some alcohol to disinfect the wound. All the kit had, though, were wipes. She had to have more. Yes, she did have a small bottle of experimental alcohol she'd brewed back at her first camp. She found it, opened and hesitated. It could cause plenty of pain, possibly making the animal thrash and hurt himself even more. Yet, she had to attempt it. Holding the bottle above the open wound, she slowly poured a little in. The horse did not react. She poured more, watching it fizz around the edges. She continued until the lesion was filled with alcohol, then wiped the outside of the wound as well. This took the rest of the bottle, for the fur here was very soiled. In the meantime, old red blood burbled up, cleaning the inside.

Julie stroked the horse, talking quietly, reassuringly. Slowly the hypo's chest heaved up and down. When at last the fizzing stopped, she needed to get the alcohol out. Thus, wiping the forceps off and taking a piece of sterile cloth from the kit, she inserted it into the wound, absorbing the liquid, then removed it, squeezed it out and reinserted, repeating the process until there was no more.

Now she looked for some antibiotic cream. There was a tube. Walking to a small stream, Julie washed her hands, then returned and coated her index finger with antibiotic. She inserted it and swabbed around, unsure of how much to put in. When she thought it was enough, she stopped. Lastly, she needed to close up the wound. Taking out the needle and surgical thread, she paused, squeamish. Finally though, gritting her teeth, Julie began to push the needle in on one side of the opening. The Hypo, unconscious, shuddered and neighed.

"Sorry, baby. I'll try to make this as fast as I can," she promised.

Over to the other side, then down again. Back and forth went her hand, one side to the other, each time pulling the thread tight. The skin did not come completely together, but blood underneath filled the empty spaces. Julie wiped again, trying to dry it, and hoping that she'd done a good enough job. Then she got out a square, self-adhesive patch bandage.

She peeled off the backing and placed it over the wound. It held firmly.

When she was done, Julie was surprised to discover that she'd been sweating profusely. She was dripping. Another surprise was to find that more time had passed than she'd thought, as the sun, now mostly shrouded by clouds, was higher in the sky than it should be. Also, the herd of Paras was back. They grazed around the two of them, keeping a watch on her, this strange biped. Though they knew the Hypo was not one of them, still, they knew it as *horse*, as brother. Their concern touched her deeply.

The Hypo slept, perhaps in a pre-death coma state. It felt hot. Julie got some water and brought it back, pouring some on the animal to cool it. Unusually, the horse made drinking and swallowing motions with its mouth. Possibly it had had no water since the shooting and was dying of thirst. Julie lifted the horse's head ever so slightly and poured some in. Immediately the horse began to swallow. A lot went on the ground, but some was making it in. She went back to the stream with her skin bottle and refilled it, then brought it once more to the horse's mouth. Again it swallowed. It drank a lot, drank until Julie worried that she might be giving it too much. So she stopped.

As the proximity of the Paras hid the Hypo from the eyes of predators, Julie felt that she could leave to take care of personal business. She needed a bath, and to eat. She'd had nothing since the day before and was suddenly ravishingly hungry. To her surprise, the herd did not bolt when she rose, but stayed and continued grazing. They seemed to know that she was not carnivorous. Perhaps it was her scent. Calmly, she walked through them and down to the lake. There she stripped and waded into the cool water.

A light pattering of rain began to fall on and around her, rippling the surface. After a few minutes, it stopped, seemingly waiting for just the right conditions to really let go. She bathed there in the cloud light, using the sand under her feet as soap. When she was done, she walked west toward an inviting stand of trees in hopes of finding something to eat in between. A stash of pine nuts and avocados provided her some protein, while at the trees she found a species of fruit she'd never seen before. It was purple and star-shaped. She tasted it speculatively with little nibbles. It was sweet. Deliciously sweet. She saw that the lowest fruits, the ones within easy reach of most of the fauna, had already been taken. Dung around the tree site, which contained pits of the fruit, told her of its edibility. When she was satisfied that they were safe to eat, she ate heartily. Then she carried a load back in her arms to have later, dropping some along the way.

She went to the Parapliohippus, and to the Hypo lying on the ground. The Paras, seeing the delicious fruit she was carrying, closed in around. That unnerved her, but she said nothing except a timid, "Uh, hi..." Soon there was a score of them encircling her. Julie reached out a hand with a fruit in her palm toward the closest horse. It sniffed the fruit, then slowly took it and began to munch, dribbling purple juice from its mouth. She did the same with the others until there was no more left. The horses now regarded her, some sniffing at her back or snuffling in her hair.

"Um, that's it, I'm out, see?" Julie spread her arms to show that she had no more of the delicious star fruit. They stood staring at her, then one began to lick her palm where the scent of juice was. It tickled and she laughed. The abrupt sound jolted them and slowly they began to wander off to graze elsewhere. The Hypo she'd operated on still slept. She walked to it and touched its face.

"I'll be back," she said softly. She'd not planned on giving away all of her food, so she went to the wood for more. Now back under the purple spotted vine, she ate, and, with a mouth full of fruit, she studied them, trying to classify what they might be. Certainly she was aware of yellow star fruit from the Pacific Islands. She wondered if this might be a distant relative. Besides being delicious, it was wonderful to look at. Almost translucent, purple with reddish highlights, the tight skin broke gently to slight pressure from her fingernail. It was juicy, being full of water, and it was warm, thanks to the day. She couldn't get enough of it.

"A person could make a fine liqueur from you," she said. Julie grabbed another armload, and this time took them to the cave. On the way, rain began again to fall, though harder now. After depositing the fruit, she went to fetch her pack and check on her Hypohippus. There was no change, except the horses had stopped grazing, choosing to wait out the rain. As typical, they lowered their heads to snooze and let the water run off.

Her Hypo was still alive, still asleep, so she grabbed her pack and ran back to the cave, leaving it under the rock shelter to keep dry. Then it was back out again, back to the injured horse. She sat near it, and, like a horse, dropped her head to let the rain off. Water pattered all around her, while the warm smell of the earth filled her nostrils. Sleepy, she lay down on the other side of her Hypo, the short grass downy soft under her. The rain was warm and rhythmically soothing.

When Julie awoke, it was still raining, though only lightly now. She turned on her back to stretch and saw a horse standing above her, head bowed and eyes closed. She looked around for the others, but they were away. She looked back at this one. The diagonal stripes, and on the left flank a white patch. The bandage. This was her Hypo! It had recovered! Or, was *recovering*. Its temperature was down, and the pain was gone. That and hydration had worked wonders.

Slowly, Julie rose and stood on her feet. The Hypo opened its eyes and lifted its head, but made no move away from her. He was a large specimen for a Hypohippus, his head coming almost to the top of hers. She'd not realized his full stature while he lay on the ground, but now he was standing and she was ecstatic, though she kept it discreetly hidden. Instead she stepped toward the horse and slowly reached out a hand, touching his neck. She felt it tense up, muscles tighten for ready flight. Nevertheless, it again made no move away from her. So she spoke to it in sweet undertones.

Twenty Eight

Two weeks had passed since Tom and Little crossed the northern corner of the great Temblor Sea. Though he'd taken the sail, he left the raft where she'd run ashore, thanking her for the voyage. Then they set out once again on foot. He would have preferred to go the rest of the distance on the raft, but after the incident with the Megalodon, he ruled that avenue out.

The going on the beach was easier than the forest, as there were fewer obstacles to have to climb over or around. Yet there was still some of that, seeing as the tide carried every fallen tree back to the shore to roll endlessly in the waves or to block a path with lateral obstruction. Soft sand could bog one down too, so when they could, they stayed on the wetter sands near the tide.

As the miles dropped away, Tom discerned that, where on the plains they'd trekked in almost uniformly hot weather, now, with the coastal influence of the Temblor, the temperatures were mild and splendid.

As expected, there were a variety of coastline denizens to navigate. More marine crocodiles, for one. When rounding a headland and noticing them, Tom immediately stopped, then backed up. He and Little then climbed and scrabbled, with some difficulty, up the gravelly hill behind the foreshore and walked above them.

On the bluffs, they encountered bunches of Giant *Coreopsis*, with attractive yellow flowers on tree-like trunks that stood ten feet tall, and Tree Lupine, also with yellow florets and similar height. After passing through them and past the band of crocs, they were presented with a choice: either climb back down, no easy feat, or continue along the rise above the beach.

Because it was mostly open land with only small inclinations, Tom decided upon the latter.

The hillock afforded dazzling views of the vast sea, the sun glinting from it like a million blinding diamonds. Looking south with the binocs, he thought he could see where the other side of the Temblor ended in the far distance, but a haze there made it hard to tell for sure. As there seemed to be less obstacles and fewer fauna to deal with here, except for some small species of Tomarctus hunting nesting shorebirds and a few other minor animals, they kept mainly to this route for the next two weeks. However, gullies frequently forced them either to moderately higher ground or back down to the beach.

Fortunately, there was only one other group of the violent Paleoparadoxia, which they happened upon a few days after leaving the raft. It was a much smaller band, though, and these were considerably less animated; contented to simply lie on the beach and sun themselves. From the safety of the overlook, Tom got a mischievous air and lobbed a rock down at the biggest one. It bounced off the tough, blubbery hide and the great animal lifted its head, but not finding the culprit, set it back down and went again to sleep, no harm done.

There was yet another delight in store for Tom which first began to manifest itself a week after rafting day. The tide, the waves of water that rushed onshore, were actually glowing a luminous phosphorescent blue/green, a phenomenon especially apparent on moonless nights, and he wondered what in the world could be causing it. After the first night, they went to the beach at sunset the following day and waited for it. Tom strode into the water to wash cakes of sweat and sand off and Little caught crabs to eat. She knew better than to get near the largest of them though. Tom dug up giant oysters a foot and a half long, with shells an inch thick. Little tried her best to open them, but her human, fearing a broken tooth, forswore her this pastime. He ended up reburying them.

When it was dark enough, they sat and watched the bright emerald waves with delight. Then, deciding to go for a stroll, he walked along the wet sands for a while. He was soon startled to see that their every step ignited in olivine radiance.

What he didn't know was that the green he saw was being caused by dinoflagellate "blooms", billions of microscopic, bioluminescent plankton, later called *Lingulodinium polyedrum,* or similar species, and diatoms, which were in turn caused by the presence of nutrients in the seawater washed down from the mountains and valleys by the frequent rains. What they were seeing, though, was but a scaled down representation of the truly huge blooms on the outer coastal Temblor and Gabilan ranges by massive amounts of phosphorous and other organic nutrients.

The phosphorus was churned up by "upwelling", an upward movement of seawater from the bottom to the surface, present along the California coast during middle Miocene. Offshore winds, aided by a strengthened California Current, pushed the water away from shore, forcing cold, nutrient-rich deep waters to the surface. The current itself was triggered by the gradual cooling of the globe. Phytoplankton fed on the nutrients, and when these organisms died they accumulated on the basin floor in truly epic numbers to create organic-rich shales that in times past included the Eocene "Kreyenhagen," and now the Miocene "Monterey Formation." With time, heat and pressure would act on the buried organic matter within these shales to create oil and gas, the source of California's famous rich reserves.

In the middle Miocene though, when the formation was still in its infancy, sea birds, whales, and fish converged in these zones to feed on the sardines and anchovies, which were in turn attracted by the plankton and krill.

It was a spectacular show, and, once again, Tom marveled at the beauty that was; and although a long way off, he mourned the eventual loss of that beauty in the future.

There was an unforeseen cost to his choice of this pathway by the sea, and Tom discovered it one afternoon after having to remove his shoe for the third time in a short while to let some minute, but annoying, debris out. Salt water had been working on the resins that held the shoe together.

Disaster! One of my so-called "indestructible" shoes has split. It now admits water, sand, stones and small sticks. Further, the tread on the underside of both has worn down. So much for technology. Will have to figure out a way to repair the bad one or replace it. If that weren't enough, all of my shirts and pants are ripped. Those I can sew, but I'll have to consider the long term. Argh!!!

Tom's selection of solution for his shoe, tying a piece of cloth around the toe end, was short-lived, as he suspected it would be. He tried to sew it, but snapped one of his needles off attempting to push it through the polyurethane. As he only had three needles total, he didn't want to risk another. So he stuck a wad of cloth inside and kept walking. Meanwhile, he put his mind to a solution. Certainly, when preparing him for the trip, Karstens had not anticipated that Tom would be doing so much traipsing. The shoes were meant to last a good while of normal use, longer than the best commercial brand, but sooner or later he'd have to replace them. Looked like it might be sooner, than later.

Tom tried several concepts, he found a piece of bark from a large tree and kept it soaking in a stream while he explored an area of sun and shade. Hours later, he returned and removed it, finding it appropriately soft for cutting. He shaped it roughly according to his shoe size, then he smoothed the inside. Lastly, he tied some string around it to hold it on, finishing his sandals.

Lashing them to his feet, he was eager to try them out. But after a few dozen steps, the uncomfortable things began to fall apart. Tom swore and kicked them off, then, head resting in his hands, he thought. The bark was too dry; maybe he needed fresh, inner bark. Procuring it, though, would be something else. He would have to keep a look out. Meanwhile, he hit on an idea almost as good. Hanging from some species of palm trees were woody, half-oval shaped structures, two to three feet in length and a nearly a foot wide. They were the tree's flower bracts. After safe development within the hard structures, the bracts opened along a seam, allowing rows of small flowers attached to a stem to come out. Upon pollination, the flowers became fruit and the bracts then dried and fell from the tree. While tough, the bracts were smooth inside. Their thickness was about a quarter-inch.

Tom attempted to carve them, shaving long strands off with his knife, but it was crude. He tried the soaking method again, weighting them with rocks in a stream, and again it helped to soften the material. When it was soft enough, he carved it into a shoe shape, curving it around, then tying the two sides together at the top with some string. The string he wove through holes he carefully punched with his scissors. Socks he wore aided in preventing skin to shoe slippage and thus blisters. Then, after drying them in the hot sun while still on his feet, he tried them out. They worked tolerably, and he justifiably felt a certain pride in his craftsmanship.

"Well," he said to Little, lifting a foot and turning it

around for her benefit, "What do you think?" She sniffed at it, then seemed to shrug her shoulders as if to say, "What do you need those things for?" and with that, ambled off to something more interesting. Tom harrumphed. Now having alternative footwear, he wrapped them in a cloth and tied them to his backpack. He'd use those he had on until they were too worn to keep.

Like a meandering river, the weeks and months drifted by, and Tom lost all track of time. Just the same, he became an astute student of all he saw. They followed cliff birds to their homes massed in caves, carvings and overhangs in the crags and bluffs. Wandered mysterious paths that wound in and out of eerie shadows, full of enigmatic secrets. Took side trips to explore endings and beginnings. Rivers, canyons, pasturelands, highlands, escarpments and lowlands. Always, though, he was conscious of his Southward calling. Some places tempted awfully, begging for exploration, but, regarding them from grand overlooks, he demurred if he could see that their peregrinations would take them too far out of the way. Even so, interspersed with the more straightforward regions, were numerous setbacks and reversals when they'd come to an impassable section, or high precipice, and were compelled to find a way round. All told, these diversions cost the pair a lot of time.

In an empty riverbed, Tom, roaming through an area where one summer dried watercourse joined their own, heard a plaintive cry up the other and decided to check it out. The ground here was parched and cracked, and yet Tom got a feeling, an indefinable sense, that all was not as it seemed here. Something - deceptive.

The bleat came again, louder now. Little ran ahead to see,

and intercept if necessary, but Tom, on a hunch, called her back. *She's a fine companion*, he thought, *and now obeys me without argument.* Coming around a bend in the waterless river, he soon realized the mistake he'd made. While the surface was indeed cracked and dry, *below it* the ground was saturated. It could have fooled anyone. His steps sank just a bit; a moment later, he was in up to his knees. Any further and he may never get out. Quicksand. Ahead of them was an antelope, a *Cosoryx*. It was caught and had sunk to its chest. Twelve feet away were two canines of the Tomarctus clan. They were standing at the bottom of a sandy bank just outside the hazard area, pacing, trying to think of a way into the mud and to their next meal. Seeing Little though, they both lit up the side. At the top, they turned again to see if they were being pursued.

Tom tried backing up, but the mud held his legs tight. He thought he might lose his shoes in the suction. With much exertion, though, he did get loose and now stood considering the situation. Evidently, the Toms had been pursuing the hapless antelope, which, in its flight, had jumped clear of the bank upon which they now stood, and landed, unfortunately, in the quicksand.

The Cosoryx continued its pitiful bleating. Its voice somewhat stifled, a gasping rasp between cries was now audible. The weight of the mud was pressing against its chest, making it hard to breathe. In another hour it would be dead from suffocation - if the Toms didn't get to it first. Should he shoot it and put it out of its misery? *No.* He decided to rescue the poor lope instead.

Across the dry channel, on the other side, was a big rock. Retrieving his rope, Tom tied one end firmly around it and walked back to the edge of the hazard. He made Little lie down, then removed his shoes, and, with no small amount of fear, slogged in. Little did as she was told, but clearly was not happy about it. When he was again at knee depth in the muck and heading toward the frightened Cosoryx, she stood back up and walked to the edge of the quicksand.

"NO!" Tom commanded. "SIT!" So she sat - and whined. Tom pulled on the rope to assure himself of its security and continued in. When the sludge was mid-way up his thighs, he was no longer able to move. In fact, he too was sinking. But he was seven feet from the Cosoryx. He needed to get the rope around it. Tom tossed the line and it slapped the antelope against the side of its face. It bleated, then made pathetic feints toward Tom with its head, trying weakly to ward him off.

"Sorry, my friend," Tom apologized. No, he couldn't get the rope to swing all the way around the animal's head and back to him. He needed to make a loop and get it over its antlers. So, slowly sinking, Tom made a circle with the rope and tied it with a square knot. Then he tossed and re-tossed. It took him fourteen tries before it fell around both antlers.

Above his waist now, Tom shouted "YES!" Now he had to get himself out. He wrapped the boulder side of the rope around his wrists and pulled. A flash of panic shot through him when he found that he couldn't free himself with just that gambit, so, after a moment's thought, he bent at the waist and lay upon his front, then straining on the rope, began to pull one, then the other, leg upwards. He wanted get level on top of the mire. Instinctively, he knew that if he did this he should be able to extract himself, crawl on, and out. It was easier in concept than practice, but after a couple of minutes, he was clear and hauling himself across. At the other side, he stood, covered head to toe in mud. Little greeted him by jumping up, almost knocking him back into it.

None too sure that he'd be able to do it, Tom now gently drew the rope taut, then braced himself and began to tug and pull. At first the Cosoryx resisted and pulled back, but then it changed course and put its flagging energies into trying to extricate itself.

With great effort, it jerked up and flailed. Tom pulled harder now. In a minute, it was mostly out.

It continued its wrenching, but fatigued itself quickly, breathing hard, tongue lolling to one side. Tom pulled again and dragged the antelope further. When finally it was free, but lying on the ground, Little came around for an inspection while he removed the tie. She sniffed at it, but seemed to understand that this was not going to be food. So, sitting on her haunches, she stared, mouth in a wide grin. The poor Cosoryx, seeing the Aelurodon that close, lay still, ears flat against its neck, and barely moved. Like Tom, it was gray-brown with muck.

"Are you alright now?" Tom asked. He looked up to see the two Toms still pacing at the top of the bank. He knew that, sure as the sunrise, soon as he and Little left, those two would be after the Cosoryx again. But he did not just risk everything for nothing, so he shouted at them to be off. Failing that, he threw rocks. Finally, he sent Little out after them. She made a strange yowling noise at his command, then ran at the bank they were on. The Toms jumped in alarm and back. Little dashed up a narrow slope and after them. Tom knew that she hadn't much chance of catching them, but that wasn't what he wanted. He only wanted them gone long enough to allow the Cosoryx time to recover and be on her own way.

Minutes passed, after which, perceiving that she was no longer in mortal danger, the diminutive Barstovian deer stood. She allowed Tom to reach out and scratch her ears. "Now don't go falling into anymore quicksand, little one," Tom admonished. "Okay?" With shaky, halting steps, the Cosoryx turned and tiptoed away. It climbed a gentle slope on the other side, turning for a last look, before passing from sight. In the meantime, Little had reappeared and now stood on the same bank-top the Toms were at just before, and watched her go. She was puffing and too tired for a chase anyway.

Tom felt good; he'd done a good deed. Climbing out of the dry riverbed, he walked to a shaded grouping of trees, and in a pool of water, washed out his clothing, hung them up to dry, then lay down for a rest.

And thus, on they went, while the days blurred together, marvelous suns, magical moons, and Tom felt that he was becoming a part of this land, a part of this time. In truth, he was already half-feral. He knew the animals now by sight, by their call. Knew which plants were edible and which to avoid. Knew the best times to travel and when to stay put. Tom had learned empirically what others learned only through years of study in books.

Like tallgrass in the breeze, he was moving with Opal's rhythms. And with each sunrise, the future seemed more and more remote, increasingly unreal as, one by one, the angers and hates, the fears and worries, the pains and regrets - the hallmarks of man - were dissolving away.

For a certainty, there would be more hazards, yet Tom was adapting. Adapting his mind. Adapting his heart. He was changing to meet the earth, not the other way around. Wildness was not far behind.

A raven sounded above. Tom looked up and sun fell on his face, in his eyes. He shielded them, caught the edge of wings as they glided by. The land was drying now, getting hotter. On the plain, a dust devil wound up and spirited away, dancing lightly over the ground. Half a mile beyond was steep, oak covered mountain. At its margin, where it met flatland, a river curved. Within those trees, all manner of fauna abode in precarious truce, panting or sleeping out the hot afternoon. Tom and Little walked along the waterway, in and out of the sun.

O Land, O Earth, O Sea, O Skies, how beautiful you are to my eyes.

Twenty Nine

The Hypohippus had continued to make a recovery, and though jittery, seemed to be stabilizing, both physically and emotionally. Its lameness and limp became less pronounced with each passing day. In the meantime, Julie did what she could to make sure he ate and drank, daily bringing armloads of brushy foliage and water. The latter she poured into a sedimentary depression on a boulder nearby from which the Hypo drank. She also continued to bring some of the purple star fruit and enjoyed the excitement of her Hypo and the Paras when she returned. His clan still several days south, back at the other meadow, he'd taken to the Paras and they to him. They were his new clan. Yet, though a stallion, she knew that he would never lead a herd of Parapliohippus. Perhaps if others of his species came along. But for now, they were absent here.

She and the Hypo were spending a lot of time together. He browsing nearby, always keeping her within sight, while she sat on the grass in the shade under a tree, writing or sketching in her notebooks and journal.

Julie also spent a considerable time investigating, cleaning and outfitting the cave, beginning with enlarging the entrance. And she swam. She knew she should be going, instead, to meet that blue dot, but something in her told her to stay. He would come to her. As long as she continued to remain in contact with the caller, he would find her. In any case, she was safer here than exposed. In keeping with that, though, she'd later decide upon a new tactic. Rather than immediately respond to the signals, then quickly switching off, which could still ultimately lead Jaqzen to her hideout, once a week she would hike to some place miles away, then send out her own call and wait for blue's reply, hastily switching off afterwards. That way Jaqzen would not know her whereabouts precisely. Eventually, as the other drew close, she would have to find a way to meet him, potentially a big risk, for the same signal that gave the blue dot her location would also be supplying Jaqzen with it.

On her journeys she always brought along her notebook and recording devices. There was so much to see and do! It was a shock and happy surprise for her when, having completed her first exploratory trek in days previous, as she was strolling away again to a new destination, she turned at a sound, and found that her Hypo was following her. She waited for him, and he came to her, his limp all but gone, and nuzzled her hand. She dug out one of the fruits and gave it to him, which he ate gratefully. Then he pushed at her pack from which the stuff seemed to magically come. Julie laughed and got another, feeding it to him. She scratched his neck and the Hypo sniffed at her face, her hair, her body. While she was recording those things around her, he was recording Julie, lodging her deep in his brain, in his heart. Friend.

Julie looked at his three-toed hooves. They had regrown since his big run. He could walk. Wondering what would happen, she turned to continue on her path. Today, she was going out ten miles to the northwest - something she wanted to see. Her Hypo continued to follow, at first walking behind, then beside her. It felt good to have a friend along for the trip.

Though mostly hidden, Julie had spied the high peak of a distant volcano above the trees, with a wisp of smoke issuing from its top. The Conejo Volcano, she suspected. Just off the coast, its elevation rivaled that of the haughtiest Sierran mountain. It stood at the fore of the Transverse Ranges, a block of mountains that had once oriented North and South like other California cordillera, but which then began rotating clockwise, caught as it was between two oppositely moving land masses. By the Anthropocene, it would have spun 90° from its original bearing.

"I should name you," Julie said, gazing at her horse. "Let me think about it."

Every now and then, Julie stopped and allowed the Hypo to browse. At these locations she'd find a place to sit and watch him. Watched how he interacted with his environment. He was certainly a beautiful animal; coat sleek and clean, striping wild and distinctive, tail un-matted, mane long and flowing. And he was a good-sized beast too, over a quarter ton of solid muscle, and very alert, constantly lifting his head to check for danger. Julie sketched him. Under that she wrote:

Hypohippus. A beautiful and noble beast.

The walking seemed to be actually *helping* the Hypo, and when next she looked, he was no longer limping. When they got to a wide open area, another, vaguely bowl-shaped grassland with knolls and hummocks, dunes, banks, dips, ridges and knobs, the place seemed to inspire the Hypo and he began to run. He ran up, then back. *There is nothing as fast as I,* he seemed to be saying, and indeed he was fleet. Coming back to Julie, he pawed at the ground. Seemed to want her to run with him. As she had her pack on, running was not an option. So she jogged. It was awkward and riled up the Hypo, who nickered and galloped by her, throwing dirt on her legs. Again he was inspirited, and ran to her, which caused her some alarm, then, turning his side, pressed against her and pawed at the ground.

"What do you want, boy?" Julie asked. The Hypo whinnied. It was the first time he'd done so. A lovely tenor. Julie cracked a smile to one side of her face, then she squinted at her Hypo. "Do you want me to *ride* you? Is *that* what you're saying?" she asked. The horse went again to her side, pushing her roughly with his. Then he stood there. "I don't think I can do that," she said. "For one thing, you're too small. For another, I've been on a horse but once in my life, and I was seven at the time and the horse a pony. My father walked beside me and we went round and round in a circle." Julie remembered the pity her father felt for the ponies. What a life. Not a life for a horse. Still, he wanted her to have the experience. By the time she'd grown, horses were gone, eaten, along with so many other non-human species when food became scarce.

The Hypo whinnied and pawed the ground again. *Is there just some instinctive connection between horses and people?* she wondered. *He truly appears to want me to get on his back. But how can he know?*

"Okay," Julie said, "I'll give it a try if you promise not to kill me." She backed away and set her pack on the ground, then walked to his side. Now, how was she going to get up? Julie put her hands on his back while the Hypo stood very still, watching her. She pulled herself higher, then back down again. A few more times of that, and she was up, lying perpendicularly across the horse's back. Still no movement. After a minute of this, he impatiently nipped at her butt.

"Ouch!" she said, "That hurt." Apparently, she was taking too long. Now, quite nervous, she slowly raised herself up and swung a leg around. She was sitting afore his stomach and behind his front legs. The Hypo, evidently none the worse for the extra weight, turned his head to look forward. Then he began to walk. Almost at once, Julie started to slide to one side. She was falling off.

"Whoa!" she said. The Hypo stopped. She raised her eyebrows, then without thinking too much about it, scooted herself back atop the horse. "Let's try that again," she muttered to herself. Again the horse stood motionless, head regarding her. Now she tried to hold on with her legs while also holding onto his mane. Again, he walked. Really, it was more of a trot, which she thought of as a proud strut. She bounced on her "seat." Though only half the size of a modern horse, this was a powerful animal, and she could be injured. Julie gulped. Then his speed began to increase. His rider was alarmed, but afraid to speak, instead emitting a series of "whoas," little *"yeows"* and muffled shrieks. When he thought that she had the hang of it, the Hypo began to run. Now Julie did yell. She held on with tight fists to his long mane.

They were flying now, hot wind in her face. Julie was in a near panic, but she did not fall. It seemed that each potentially dangerous mistake on her part was countered by an opposing move on the Hypo's that saved her from going down. Still, it was mostly a straight line. This went on for minutes. After a while, she began to get a better balance. When she thought that they had gone too far from her pack, she began to pull on her Hypo's mane. She tugged and leaned to the left. In response, the horse made a slow circuit back in that direction. Then he was running again. When they were closing on the spot where her pack lay, Julie pulled back once more while saying, "Whoa." She remembered reading that that was how you stopped a running horse. And it worked, for the Hypo slowed to a trot back to their starting point, finally halting a few feet away. But he pawed the ground. He wanted to go again. Heart thudding, but more confident, Julie shook her head, then said, "Okay, let's go!" and off they went.

Around and around they galloped, a little further each time, pounding a circular path in the soil, and Julie honed her budding riding skills, while her Hypo learned how to read her signals. Truth be told, Julie thought as they raced along the ground, that he was one smart cookie, as intelligent as any animal she knew, if not more. A half-hour later, she was ready to get off, and she thought her Hypo was as well, for he was dripping wet under her. She glided him back to their starting place, all the while speaking to him, then, when he was stopped, she sat a moment and pet him. At last she slid one leg over and slowly dropped to the ground. Her thighs hurt, and, walking a few feet away, she sat down, then lay back in the grass. The Hypo walked to her and lowered its head to sniff at her face. Then walking off a few feet, it put its head down to browse.

When Julie had recuperated, she walked to a small stream that wound its way through tree and glade. Her Hypo followed, and as she lay to drink of the cold water, he did the same. Then she stood and went back to her pack. She already had a name for her Hypohippus. It had occurred to her while she was still on his back, wind blowing his mane, and her own mane, behind them, warm sun on her skin.

"*Zephyr* will be your name. A gentle wind from the West."

In the days before her big adventure with Zephyr, one of the things Julie had done to outfit the cave was the construction of a bed. She'd had enough of sleeping on the ground. Even sleeping in soft sand had its limitations. What she did was to gather small logs and branches, each similar in size to the other, and cutting the ends off, tied them together. When she had it, she lifted her framework of thin logs and set it on four "posts" of equal height. If one was a little taller than the others, she dug into the sand and buried it a bit until all were the same. Making the posts took a good deal of time as they were thick and hard to work, but, finally done, she tied them to the four corners. Next, she gathered some mud, and into that mixed dry straw. This she slathered in between the framework logs until the "platform" was whole and level. Following that, Julie piled a one foot thick covering of straw on top, then sewed together the washed and dried skins of various kills she found, fur side up. There were several layers of this, and another for the blanket. It took her a week to find enough skins. Zephyr kept his distance as she dragged the smelly things across the landscape, but did not otherwise seem terribly perturbed. And she had her bed.

For her pillow, Julie found another skin, an especially beautiful and soft fur, and stuffed it full of Cattail cotton from the abundant, fluffy seed heads at the top of each plant. They pulled apart without difficulty and floated on the air with ease. When the time came for their replacement, she would let them go back to the wind and gather a fresh batch. Julie was aware that in the future the wearing of furs would be a sign of calloused indifference to the suffering and death of other living beings, but in her case she had not killed these animals. Too, there was not exactly a department store around from which she could obtain an alternative.

It was *oh so luxurious* to have a bed for the night. By chance, the day after she finished, it began to rain. This rain, however, was no ordinary shower; it was a tempest. Big, billowy clouds, dark and foreboding, gathered, while a few ominous booms sounded distantly. Shortly, drops began to fall. When lightning flashed and thunder crashed, it fell harder, then pelted down, followed by a strong gale that tossed the trees outside to and fro, battering the wildlife, including poor Zephyr, who stood next to the cave mound. Fortunately, the hummock blocked the bulk of the winds that blew over the top, but when they changed direction, there was no such protection. As other horse species, he simply stood unprotesting in a semi-stupor with his back to it.

Julie, meanwhile, had a fire going inside her cave with wood she'd gathered days before. The smoke was easily sucked outside by the howling winds and over the lake. Safe and snug inside, she lay on her bed, sipping mint tea, and looked out, marveling at this wild Miocene monsoon. She wondered if it was another sign of the coming global deterioration in climate. The existence of a bed soon made her think of

Tom since they both shared one back in the future. She prayed again for a miracle to bring him to her. Then she was asleep.

It rained for two days. A warm, late summer rain. Yet, the world was on the cusp of change; gradually summer rains would end in the West, though they'd continue in the East. Then it would fall predominantly during the winter months.

There was something about the moment, of sky filled with dark, heavy clouds, of rain coming down, sometimes gently, sometimes in torrents, cleansing the land, giving it life. Distant flashes. Rumbling, like French horns and bass drums. The always present sound of water falling into the lake from somewhere unseen. And in between all of that, the quiet. The peace. The delicious sounds of nature.

When things calmed a bit, Julie picked her way along the banks in bare feet, wet mud oozing between her toes. She loved the feel of the water upon her skin. To her right, a few hundred yards away, was the herd of Zygos, their outlines blurred by the rain. Gray hulks, unmoving, like monuments. She walked toward the group of trees they'd been at previously. A strange mist was rising from the area. Curiosity, and a need to get out for a bit, impelled her. Along the way, there were blackberries to eat as they spilled over the sides of overhangs and ledges just feet from the waterline. Frogs leapt into the murky depths from their perches on rocks when they noticed her. Others droned from across the lake. A lone bird peeped blue notes rhythmically from the top of a tall tree.

When she reached the stand of trees, she found, as usual, that the place was larger than it looked from the cave. It was a riparian gorge with riverine plants growing in abundance. Small, red berries, attractive to birds, possibly the same red fruit as those on the other side, dripped with moisture. There were grapes, too, which hung in big bunches from the trees above. She could see that the gorge continued on upslope as it cut back into the escarpment. Grape vine was thick within, where it was out of reach of the Zygos. Below, at the bottom, were the falls she'd perceived since arriving, a cascade of water pouring over a rocky shelf and into a deep limestone bowl. Steam rose up from these falls as they coursed over rocks. She reached out and touched it, then withdrew her finger, *hot*. The bowl had a turquoise color to it. Mineralization. Here, searing waters mixed with the cooler lake water. Hopefully, Julie stuck in a toe. It was wonderfully warm. *It would make a fine bathtub,* she thought.

Something splashed and she looked up, then moved around the thicket to see what it was. Another splash. *Legionarictis fortidens,* a primitive otter-like critter. There were three of them. They were sliding down the wet, flattened grass of the highland on their bellies and straight into the lake. Then they'd swim and climb out and do the whole thing over again. Julie laughed. There was no obvious evolutionary reason, no survival need to do this that she knew of. They were simply having fun.

The lake bent around a jut of land at the end. She walked to it. Here the main source of the water to the lake, a strong river, ran. Past it, hidden by the slope of the land, the lake went a bit further east, maybe a hundred and fifty feet, and terminated in a pointed bank of sand. In the water were a number of animals, but Julie couldn't tell right off what they were. They were up to their necks and slowly milling around. She found a spot on a rock under a tree to sit and observe them.

The shower, which had stopped, started again. One of the creatures spied her and began to slowly make its way toward the bank. It climbed out, then shook itself, which didn't do a lot of good as the rain soon made it wet anew. An Oreodont. It was *Ticholeptus*. Julie guessed its weight at about three hundred and fifty pounds, a big one. Now it stood with its back to the water and waited for the rest of its kin to follow suit. They were in no hurry to leave, however. The one that waited now called to them, emitting a loud and un-melodic tuba-like bellow. Still, they remained. It continued to call, closing its eyes and lifting its head each time. Julie stuck her fingers in her ears. After a while, the beast gave up and walked back into the water to rejoin its group as if it had never seen her.

She walked under the tree and up the incline. It was open grassland here. Horses grazing. And there was Zephyr among them. He lifted his head and whinnied at the sight of Julie. There were other animals in the fore-distance over a small rise to her left. A group of five of them. Short, but heavy and powerful looking. Rhinos, *Peraceras,* all females. Julie clapped her hands involuntarily and took out her camera, snapping some pictures. These were the first rhinos she'd seen. She'd suspected that they would be rare on this side of the Sierras, and they were. It was a pleasure to finally see some, though. They browsed in equanimi-ty, ignoring the rain, with their heads in the shrubbery. Though they grew up to half a ton, considerably less than other rhinos like *Aphelops,* still, they were big, and short-tempered enough to deter most attackers. Their young, on the other hand, were always in danger. But what these lighter weight rhinos lacked in bulk they more than made up for in agility. It would have to be a desperate animal to attempt a rhino-napping. And, indeed, there was a young one. It nibbled in the middle of the Peras. *All females,* she pondered again. *The males are probably solitary.*

Julie began to sing. It was David Downes' *The Voice.*

The rain stopped and sun began to show behind the clouds. Eastward in the sky, a rainbow slowly formed. As she watched, it crept downward to the earth. A vivid arc of color. She'd seen many since she'd been here, but this one in particular seemed *especially* bright, *especially* lovely. Perhaps it was the atmosphere - not just that in the sky, but the atmosphere here, in this special place.

Birdsong abruptly sounded, a gliding, undulating melody full of ripples and swirls. Julie glanced up to see that it was the same bird on the same high branch as before. The one that only peeped. Now, though, it sang a much different song. Listening to it in awe, Julie thought that it must be the most beautiful song a bird had ever sung, there were so many variations, so many inflections in note and tone, all crisp and clear! The little bird was just singing its heart out. Singing, it seemed to Julie, for the pure *joy* of it. The song rang across the land, lifting spirits still dripping with wet. She tried to see what kind of bird it was, but it was too high in the tree. It looked about the right size though, and she wondered if it might be the late Miocene songbird *Palaeoscinis turdirostris.* If so, it was a bit early.

Now that she was here, Julie had begun to dislike the cold, sterile, and often ugly scientific names for the many animals she had seen. Names that spoke of calloused objectification and dissection. Of bodies under pins, or behind bars. Certainly she would continue to use these names in her notes, but privately she had other ideas. The stunning beauty of the song made her think of the name *Aria* for this little one. And thus she named it.

Another Aria began to sing from somewhere distant, answering the call of the first. They sang in concert then, each filling gaps in the other's song.

It was an extraordinary performance, and Julie wept for the splendor of it, suddenly overwhelmed with gratitude. She still could not believe that she was here, in this land of dreams, of *her* dreams. *This is what life was supposed to be. For the first time in my life I know what true happiness is.*

And she knew something else: This was home.

Thirty

Tom had been following Julie's leads daily for some time along the Temblor's marshy shores, across rivers, through coastal fogs, and swaths of Taxodium/Nyssa forest, when the calls suddenly stopped. At first, when four, then five days went by with no return beacon, he panicked and thought the worst. Then he began to run. After six days with no contact, Tom was beside himself. He was also exhausted and sore. He'd taken several spills, and just the day before, had slipped and fallen from a fifteen foot bluff, landing on a hard sandstone slab and twisting his ankle. Now he was limp-walking. He knew that he'd been lucky though, very lucky; he could easily have broken a leg. On the seventh day he got his call.

In a flash, he dropped his pack and whipped out the PinPointer to see Julie's blinking green light. And there was Jaqzen's red. He let out a cry of startlement and fell to his knees. Quickly, he switched on his own beacon. A few seconds later, green switched off, but not before he'd made a calculation. Jaqzen was now a mere 14 miles away from her, while Tom was 355.

The next week was a repeat of the last, communications wise, and Tom concluded that Julie was intentionally limiting her calls for fear Jaqzen would find her. At the end of the week, she called from a different locale than previous, this time 20 miles southeast of the other. The third week she called from ten miles to the right of that one. And so it went. She was trying to keep Jaqzen guessing. Yet, even though she never signaled from the same place twice, in venturing out this way, in this spoke-like fashion, making her calls at the end of each spoke or trek, Tom was able to guess her probable base camp at the center of the hub. It alarmed him. He dearly hoped that Jaqzen had not figured it out as well.

As they continued, the terrain beyond the marshlands began slowly to dry out. Fresh grass was now mostly burnt yellow or brown. Trees were also thinning, and the species changing. While oaks still dominated, pines and other such conifers were being supplanted by chaparral and broad-leaf sclerophyllous shrubs with hard, thick leaves that held onto water longer: Manzanita, Ceanothus, Silktassel, Coffeeberry, Sumac, Mountain Mahogany, Flannelbush, Toyon, Barberry and Tree Poppy. There were even a few Joshua Trees and cacti present. In the mountains though, starting at 1,000' - 1,500' to about 2,400' were Madrone, Maple and Alder while below them were more Populus, some Maple and Sour Gum (Nyssa).

The change worried Tom, as the availability of water for he and Little was lessening. It was still to be had, but the pools were spacing farther and farther apart. Further, the water quality was dropping as well. Where before they had no trouble finding clean sources, and the rivers and streams that fed them, now water was often stagnant and rivers nonexistent. At these water holes, Tom would drink as much as he could, always through his filter, and top up the bottles. Little, too, drank deeply, waiting, as instructed, for her human to clean it first. Then he would climb a hill to try to get a view of the way ahead. It didn't look good. Tom wondered if he should set back out for the mountains again, but their distance and rugged appearance deterred him. So he decided to continue along the coast. He knew he couldn't drink the water, but at least the weather was a little cooler.

As the year wore on, the area of the shallow Temblor sea nearest the shoreline had begun to evaporate and turn boggy. Tom began to come upon the remains of various animals that had gotten stuck, perhaps trying to get at the green eel grass. Indeed, their own feet sunk in the mire, and they were forced once again to move inland.

After a day of this, Tom was truly apprehensive. Though he could still see rain coming down in the mountains and valleys behind him, forward it looked only dry. The lowlands had not seen rain in over a month. Further, he saw none of the eastern rivers that normally ran to the sea. His worry was compounded by the increasing presence of sand dunes, remnants of an ancient beach? Evidently, there was a time when the shoreline was even higher.

When the scenery had begun to change, Tom started to ration his intake of water. It wasn't optimal, but he saw no other choice. As he was sweating more, he also upped his intake of salt and put some in Little's water. But it was running perilously low, so he decided to try something else, something he'd once read about. Thor Heyerdahl, the famous archaeologist, in his journey across the Pacific on the Kon Tiki, when he and crew needed salt, they'd mixed fresh and ocean water at a 60/40 ratio. Tom did the same. He'd have *it,* while Little would have a separate container for fresh water.

The girl looked to be suffering, with large gobs of drool hanging from her ever panting mouth. She was most definitely out of her element here. Still, she slogged on beside, then behind him. What's more, neither had eaten since the day before, and hunger gripped their stomachs like a vice.

By the third day, Tom looked again toward the mountains. Green was there, and that meant water. But they'd have to climb past the dry zone. It looked quite steep and angular, and he saw no way onward once they got there. *If* they got there. In the dust he sat and shook his head. Sweat and grime clung to him, smeared on his face. Dirt in his teeth. He refused to give into panic, yet they had only half a bottle of hot water between them. By the next morning it was all but gone.

"So this is how we shall die," he said dolefully to his friend. With that, he began to weep, shedding tears for Little who had so faithfully entrusted herself to him all this long journey. He wept for himself too and the loss of his hopes and dreams. But most of all, he cried for Julie, for now her help would never come.

With that thought, a fierce anger seized Tom and he swore at himself, at his blasted self-pity. Commanding Little to remain where they'd stopped in the shade of a scraggly poplar tree, he stood, dusted himself off, then walked to and climbed a sand dune nearby, this one higher than the others. It was hard going. Seemed for every two steps he took up its side he slid back one. His face fell at the scene from the top. Baking brown land and sand almost to the horizon. Yet, squinting, hand blocking the glare, he saw that there was something else too. *Far* out there, how far out he couldn't tell, but many miles away was what appeared to be - water. A large body of fresh water.

Or was it a mirage? Rubbing the stinging perspiration from his eyes and off his brow, looking past the water, it seemed the land turned green and blue again. So this dry section had an ending? Hope wasn't dead then. Yet.

Who was he fooling, even if it *was* water, they'd never make it. Both were weaker than they'd been in a long time.

To his right, out at sea, the distant fog had finally passed, and now he could make out the low slopes of what appeared to be an extended island chain, or perhaps it was one long range on the Temblor's western side. It swept north out of sight and ran south, paralleling this thirsty land. He gazed again at the green far away.

So far.

Tom looked over toward Little, lying still under the tree facing his way. It would be hard, truly hard to go that distance.

The girl had been dragging for the last day and a half. Could he really expect her to go on? Should he perhaps leave her here, go fetch water himself and bring it back? He doubted that she would understand to wait for two days, for that's what he expected it to take, at a premium pace. Three days seemed more likely in his depleted state. She could not be without water for that long.

He decided they'd travel at night again, like they used to. If they could do most of it tonight, one, long, miserable effort - maybe.

His feet sinking in the burning sands, Tom walked back down the hot dune. He sagged under the tree and lay back, drained and bone-tired. Little had her eyes closed and mouth open, breathing hard. Feeling a wave of love and pity for her, Tom took out the water bottle and poured the rest into her bowl, shaking out the last droplets and adding another salt tablet. Hearing it, she opened her eyes, looked, and then began to drink. Tom held the bowl for fear she would knock it over and lose some of the precious liquid.

"Tonight, my friend," he said.

When evening fell and the temperatures dropped, the two left, and as they paced the drylands, feet dragging, kicking up dust, Tom kept a look out for more water. There was none. Still, the night was cool, and, desperate though they were, lovely. Both man and beast plodded, afraid to stop.

The sun rose chill, but in a half-hour's time, was hot again. Tom climbed another dune to look out and saw the blue; *No, not a mirage*, he told himself. It was closer now, perhaps ten miles away. He walked back to Little. She lay panting again in the checkered shadow of a dead tree. Tom knew she could not make it another day walking in this heat. He had to take a chance. He would go alone to the blue and bring some back. He told her then to stay, that he would return tomorrow with water. But when he began to walk off toward the South she dragged herself up and began to follow.

"NO!" Tom shouted. "STAY! I'll be back." But again, she followed. This time Tom, angry, did something that surprised even him - he struck her. She looked surprised for a moment, then afraid. Tom's eyes immediately welled up and he bent down and put his arms around her. "I'm *sorry* girl. I didn't mean to hit you," he said, holding her, tears wetting her fur, precious water spent for love. "I'm sorry that I brought you here, to this place to die. You're the best friend a man could ever have." Little sat again, panting heavily. "You have to stay." A look passed over her, different from any expression he'd seen on that big face before. He didn't know what it meant. Tom bent to kiss her head, but she was stiff. He pet and reassured her again that he was coming back. Then he stood, turned and left.

An hour after leaving Little, Tom's mouth grew dry. By two, it was his tongue, so moistureless it stuck to the roof of his mouth. By midday, his lips were cracked and bleeding. He'd not had a drink in a day. Hadn't eaten in two, either, yet food was not his main thought. Tom was so thirsty he was in a torment for water. Still, he trudged on, his world focused on one thing and one thing only. Slowly, as the fluid left his body, its equilibrium fell out of balance. On his head he wore the hat to provide shade from the beating sun. But it also held the hot in. Every so often, he lifted the brim to let it out.

There were frequent rests when Tom bent over, hands on knees, and panted. His head ached. He didn't know that he was in the throes of heat exhaustion with heat stroke not far behind. He began to see things, visions of water that wasn't there, giant

473

black birds circling high overhead, someone following him. And he saw bones, a ceaseless array of bones and teeth along the shore. Mile after mile. After mile. More delusion.

The day scorched on and the sun bore down mercilessly. *It must be a hundred and thirty degrees out,* he thought. Still, Tom put one foot in front of the other... in front of the other... in front of the other. By late afternoon, he sat down in the shade of a large rock, utterly spent. Dizzy, his head swimming and perception waning, he lay back. Nausea threatened him with dry heaves. If he gave up now, he thought, it would be easy. Just go to sleep.

No. Again, he cursed his weakness. But when he tried to get up he found that he couldn't, or he could, but only with the greatest difficulty. *Wait,* he told himself, *wait until dusk.* He thought about Little. Was she still waiting for him, or had she wandered off to an uncertain fate, convinced that he'd abandoned her? He couldn't stop. Shakily, Tom stood, and trembling, he walked on; time, and consciousness, fading in and out.

It must be farther than ten miles, he pondered dully. *Maybe fifteen.* Pulling over a rise now, he stopped still. There it was in front of him. The lake, or more accurately, the big waterhole. His spirit tried to leap, but even that took too much energy. Walk.

Step, by dragging step. Panting. Something was lying in the water near the edge. Some *things.* Enormous and black, they turned and looked at him, then rose at his fearless advance. Snarling. Vicious. *Entelodonts.* Three of them. Querulous, there were deep scars on each of their heads, injuries inflicted by the others whenever they were feeling testy, which was fairly often. They'd not eaten in a week and had camped out here anticipating the inevitable appearance of a thirsty animal. Something so parched that it would ignore the danger, trade its life for a taste of water. The trio came at him confidently. Without a second thought, Tom pulled out the pistol and, with unsteady hand, managed to shoot the lead one square in the forehead. It fell on the spot. The others jerked and stopped in their tracks. He shot again, this time at the ground in front of them, sending a spray of dirt in their faces. That was enough, and the giants were gone, running and squealing in anger, short, thin, black tails up in the air, onto the baking plain.

Tom dropped his pack, fell at the water and was about to drink when a tiny thought encroached. Toiling, he sat, opened his pack and dug out the purifier and cup. Then he began filling it and drinking. One after another. Cup after cup. Shortly, a pain in his gut, he stopped. Instinctively, he knew that he would do more harm than good if he didn't. He had to go slower, measure it out. And he did, yet he continued to drink. In an hour's time, he was feeling better. Not a lot, but better. Next, since he'd not eaten in two days either, Tom walked to the black mountain of pig and cut off a chunk with his knife. In normal times he would be loath to do something like that, but this was an exception. "I'm sorry," he said. Tom lifted the meat to his face and drank the warm, salty juice. It was what he needed. Then he cooked another large piece. *That pig gave its life for mine,* he thought. *Thank you.*

Using a bowl, Tom buried the animal in mud to hide it from other predators, then he disrobed and waded into the pool, scrubbing himself clean with sand and washing his clothes. By sundown, he had improved. Should he continue on, he wondered briefly, on toward Julie, or should he go back for Little? He dismissed the perfidious notion at once; there was *no way* he could leave his friend. None. He *had* to go back. Little was a part of him, something he could no more abandon than his right arm. Tom filled every container he had with water and sliced off another large chunk of entelodont. It would be for Little. He left immediately.

All night long he walked, though his body demanded sleep. Step after step. The extra weight was taxing. This time, though, he drank when he needed it. The crazy illusion of bones along the beach was still there, gleaming whitely in the full moonlight, and he marveled at it. It was morning when he dropped into the basin where he'd left the girl.

She wasn't there.

"Little?" he called out, then "Little! ... Little!" There was no movement, no sound in response, nothing but the sun pounding down and heat waves climbing.

Oh no, he thought. Had she left to go after him? Or perhaps his scolding of her, and then leaving, made her think that he was saying goodbye. Tom let go his pack and ran toward the dead tree. "LITTLE!" he yelled, *"LITTLE!"* Gone. Frantic, he ran to every bit of shelter he could see: trees, boulders, the side of the dune he'd climbed the day before.

And there she was, a dark mound lying in a sliver of shade. She looked near death, rapid panting, tongue dry, swollen and hanging out the side of her mouth. The sun advancing over the sky had forced her to move from the even feebler shade of the dead tree to this spot on the lee side of the drift. She lifted her head faintly at his approach, even managing a weak wag of her tail, then lay it back down. Tom ran back to his pack and, grabbing it, raced toward the girl. He found her bowl and splashed water into it. She did not drink. Distraught, he opened her mouth and poured some in. He also poured some onto her head and fanned her with his hat, then a bit more into her mouth, encouraging her with comforting words. She swallowed. He poured more and she swallowed again. And again. After another swallow, she refused any more and simply lay, puffing. Terribly worried, Tom continued to fan, thinking it best not to force her.

~ The day sweltered ~

Five long minutes later, Little, grunting with effort, rolled onto her chest. Tom, awash in relief, cradled the bowl for her. With difficulty, she drank.

"Good girl!" Tom said, tearfully. "You drink *all* you need." He opened his pack and got out the chunk of meat he'd brought her, then cut off a piece. It sliced easily with his knife. He placed it before her. She ignored it. He poured more water, crushing and dissolving a salt tablet in it. She drank. When he worried that she was drinking too much, he held off, and stroking, continued to talk gently to her. As the minutes fell by, and Little was rehydrating, Tom was amazed to see that her tongue was shrinking.

At last, she lay back on her side and closed her eyes, happy that her human had returned. Tom stretched out in the dust beside her, and together they slumbered the rest of the long, hot day in the shade of the dune.

By evening, they were well enough to find better cover where they would rest until the following evening. Tom wanted to take advantage of the cool nights. Still, he was cognizant that they needed to get to the pond as soon as possible. The water and food he had left should just last till then. Hopefully, they would find more water holes after that.

They sweated out the next day. Just being. Existing. Recuperating under the white-hot star without thought. It seemed the world waited with them. That night they were ready and once more returned to their quest.

"A very strange phenomenon. There are bones everywhere along the shore and within the waters of the coast. A variety of bones. And teeth. Especially teeth. Millions of them. Billions perhaps. Sharp, some very large, big as my hand, resembling those of that thing that nearly had us for lunch. We go, crunching over them, and the bones just keep coming. There is no end in sight."

After miles of nocturnal walking, tripping and puzzling over the teeth and bones, Tom thought to check with the Pin-Pointer, and switched on the overlay. It could be done without activating the beacon. He saw their location on the map screen, his blinking blue light. He was in what would become central California. There was a word near the blue light. Placing his fingers on the screen, he expanded and brought the word closer.

Sharktooth Hill

Tom tapped on the word and the information came up.

STH "bonebed." An accumulation of terrestrial, and especially, marine osseous deposits, averaging 200 bones per square meter. Famous for the abundance of shark's teeth found therein. Thought to have been formed sometime between 15.9-15.2 million years ago. It is unknown precisely what caused the massive buildup. Hypotheses range from calving grounds, volcanic or red tide poisoning, shark predation, massive acid rain, near surface magmatic hotspot, which superheated the waters, gradual buildup over millennia, or some combination thereof. Slow, steady accumulation, via time and tide, is the currently favored view.

There was a picture of a man holding a large tooth, and next to that, a sketch of the animal it came from. A mammoth shark. Tom was astonished. It was the same beast that had attacked them. *Carcharocles megalodon.* It was gigantic. The memory of it made him shudder.

By daylight, they had again reached the water hole. This time no entelodont stood guard, except the dead one under a now hardened mound of dried mud. Other Barstovian denizens were there though, camels and a rough-looking species of antelope with scraggly fur, drinking and lying by the waters. At the sight of Little they retreated. The girl, however, wasn't interested. Instead, she headed immediately toward the water, where she lay, and lapped at the life-giving fluid. Tom, too, drank until sated.

After drinking, the aelurodon began to nose around. There was something here. Then she found it. It was buried in a mound of mud. She dug at it until the big black thing was partially unearthed, then began to feast. She didn't object when Tom walked over and cut out some large pieces of choice meat and draped them over a willow pole he'd erected above a fire. The tips of the flame just reached the bottoms of the meat, but went higher as he heaped more dry wood on. Fat dripped, crackling on the coals. He sat in a shade and watched the rivers of diaphanous heat shimmer upwards, rising at times to turn the meat over, or snatch a bite to eat.

Even here, a quarter-mile from the shallow sea edge,

there were sharks teeth. Shiny and perfect, they were uniformly distributed in the searing white sands around him. He could merely push hands into it to find them.

A shadow fell over the land and Tom looked up. Clouds were slipping by from the North and had just covered the sun's scorching face. Behind were more. Dark and full. A cooling breeze followed. It tossed his dirty hair and fluttered his torn shirt, blowing the oppressiveness away.

"Yes ... *Oh please, yes,*" Tom said, watching the sky. It seemed a battle, and briefly the sun shone again in patches, threatening a full reemergence. Yet, the growing mantle of clouds would not be stopped. They were filling the heights and blowing south.

The fire still burned, but now it was brighter in contrast to the darkening atmosphere. Tiny pinpricks of moisture fell on his face and hands. Tom, worried that the sky would open up and spoil the meat, went to check on it. It was well done. Both sides. With a willow skewer he lifted them off the pole and laid them on a still hot rock. Then he fetched his pack and found something to wrap them in; an old, torn shirt, which he'd cleaned and kept. He wrapped each one, then folded the cloth around them. Juice and oils began to show through. He'd need to wash the pack at some point to remove the odor, lest it attract something he did not want to attract. He zipped it up, then looked around for somewhere to duck out of the rain, which began lightly to fall.

There was a mass of boulders with mesquite growing in between two of them. In the center was a sheltered area. Tom, slinging the pack over his shoulders, ran toward it. Though the pack was water-resistant, and he himself could use another wash, he felt an instinctual desire to be out of the weather. Under cover, he dropped to his haunches to wait it out. Little, seeing him run, ran after him. She sniffed at the pack, then licked his face.

This is mine, girl, Tom thought. *But don't worry, I'll cut you more before we go.* The rain began to come down harder now, causing the fire to sputter and sizz. After a time it went out, leaving glowing red coals. By and by, though, they too gave up the ghost, with only smoke to ascend skywards.

Rain fell for half an hour, then the clouds were gone above and the sun beamed, though now with less intensity. In the distance, Tom could see great sheets of water still falling, slowly at an angle, to the ground. He prayed it meant that there would be drinking water available through this desert-like land. Little went back to her entelodont, gorging herself until her sides bulged. Tom removed one of his fat steaks and ate it all, licking his fingers at the end of it, satisfied. In minutes, his eyes began to droop. He lay down in the dry sand under the boulders, using the pack as a pillow, and closing his eyes, slept the sleep of the dead.

A day after the pond, on a cool, blue morning, Tom and Little came upon a mighty river. The map told them that it was the *Kern*. Apparently, other rivers that would have flowed separately down their own paths to the Temblor and provide them with water, had, for some reason, instead joined the main far upstream to become this roaring torrent. It explained the dry patch they'd walked through. Before it reached the sea it became a broad, fan-shaped delta.

Yet again, Tom was presented with a body of water they had to cross. This time, however, when he walked to the marshy edge, he saw that, though wide, it was not terribly deep and could, in fact, be negotiated. The presence of various terrestrial wildlife standing on reedy mounds at certain points within attested to its shallowness. The solution for he and Little was quicker than the first time too. Tom found a thick, flattish piece of driftwood, roughly five feet long by four wide that would serve as their craft. Then he located a long, thin log that had been felled by some Zygolophodon. This he stripped of branches and bark: the rafting pole. And, without further ado, they boarded her.

The voyage was serene and uneventful, lasting an hour or so. Only the pole as it hit the water, the occasional plop and tinkle of frogs and turtles jumping in from boulders, floating bits of wood and vegetation, and the call of bay birds breaking the hush. They stayed close to shore, in waters much too shallow for the Temblor's larger marine denizens. Though the water increased in swiftness as they approached midpoint, this was offset by the Kern's width. As they rafted by, a solitary, and now peaceful *Paleoparadoxia* lifted its heavy head mid-mastication, mouth full of reeds hanging down on either side, to gaze at them, then, failing to comprehend, went back to its grazing. A group of *Blastomeryx,* diminutive hornless ruminants with downward facing tusks, swam to and stood on a little island of flattened sedge, munching something there. Brightly colored dragonflies and hummingbirds danced and zoomed just over the glassy, clear waters, their depths teeming with moss and fish. Shafts of sun, now kind and lovely, shone through trees, which grew on a narrow peninsula that tapered into blue tranquility.

Lifting the raft onto another patch of flattened reeds, Tom slipped into the bay and swam soundlessly, while his cares washed away with the dirt. Little, too, dog-paddled in joyous circles around him. When she was out, she shook a million rainbow droplets to the four winds. It was a magical hour in an enchanting place he would never forget.

Back aboard, they poled around the point and Tom was instantly stunned by the vista that met their eyes. Past the peninsula, an old sandbar had cut off a long section of beach and it sat isolated from the fresher waters around them. Here it was much saltier and shallower, but still navigable. Yet, it was what lingered in their hundreds that shocked him the most. Between the surf grass in the tide pools at the beach, and the grassy banks just back of the shore, were row upon row of tall, bright pink birds, standing, walking and sleeping. His jaw dropped.

"Oh ... my ..."

Completely ignorant of their provenance, he quickly took out the P.I. and snapped a picture.

Megapaloelodus, family Phoenicopteridae

Flamingo

Their color was truly shocking. Feathers, legs, even their eyes. The most exquisite pink he'd ever seen! Surrounded by green, the effect was electric neon. The birds were three to five feet tall, with downward curved bills, graceful and elegant. As they glided slowly closer, Tom gaped through his binocs. At their feet was an evenly spread out layer of what appeared to be white, snail-like mollusk shells.

The birds, a little edgy at Tom and his aelurodon companion, strutted the shoreline in long strides. Finally, at some invisible signal, the whole took to the air, a pink cloud swirled in blue. When at last the two passed, the flamingos circled around and landed back in their place.

The whole filled Tom's heart, healing it after the last day's misadventures.

Opal, I love you.

It took them another two days of hiking before the numbers of bones and teeth began to diminish. Finally, they were gone. In all, Tom guessed they'd strolled by fifty miles of them. On the way, he couldn't help but collect some specimens as souvenirs. One he tied with a length of entelodont sinew, and, making a loop with it, placed it around his neck. It hung proudly on his chest, a shiny, three-inch tooth from *Isurus hastalis,* a giant mako.

"What do you think?" he asked Little, holding the tooth up for her inspection. She sat on her muscular hindquarters and looked at him bemusedly, then opened her mouth in that wide smile of hers. He, in turn, considered her as well. She had gotten big in the months they'd been trekking. He guessed her weight now at 125 pounds and growing. Solid muscle. And heart. Her fur was lustrous, her tail full, upright and proud. He was proud to have her. What a fine companion she'd been to him.

By the end of the week, the countryside was regularly green again. Thanks to that rain and the river, they'd indeed had water enough to see them through the last of the dry lands. Rather than the flat world of the barrens, gently rolling hills greeted their eyes, and endless miles of delightfully scented, tall grass prairie, strewn with wildflowers, waved in concert to the warm winds, sounding almost like a quiet ocean tide. Naturally, with the grass came the grazers in a diverse variety, and their numbers spread far out. Too, pools of water and small lakes became more frequent, as did Live Oak, Laurel, Palm and Pine woodlands and sclerophyllous shrubs. And fruit trees. Tom was overjoyed to have the avocados, sweet fruits and nuts back. He realized something else then: month after month, all this long journey, there had always been flowers. Even in the barrens! *With the equable climate, flowers must bloom all year here,* he surmised with a smile.

Still, had they continued due south or southeast, they would have entered the Mojave region. Yet the Miocene

Mojave was little like the dry desert it would become much later. Now, it was a cooler, wetter place. It would take another ten million years, and the uplift of the San Gabriel, San Bernardino and other, more southerly ranges, creating a rain-shadow effect, together with the development of the Pacific gyre and cold California Current, before true desert would become established there. In the middle Miocene, the Mojave was greener and water abundant.

In time, however, its flora of willows, cottonwoods, pines, palms, oaks, magnolia, walnuts, avocados, maples, nutmegs, plum yews, etc., and their dense and diverse understory of shrubbery, would be replaced by an arid thornscrub community, a developing ecotone. Then, lonely herbage such as *Stenocereus thurberi*, or Organpipe cactus, *Pachycormus*, the Baja Elephant Tree, *Brahea*, drought resistant Fan Palms, *Lysiloma*, also known as fern-of-the-desert, *Prosopis*, more generally known as Mesquite, *Fouquieria*, commonly Ocotillo, and *Dodonea*, aka Hopseed Bush, as well as various junipers, buckthorns, soapberries and others, would take hold.

Nevertheless, while departing *these* dry lands, they were also beginning to move away from the coast now, at last leaving the great Temblor, as, having reached its southern limit, its shore continued due west. They were going southwest though. According to the PinPointer, Julie was near the coast, but the most direct path lie straight ahead. They still had two hundred miles or so to go. While the terrain behind them had been tough, Tom hoped that, if the territory ahead remained roughly like this, rolling grassland, and scattered lake and woodland, and there were no other major mishaps, they might make it to her camp in two to three weeks time. The prospect thrilled him.

Tom began to think more about what he would do if and when he confronted Jaqzen. The red light no longer glowed when he switched on the PinPointer. It hadn't for a couple of weeks now. He wasn't sure what to make of it, but thought it probably some sort of ruse. And it was likely that the Neanderthal had been keeping track of *his* advance too, and was preparing to cut him off. Or maybe he had finally discovered Julie's trick and was triangulating. He prayed it wasn't that. He had to keep on the lookout. Thus, Tom found himself watching the horizon closer, checking behind things, and listening for that which he'd not heard in a long time, another human voice. Jaqzen's, though, was not a voice he wanted to hear. He kept the lock off his gun.

The stress of the impending events taxed Tom's energy almost as much as if he were suffering from dehydration. When he recognized it, he made himself stop fretting. If experience was the mother of knowledge, then preparation was the mother of courage. He'd experienced and learned a lot in his time on the trail. He'd grown. In many ways he was not the same man he used to be. He was stronger now, in body and mind. Maybe he wouldn't be able to beat Jaqzen in a physical fight, but he was certain he could outthink him. That would have to be his strategy.

My dear Julie,

If only you knew what is going through my heart these days. I am changing. Transforming. Yet my love and admiration for you only grows. I just hope you will see that in my heart I am still the man you married, and that you will still love me for it.

Be safe and strong and know that I am coming.

Thirty One

Since he'd arrived, Jaqzen had thoroughly enjoyed himself. Indeed, the Miocene had turned out to be everything he'd hoped it would be. There was no limit to the game to be taken, and he'd left a long line of carcasses in his wake, most killed for the sport of it. If one wanted to, they might be able to find him via his trail of carnage. He only regretted that Julie hadn't seen it.

How he had hoped to get his hands on her, yet somehow she'd managed to elude him. He wasn't used to tracking human prey in wilderness, but on city streets. Even so, it was inevitable, she would be his. He almost had her in that tableland, but she was cleverer than he'd assumed and had sent a stampede of horses his way. He shot to wound and drop her, then turned to flee and was knocked over and almost trampled. In a rage, he cut one of them down, but was aware that he was wasting valuable ammunition. Maybe that's what she *wanted*. In any event, by time the dust settled she was gone. Eventually, though, she would tire of the chase and he would have her. Of that he was confident. It was only a matter of time.

And now that time had come; although it had taken him a while to figure it out, he knew where she was. At first it seemed that she'd been sounding from random points in her dash away from him, yet, in the last several weeks, a pattern had begun to emerge. She was not still heading north, north toward that blinking blue light, but was hovering somewhere inside about a twenty-mile radius. He knew that because her signals stayed within that same general area, week after week. True, they moved around, yet they never left that circular domain. She was in there somewhere, he knew, and he would find her. And when he did...

It made him laugh, this vision of his, jamming meat down her vegetarian throat. She'd gag and wail, of course, like a baby. *Sue me!* he'd chortle. Then he'd take her and violate her, as he'd wanted to since he first laid hungry eyes on her. Like a wild horse he'd break her, break her spirit. Then, and only then, would she surrender, would she be his. No more of that uppity "professor" stuff here. There'd be no one to stop him, no one to protect her. He didn't want to do it, but it was the way it had to be. *Naw,* he laughed to himself, he *wanted* to do it, and in the worst way.

First though, he'd have to take care of whoever it was that was coming. That pulsing blue dot. Seemed they'd gotten his Strong Box note and decided to send someone anyway, but from a safe distance. Hundreds of miles. He chuckled. They must *really* be afraid! He hoped they liked that *other* note he left for them in his bungalow on the de Physica grounds.

So who could it be, he wondered, *another tracker like himself? Peterson maybe? Vegas? Or perhaps Abramowitz or Mossuel. It mattered not. Let him come. Jaqzen has no equal. More sport. And when I'm done with him, I'll get the human race going again, bring back some civilization, my bitch and I. Then I'll be King of the World.*

With a clever smile, he turned off his beacon.

~~~

Now that the blue light was getting closer, Julie began to think about what she had to do. Would she be up for another long odyssey, for surely that was what was to happen? The Institute had sent another expert to bring her back, but they'd not wanted to risk landing him in the vicinity of the original Strong Box. Yet, why *so far away* she couldn't guess.

And now she was torn, for as much as she wanted to be

reunited with her husband, she wanted to remain here, in her home. How could she go back to that nightmare world? It was likely that if she did, she'd never be allowed to return to the Miocene. The thought made her shudder. But on the other hand, maybe once they had everything they wanted, the samples, the video, her notes, they'd be grateful enough to let her and Tom come back here to live as repayment. They could keep their money. She'd have to wait and see what the blue man had to say. In the meantime, she readied herself for anything.

Julie noticed that the red light that meant Jaqzen had not appeared in the PinPointer for weeks, and it worried her. Now she didn't know where he was. Furtively, throughout these days, she glanced around, imagining him coming at her from anywhere. She wanted to keep Zephyr nearby, so that in a pinch they could make a rapid escape, but it seemed the boy was wandering farther away lately, toward a small herd of other Hypohippus that had shown up one fine day.

On the other hand, maybe the end of Jaqzen's beacon meant the end of Jaqzen. Much as she hated to think of herself as a vengeful person, she was astute enough to know that as long as he was alive she would have no peace. Or maybe there was a simpler explanation for the ending of the red beacon, maybe he'd simply lost or broken his PinPointer.

That was certainly a possibility. In that case, perhaps he was still heading north, thinking he was on her (imaginary) trail. She hoped he hadn't figured out her subterfuge.

Day by day, Julie continued to refine her riding prowess. She spent two hours each afternoon on her stallion, for that is what he was, she noted, when he began to herd a group of females with him. He was a beautiful boy too, having fully recovered from his wound, and truly seemed to enjoy being brushed, whinnying his approval, prodding her when she lagged. Proud and strong, his tail stood erect whenever they rode. Then with the whole group, Zephyr, Julie and his five females, they'd run. The thunder of their galloping made every other animal, with the exception of the proboscideans, move out of their way. Afterward, dripping with sweat from their necks and sides, and the satisfying release of pent-up energy, they'd return home to drink at the lake and sample the swaying grasses.

Julie made another friend during that time. The Miocene field mouse, *Copemys*. She woke one morning to find it sitting on the pillow near her head, chewing a pine nut she'd dropped. A slight shift by her sent it dashing under the blankets and she let out a yelp, pulling them off. It ran, but the following day was back, munching another seed she'd carefully placed next to her. Then, from beneath the covers, she slowly brought out more. And hence the start of a ritual: every morning the little mouse turned up and she'd feed it. Soon she was holding it, a tiny, quivering, ball of warmth.

Always the scientist, Julie made a further discovery, wondering what had taken her so long. The broad-leaved deciduous trees in the mid-Miocene, or trees that *would* be deciduous in a colder world, were *evergreen* here. She happened upon the idea while noting that, unlike the deciduous trees of the future which lost all their leaves at one time, *these* trees, often *the same species*, dropped and regrew their leaves all year long like evergreens. *Of course*, she realized, *why drop all your leaves when there's no need to, when you can still harvest sunlight, when you can still grow?* That, in addition to the extra CO_2 from volcanoes, also helped explain the generally larger size of trees here. Leaves that stayed on trees longer made use of a longer growing season, and that would naturally mean more growth. And while already here, geologically speaking the spread of grasses would *coincide* with the coming seasonal leaf drop, and by ensuring a continuous food supply, aid in the transition from browsing to grazing in mixed-feeder communities.

At any rate, it was only when the year had advanced toward "winter" that leaves began to turn brilliant color before falling. Yet what a glorious color it was! Then she'd stroll through her forests in rapture, as almost every hue of the rainbow fluttered and waved.

Thus Julie remained, loving the earth, learning her ways. But the feeling of fear and expectancy, dread and anticipation, only grew.

~~~

It had been many months since Tom first set out. Far longer than he'd expected. And of miles, he had no idea. He'd not even remembered the pedometer until weeks after he left. By then he thought, why bother? That original 653 miles - as the crow flies - likely had become a thousand, or more.

As they closed in, Julie was taking a chance by signaling more often. Every three days or so. It was a big risk. Still, Jaqzen had not found her.

Yet, what an experience it had been! When he thought back to all of the adventures, everything he and his best friend, Little, had been through, he marveled. Terror and elation, sickness and strength, danger and profound peace. In less than a year's time, Tom had learned more than he could in a hundred future lives, had faced more than any other person from the Anthropocene ever could.

He recalled, with a shake of his head, all of the many false starts they'd endured, the near tragedies.

There was the time he'd almost burned down a forest. The days were long and hot and the grass dry. Having built an evening campfire as usual, Tom sat on a log near it, bone tired and head nodding. Oblivious, he had not even heard Little's bark, had no idea until she physically yanked him backwards by the collar. He jumped up, and, seeing the spreading blaze, stomped it into oblivion. His palm tree shoes, though, were toast and his feet burned. But it forced him to fashion his first pair of moccasins, a shoe type which he still wore.

On another occasion, while on a jaunt through a canyon in the Mojave, Tom looked up to the sound of rolling thunder. It hadn't rained for sometime, then suddenly did that morning. Yet, now the sky was sunny and clear. It puzzled him. An earthquake? Still the sound of thunder increased. Then he thought that it must be a stampede. Up, he and Little ran, up the side of the gorge, just as a wall of water shot by, a flash flood that fell over itself in a mad rush down the ravine, pushing a host of rocky and woody debris ahead of it. And, suddenly as it came, it was gone. "Well," he'd remarked to Little, "*that* was interesting!"

Then there was the Amphicyon battle they'd witnessed months previous. In an opalescent woodland they'd ambled, through sun and dappled shade, light and shifting shadows, heading toward a crystal pool in a clearing. The sky was a sweet, turquoise blue, the air, breezy and cool, and Tom, in another rapture, was humming and strumming his board piano. But it could be dangerous to let one's guard down in the Barstovian. From nowhere, a tremendous roaring, a horrible snarling spun the hiking pair round. Two big males that happened to cross territories, and then paths, were now engaged in a fight to the death.

The hikers dashed behind some trees and Tom ripped the gun out of its holster. The volume of roaring was so tremendous however that, as he had at other times, Tom stuck fingers in his ears, this time dropping the gun. Fortunately, it did not go off, and he picked it back up. Little was on maximum alert, her hackles fully raised and eyes wide. She'd wanted to run, and almost did, but returned to stay by her human. Then he saw them, the terrible beasts, as they bit and locked onto each other again and again, their eyes mad with fury. The movement was incredibly fast, and within seconds, blood flew in sprays coming from both beast's shoulders and necks. Suddenly, one stood on hind feet and swiped a mighty paw at his opponent, knocking him down. A hit like that would have ended Tom, he knew. Or Little. But the other sprung up again at his enemy's throat and sunk teeth in.

Tom did not want to wait around to see the outcome, fearing that the dreadful winner, still amped with adrenaline, might come after them. Quickly, using the trees as cover, they ran, and continued running until they were past a hill and deep into a canyon, far from the awful clash. Tom's heart and muscles, though, were strong, and at the end of it, rather than exhausted, he felt invigorated.

In all honesty, however, these episodes of fright were the minority, and though they stood out in his mind, most of the time peace reigned in the Luisian.

One occasion that Tom remembered with particular fondness, was the time they happened upon a huge, hanging honeycomb, full and dripping gooey golden goodness. It was while they were still in the forest, before their sea crossing. He'd been in a funk for several days about the journey in general and all the hurdles they faced, when, hearing a loud buzzing, they found it. Five feet long by three wide, it was swarming with thousands of bees, yet these bees were non-aggressive and paid no mind to the small animals that eagerly nibbled comb and lapped honey that had fallen to the ground. As Tom watched, a chunk of comb suddenly detached and swung loose, dangling. Gobs of amber sweetness plopped down on the heads of the diners below, who then cleaned it, each from the other. Before the comb touched the ground, Tom walked over, and, with nervous eyes on the oblivious bees, gently took hold of it and pulled slightly. Then he had it, honey coating his hand and dripping into Little's mouth. To be sure, they came across other hives and sampled other honeys, but this one cheered his soul when he needed it most.

As Tom closed in, doubts had begun to creep into his mind. What if he'd had the big man all wrong, had prejudged him out of jealousy? Maybe Jaqzen's brusque manner was simply impatience with the pettiness of a husband overly concerned about his wife. After all, he had bigger things to worry about. And there could be a logical explanation for why they'd failed to reappear when they were supposed to. It was entirely possible that some technical glitch somewhere had marooned the two back in the Miocene. Probable even. Still, how to explain the fact that Julie and Dietrich had been separated all this time? Whatever the case, he shouldn't go in with guns blazing. Find out first what had happened, get the facts. Yet, though his logical mind entreated, his gut told him that his mind was wrong.

He knew he was finally getting near when the unmistakable signs of humanity, of Jaqzen, began to appear. Garbage and destruction. It was a shock at first, and Tom stood dumbfounded as he stared down at the crumpled pack of cigarettes on the ground. Then he noticed the Cosoryx head lashed to a tree.

It was destroyed, obviously Jaqzen had taken out his rage on the thing. There was a blood stained note crudely scrawled in gore beneath.

You were warned

The carnage looked recent. The ape-man was here, and knew Tom was too.

There was another Amphicyon battle they'd witnessed one evening while sitting atop a low hill. Tired after a long day's trudge, something caught his eye, something out on the dry grasslands. Dust being whipped up. It spun high and dispelled in the air. Below it was movement. Rapid. Running. An Aepycamelus loping with one of the great beasts in hot pursuit. *Oh no*, thought Tom. *Not them*. It was clear that the Aepy would be caught as it was no match for the Amp's much greater speed. When the carnivore was almost upon it, though, the camel made a quick turn to the right while the brute went past. The Aepy continued on in its path, hastening fast as it could, but the Amp came back again at full charge. Its speed was mind-boggling, the power in its pumping legs was evident, almost catlike.

It was a terrifying scene, especially for Tom, who had a natural aversion to violence. He braced for the worst. But not all fights are predictable, and when the Amphicyon sprang, claws bared and fangs ready, the very instant before it was to land upon the camel's back, an amazing thing happened. The Aepy kicked.

The timing was perfect. A second sooner, or later, and it would have been all over. Any other day, and it would have been all over. But not *today*. The camel's rear feet caught the Amp, one in the chest and the other in the face, twisting it abruptly to the side. Tom heard the kick, a moment afterwards. Then the Amp went down. It stayed down, and would not be rising, its neck broken. The Aepy continued to lope for a way, but seeing it was no longer being pursued, stopped. It stood for a time then, mouth open and tongue lolling, while it caught its breath. Then, slowly, redeemed, with one last look at the Amp, it walked away toward the lengthening shadows of a hill that angled up between the savanna and a wood. A lowland species, Tom thought, its fur was shorter and darker than those he'd seen back in the nascent Sierras. Reaching the point, other Aepys strode out from the trees to meet it. Its harem and young. It had lived, lived to love another day and pass its genes on to one more generation.

Now as he stood looking down at the plastic wad, at the horrible head of the Cosoryx, his blood hot with fury, Tom remembered the Aepy. Would that he'd be so lucky. He picked up the trash, a feeling of horror in his gut. Horror at what could, *would* happen, if people like Jaqzen were to travel back in time. Heaven into Hell.

Pulling a fire stick out, he lit the trash, watched it burn until it was nothing but ash. The same as he'd done the rest of the waste he'd carried. When the item was used up or broken it was his disposal method of choice. He always waited until only ash remained. Then he'd stand and walk away. In this way, one by one, Tom was shedding the last residues of man.

From this point on, Tom's bearing changed. Gone was the casual comportment he'd settled into these past months out of ignorance of the full situation. Time, it seemed, had dulled his memory. Ambling through paradise in a world to oneself, a person could forget his mission, the reason he was here, the reason others had sacrificed their lives for him. The message on the tree brought it all back in a flash. Suddenly, realizing what Julie must have endured, the fear, the exhaustion, the pain of loss, filled Tom with guilt. He could have come sooner, *should* have. *Now*, though, was not a time to rush.

As they walked, Tom kept a sharp look out, eyes penetrating the mists and shadows of the forest that fell on either side of them, ears listening for the slightest hint of aberration, something *out-of-place*. Even Little sensed that the air had changed. Maybe it was the lack of birdsong, the unusual silence that often presaged disaster, eerie quiet, as if the world were waiting for *it* to happen.

A strong smell of ammonia. Strange. Little investigating, hackles raised. They were walking down a narrow path, perhaps twenty feet wide. The previous day, standing on top of a bluff, Tom had spied this trail. Bottomlands, thick, heavy jungle dominated here. Yet, running down the middle of it was a ribbon of bare land, well trod, a natural path. Looking down, he could see the tracks of many different animals, especially the heavy Zygos. And there were Jaqzen's, large, like the man. Tom compared his foot size, was shocked by the difference. Soon enough, though, the Zygos would obliterate them.

Trees had been felled by the zygos and the gomphos, forcing Tom and Little to climb over or go around. In time, the proboscideans would thin the forest, and, with the help of horses and other grazers, in addition to the changing climate itself, aid in the spread of grasslands, especially on the Great Plains.

From Julie's beacon pattern, Tom had deciphered her technique. Unless she changed it, he knew about where she would be the next time she signaled. Then she'd turn to find him there, and, at last, after fifteen million years, they would be reunited. That day was tomorrow.

First, though, he'd have to meet Jaqzen. Much as he tried not to let it, apprehension crept into his thoughts. Though he'd toughened over the past months, still, Tom doubted that he was a match for the Neanderthal. The man was obviously psychotic.

Likely, he was prepared and waiting, had worked jobs like this a hundred times before. *Piece of cake*, he could almost hear the ape-man say. But maybe that was his weakness. Overconfidence. He noted the cigarettes. Must have brought quite a stash; how had he gotten them past the people at the Institute? With some help, possibly. He wondered what Jaqzen's lungs looked like, about the shape he was in. Perhaps not as good as a year ago.

Tom looked over at Little. Almost full-grown, she now weighed a hundred and seventy pounds. A hundred seventy pounds of fearsome power. Fast and strong, when she hunted now, she went after larger game, pulling them down and ending the chase quickly. Suffering was minimal, though he would never enjoy watching it. In the meantime, he'd become well acquainted with Luisian, non-meat, fare, and had begun to switch back to a mainly vegetarian diet. But not completely. Eating with Little was a bond he'd not break.

They were as one now, Little and her human. Knew each other's quirks and ways of thinking - when one was happy or angry; when a situation called for speed or stealth; when to take the low path rather than the high one. Tom knew that he could count on Little's help should it be required. That she too was a killer, would act in a second at his barest call. Two against one, they would prevail.

He couldn't do it. He'd not risk her life to save his own. This was something he had to do by himself. And when it was over, should he die, he knew his companion would protect Julie.

Thus Tom ruminated, as his foot touched the thin, nearly invisible wire, almost setting it off. Little was behind, guarding his rear, growling her low, deep growl, hackles up.

When his other foot pushed hard against the metal line though, Tom looked down, saw it, then up again at the sound of something coming fast at them. A shape, large and heavy, square with pointed stakes, was whooshing rapidly. Without a thought, Tom dived for Little, knocking her down and past. The square side of the death machine slammed into him, but the stakes missed. The next thing he knew, he was lying on the ground in a heap, pain shooting through him as the swinging trap swayed back and forth until finally gravity brought it to a halt.

Little, whining, rushed to her human, not comprehending. She jumped on and licked Tom's face, ears flattened in a way that spoke of acquiescence, fearful of reproachment.

Slowly, Tom straightened, and sat, grunting with pain. With one hand he clutched his stomach, the other he put on his faithful companion, glad to see that she was unhurt, then turned to look at the hanging contrivance. So, Jaqzen had set a trap. It hadn't worked though; they were still here. *Just.* It was his backpack that had borne the brunt of it. Nevertheless, he'd had the breath knocked out of him.

Still sitting, Tom slung the pack off and looked at it. A rip along the width. It was high enough, though, that nothing was coming out. It could be repaired later. But the pack was wet. He opened it to inspect the inside. The water bottle was smashed and was now rubbish. Tom considered it grimly. Well, they still had the skins. Pulling other things out, he saw no further damage. Then he opened the pocket that contained the PinPointer.

"No," Tom said as he removed it. It was now in pieces, one falling from his hands to the ground trailing wires. It would never work again.

Seeing that, Tom felt a devastation he'd not ever known. *"God, NO,"* he repeated, his hands shaking, then he let out a roar.

Stay calm, Tom told himself, *just gotta stay calm. And alert. Nothing's changed.* After reloading the pack and picking himself up, he and Little continued on. It had now been an hour, and no more traps. Maybe that was *it*, he hoped, Jaqzen's best shot.

Tom knew that he had but one chance at this. He was heading to Julie's north-easternmost post, the one closest to him. She'd been doubling up on her beacons, had made the circuit and was due to arrive there again. The last time she called from it, two weeks ago, he noted the location. Yesterday he decided to double-check the distance. There were now 42 miles between them and it.

He concluded that she'd been making these calls precisely at noon, or around 12:00 PM. He assumed that based on the position of the sun. It was near zenith. She'd have a chronometer and was likely timing her signals by it. And while he knew he shouldn't, he returned her signal; he wanted to make sure she knew he was approaching and would wait for him. Now he was glad he did.

He needed to guesstimate how far he and Little traveled since then. To do that, he had to know what the time was when he stopped last night and started this morning. He shook his head, unsure. Then he tried to think what time of year it was. As things were pretty uniseasonal in the mid-Miocene, it was hard to tell. Still, he thought that it was just past winter. He based this more on a hunch than anything else. The past several months, things had been slightly cooler than before and now they were heading toward a bit warmer. March? What time does the sun set in March? He guessed about 6:00 PM. They'd stopped at sundown. Six hours of hiking then? From an earlier calculation some time previous, when he'd played with the pedometer, he tagged his average walking miles per hour at 2.5. So at 2.5 miles an hour, they had gone roughly 15 miles. This morning they started out again at sunrise. He guessed that the sun rose at 6:00 am.

Tom looked at the sky. The sun was a few degrees before

noon. Maybe 11:00. Five hours had elapsed since the morning. 12.5 miles. Adding the two, he came up with 27.5 miles since Julie called. He had 14.5 miles, or nearly 6 hours more, to go. It was *a lot* of guesswork, so the margin for error was high. Tom prayed that he wasn't *too* far off.

If there were no other setbacks, and if he pushed himself, Tom thought they could make it to Julie's general signaling area just about an hour before sunset. She'd show up tomorrow and he'd look for her. But there were so many doubts.

A small deer. It was pinned to a tree, speared by a long shaft that was sent hurtling toward it after the poor animal found another of Jaqzen's trip wires. Its head down, blood dripping from its mouth, it was dead, having inadvertently sacrificed its life to save them.

They walked on for another couple of hours, stepping over two more traps, while the forest drew in closer to the trail. Trees towered above, casting it in ominous shadows. Foreboding. Anxious, gun in hand, Tom peered into the wood, expecting Jaqzen to jump out at any minute.

In her school days, Julie had once been assigned to read and compare two stories, *Young Goodman Brown* by Nathaniel Hawthorne, and *How to Tell a True War Story* by Tim O'Brian. Stories that dealt with shadows and imagination. With nature and nightmares. She'd written an essay about it, and now Tom remembered it. He'd read it that day back at their apartment. Back while he waited for her return. It seemed a world away.

At first she was puzzled by it, this comparison, then slowly it began to dawn on her.

"I was suddenly struck with the realization that both stories seem to be revealing, via their disparate plots, the same very interesting thing. A base alloy of the human mind. It has to do with unconscious and instinct. It also has to do with fear and our genetic history. One could perhaps reduce it down to strict zoophobia (fear of animals) and nyctophobia (fear of the dark) and try to treat these (separately or together), but that would not explain their origins.

"What am I getting at? Simply this. Humanity's 10,000 year separation from nature (we've been here much longer, but it was at about this point that we began to segregate ourselves away from other species and live citied lives) has had long-lasting and profound negative impacts on its psyche. We continue to confuse nature, dark and mysterious, with evil, and still lack understanding on the underlying cause for much of our fears and prejudices. But could these fears and prejudices, which have given convenient excuse to many to clear-cut forests, pave over wild lands, and even hunt species to extinction, actually be based on 'genetic memory' and encoded in our DNA? A memory that stretches back millions of years to a time when survival in nature was a continual, often frightening struggle? An open question, but judge for yourselves.

"Let us first compare how nature is treated in both stories. Hawthorne wrote of Goodman

Brown on his way to meet the devil,"

He had taken a dreary road, darkened by all the gloomiest trees of the forest which barely stood aside to let the narrow path creep through, and close immediately behind. It was all as lonely as could be; and there is this peculiarity in such solitude, that the traveler know not who may be concealed by the innumerable trunks and thick boughs overhead; so that with lonely footsteps he may be passing through an unseen multitude.

"And now this from *How to Tell a True War Story* in a description of the Vietnamese jungles,"

So what happens is, these guys get themselves deep in the bush.... And I'll tell you - it's spooky. This is mountains. You don't KNOW spooky till you been there. Jungle, sort of, except it's way up in the clouds and there's always this fog - like rain, except it's not raining - everything's all wet and swirly and tangled up and you can't see jack, you can't find your pecker to piss with. Like you don't have a body. Serious spooky. You just go with the vapors - the fog sort of takes you in.... And the sounds, man. The sounds carry forever. You hear shit nobody should ever hear.

"Already one begins to see how, in both narratives, the mere presence of the natural world, its benign features amplified and transformed by the imaginations of the characters involved as night approaches, is influencing their perspectives. Were it broad daylight at the local city park, the eerie conclusions they draw, really the basis for both stories, would have been different. So are these really stories that perhaps say more about our fear of nature? Let's continue. From *Young Goodman Brown,*"

> *The whole forest was peopled with frightful sounds - the creaking of the trees, the howling of the wild beasts, and the yell of Indians; while sometimes the wind tolled like a distant church bell, and sometimes gave a broad roar around the traveler, as if all nature were laughing him to scorn.... "Ha! Ha! Ha!" Roared Goodman Brown when the wind laughed at him. "Let us hear which will laugh loudest. Think not to frighten me with your deviltry. Come witch, come wizard, come Indian powwow, come devil himself, and here comes Goodman Brown. You may as well fear him as he fear you."*

"This may seem an inconsequential point, until one realizes that many terrible acts have been committed throughout history based solely on superstition and fear. One might also wonder how many forests have been razed, how many mountains leveled, how many species driven to extinction merely because of some gut-level fear of them - the darkness, those howls, al-

504

most demonic at night, bears and lions which must kill to eat and to feed their young. And is it just such an unreasoning terror these tales betray? The answer is important, for the life and health of a world is at stake.

"After describing a variety of weird sounds, 'voices' the troops thought they heard coming from their jungle post in O'Brian's account, the story goes on to say that they were,"

> *not human voices, though. Because it's the mountains. Follow me? The rock - it's TALKING. And the fog, too, and the grass and the goddamn mongooses. Everything talks. The trees talk politics, and the monkeys talk religion.*

"It seemed that as night came on, some instinctual agitation, some remnant from our remote past took over."

> *The dark was coming hard now, and off to the west I could see the mountains rising in silhouette, all mysteries and unknowns.*

"How much of this fear is due to the fact that most predatory animals hunt mainly during the night when it's cooler and when they are less likely to be seen? Was there a time before we began to band together and learned to make weapons, that we, as an earlier primate, sat out the hours of darkness on some high tree branch trembling at the sounds of the night, listening to the frightful cries of those caught in the jaws of fate? Huddled together and whimpering, we grew into man, and those glimpses of the awful fanged creatures below were surely like glimpsing devils (thus the origins of the horrible demons of world religions? Of our literary and cinematic fascination with monsters?) And so the child asks its mother, the child who has known only love its short life, to please leave the light on at night. 'The vapors, man. Trees and rocks - you got to listen to your enemy', says our narrator in the war story, a war against the ghosts of long ago. Ah, the key: Nature is the enemy, and so what action do the panicked troops undertake?"

The guys can't cope. They lose it.... They call in air strikes.... all night long, they just smoke those mountains. They make jungle juice.... They blow away trees and glee clubs and whatever else there is to blow away. Scorch time. They walk napalm up and down the ridges. They bring in Cobras and F4s, they use Willy-Peter [white phosphorus] and HE [high explosives] and incendiaries. It's all fire. They make those mountains burn.

"Rather than seeing the beauty of the lush greenery around them, they saw only shadows and what might be lurking in them. They saw insects and leeches; downcast amid downpours. They had reason to, of course, because those trees and shrubs could be hiding enemy fighters. The wild sounds that they heard might have been the disguised calls of an unseen horde.

"This Garden of Eden was instead for them a 'Garden of Evil' as O'Brian describes it. The 'dark world', into which Goodman Brown ventured, was full of 'wickedness.' But which is the devil here, nature - or our fear of it? Says Hawthorne in *Young Goodman Brown*,"

The fiend in his own shape is less hideous than when he rages in the breast of man.

The trees were so high and thick now that Tom couldn't see the sky. The trail was narrowing too. Up ahead, two rocky outcrops forced the fauna through a space little wider than an elephant, and he imagined them walking through single file. Like those people in the stories Julie had written about, Tom was spooked. He'd walked dark paths before, but never with such a feeling of disquiet.

Little had gone ahead while Tom scanned the forest. Shadows there were moving, keeping up with them, just back of the trees. Or so it seemed. There was a cry and Tom's head shot around. Little was gone. Was she the other side of the monoliths?

"Little?" Tom called out. She did not return. "Little!" he said again. Something was wrong. Tom jogged to the large stones, but when he was almost upon them he saw that there was a gaping hole in the ground between them. The tarp and branches that had hidden it now within.

"YI!" Tom shot, *"LITTLE!"* Reaching the edge, Tom looked down into the pit. Ten feet deep, it was full of upraised stakes, like the ones that had almost gotten them earlier. And there was Little, lying on her side, blood oozing out of her. She looked up at Tom, then lay her head down again.

"NO!"

Tom threw off his pack, then quickly found a stout vine and tied it off. Tears welling in his eyes made it hard to see, even so, he lowered himself fast as he could into the hole, just missing a sharpened pike. There was a small gap at the edge with footprints, Jaqzen had left this part bare, as that was where he stood when he'd finished, then pulled himself back up. Tom, crying now, yanked stakes out and threw them aside as he went to Little. Her eyes were open. Crouching down, Tom looked at her. There were deadly pikes all around her. She must have fallen on one, impaled.

Tom felt under her, wiping the tears that flowed freely down his face. No stake. He felt again, and again found nothing. Huh? But the blood? Now he saw that on her way down, she had grazed one of the points. That was all it was, a graze.

"Girl, are you all right?" Tom asked. Little made to get up, lay her head back down, then a second later, tried again. *Oh please, not a broken back,* he thought in fear. When she tried a third time, she stood, trembling. Tom threw his arms around her and wept. Then he felt for broken bones. None.

"Let's get out of here!" he said. Now Tom did something he would never have been able to do in the Anthropocene. Lifting her hundred and seventy pounds over his shoulder, he began to pull them both up as, hand over hand, he climbed the rope. It was a Herculean feat, and even he, as they broached the rim, marveled at the ease with which he did it. At the top, he set Little down. Now she stood, then shook, looking roughed up, but none the worse for the fall. Tom stared back down into the pit. Saw where she had fallen. It was impossible! Though there were gaps between the stakes, he didn't know how she

had managed to fall in the small space between seven of them without being run through. He looked at the vine. It wasn't *that* strong looking. How had it held their combined weight? He checked her over again. Nope, just a graze, then he hugged her, kissed her head.

They were past the rocks now, looking south, down the path. How had the ape-man kept animals from spoiling most of his traps? Little was sniffing at something just feet away. A strong smell of ammonia. Like before. *Ah, predator pee.* He probably killed something, removed its bladder, then poured it here. The strong smell kept most of the others away. He thought back to the savaged Cosoryx head, then Julie's essay.

"We have evidence for this hypothesis as we witness the slaughter, without qualm, of a baby water buffalo by the panicked troops. Do they have good reason? I won't say. It's a question which humanity as a whole must answer.

"It is a war in which we have been engaged, a war against nature, payback for ages of fear. But we're rational now (aren't we?) and it's time to end the war, time to look back and realize that what we've done, the way we've behaved toward the earth, and each other, was based on childhood ignorance. Time to grow up.

"The forest was 'haunted' before (*Young Goodman Brown),* but the demons now are those of our minds, and our hearts. Thus, the storyteller in O'Brian's tale clarifies the point for us regarding his Vietnamese experience: '...It was a ghost story,' he says.

"'The forest is of course his own mind', says Frederick C. Crews in *Modern Critical Views: Nathaniel Hawthorne*, referring to another Hawthorne character, 'Reuben,' and alluding to Goodman Brown,"

> *in which is deeply buried a secret spot, a trauma, to which he will have to return. He thinks he does not know the way back, he resists the opportunity to go, but ultimately is overruled by the strength of what he has repressed. Self-knowledge is knowledge of what lies almost inaccessibly remote in the forests of the mind, and Reuben* [or Goodman Brown] *will not be free until he has reached this point and released what lies imprisoned there.*

"This, I submit, is sound advice for the rest of us as well."

Looking farther now, Tom could see the end of the forest path, for five hundred yards away was an opening. A misty patch of light there told of a finish to the narrow death trail. Between he and it, though, was darkness.

The constricted passage had been a perfect place for Jaqzen to set his traps. Possibly there were more. Though it was choked with growth, they'd go through the trees.

Tom immediately cut straight into the wood, and anticipating that Jaqzen might have rigged the perimeter of the trail too, they kept going until they were a good ways within. Had he not, they could have easily stepped on one of the other mines Jaqzen had laid. But pushing through solid forest wasn't easy either, and without a view of the sky, he had to guess the direction they'd be heading. By now, however, Tom had an instinctual feel for direction. Problem was, taking this route would throw off his timing. He'd have to adjust.

It took Tom exactly 3943 seconds from the time he diverted his path until he finally emerged from the thicket and into the open. He'd counted them. He estimated that, were they to have slowly walked the path they'd been on from the rocky outcropping to its end, it would have taken them five minutes. Had they survived, that is. The detour took sixty-five. Thus, it cost them an extra hour. That meant they should arrive close to sunset. That would be their stopping point, then. Dusk. He looked up at the sun, guessed they had three hours to go. Then they'd camp out. First thing tomorrow he'd begin his watch for Julie.

Thirty Two

Tom looked out at the way ahead. Something was bothering him, had unconsciously nagged him since he first saw the note. Now, like magma slowly rising to the surface, he realized what it was. Since Jaqzen had already been here, that meant that he too knew about this signaling station of Julie's. Then why hadn't he grabbed her? He thought hard. The last time she'd used it was two weeks ago. She'd made the rounds and was back here again. It could only mean that Jaqzen figured out her system just within the past two weeks. He knew that she'd be back, and when. That gave him time to dig the pit and set his traps. He knew also that, whoever it was that was coming from the North, he'd have to use that trail, inasmuch as the forest on both sides was nearly impenetrable.

Of course the ape-man is here and will be waiting for Julie too. But will he be watching the death-trail's terminus for the interloper or stalking Julie? No, having had such a difficult time bagging her up till now, that would be his priority. So then he'd have to trust that his traps worked, expected they would. That meant that since they didn't, he could be caught off guard. Tom had the advantage.

On the other hand, though, maybe he *could* do both, watch for Julie *and* Tom merely by swinging his binocs around. Tom made a strategic change to his plans. Julie wouldn't be at her signal station until noon tomorrow. He had plenty of time to get there. He'd wait the three hours until sunset, then set out in the dark for another three hours to make up for it. That would get him his distance. He hoped Jaqzen's binocs weren't night vision capable.

When the sun finally went down, Tom and Little got up and began to walk. They proceeded straight as from the trail. He'd know it was three hours by again counting the seconds, all 10,800 of them. It would be a *long* three hours.

Warm night. Were it not for the impending trouble, he'd have said a lovely night. A crescent moon rose, giving just enough light that Tom could see his shadow as it stretched out darkly behind and to his left. Little padded along beside him, serene. Looking about them, Tom could make out the faint shapes of things, scattered trees and shrubs, rocks and plain. In the drier patches, his feet crunched gravel underfoot. The stars were bright and occasional zippings of luminous insects reminded him that, despite his petty troubles, life went on.

Step by plodding step they went in silence, while time dropped away. Tom found, to his dismay, his apprehension was rising, like a cobra in a charmer's basket. There were any number of things that could go wrong. He did not, in fact, even *have* much of a plan past simply intercepting Julie before the enemy did and shooting him should the situation demand it. *"Give me a gun and I'm as strong as that guy,"* he'd told Julie before she left. Now he supposed he'd find out if that was true.

No, no more of this. He shook from himself for a final time his vacillation. The man had been stalking his wife for more than a year. Had nearly killed Little. He knew what he had to do.

There was movement at the edge of his vision. He looked that way, but it was only a rabbit-like animal. At their approach, it darted off. Little made no move after it, sensing, somehow, that *now* was not the time.

Two low hills were coming up, darker than the night, with a quarter-mile span between them. Half a mile past them and around, a long, low line of trees circled this pocket of subtropical scrubland within the forest. He guessed they'd be upon the hillocks in ten minute's time. He was at 9,655 seconds. Were they *it?* If so, his calculations weren't terribly far off. Tom shuddered at the more likely scenario, though. That he was nowhere near the signal post, might miss Julie entirely, in which case Jaqzen would catch her, and that would be that. The end of his world.

Almost unwelcomely, however, he found that he was right. In contrast to the black of the hills, a tiny light suddenly popped on halfway up the left one. *Another lightning bug,* he wondered? He watched it as they continued on. There was something different about *this* bug though, it was staying put, not zipping away. Tom crouched and dug the binocs out of his pack, then brought them up. He focused there, on the dot of light, bringing it closer. The little gold glow simply sat there on the dark face of the hill, then, strangely, it increased in intensity, dimming again a moment later. It followed this pattern, brightening and dimming, brightening and dimming over and over. Suddenly, it flew off, shot a few feet away, and landed, still alit on the ground.

Tom scratched his head, perplexed. Then another gold light flared on, resuming the pattern, and suddenly he knew. It was Jaqzen, and he was smoking. Tom's heart began to beat suddenly in his chest, his reactions insanely mixed. On the one hand, and most importantly, it meant that he was probably in the right location and that Julie *was* coming. On the other, it meant that he'd be dealing with Jaqzen sooner than he'd planned. Repacking the optics, he stood and headed for him.

As if from nowhere, a wind began to blow, strong and straight, throwing sand and grit ahead of it. Fortunately, it was a northerly, so it was at his back. Still, Tom bent over and pulled up a tattered collar to keep the stinging particles from pelting his neck. A dust storm, it pushed at them, forcing them on with an eerie, almost haunting sort of howling,

A small species of tomarctus loped by, just fifty feet ahead, driven to exposure by the fusillade, wan moonlight barely showing it up.

~~~

Julie got an early start that morning. Though by her past actions she could be expected to appear at noon, she *wanted* to be early, and hopefully before anyone else. She did not want to be surprised. Thus, she rose in the wee hours, and, with her pack, walked out to find Zephyr. She was relieved to see him there in a standing sleep just outside her cave. Though it was his usual place to be this time of night, that wasn't always the case. Sometimes, as the night wore on, he spent it in the fields above.

Zephyr lifted his head and nickered as Julie crawled out of the cave entrance, pulling her ruck behind her.

"Hi, baby," Julie said, "thanks for staying by." Indeed, she'd asked he remain there that night. "We're taking an early trip today, you and I." Julie walked off to take care of business, then went to the river for a drink. An owl hooted in the trees on the lake's west side. Zephyr pulled at some leaves growing in the flow, banging the clod of mud off that came with it. Julie put her hand on his neck, kissed his head.

"Today's the day, Zephy, the day we find out what's going to happen, who that blue light is, and if I have to leave." Here she paused. The thought of leaving everything she loved was painful, too painful to contemplate. Well, almost everything. Tom was still stuck up there in the Anthropocene, waiting and probably despondent. Would she be allowed to return to him, or would she be killed, like Jaqzen had said? Would she have to take a long trip back upstate? And what was up with *that* anyway?

A noise sounded overhead and Julie jumped, then saw that it was only her stallion's harem looking down on them from the top of the mound above her cave. "Look at me, I'm just a flutter of nerves," she said.

"If I have to leave, Zeph, you'll have to make your way back here. Don't abandon your family to follow me, okay?" she urged. Julie knew that that was a possibility though, and that she should be making this trip alone. But selfishly, she couldn't say goodbye. Not just yet. Goodbye, then a long walk in the dark.

Julie slung her pack on, then climbed up Zephyr's back. It was a load for the boy, but he was up to it. She looked out at the lake, her lake, moonlight shimmering off of it like silver starlight. A tear formed at the corner of her eye. Dropped. She breathed in, then out, her voice quavered. Finally, she whispered, "Let's go."

~~~

Jaqzen had been there in the little desert basin for over a week. In that time he'd worked nonstop. First, he had to make sure that no one would make it through that narrow path.

It was perfect and he laughed when he discovered it. He knew hit men, even *they* had their fears. Fears of tangled jungles and beasts skulking in the dark. Most were citified, not experienced game hunters like him. They probably shook all the long journey down the state, blowing away every twig that fell from a tree. Thus it was serendipity that the way to this signaling station would necessarily be via that spooky trail. *Pure serendipity*. Once on it, they'd *never* venture into the deep forest on either side. Only *he* had that confidence; yet even he found it menacing. There was something about it, that long length of gloom, that seemed malevolent, as if something were lurking in the shadows, watching, weighing, readying an attack.

And yet, he'd survived it, those days spent digging and rigging, and scoffed at his own superstitious nature. It was satisfying to know that eventually man would take his revenge. In the meantime, he'd been doing his part to strike at the heart of the evil in nature. Setting fires, clearing the land, killing its denizens. Even the mighty Amphicyon now avoided him, his scent. Jaqzen relished his role as top predator in this wild world, marking trees with his own urine, delineating his own territory. *Cross that line and your mine!* he'd think after each pissing session. No one else was as fit for this world as he. He and Julie. And now he'd have her, at last. She'd put up one hell of a fight, and thus earned a measure of his respect, a fitting match. But that was all about to end. He'd enjoyed the cat and mouse, but ached to bed a woman, then teach her her *rightful* place.

"I'm excited as a school girl!" he said huskily, laughing as he sat on the other side of the signaling hill, taking a drag on his cig. He picked up his rifle and scope and swept it slowly over the night landscape, finger on the trigger, ready to shoot just in case. While he doubted anybody could make it through the trail, one couldn't let one's guard down. Later, he'd go to have a look and see what he'd caught.

Ah, movement! Just at the limit of his scope's night vision capability. He trained his rifle there, but it was only a tomarctus loping by.

"Damn dog!" Jaqzen spat. Then he aimed, placing it within his rifle's crosshairs. Suddenly a strong wind rushed his way, assaulting him with gravel that stung his face. He lowered the gun and put up an arm to cover his eyes. *"What the freak?"* The bombardment seemed to come from nowhere. He waited, but it didn't stop. He let fly a volley of curses, shaking his fist at the sky.

~~~

Tom had continued on toward the hill where Jaqzen now sat. He'd stopped counting seconds soon as he knew it was the Neanderthal. All the way, the wind howled and sand blew around them. Yet the dark of the hill was still apparent.

And now he was there at the base. The wind had ceased, and there was no sign of Jaqzen. Tom re-holstered his pistol and began to climb. Little was on high alert, sniffing the ground, low growls emerging from deep within. Her ears were forward and eyes fierce. If Tom were someone else, he might have sent her off to find and damage his enemy. But he was Tom, and he loved his aelurodon second only to Julie; he kept her on a tight restraint. Even so, she pulled him up the hill with ease until, a minute by, they were standing at the place where the ape-man had been. Cigarette butts littered the ground, his calling card.

Tom glanced around, eyes narrowed and mouth firm. Ape-man had left to avoid the windstorm. What did that mean, "left?" He was probably even now sitting on the other side, only a few hundred feet away. Tom again removed his gun, and together he and Little picked their way along the semi-steep side of the hill. In contrast to just before, now everything was unnaturally quiet, deathly quiet, and Tom cringed at the sound of each leaf crushed underfoot. As he came closer to the southern face, moonlight luminous there, he slowed his pace and raised his pistol. But no Jaqzen. Tom spun around, expecting that he'd been outwitted and would find the fiend standing behind him. Not there. He walked clear around the hilltop again, but no.

Then he looked down toward the South, back into the basin. Did a double take. It was dark, but he thought he saw movement.

Yes, movement! Yet, it wasn't the big man, it was something else. He strained to see, something silently running, coming toward them. Tom hurriedly got the binocs and pointed them at the shape in motion. A horse. Wait, something ... some*one* else! A sound burst from his throat, an exclamation. *IT WAS HER! JULIE!* She was on the back of a horse! Like an apparition, her hair was long and flowing behind her in the wind, and she was coming straight toward them!

Tom said something that was nothing and was about to dash down the side when he saw other movement. He'd forgotten about Jaqzen, but there he was at the bottom of the hill, three hundred feet down, hiding behind a boulder, waiting, a predator ready to pounce. Tom judged he'd have to run down to make it. Quickly, he tied Little to a tree, commanded her to stay, dropped his pack, and set off. She squealed and pulled to get free, but did not bark. Tom realized that those precious seconds tying her meant that Jaqzen would be at Julie before him.

It wasn't easy running down a semi-steep hill in the dark and he tripped in a hole, falling hard and painfully, but was up again in a flash, racing downside. Now the sound of galloping hooves was audible. A hundred feet from the bottom, Julie and Zephyr caught sight of the running figure coming their way down the hill and the boy spun to the side just as Jaqzen burst from behind the rock, knife in hand to slay the horse.

Tom's mind went into slow motion again as it had at other times of crisis, and all sound ceased, only his legs pumping, his heart beating like the pounding of those hooves. Leaving his gun holstered, he pulled something else from his belt, something he'd taken back on the trail. A silent vow he'd made. Now he held it in his hand as he raced toward the barbarian.

Zephyr ran fast as he could, but reversing their direction had cost him time. And Jaqzen was on him, slashing like a madman with his knife. He missed though, while the horse did not. Zephyr kicked, catching the big man full in the chest, cracking a rib, and he faltered, falling to one knee. Even so, he was able to pull Julie down by her pants, refusing to let go. She screamed and kicked at him, a hard snap at his head, throwing blood to the other side of his face. Still, he held on.

"I got you, Bitch!" he rasped, "Ha, Ha. *I got you!*" Standing back up, he held one arm across his stomach and the other, Julie by her hair. "I told you I would, didn't I? You never stood a chance!" Putting his hands around her neck, he gripped tight. In that moment, his moment of bloodlust, he might have killed her, wanting only the immediate satisfaction of his blinding fury. Then Zephyr came at him again, ramming from behind, and once more knocked him to the ground, forcing him to release his hold on her. Julie let out another exclamation. There was the other, the running figure, just back of the ape-man. Half up, Jaqzen turned, instantly regretting it, imagining it a trick. He was about to turn around, then his eyes grew wide, at first with fear, then amusement.

"What?" he said, "What? ... *You?*" And suddenly he knew. Despite the dark skin, flowing beard and tattered clothes, he knew who this was. *To think that all this time I'd been worried about* you! he thought, and with that he began to laugh. "Look at you! You're an animal!"

Tom, on the slope behind, was now level with Jaqzen. He raised his left hand to strike and Jaqzen caught it with both of his. "Haven't we been here before?" he growled.

"This ought to even the odds, then," Tom said, as, instantly, he brought up his right and struck, sinking the stake, the same stake that had grazed Little in the pit, into Jaqzen's chest. It went deep enough to lodge between two upper rib bones, the point puncturing a lung beneath.

"Die, you fiend!" Tom said, as he swung at the ape-man's face, hitting it fully and soundly with a satisfying crack. Blood began to pour from his nose. Jaqzen staggered back, then fell again, clutching at the stake. He wasn't done yet, though, and he yanked it out, throwing it away.

"Come on, then!" he bellowed, rising. Tom obliged and began to pummel the man's face with his fists, feeling the skin give under every blow.

Jaqzen swung forcefully with a leg, knocking Tom off his feet, and he fell hard on the ground. *"That the best you got, little man?"* he roared, regaining his momentum. *"That's it?"* Tom, up again, came back at him, fists flying out rapidly. Then, grimacing, Jaqzen grasped Tom by the throat and began to squeeze. "You had your shot, Mouse, and it wasn't bad, but now you go bye-bye." Tom reached for his pistol, but found that it was missing. It had fallen out when he'd tripped on the hill. He tore at the big man's eyes, but already was beginning to feel faint. Julie, frantic and crying, cracked the ape-man on the back of his head with a fallen branch, but, dry, it broke in two.

"I'll be dealing with you in a minute, Bitch," Jaqzen promised, *"soon as I finish off dear hubby."* His entire head was dripping in blood. Julie looked around desperately for something heavier, a rock, but there was only sand.

To the end Tom fought, until, asphyxiated, he succumbed, his knees buckling. Jaqzen, now recovered, laughed. "Bye, Mouse!" he said.

That's when it happened. When lightning struck. Well, not lightning exactly, an Aelurodon with a chewed off piece of rope around her neck. The first pass knocked the big man off her human and sent him sprawling to the ground. Julie rushed to Tom.

"What's this?" the ape man said, *"You brought your puppy, too? All the merrier!"* Little now faced the monster, teeth bared and snarling, spitting ferocity. *"Come on then, I like a challenge!"* Little sprang and Jaqzen swung, crashing a meaty fist into her muscled side. There was a loud snap.

"Ahhhh!" Jaqzen yelled out in pain, grabbing his wrist. Little turned to spring again and Jaqzen kicked wildly. Little caught it, tripping the big man, who fell heavily onto his back. Then, with her powerful jaws, she crunched down solidly, tearing muscle, cracking bone, and shook viciously, ripping open the leg, and an artery. To the big man's horrible shrieks, she continued to shake, flopping him around like a rag doll. His leg shredded, she dropped it, and approaching, stood over him, daring him to look her in the eye. Jaqzen, incredulous, tried to back away, but when she growled, he stopped. One could almost sense that she was going to enjoy this. Unknown to Tom, she'd intuited for some time that this battle was coming.

Tom came to then, and turned to see his journey companion about to strike. "LITTLE!" he yelled.

The big man lay on his back, while his blood, pouring from multiple wounds, was pooling beneath him. His life ebbing away with each beat of his heart. He put his hands in the air between he and Little, a look of true fear now on his face.

"No! Look, hey, I'm sorry," Jaqzen pleaded, voice quavering *"I - I didn't mean it. Any of it. I'm sorry!"* Suddenly, all the bravado gone, the man looked small and pathetic. Little, her eyes red with rage, mouth working, dripped saliva into the madman's face. A strange rumbling emerged from deep in her chest, like thunder. She was, after all, an Aelurodon, a wild Barstovian beast.

"No! I'll do anything you ask. I'll - I'll be your slave!" Jaqzen shrieked. Tom, uncertain, fought to decide. Bad as Jaqzen was, could he do it, could he let her kill another human

being? He almost called Little back, then stayed himself. No, this has to happen. This diseased man, symbol of all that had gone wrong, of the cancer of the future, had to leave. He felt something warm in his pocket, withdrew the opal to find it glowing. He held Julie away from the carnage

Finally, spitting blood and cursing, Jaqzen screamed, *"We're gonna win, Pine! We're gonna win in the end!"* followed by a hysterical, gurgling laugh. Tom shook his head. Clearly the man was insane; deranged product of a deranged time. In spite of everything, he pitied him then. Pitied a race that would fall so out of balance with the natural world around it.

Forgotten in Little, though, was any sense of the propriety she'd learned all her long time with Tom; even had her human called her back she wouldn't have heard. And thus, lips curled and fangs bared, she leapt. The man tried to fight, but with his injuries he was too slow. With blinding speed and precision, she tore at Jaqzen's throat, ripping it out like any prey animal's, and when he was dead, continued to rip him to pieces. Then, as before, Tom turned away from the scene.

It had happened so fast, and when at last it was over, a strange peace came upon him as he held Julie in his arms. It was done; what had seemed nearly impossible so long before had actually been a fait accompli. Tomorrow, the vultures and scavengers would come. By day's end, there would be no sign of the man here.

> *"After a firefight, there is always the immense pleasure of aliveness. The trees are alive. The grass, the soil - everything. All around you things are purely living, and you among them, and the aliveness makes you*

523

tremble.... Freshly, as if for the first time, you love what's best in yourself and in the world, all that might be lost. At the hour of dusk you sit at your foxhole and look out on a wide river turning pinkish red, and at the mountains beyond, and... you find yourself studying the fine colors on the river, you feel wonder and awe at the setting of the sun, and you are filled with a hard, aching love for how the world could be and always should be, but now is not."

Tom, Julie, Little and Zephyr walked to the other hill and waited for dawn, saying nothing. Normally, a Barstovian horse would never be this near an Aelurodon, yet these two would become inseparable. Perhaps a beginning to the natural friendship that would develop much later between horses and dogs.

With the moonlight in her hair, in her eyes, Tom thought Julie stunning. Ravishing. He held her tightly, unable to let go.

"Thank you," she whispered, a tear running down her cheek.

"For what?" Tom asked.

"For coming," Julie answered. But she was also thanking the earth, thanking Opal for answering her prayers.

"Thank you for being here," Tom replied.

"I love you," Julie said. It was something she'd needed to say for too long now. "So much."

"I love you too, baby."

When the sun's rays began to stretch across the sky, heralding a new day, Julie said, "Let's go home."

Epilogue

Tom knew it was silly, that they'd never find it. In fifteen million years, the slow process of erosion would erase any sign of it. Still, he carved the words in the rock. It was a message to the future, the far future of man.

Save the earth

Below them, wedged in a tiny crack between the heavy boulders, he stuck a note.

You know how some days, rare as opals, just have a special feel to them, in the morning when the day is fresh and new or after the first spring rain, when tender leaves hang heavy with drops? The sun, a breeze, even clouds, whatever. You don't know what it is, but it just feels right and you smile. That's everyday life in the Luisian. There's just something about a Miocene sun! You can almost hear the music, Opal's song.

Love her, protect her, and she will you.

Tom turned and headed out, disappearing over a grassy rise. Back to Julie. Back to life.

Miocene Horses © Marianne Collins

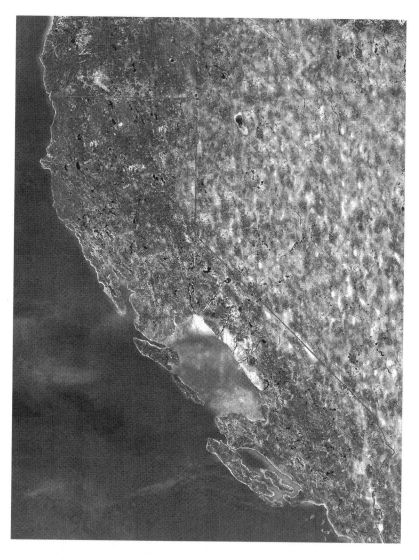

Miocene California, Rod Rayborne

Quotations

Quotes about the Middle Miocene

"Clarendonian Chronofauna: Grassland Savanna Land mammal diversity in North America reached its zenith during the Barstovian mammal age.... These mammal ages are thought to indicate a savanna optimum in North America, with a rich mosaic of trees, shrubs, and grasses supporting an extraordinary variety of large and small, grazing and browsing, ungulates. It is not uncommon during this savanna acme to collect in a single site 20 genera of ungulates of which half are Equidae."
~ S. David Webb and Neil D. Opdyke. *Effects of Past Global Change on Life.* [chapter] *Global Climatic Influence on Cenozoic Land Mammal Faunas.* p. 193

"During such robust chronofaunal intervals the continental mammal fauna stood near its ecological capacity.... The acme of land mammal diversity, dominated by horses and other savanna herbivores, is attained in the Barstovian.... the land mammal faunas experienced high diversity and long stable community development (chronofaunal evolution). This lends credence to the view that the ecosystem was near capacity during the Barstovian acme" ~ *Effects of Past Global Change on Life.* p. 203

"Horse diversity increased so dramatically that at some fossil sites from fifteen million years ago as many as a dozen species can be found. Today the world's horses (and their relatives the zebras, asses and onagers) are reduced to the single genus Equus, whose wild members live only in parts of Asia and Africa.... the familiar horses, zebras, asses and onagers that share our modern world represent but a single surviving branch on a once luxuriant equid family tree that reached its full glory during the Miocene." ~ Bruce J. Macfadden. *Natural History* 4/94. Article: *The Heyday of Horses.*

"Canids experienced their second spurt of diversification in the middle Miocene... their maximum ecological breadth during this time." ~ Wang and Tedford. *Dogs: Their Fossil Relatives and Evolutionary History.* p. 127

"If west coast marine tetrapod evolution in general had a peak, a time when it went as far as it could go, the mid-Miocene may have been it." ~ David Rains Wallace. *Neptune's Ark: From Ichthyosaurs to Orcas.* p. 105

"Changes in the productivity and species richness of terrestrial vegetation must have affected herbivore communities. Hoofed herbivorous large mammals on the North American continent show a maximum diversity during the middle Miocene climatic optimum... This maximum in both local and regional diversity greatly exceeds the diversity of ungulates in any present-day habitat, which implies a greater primary productivity than is seen today. Preliminary review data suggest that the pattern of elevated ungulate diversity is a global phenomenon, and, therefore, a global driving force is the most likely explanation. CO_2 fertilization during the middle Miocene climatic optimum may have made possible the expansion of high-productivity terrestrial biomes that supported high-diversity browser communities." ~ Wolfram M. Kürschner, Zlatko Kvac̆ek, and David L. Dilcher. *The impact of Miocene atmospheric carbon dioxide fluctuations on climate and the evolution of terrestrial ecosystems.* p. 452

"The later Tertiary mammalian fauna of the World Continent was perhaps the richest that has ever existed on the face of the earth. It is as if mammalian life had been proliferating in ever increasing numbers, exploring every ecological nook and cranny that could be populated, testing how large or small you could get, how best to adorn yourself with tusks or horns, how to fly, swim, climb, run, dig, jump, hunt, eat, kill and defend yourself, better than ever before. All the manifestations have a single keyword: adaptation. Most of the evolutionary lines of the later Tertiary had a fairly long history behind them: they had got far enough to attain basic adaptation for a given way of life. What remained now was to perfect it. And so, in the late Tertiary, the mammals were increasing in efficiency, under the constant supervision of natural selection - a perfectionist potentate. And in general this would also involve an increase in beauty, in gracefulness, in elegance." ~ Björn Kurtén. *The Age of Mammals.* [chapter] *The Miocene: Epoch of Revolutions.* Columbia University Press. 1971

"Looking back the Pliocene [or the timeframe within the Pliocene now called the Miocene] is something of a paradise lost, a climax of the Age of Mammals before the coming of the cold; a time when life was richer, more exuberant than ever before or after." ~ Björn Kurtén. *The Age of Mammals.* [chapter] *The Pliocene: Epoch of Climax.*

Quotes about the State of the Biosphere

"Human beings and the natural world are on a collision course. Human activities inflict harsh and often irreversible damage on the environment and on critical resources. If not checked, many of our current practices put at serious risk the future that we wish for human society and the plant and animal kingdoms, and may so alter the living world that it will be unable to sustain life in the manner that we know. Fundamental changes are urgent if we are to avoid the collision our present course will bring about.... Our massive tampering with the world's interdependent web of life -

coupled with the environmental damage inflicted by deforestation, species loss, and climate change - could trigger widespread adverse effects, including unpredictable collapses of critical biological systems whose interactions and dynamics we only imperfectly understand.... We the undersigned, senior members of the world's scientific community, hereby warn all humanity of what lies ahead. A great change in our stewardship of the earth and the life on it is required, if vast human misery is to be avoided and our global home on this planet is not to be irretrievably mutilated."

~ *1992 World Scientists' Warning to Humanity,* signed by 1,700 of the world's leading scientists, including the majority of Nobel laureates in the sciences.

"During a remarkably short period of time, we have lost a quarter of the world's topsoil and a fifth of its agricultural land, altered the composition of the atmosphere profoundly, and destroyed a major proportion of our forests and other natural habitats without replacing them. Worst of all, we have driven the rate of biological extinction, the permanent loss of species, up several hundred times beyond its historical levels, and are threatened with the loss of a majority of all species by the end of the 21st century." ~ Peter Raven, past President of AAAS (American Association for the Advancement of Science) in the Forward to *AAAS Atlas of Population & Environment.*

"Among the environmental trends undermining our future are shrinking forests, expanding deserts, falling water tables, collapsing fisheries, disappearing species, and rising temperatures. The temperature increases bring crop-withering heat waves, more-destructive storms, more-intense droughts, more forest fires, and, of course, ice melting. We are crossing natural thresholds that we cannot see and violating deadlines that we do not recognize." ~ Lester Brown. *Plan B4.: Mobilizing to Save Civilization.*

"The wetlands, forests, savannahs, estuaries, coastal fisheries and other habitats that recycle air, water and nutrients for all living creatures are being irretrievably damaged. In effect, one species is now a hazard to the other 10 million or so on the planet, and to itself. 'Human activity is putting such a strain on the natural functions of Earth that the ability of the planet's ecosystems to sustain future generations can no longer be taken for granted.'" ~ Tim Radford, science editor. *Two-thirds of world's resources 'used up'. The Guardian*, 29 March 2005, reporting on the *Millennium Ecological Assessment.*

"The flip side of urbanization is what we are leaving behind on our way to a world of hundred-story office buildings, high-rise residences and landscapes of glass, cement, artificial light and electronic interconnectivity. It's no accident that as we celebrate the urbanization of the world, we are quickly approaching another historic watershed: the disappearance of the wild. Rising population; growing consumption of food, water and building materials; expanding road and rail transport; and urban sprawl continue to encroach on the remaining wild, pushing it to extinction." ~ Jeremy Rifkin. *Washington Post*. Sunday, December 17, 2006. *The Risks of Too Much City.*

"We have always had reluctance to see a tract of land which is empty of men as anything but a void. The 'waste howling wilderness' of Deuteronomy is typical. The Oxford Dictionary defines wilderness as wild or uncultivated land which is occupied 'only' by wild animals. Places not used by us are 'wastes.' Areas not occupied by us are 'desolate.' Could the desolation be in the soul of man?" ~ John A. Livingston, in Borden Spears, ed., Wilderness Canada. 1970

"Time and space - time to be alone, space to move about - these may well become the great scarcities of tomorrow."
~ Edwin Way Teale. *Autumn Across America*. 1956

"We never know the worth of water till the well is dry."
~ Thomas Fuller. *Gnomologia*. 1732

Quotes from Astronauts about The Earth

"A Chinese tale tells of some men sent to harm a young girl who, upon seeing her beauty, become her protectors rather than her violators. That's how I felt seeing the Earth for the first time. I could not help but love and cherish her." ~ Taylor Wang

"The colors are stunning. In a single view, I see - looking out at the edge of the earth: red at the horizon line, blending to orange and yellow, followed by a thin white line, then light blue, gradually turning to dark blue and various gradually darker shades of gray, then black and a million stars above. It's breathtaking." ~ Willie McCool

"A tear-drop of green." ~ Ron McNair

"Suddenly, from behind the rim of the Moon, in long, slow-motion moments of immense majesty, there emerges a sparkling blue and white jewel, a light, delicate sky-blue sphere laced with slowly swirling veils of white, rising gradually like a small pearl in a thick sea of black mystery. It takes more than a moment to fully realize this is Earth . . . home."
~ Edgar Mitchell

"My view of our planet was a glimpse of divinity."
~ Edgar Mitchell

"If somebody'd said before the flight, 'Are you going to get carried away looking at the earth from the moon?' I would have say, 'No, no way.' But yet when I first looked back at the earth, standing on the moon, I cried." ~ Alan Shepard

"The Earth reminded us of a Christmas tree ornament hanging in the blackness of space. As we got farther and farther away it diminished in size. Finally it shrank to the size of a marble, the most beautiful marble you can imagine. That beautiful, warm, living object looked so fragile, so delicate, that if you touched it with a finger it would crumble and fall apart. Seeing this has to change a man." ~ James Irwin

"We came all this way to explore the moon, and the most important thing is that we discovered the earth." ~ William Anders

"Before I flew I was already aware of how small and vulnerable our planet is; but only when I saw it from space, in all its ineffable beauty and fragility, did I realize that human kind's most urgent task is to cherish and preserve it for future generations." ~ Sigmund Jähn

"Oddly enough the overriding sensation I got looking at the earth was, my god that little thing is so fragile out there."
~ Mike Collins

"For the first time in my life I saw the horizon as a curved line. It was accentuated by a thin seam of dark blue light - our atmosphere. Obviously this was not the ocean of air I had been told it was so many times in my life. I was terrified by its fragile appearance." ~ Ulf Merbold

"On the one hand, we can see how indescribably beautiful the planet that we have been is, but on the other hand, we can really, clearly see how fragile it is.... The atmosphere for instance...the atmosphere when viewed from space is paper thin, and to think that this paper thin layer is all that separates every living thing from the vacuum of space and all that protects us is really a sobering thought." ~ Ron Garan

"To fly in space is to see the reality of Earth, alone. The experience changed my life and my attitude toward life itself. I am one of the lucky ones." ~ Roberta Bondar

"Now I know why I'm here. Not for a closer look at the moon, but to look back at our home, the Earth." ~ Alfred Worden

"When you're finally up at the moon looking back on earth, all those differences and nationalistic traits are pretty well going to blend, and you're going to get a concept that maybe this really is one world and why the hell can't we learn to live together like decent people." ~ Frank Borman

"The first day or so we all pointed to our countries. The third or fourth day we were pointing to our continents. By the fifth day, we were aware of only one Earth."
~ Sultan bin Salman Al-Saud

"This planet is not terra firma. It is a delicate flower and it must be cared for. It's lonely. It's small. It's isolated, and there is no resupply. And we are mistreating it. Clearly, the highest loyalty we should have is not to our own country or our own religion or our hometown or even to ourselves. It should be to, number two, the family of man, and number one, the planet at large. This is our home, and this is all we've got." ~ Scott Carpenter

"I left Earth three times and found no other place to go. Please take care of Spaceship Earth." ~ Wally Schirra

Acknowledgements and Credits

The author wishes to thank the following people for their kind use of the quotations in this book:

Excerpts from "How to Tell a True War Story" from THE THINGS THEY CARRIED by Tim O'Brien. Copyright © 1990 by Houghton Mifflin Harcourt Publishing Company. Reprinted by permission of Houghton Mifflin Harcourt Publishing Company. All rights reserved

For quote by Wolfram M. Kürschner, Zlatko Kvac̆ek, and David L. Dilcher in *The impact of Miocene atmospheric carbon dioxide fluctuations on climate and the evolution of terrestrial ecosystems*, p. 452, Copyright © 2008, National Academy of Sciences, U.S.A., Kay McLaughlin for Diane Sullenberger, Executive Editor PNAS

For quote by W. David Lambert: with kind permission from Springer Science+Business Media: "Ecosystems", *Functional Convergence of Ecosystems: Evidence from Body Mass Distributions of North American Late Miocene Mammal Fauna, Volume 9, Issue 1, pp 97-118, February 2006, W. David Lambert*

For quote by Lester Brown: Earth Policy Institute

For quote by Thomas Berry: The Forum on Religion and Ecology at Yale University

For quote by Peter Raven: Peter Raven, Missouri Botanical Garden

For quotes by S. David Webb: S. David Webb, Florida Museum of Natural History

For quote by Björn Kurtén: Marina Kurtén, MA, Translator, Information liaison, Department of Computer Science, University of Helsinki

For quote by Jeremy Rifkin: Christian Pollard, Technical Publications and Media Coordinator, Office of Jeremy Rifkin, Foundation on Economic Trends

For quote by Tim Radford: Helen Wilson, Content Sales Manager, Syndication, Guardian News and Media Ltd.

For quotes by David Rains Wallace: Greta Lindquist, Subsidiary Rights Assistant, University of California Press

For quote by Bruce MacFadden: Bruce MacFadden, Florida Museum of Natural History

For quote by Frederick Crews: Frederick Crews, University of California, Berkeley

For quote by Edwin Way Teale: Deana Dupree, Permissions Manager, St. Martin's Press / Macmillan Children's Publishing Group

For quote by Edward Abbey: Reprint by permission of Don Congdon Associates, Inc.
© 1987 by Edward Abbey.

The Voice was written by Brendan Graham, Peermusic (UK) Ltd.

It's In the Rain and *If I Could Be Where You Are* are Enya (Ni Bhraonain) songs, and were written by Roma Ryan, EMI Music Publishing / Sony/ATV

Special thanks to the following people for their assistance

My wonderful daughter, Carissa Rayborne,
for finding and correcting errors throughout

My brother Rod Rayborne, for his outstanding artistry in the
creation of the cover of this book and "Miocene California",
and for patiently putting up with my pickiness

Paleoartist Marianne Collins, for letting me use her beautiful
Miocene painting

My college English instructor, Lynn Steiner, for her
inspirational teaching, and for graciously giving me two weeks
of her time to edit *Opalescence*

Those scientists who kindly allowed me to ask and answered
my questions, including (but not limited to):

S. David Webb, Ph.D. Distinguished Research Professor and
curator, Florida Museum of Natural History. President, Society
of Vertebrate Paleontology

Jere Lipps, Ph.D., Director of the John D. Cooper
Archaeological and Paleontological Center, Santa Ana, and
Professor Emeritus, Department of Integrative
Biology, UC Berkeley

John Wakabayashi, Ph.D., Associate Professor, Department of
Earth and Environmental Sciences,
California State University, Fresno

William L. Bilodeau, Ph.D. Professor of Geology and Chair, Geology Department, California Lutheran University

Jeffrey A. Myers, Ph.D. Department of Earth Science, Western Oregon University

~~~

The lovely Lisa Kelly of Celtic Woman, whose incomparable singing so inspired me

Los Angeles Times Book Reviewer, Michael Harris, for reading and commenting on a draft copy

The publishing teams at Smashwords and Amazon for patiently walking me through the process

R.C. Butler at Bulldog Press, for graciously helping me with the print end of this beast

And finally, to Mother Earth, which has provided so much for so long to her many offspring.

About The Author

Ron Rayborne, together with his brother Rod, has always felt a special affinity for our unique planet. A long-time California hiker, many of the experiences within *Opalescence* are actual occurrences. Ron is an interested non-scientist.
To learn more go to:

midmiocene.wordpress.com

If you liked this book, please review it at your favorite online bookseller.